THE BROPOSAL

THE BROPOSAL

SONORA REYES

FOREVER
New York   Boston

Copyright © 2025 by Sonora Reyes
Reading group guide copyright © 2025 by Sonora Reyes and Hachette Book Group, Inc.

Cover illustration by Charlotte Gomez. Cover design by Daniela Medina. Cover copyright © 2025 by Hachette Book Group, Inc.

Forever
Hachette Book Group
1290 Avenue of the Americas, New York, NY 10104
read-forever.com
@readforeverpub

First Edition: January 2025

Forever is an imprint of Grand Central Publishing. The Forever name and logo are registered trademarks of Hachette Book Group, Inc.

The publisher is not responsible for websites (or their content) that are not owned by the publisher.

The Hachette Speakers Bureau provides a wide range of authors for speaking events. To find out more, go to hachettespeakersbureau.com or email HachetteSpeakers@hbgusa.com.

Forever books may be purchased in bulk for business, educational, or promotional use. For information, please contact your local bookseller or the Hachette Book Group Special Markets Department at special.markets@hbgusa.com.

Print book interior design by Taylor Navis

Library of Congress Cataloging-in-Publication Data

Names: Reyes, Sonora, author.
Title: The broproposal / Sonora Reyes.
Description: First edition. | New York : Forever, 2025.
Identifiers: LCCN 2024026581 | ISBN 9781538766682 (trade paperback) | ISBN 9781538766705 (ebook)
Subjects: LCGFT: Romance fiction. | Gay fiction. | Novels.
Classification: LCC PS3618.E939 B76 2025 | DDC 813/.6—dc23/eng/20240715
LC record available at https://lccn.loc.gov/2024026581

ISBNs: 9781538766682 (trade paperback), 9781538766699 (library hardcover), 9781538766705 (ebook)

Printed in the United States of America

LSC-C

Printing 1, 2024

For R,
In memories you'll live forever, just like a jellyfish.

TRIGGER WARNINGS

ICE/police/racial profiling/immigration issues
Injury/breaking a bone (ankle)
Physical and emotional abuse
Queerphobia
Addiction-related death
Sex

AUTHOR'S NOTE

While this book deals with the very real experience of living as an undocumented person in the United States, it is not meant to be educational or informative. Immigration laws and experiences vary widely and can be enforced differently from year to year, state to state, and person to person based on myriad factors, none of which are universal. A novel also necessitates a shorter timeline, and some details have been adjusted accordingly.

This story is so close to my heart and is told with tremendous love and care. That said, the focus is primarily on *feelings*, not logistics. There will be no play-by-play on how to get a green card or detailed descriptions of immigration law. However, if you'd rather laugh and swoon (and possibly cry?) over a love story between an emotionally constipated himbo and his sensitive people-pleaser best friend, look no further.

CHAPTER ONE

HAN

Hello? Han? Are you listening?"

I jolted, realizing I was paying more attention to the fake bioluminescent jellyfish in the tank next to my desk than the email on my screen or the girlfriend talking on my phone. Well, ex.

Even if the ones in my room weren't real, jellyfish were a hell of a lot more fun to think about than getting fired or breaking up, even if I was the one doing the dumping. For one, jellyfish were pretty fucking rad.

Jellyfish didn't have girlfriends.

Jellyfish didn't have to work for a company that promised to sponsor unsuspecting immigrants' work visas only to fire them over email without warning.

Jellyfish didn't even age, bro. Those Benjamin Button motherfuckers can just de-age themselves back to childhood, to their polyp stage, whenever they're in severe stress.

"Hello? Are you still there?" Tatiana asked over the phone,

reminding me yet again that I'd just zoned out in the middle of dumping her.

"Oh, uh, yeah."

"So, we can still go to the ball, right?" she asked, as if she hadn't heard the words *I think we should break up*. We'd planned to go to a drag ball together since my cousin Leti would be emceeing tonight. "One last date?"

I paused to think about it. Scoring another date with the girl I just dumped was definitely not a part of the plan, but what the hell? We'd only been together-ish for a few weeks, so it made sense that she wasn't too, well, *broken up* by it (heh). But I had still expected at least a little bit of pushback. Whatever. As long as Tatiana knew we weren't together, I didn't mind hanging out as friends. Especially if it'd get my mind off my newfound lack of a job. Without the ball to distract me, I would have beaten myself up all night. Maybe my boss found out I'd been applying for other jobs that would have also sponsored my work visa. A fireable offense, apparently.

I was happy to go to the ball with Tatiana instead of spiraling about the universe wanting me to suffer.

"Oh, uh...sure? Yeah, let's go to the ball," I finally said, quickly shooting Kenny a text saying Tatiana would still be needing a ride even though we were broken up.

"Good, I was really excited for that." I could hear Tatiana's smile over the phone, completely unfazed by having been dumped.

"Me too," I admitted, chuckling to myself.

If commitment didn't scare the living shit out of me, I might have ended up with someone like Tatiana. According to my best friend/roommate/honorary family member Kenny, she was perfect for me. Even though she worked at the same restaurant as

Kenny and was good friends with Leti, it never annoyed me to spend extra time with her. What more could a guy ask for in a relationship?

Not to mention, she was beautiful. Her dark brown skin matched the shade of her eyes almost perfectly, and she wore her makeup like art. She really was the whole package. If I was ever going to fall in love. Which, let's be real—wasn't gonna happen.

Because, as with all the other girls I dated, I felt nothing for Tatiana. It didn't matter how perfect she was; the spark and passion just never came. And even if it miraculously did one day, it wouldn't change a thing. It wasn't that I didn't like the *idea* of romance. But *real* romance—the kind you could completely lose yourself in, the kind people spent entire lifetimes maintaining, wanting nothing more in life than each other—it just wasn't in the cards for me. It was too dangerous. Too risky. So, I always made sure to end things before they had a chance to get there.

Besides, being undocumented, I would rather not get close enough to trust anyone but family. Sure, I didn't really trust anyone but family (Kenny included) with *most* information about me, but especially this.

"So, you're not mad?" I had to ask, or I'd be convinced I was imagining the whole situation.

"It's actually good timing. I think I might be catching feelings for someone else, so it all works out."

We both laughed, and somehow it didn't feel forced or awkward. The two of us were definitely better as friends.

"I'm so excited! I've never been to a drag show before!" Tatiana said, her voice sounding a little far away. I was probably on speakerphone while she finalized her costume. Neither Tatiana nor I would be performing, but it was Halloween, so we were all dressing up.

"It's technically a ball. But yeah, there's definitely drag. You'll love it."

I'd been to plenty of drag shows and underground balls alike to support my cousin Leti, who was basically my sibling. Leti performed almost every week, but tonight they were more than performing. Tonight, Leti was the emcee.

I had to admit I was relieved Tatiana still wanted to go. Kenny was bringing his girlfriend, and the three of us alone was bad news. Hell, me around Jackie at all was bad news.

"Oh, Kenny's here. See you soon!" Tatiana said before hanging up the phone. Since she lived closer to Jackie's house than our apartment, Kenny would be picking Tatiana up first, then me.

About fifteen minutes later, Kenny's car horn in the parking lot beckoned me. I took one final look in the mirror before leaving. I was already in my costume, since I'd planned on going as a third wheel with Kenny and Jackie after breaking up with Tatiana.

Cowboy—an easy choice. All I had to do was raid my tío Nacho's closet for boots, a belt, and a cowboy hat—Nacho's go-to outfit.

The blue minivan—Kenny's dream car—was waiting in the apartment lot as I made my way downstairs. As soon as I opened the back door and scooted in, Jackie looked at me and then turned back to Kenny.

"What's he supposed to be?" she asked. Jackie was the type of person who talked about me instead of to me when she was in a mood. Meaning, she was still mad at me from the other day, when she asked why I never laughed at her jokes and I made the mistake of telling her the truth: I didn't find them funny.

"*He* can hear you." I didn't bother hiding my irritation. "And he's obviously a cowboy." I knew it was risky to get snarky with Jackie, but what did she expect? Her cold shoulder thing kind of depended on me being the only one to notice. Calling attention to it just made her look like an asshole, and with Tatiana as a newly introduced wildcard for Jackie, she wouldn't want her first impression getting too tainted. As expected, she turned to respond to me directly.

"No offense, but if you're going with the Wild West theme, wouldn't a Native American costume be more appropriate?"

"Seriously?" I rolled my eyes, and Tatiana shifted uncomfortably next to me.

"Babe, that's a little..." Kenny started, but Jackie was already backtracking.

"I was joking!" Jackie threw her hands up in exasperation. She sounded casual, but her usually pale cheeks were now almost as red as her hair. "Jesus, tough crowd. Let's just go."

Kenny obeyed, and Tatiana was quick to change the subject.

"So? How do I look?" she asked. Tatiana's gold tiara kept the long black hair of her wig out of her face. She looked like she belonged on the big screen.

"You look hot," I said. "Err, am I still allowed to say that?" I rubbed the back of my neck. I'd never been an expert in saying the right thing.

"You're allowed to state facts, yes." Tatiana grinned, and I let out a little laugh.

It didn't take long for me to notice that neither Kenny nor Jackie was in costume. Even though I knew Kenny had planned an outfit—I'd helped him make it and everything. Instead, he was wearing his usual oversized sweater and ripped jeans.

"What happened to Dracula?" I blurted out.

Kenny slumped his shoulders, but Jackie responded for him.

"I just don't love Kenny wearing makeup, you know? Doesn't suit him right," she said, as if it were totally normal to keep Kenny from wearing what he wanted.

"You know there'll be dudes in makeup where we're going, right?" I said, trying not to sound antagonistic.

I could hear Jackie's eye roll in her tone. "Obviously. *Kenny* is different."

"He's not—" I started, but Kenny finally spoke up.

"It's okay, Han. You did a great job on the costume, but it was a little itchy. That part was my bad. I'm fine going casual," he said, talking slightly faster than normal.

"Nothing wrong with going casual," Jackie said, turning to give me a glare that said I needed to shut the hell up. But her eyes found the backpack on the floor by my feet, and her face turned bright pink from embarrassment before snapping to the side. She stared stiffly out the window so her blush wasn't too noticeable, but I saw it.

The backpack was Kenny's "sex bag." He had this bag stocked with condoms, lube, even things like handcuffs, rope, and sex toys—Kenny was a kinky motherfucker—and he would take it with him whenever he was meeting up with Jackie. I guess it was more convenient than just carrying condoms around in your pocket? I don't know. Apparently, Jackie wasn't fond of Kenny leaving it in the car when there were other people around. I had half a mind to rummage through it, pretending to be looking for a snack or something. She'd just take it out on Kenny though.

Once we made it to the main streets, the world outside the car windows started to zoom past faster than I was comfortable with.

"Whoa, slow down, bro." Kenny tended to have a lead foot when he was stressed, but I couldn't stand being in a speeding car. We'd be more likely to get pulled over, and that meant cops. I couldn't be too careful, especially when US citizens were getting thrown in cages indefinitely for not having their papers on them.

"Sorry, Han," Kenny said, his tone a bit flustered. But he slowed down, no doubt understanding the edge in my voice for what it was. Still, my anxiety took a few minutes to settle.

"Quit back-seat driving," Jackie said when she noticed me glancing at the speedometer.

I wanted to defend myself, but I couldn't say *why* I needed Kenny not to speed without outing myself as undocumented. So I held my tongue. If it was anyone but Jackie, Kenny would have defended me in a heartbeat, but he kept quiet. I shifted my focus out the window, ignoring the pang in my chest.

Now seemed like a good time to channel that jellyfish energy. If I tried hard enough, I could go back to polyp, too. Replacing stress with a calming childhood memory was a trick I'd been doing for as long as I could remember.

Close your eyes. Breathe steady. Remember where you came from.

My breath slowed, the sound of cars zooming past enveloped my imagination, and the scene filled out.

Zooming child-sized cars raced all around a large fountain in the middle of my favorite childhood park in Mexico. Children laughed and screamed as they pedaled for their lives. One of those screams was my own.

"Alejandro!" an anxious voice called as I lost control of the wheel and fell out of the circular formation.

I didn't stop screaming in joy as the play car zoomed down the hill, going faster and faster until it was suddenly stopped by a thick tree.

"Alejandro!" the voice called again from a distance, though as she ran closer, her face was no clearer to me, even if I knew instinctually she was my mom.

The real car pulled to a stop much more gracefully than the one I'd crashed into that tree all those years ago.

Thanks to Kenny's initial speeding, we got to the ball well before it started, so we were able to catch Leti before they got too busy.

Kenny and Jackie trailed behind as Tatiana eagerly pulled me inside. Tonight's ball was at an art center that'd been decorated for the event. The walls had cobwebs, and there were pumpkin decorations on the tables. A stage and makeshift runway were set up in the middle of the room so the competitors could show off their personas.

All the categories were spooky. Kinky Kanines (werewolves), Sexy Spirits (ghosts), and Alluring Undead (zombies) in drag were scattered around, waiting for their turn to shine. Ballroom music played through the speakers, the bass shaking life into my veins. I wasn't a Halloween fanatic or anything like that— that was all Kenny, at least before Jackie got weird about the makeup—but I always enjoyed Leti's events, whatever season they came in. Being autistic, you'd think the loud music and crowds would be overstimulating, but these particular events were so familiar, they just felt safe.

I took Tatiana's hand and guided her behind the stage to find Leti.

"Han! Tati!" Leti waved enthusiastically from across the room, then made their way toward us in style. They walked slowly to draw attention, snaking their hand around the shoulder of a would-be contestant and dipping, then twirling as they reached us. They wore a sparkling purple catsuit, a long pink wig, and a face full of drag makeup.

"My God, Tati, you look gorgeous!" Leti winked, "And, Han, you look... like my dad."

I grinned, and Tatiana giggled at the compliment. She suddenly seemed way more Diana Prince than Wonder Woman. Still cool and confident but less like the star of the movie. Now Leti was the star.

"You look pretty great yourself," Tatiana said, playfully touching Leti's arm.

"As always." Another wink. "So, Han, where's your husband?"

"He's with Jackie." Kenny and I were voted "most likely to get married" in high school as a joke, but people still played it up whenever Jackie wasn't around. She *hated* being reminded Kenny and I got that vote, considering she and Kenny were dating back then, and I doubt anyone voted for *that* pairing.

"Jealous she's hogging up your hubby?" Leti gave me a fake pouting face, and I rolled my eyes. I knew they were joking, but just because I wasn't a fan of my best friend's cartoon-villain girlfriend didn't mean I was jealous.

"Five minutes." Someone came from behind Leti, tapping their shoulder. Leti peeked over to the common area, which was getting crowded. They nodded and shooed us away.

We walked back to find Kenny and Jackie at a table next to the runway, so we'd be getting a great view. Elaborate costumes were everywhere, some folks sitting at tables and some standing idly around. I was surprised Jackie had agreed to come. She was the type of girl who made fun of Kenny for being soft and expressing his feelings "like a woman."

Still, inviting Jackie was the only way Kenny could come. She bounced her leg and bit her nails. If I didn't know better, I'd think she was anxious, but that wasn't Jackie. She was just way out of her element. Who even knew what Jackie's element was—she seemed to hate everything that wasn't her job or being alone with Kenny.

I caught eyes with Tatiana, who glanced at Jackie and back at me.

She okay? she mouthed. Tatiana just didn't know Jackie for the judgmental asshole she was.

Before I could respond, Leti stepped onstage.

"Welcome to the Ghoul Ball," they said in a deep, sultry voice I'd only ever heard them use for moments like this. As they introduced themself and the judges, I got distracted by Jackie again.

"Sorry, he's straight," she called out to a drag queen who was making eyes at Kenny from another table. The queen rolled her eyes and got back to her conversation, but I couldn't push down the embarrassment in my chest.

"What was the point of that?" I said, arms crossed. "He's not even—"

"Kenny can speak for himself," Jackie said, and I let out a bark of a laugh at her inability to see the irony.

Kenny looked a little offended, and I realized he might have thought I was laughing at the idea of him having his own agency, so I went on to clarify. "You're right, so why did you say he's straight?"

"Because he *is*," Jackie said through gritted teeth.

"I'm not though?" Kenny said, shifting uncomfortably. "We've been over this, babe..."

Jackie rolled her eyes. "Of course you are. You're with me, and I'm a woman. So you're straight."

As a straight man, even I could tell Jackie was completely missing the point. "That's not how that—" I started, but Jackie interrupted, again.

"I'm sorry, was I talking to you?"

"Guys, stop," Kenny pleaded. "Can we just have fun for one night?"

Shit. I had promised Kenny I'd play nice with Jackie tonight, then immediately did the opposite. And there Kenny was with his goddamned kicked-puppy eyes.

"Sorry, bro," I conceded.

"Is Kenny really the one you should be apologizing to?" Jackie said, arms crossed.

"Yeah," I answered matter-of-factly. Why the hell would I apologize to Jackie? "You should apologize to him, too."

Jackie looked like she was about to jump over the table and strangle me, but I elected to ignore her, turning my attention back to Leti, who was introducing the next round of contestants.

"Kinky Kanines..." they said suggestively, and three performers dressed like werewolves stepped to the stage. They had two minutes to dance, pose, and vogue their way down the runway in an attempt to upstage each other and impress the judges.

Once the music came on, the werewolves started voguing their asses off. One with furry thigh-high boots duck-walked down the runway to the judges' table, then jumped up and landed in a shablam, her leg held up high. The other two faced off, posing high and low, trying to outdo each other with every beat. They twisted into positions that made my back and shoulders hurt just looking. Leti counted down on beat, and the music stopped so the judges could choose their winner: the duckwalker.

Between acts, Leti held everyone's attention by clowning on the audience members' costumes. Once the category with sexy Freddy and Jason lookalikes concluded, Leti looked at Kenny and shook their head in disappointment.

"I'm not usually one to go after family, but how can I not when this guy shows up to a *Halloween ball* like *that*?" Leti gestured their arms in Kenny's direction. The audience booed, but Kenny didn't miss a beat before standing to pose for them, which had a few in the crowd catcalling and whistling.

"Sit *down*." Jackie tugged the sleeve of Kenny's sweater.

Luckily, Leti moved on quickly by introducing the hero category.

We got another Wonder Woman (whom Tatiana whistled loudly for), a Hawkgirl, and a Sailor Moon.

Before the category was over, Jackie cleared her throat once the music stopped.

"I'm leaving," she said.

"But the show just started," Tatiana replied.

"This isn't really my scene. Kenny?"

Kenny gave Jackie a guilty look. "Babe, I'm their ride."

"Can't they take an Uber?" Jackie asked.

My jaw clenched. Sure, I'd take an Uber if I had to, but it was kind of ridiculous for Jackie to expect that when we all came together.

When Kenny took too long to respond, Jackie snatched her bag from the table. "Fine. *I'll* take an Uber. Seriously, Kenny, it's like you're *his* boyfriend." While it was usually a joke, Jackie saying it made my face burn.

"We'll take an Uber. It's fine." I felt myself getting defensive.

"No, no. I'll drop Jackie off, then come back for you guys," Kenny said.

"Jackie, are you sure you want to leave?" Tatiana asked, not knowing that reasoning with Jackie was like breathing and swallowing at the same time.

Jackie frowned. "Yeah, I should get to bed since I have an early day at work tomorrow. Some people's jobs are important." I wasn't sure if that last comment was meant as a jab against me or Kenny (and Tatiana by extension), since they worked at a restaurant and I was at a boring office job before getting fired—not that she knew about that.

I wanted to defend myself, but...she wasn't wrong. She worked at a shelter for abused women, which *was* an important job. And Jackie knew it and never let anyone forget it.

She turned away, firmly grabbing Kenny's arm as she led him outside. I wanted to walk after them and tell Jackie off for putting her hands on Kenny like that. But I knew getting involved would only make things worse.

Jackie was the type of girl who needed constant reassurance that she was a good person whom people liked. Calling her out on anything she did just reminded her I was one of the few people who never gave her that validation. We had a hard enough time around each other as it was. I didn't want to go making things worse.

I should have been annoyed, but it was honestly a relief to be rid of Jackie. Finally, I could properly ignore my problems and relax into the performances. It sucked that Kenny had to leave, but I would take alone time with Tatiana over a whining Jackie any day.

"Is Kenny okay?" Tatiana eventually asked.

I didn't know how to answer. Kenny would have said yes, of course he was okay. But I wasn't so sure.

"I don't know why he won't break up with her. She's way too controlling." I ran a hand through my hair. "She wants him to break our lease so they can move in together."

Then again, if I couldn't get another job soon, he might not have another choice.

"Oh shit. Are you gonna be okay if he does?"

"He wouldn't do that. Are you kidding? He's scared shitless of living alone with her," I said, knowing I needed to get my ass in grind to get another job now. Tatiana nodded.

"Why is he with someone he's afraid to live with?" she asked, as if it were that simple.

"Hell if I know" was all I could bring myself to say. If I knew anything about Kenny's relationship, it was that it was beyond my comprehension.

It was hard to pay attention to the show after that. It'd been a few months since Jackie first asked Kenny to move in, but so far Kenny hadn't budged. He'd lied and said it was because his traditional Mexican Catholic parents wouldn't approve of them living together before they were married, but Jackie wasn't buying it. (Kenny's parents were the farthest thing from traditional.)

Lie or not, Jackie was getting fed up. She was nice enough when they'd first started dating in high school, but the longer they were together, the bolder she got. By now Kenny and I could barely hang out without Jackie getting possessive.

Relationships were always fun in the beginning, but I knew from watching Kenny's that eventually it wore off and turned soul-sucking. When you let someone get close enough, nine times out of ten you ended up getting burned, and romantic relationships were the perfect recipe for getting too close. I vowed never to get to that point with anyone. As much as I cared for Kenny, no way would I let myself end up like him.

I hated that thoughts about Jackie distracted me from the show that was supposed to be distracting me from losing my job. Jackie somehow found a way to suck out the fun in everything even when she wasn't there. And when the last winner was announced, Kenny still wasn't back. Tatiana and I helped Leti and the crew clean up the venue while we waited.

Once we were done, Leti appeared behind me, throwing their arms over Tatiana's and my shoulders, holding their wig in one hand, their face now devoid of the intense makeup and their black hair braided down their back.

"Have you ever thought about doing drag?" they asked, looking me up and down.

"Nope." I couldn't act for shit, and I had major stage fright. I was definitely more of a spectator.

Leti frowned. "We need more performers for the next show."

"Sorry, Leti. I'd just embarrass you." I laughed at the idea of myself wobbling down a runway in heels. I'd probably break an ankle . . . again.

"I'm not even sure we're related. Whatever. Who's hungry?"

Leti and Tatiana debated where to get food while I wondered how much an Uber would cost to get all of us home. I couldn't be spending too much now that I was out of a job. Before I could call the Uber, Kenny finally showed up. His light brown skin was flushed and sweaty as he jogged over to apologize.

"Sorry, guys. Jackie and I had some stuff to work out. I didn't mean to miss the whole thing." He frowned, pushing his glasses up his nose with his index finger. "I hope y'all haven't been waiting too long."

"Didn't think you were coming back," I said under my breath.

"Of course I was coming back." Kenny frowned like he was offended. I shook my head and sighed. Kenny was a good dude and always intended to be on time to things, but he also lived in the moment, so he wasn't exactly punctual.

Leti leaned toward Kenny and cupped his cheeks in their hands, inspecting him closely. "Have you ever thought about doing drag?" They let go of his face and took a step back. "We need more performers for the next show."

Kenny's lips pursed to the side. "Yeah, kind of."

I couldn't say the news surprised me. Kenny was a theater kid in high school and was always looking to show off his acting chops. Plus, he was an incredible dancer. He would have no problem figuring out how to duckwalk.

"You should do it! I can do your makeup, and you can wear one of my outfits!" Leti squealed. "You have the perfect bone structure for drag. I can't wait to do your face."

I couldn't argue with that. Kenny's bone structure was... Yeah, it was good.

"I don't know," Kenny said, looking conflicted. "Jackie would hate it..."

"Ah, yes. Heterosexual opinions are very important on this matter," Leti deadpanned.

"I'll think about it," Kenny said, rubbing his arm.

"So, how *are* you and Jackie?" Tatiana asked. A bit forward, but I was curious, too. Jackie couldn't have been happy that Kenny came back for us, but his flushed cheeks, sweaty forehead, and overall glowing aura implied they might have... Let's just say they may have put that backpack to use.

"We had a really good talk actually." Kenny smiled. A hesitant, but genuine smile. I made a note to myself to ask him about that later. "Anyway, I'm starving."

"I've never been hungrier in my life," Leti said, the back of their hand raised to their forehead in a show of drama.

"Food's on me," Tatiana offered, and I had to admit I was relieved.

* * *

After getting burgers and chili con carne at Blakes, we sat outside to eat. Being as hungry as I was, I started scarfing down my chili as soon as I sat down. Midbite, I vaguely noticed Tatiana laughing about how I sat next to Kenny instead of her, my "date," even if we were broken up now. I was too into my chili to care, but Kenny turned his head and gave me a little smile that would look subtle to anyone who didn't spend practically twenty-four-seven with the dude. To me, though, that smile belonged on the face of the universal chaos gremlin mascot. Which meant a prank was coming, but because this particular smile was directed at me, it must have meant I was supposed to be in on it.

His eyes flickered down to my lips, and his tongue peeked at the corner of his mouth, as if licking something from it.

"You have something on your . . ." Kenny reached out and gently wiped some chili off the edge of my mouth. His thumb lingered on my lip for just a moment before he stuck it in his own mouth and sucked on it, his eyes never leaving mine.

I almost didn't think anything of it until I saw Tatiana and Leti glance at each other like they'd just walked in on us raw dogging it.

It wasn't that I didn't know a gesture like that would usually be reserved for someone who'd have gladly put more than my chili in their mouth, but this was *me and Kenny*. I was straight, and Kenny was in love with Jackie. Therefore, the gesture at this moment must have had a different motivation than what Tatiana's and Leti's scandalized faces implied.

"You sure Jackie wasn't right about y'all being boyfriends?" Tatiana bit back a smile.

Kenny threw an arm around my shoulder, taking my hand in his other hand and kissing it dramatically. The warmth from his finger lingered on my mouth, and the heat from his lips clung to my palm. "I mean, he's my *husband*, so no, she's dead wrong."

Then it made sense. The gremlin smile, the thumb sucking, the hand kiss . . . Kenny was making a joke.

"I can see it." Tatiana giggled. "Y'all are so cute!"

Then they all burst out laughing, but I wasn't one to laugh at a joke without being sure of the punchline. First I had to make sure I was laughing at the right thing.

"It's funny because I'm straight." My words came off deadpan, but I'd meant it as a question. The only alternative I could think of would be that Kenny was laughing at the concept of anyone being attracted to me, which was so not Kenny.

Since no one disagreed and I now understood the joke, I laughed along with the rest of them.

Kenny always seemed to laugh hardest when Jackie wasn't around, and the way the two of us laughed when we were alone was unrivaled. I didn't even know what we were laughing about anymore as we stumbled up the stairs to our apartment. Kenny had always said my laugh was contagious, but his wasn't any better. It was as if our laughs put us in a vicious cycle, alternating between noise-complaint-worthy cackling to silently wheezing and seal-clapping to make up for the lack of volume.

At that moment, it didn't matter that I'd gotten fired or fought with Jackie. I'd forgotten about all of it, and the only thing on my radar was that *laugh*.

When Kenny laughed hard enough, he'd throw himself on the nearest person, or the floor or wall, if there was no one close enough. Today (and most days) I was the nearest person, which made climbing the steps a bit of a struggle.

I pushed Kenny away when we got to the top and wiped a joyful tear from my eye. Three stray cats were waiting for me outside the door.

"You need to stop feeding the strays." Kenny laughed, but I knew he wasn't being serious. Even though I didn't have a cat of my own, I bought food for the neighborhood cats. I opened the apartment door, careful not to let them in, since my emotional support dog Luna didn't like cats, and grabbed three bowls to fill with kitty kibble and some treats to set outside. I squatted and scratched the calico's and black one's heads. The third was new-ish and hadn't warmed up to me enough for pets yet.

"Ten bucks says she'll let me pet her by next weekend," I said as I went inside.

"Bet, that little one is vicious," Kenny said, still laughing. I put on my dishwashing gloves and started rinsing the dishes Kenny had left in the sink from his dinner. "I love your little gloves," Kenny said as he slumped down on the couch.

I just sighed. There was no way I'd tell him I didn't actually *like* doing the dishes. The texture of the food gunk made me want to gag, so the gloves helped. But Kenny hated dishes more than I did, and his executive dysfunction was way worse, so I was the dishes guy.

"Hey, so... I need to talk to you about something." Kenny had stopped laughing, the contagious smile wiped from his face completely. His voice was shaky enough to spike my heart rate. Had Jackie said something about me? Did he find out I got fired? Was he moving out?

"What is it, bro?"

Kenny ran a hand through his messy black hair. Luna, being an expert in emotional support, hopped up on the spot next to him, resting her head in his lap. She may have been *my* dog, but Kenny was the one she followed around everywhere. She didn't even have the decency to *pretend* to like me more. Maybe I was just more of a cat person, and Kenny had a way with dogs. Well, my dog.

He let out an unsteady breath as he patted the brown Lab's back with one hand and chewed on his nails with the other.

I didn't sit with Kenny and Luna once I finished the dishes. If I sat, that would mean the conversation was serious, and a serious conversation couldn't have a good outcome. I didn't do well with serious. I never knew how to act when people got emotional.

I poured myself a glass of water. To ground myself, I stared at the Han Solo posters on the wall behind the couch—where Kenny got the nickname for me, my full name being Ale*jan*dro.

I tried to convince myself this talk wasn't about Jackie or me getting fired. I couldn't afford this apartment by myself, even *with* my old job. If Kenny broke the lease, would I have to go back to living with Tío Nacho and Tía Mary? I sipped my water, trying to let the thoughts float away.

"Just say it. You're freakin' me out," I coaxed, hoping my fears were false.

But what Kenny said was worse than I could have imagined.

"Jackie and I are getting married."

CHAPTER TWO

KENNY

Han! Are you okay?" I hopped off the couch and rushed over to Han to slap his back as he choked on his water.

"Fine..." he managed between coughs. "Maybe I do need to sit down," he finally said, and we both sat on the sofa. Luna reluctantly slunk to the floor and lay at my feet to make space. Han scratched his chin without saying anything. Just sitting there, disappointed in my life choices, probably. The longer the silence stretched, the farther I shrank into the cushions.

"Say something?" I urged after what must have been a full minute of silence.

"I'm just...processing." Han stopped scratching and rested his elbows on his knees. "Where did that even come from?"

I knew what he was really saying. That I didn't seem happy. But I *was* happy. Jackie made me happy. Most of the time, at least.

Besides, what was I supposed to say? That Jackie threatened to break up with me if I didn't propose? I knew Han didn't approve of Jackie, and Jackie *really* didn't approve of Han. But "no bullshit" was the only fully spoken rule of my relationship with Han. So, honesty it was.

"It was an ultimatum." Knowing Han, my admitting that part probably guaranteed he'd try to talk me out of it, but I couldn't lie to Han even if I wanted to. "It was either get married or . . . break up." Just saying the words "break up" made my throat tighten. Besides the few "breaks" Jackie and I had taken, I hadn't been single since early high school. The idea terrified me.

Jackie knew me better than I knew myself. When I wasn't sure about something, she'd make the choice for me. When I didn't know what to think or how to feel, she was right there to enlighten me. Who even was I without Jackie? Did I even have a personality of my own? Thoughts, feelings, desires of my own? I wasn't so sure, and I didn't want to find out.

I might have been as scared of being single as Han was of *not* being single. All I knew was that I didn't want to be alone, and marrying Jackie ensured that would never happen.

"And you chose . . . to get married?" Han rubbed his temples.

I leaned forward and wrapped my arms around Luna, who went limp as I picked her sixty pounds up to hold in my lap. A living weighted blanket. I wanted *support*, and Luna had plenty to offer. The weight in my lap felt like the hug I desperately needed.

"Yes." I swallowed, preparing for a lecture.

"Why?"

"She was going to break up with me . . ." The words came out before I had a chance to think about them.

"But do you *want* to marry her? What do *you* want?"

Leave it to Han to ask these kinds of questions. He always made sure I factored myself into the equation. I was usually the giver, especially with Jackie. If we disagreed on what to eat, it was her choice we went with. If she was sick, I took care of her. If she was sad, I comforted her. I would do whatever it took to make people happy, my own feelings be damned.

With Han, though, it was a different story. I still wanted to make him happy, but I never had to put myself second to do it.

I thought for a moment before answering. Of course I wanted to get married. I had always wanted the "American dream"—a wedding, kids, a house with a white picket fence. Jackie was offering me just that.

"Yes," I finally said. A shaky yes, but a yes all the same. But I felt uneasy more than anything. If I wanted to stay friends with Han, I was basically committing my best friend and girlfriend—fiancée—to a lifetime of hating each other. My chest sank. Maybe they could work it out somehow? "Do you think you and Jackie will ever get along?"

"She's low-key—no, *high*-key—abusive. You know that, right?"

"What? She literally works at a shelter for abused women. She's not abusive." Sure, she was a bit abrasive, maybe a little aggressive, but abusive? No, I could take care of myself.

"Bet she doesn't think women can perpetuate abuse, huh?" Han said, and I hated that he was probably right. But that didn't mean *Jackie* was abusive.

"She just likes to be in control. Because of her parents—"

"Nope. Nuh-uh. Maybe her parents being controlling or getting divorced was a good excuse in high school, but she's grown now."

"Trauma isn't linear, though. Just because she's an adult doesn't mean she's healed," I said, feeling oddly defensive. Han didn't know Jackie like I did. She just needed some more time and space to heal.

Before her parents' divorce, we were fine. We were perfect. We could get back to that.

"Okay, well, is she *trying* to heal, or does she expect you to do that part for her?" Han asked.

"No! I mean, yes, of course she's trying to heal. She even said she's open to getting a therapist." I gave Luna an extra squeeze, like she was the one who needed to be hugged.

"Didn't she say that years ago? Has she actually looked for one? Doesn't she have, like, a million resources for that kind of thing with her job?" I knew Han wasn't trying to be mean. He was just blunt. Didn't mean it didn't bother me.

"Well, if Jackie doesn't want therapy, I can't force her," I said. Sure, maybe she wasn't actually looking, but it was still her decision.

"My point is, she's using her parents as a shield for treating you like shit. She's abusive, I'm telling you. You know she doesn't have to outright hit you to be abusive?"

I kept my response to myself. Han didn't have to know that Jackie maybe, occasionally, sometimes *did* hit me. He wouldn't get it. I was a freaking black belt in Taekwondo, but I didn't need to defend myself against my own girlfriend. Why would I? Han didn't have to get why Jackie was the way she was. I understood her.

Han sighed when I didn't respond. "I know I can't convince you to leave her, but are you really sure about this?" he asked, eyebrows raised.

"Yes," I said, running my hands through Luna's fur so Han couldn't see them shaking. I didn't want to lose Jackie, but I couldn't lose Han, either. Did getting married mean I'd have to choose?

"Okay, then." He sighed. "I'll play nice, but I won't like it."

Han wasn't one to give a sappy "I support you" speech, but sometimes I wished he would. I needed some kind of confirmation that marrying Jackie wouldn't cost me my best friend.

"Thanks for the support," I said sarcastically, but Han didn't catch the tone. He rarely did.

"Sure thing. Love you, bro," he said. I wasn't complaining about the affection, but it always bothered me a tiny bit that Han was incapable of saying anything nice without putting "bro" at the end. I wasn't really sure why. Maybe because it took some of the vulnerability and realness out of the moment. Then again, Han wasn't exactly the vulnerable type. He gave me a firm shoulder squeeze before heading off to bed. I sat there alone, the warmth from Han's hand lingering on my shoulder in a way no one else's touch did.

I woke up the next morning to a phone call from a random number, and I groggily answered, expecting a spam call. Han would make fun of me for always answering random numbers, but you never know when it could be important, right?

And this time it was.

"Hi, I'm looking for Brandon Hawes?" the voice on the other line said, and I immediately knew something was up. Brandon Hawes was Han's boss. Why would Han give someone *my* number and say it was his?

"May I ask who's calling?" I asked before giving any information.

"Kaitlin Ford, I'm calling from the ABQ Biopark Aquarium. Alejandro Torres put you down as a job reference."

I fist pumped the air. Given Han's love of jellyfish, the aquarium sounded like the perfect fit, and it was about time he got a job he actually enjoyed. Han must not have wanted his boss to know he was looking, so he gave them my number. I jumped into gear, talking up Han's work ethic, loyalty, and how he was always, always on time. All true.

"He sounds like a great candidate!" Kaitlin said. "If you valued him so much, may I ask what made you let him go?"

The gears in my mind clogged up. Han got fired?

Why wouldn't he have told me? How long ago had that happened? Was he okay? Were *we* okay on rent?

"Mr. Hawes?" The voice sounded fuzzy through the ringing in my ears.

"My apologies." I cleared my throat, then stumbled over an answer. "Ah, well, you know how it is. Who knew corporate greed had its downfalls?"

She gave a dry laugh. "Thank you for your time, Mr. . . . *Hawes*."

Click.

Shit.

After pacing my room a few times, I swung my door open and made a beeline for the living room, where I could hear Han's music playing in the background. He sat on the couch, typing away on his laptop.

"You lost your job?" I asked as unantagonistically as I could manage.

"Got fired." Han didn't even bother looking up from his screen.

I pushed the bubbling frustration down about how Han hadn't bothered telling me. This wasn't about me. This was about Han. If he didn't tell me, there must have been a reason. I needed to be a better friend so he could trust me more. Jackie's voice rang in my ear, saying I wasn't good enough. Not for her and not for Han. I needed to be better.

A knock at the door pulled me out of my thoughts, and Han

gave me a questioning look. *Who's here?* I felt embarrassed to admit it was Jackie. After Han called her abusive last night, I hardly thought he'd be happy to see her. Still, he'd promised to make nice.

"It's Jackie," I said, cautiously gauging his reaction. He nodded, not a hint of emotion on his face as I went to let Jackie in. The moment the door opened, she threw herself into my arms, and I relaxed into hers.

"Fiancé!" she squealed as she nuzzled her face into the crook of my neck. As I squeezed back, I could almost feel Han's eyes rolling, but I didn't care. I was going to marry this woman.

When Jackie finally pulled away, I prepared myself for her to ask if we could go to my room so we could be alone, but instead, she waved.

"Hi, Han," she said as she went over and *sat next to him.*

"Hey, Jackie," Han said with a smile that didn't quite reach his eyes. I blinked to make sure I was seeing correctly. Then a huge grin took over my face. Jackie and Han were both willing to try for me. I sank onto the couch between them and wrapped my arms around their shoulders.

"I love you guys."

"Love you, too," Jackie said, planting a kiss on my shoulder.

"You too, bro," Han said at the same time. My shoulders stiffened at the tension coming from my left, where Jackie shifted in her seat. Shit. I shouldn't have said that. But Jackie didn't say anything, which was a good sign. I slipped my hand in hers and squeezed, and then she relaxed again.

"So, um, how are you doing, Han?" Jackie asked.

"I'm good," Han said.

"That's good..."

"Yeah..."

Jackie shifted uncomfortably. "Um, the weather's kind of nice, right?"

"I guess."

Jackie seemed to give up on the conversation then, pulling out her phone and scrolling through some Twitter article. I glanced down in curiosity. The headline was about ICE raids.

"So, ICE is pretty terrible, right?"

Han's shoulder next to me stiffened. Jackie didn't know about his status, but I didn't want him to think she did. He didn't answer, so Jackie kept going.

"You guys must hate them, right?" She leaned forward to make eye contact with Han.

"Why, because we're Mexican?" Han fired back.

"We don't have to talk about this," I finally butted in, but Jackie was already answering.

"Yeah, I'm just curious about your guys's thoughts, as Mexicans." Her eyes were all big and innocent. Jackie had never asked me that before, so I was a little thrown. Particularly now that she was making nice with Han. I had a feeling it had to do with me being practically white-passing (depending on who you asked) and Han being more racialized. Because I was fourth generation and extremely assimilated, maybe Jackie considered me too removed from the issue to be asking me about ICE unless Han was there.

"Babe . . ." I wished this conversation could end that second, but Han interrupted.

"Actually, I'm tired. Gonna go take a nap." And he went to his room, leaving me alone with Jackie.

"I was just trying to connect with him about something," Jackie said with those big innocent eyes. I sank farther into the couch. Whatever lightness I'd felt from them trying to make nice was gone. "I wish Han would just be honest about his feelings for once."

"He is." I defended Han on a reflex, but I had to admit Jackie had a point. Han wasn't the type to go telling everyone when something upset him.

"No, he's not. He's clearly mad, but instead of talking he just left."

"He's not mad," I reassured her. I hadn't been lying when I said Han was honest—just not the way Jackie would expect. When Han was upset, he'd give the strays an extra treat, or work out, or go for a walk, or watch a tear-jerker kid movie for an excuse to cry. He always had a tell. Which meant Han wasn't upset. Annoyed, sure, but not angry. I kicked myself for not noticing he'd given the cats some treats the night before. That was his tell that he got fired, and I missed it.

"He is. *That's* why you two never fight. It's not healthy. It's important to be open about your emotions"—Jackie leaned her head on my shoulder—"like we are."

"That's not why we don't fight." I had to resist telling Jackie she was more than open with her emotions. She could be so mean about it. But I didn't want to start a fight, especially over Han. "Do you really think fighting is healthy?"

"Of course. It proves there's love, you know? It wasn't the fighting that told me my parents stopped loving each other. It was when they *stopped* fighting. They didn't fight, because they didn't care. *We* care." She kissed my shoulder again.

"We do," I reassured her as I kissed the top of her head. I was the opposite of self-aware, but Jackie knew me. She was self-assured and had enough confidence for both of us. She was my first. If fighting was proof of love, then she loved me more than anyone. But what proof was there for Han?

Luna curled up around my feet. Han left her with me whenever I was anxious, which I almost always was. I looked around and noticed he'd already done my dirty dishes. He never guilted or judged me when my executive dysfunction caused him more work. He just did it to make things easier on me.

Everywhere I looked, the evidence was there.

CHAPTER THREE

HAN

It wasn't that Jackie bringing up ICE got to me.

It was just that... it did.

And there was no way in fuck I'd let her see me worked up over ICE, or that I lost my chance at a green card, or that I had no idea what to do next.

I'd already crossed every other path to citizenship off the list. The only two options left were to join the military or get married. I couldn't bring myself to support the militarized US state, and I couldn't use someone for marriage. Even if I wanted to, I had no prospects.

My chest tightened, and my breath hitched. Suddenly the room felt simultaneously big enough to gulp me up but also too small, like it would crush me alive.

Back to polyp.

Close your eyes. Breathe steady. Remember where you came from...

* * *

My earliest memory was of a guitar. Ringed fingers plucked the strings, a pendant I couldn't quite make out hanging from the woman's neck, bobbing back and forth as she swayed with her song. She set the guitar on the ground and pointed. I looked up at her in awe, but the memory was fuzzy around her face, and when she sang, she sounded like she was underwater. Like a distant song clouded by time, but still beautiful all the same. Logically, I knew this woman was my mother, even if I couldn't bring myself to remember her song, or necklace, or what her face looked like back then.

But I remembered the guitar, and the magic of my first time making music with my own hands.

* * *

I opened my eyes, breathing just fine. I wasn't *okay*, but I was better. I got out a pen and started writing.

I might not have been super vulnerable with any real-life person. I preferred to let things out in letters to my mom I'd never send. I'd been writing them since I was ten, when Leti, Mariana, and I got a shared laptop. Even then, I never had the courage to actually send any of the letters. My mom wasn't the type to appreciate a heartfelt letter. It always felt like she cared more about drugs than about me.

So, I wasn't exactly writing these letters for my actual mom. They were for the fictional mom in my head, who would appreciate them and write back a sappy letter of her own.

I tried writing, but my hands shook and my vision blurred. So I went to method number two for processing shit.

My guitar.

I strummed for a bit, then turned on my computer and started recording just in case genius struck. Sometimes, when I couldn't write the words on paper for my mom, I found myself singing or speaking them on a recording I'd never show anyone.

"Hi, Mami. I lost my job." Instead of singing, I just strummed while I blurted out my unfiltered thoughts. "Would you have me if I moved back home with you and Papi?" My throat tightened, but I swallowed and kept going. "I don't know what else to do. I don't think I can stay here anymore. I'm sorry . . ." I tried gulping down the lump, but it just grew, and I choked on it. I turned off the recording. Some things were too vulnerable even for the made-up version of my mom that existed only in my head.

CHAPTER FOUR

KENNY

Jackie was long gone by the time Han came out of his room, but he didn't sit next to me.

"Going for a walk," he said as he made his way to the door.

"You okay?" I asked, but he just threw me a thumbs-up before shutting the door behind him.

Shit. Walks were one of Han's tells. I wanted so badly to chase him out there and ask what was wrong, but I knew he wouldn't say. He didn't even tell me, his *roommate*, that he'd lost his job. Had I done something? I must have.

With the "no bullshit" rule, I was supposed to trust that Han would tell me if I'd done something that bothered him, but sometimes Han didn't realize himself when things were bothering him. Still, if being with Jackie had taught me anything, it was that I had one major talent: fucking things up.

I was constantly saying or doing the wrong thing. According to Jackie, she was the only one I could trust to call me on my shit, and if Han's lack of criticism was anything to go off, she was right. I might not have known *what* I did, but it was clear I'd fucked up once again, and I desperately needed to make things right.

When I was depressed like Han seemed to be, I had a particularly hard time doing chores. Maybe I could ease Han's load a bit by doing some of his?

I went to Han's room and got to work. I was surprised to see clothes on the floor instead of in his hamper. This looked more like my room than Han's. The closest I'd ever gotten to using my hamper was tossing clothes in its general direction and hoping for the best. But Han wasn't like me.

There were only a few outfits on the floor, but it felt so un-Han that I stood there for a moment before getting to work putting them in the hamper and carrying it down to the laundry room. Luckily, I had plenty of spare change for the washer from my serving job.

Han still wasn't back when the clothes were dry, so I decided to put them away. I hung up his nicer shirts and folded the T-shirts and pants before putting them in his dresser.

I must have accidentally bumped the desk, because the computer screen lit up, and a video with Han holding his guitar popped up.

I smiled. Han sometimes recorded original songs on his computer, and I loved watching him sing. Whenever Han recorded a new song, he'd casually mention it to me, then leave it on the screen and leave the room so I could watch without him having to see my reaction. He was a bit shy like that.

I assumed this was the same, so I pressed play.

He talked instead of singing, but he was strumming his guitar, so it took me a while to realize this particular video wasn't meant for me.

I don't think I can stay here anymore.

Han wanted to leave?

Just then the apartment door opened, and I quickly paused the video and shut off the computer, running out of Han's room and into the living room.

"Han," I started, but didn't know how to finish. I couldn't just beg him to stay. I wasn't even supposed to know he wanted to leave!

"You okay, bro?"

I hated that he was asking me that instead of the other way around. "I'm worried about *you*."

"What's to worry about? I'm all good. Just needed to clear my head." Han grinned, but I didn't buy it. He was thinking about going back to Mexico! And he wasn't even going to tell me. He was not *all good*. And neither was I, apparently.

I needed to be better. Needed to be more trustworthy.

"What do you need from me? I'll do whatever I can to support you," I said, sounding more desperate than I'd hoped.

"What are you talking about? We're good, bro."

I snapped my fingers as a brilliant idea came to me. "I can get you a job at the restaurant!" I hoped that would be enough to get him to stay. He'd said he might leave because of getting fired.

"Really?" Han asked, a hint of hope in his voice.

"Yeah! Two cooks got fired yesterday for fighting. And as assistant manager, I don't need permission. I can just hire you! You're already a natural with cooking."

"Thanks. I, uh, appreciate that, bro." Han finally smiled, for real.

*   *   *

I drove Han to his first shift the very next day. Now we both worked at Joe's Cheesecake, which was basically the Cheese-cake Factory, but cheaper. As a server and assistant manager, my shifts changed every couple of weeks, while Han's were expected to stay pretty consistent as a cook. Our shifts didn't overlap today.

"Jackie said our relationship isn't healthy because we never fight," I blurted out as we pulled up to the restaurant. The thought had lingered since the night before.

I wasn't quite sure why I felt the need to bring it up. Maybe I needed validation that she was wrong. That there wasn't some-thing wrong with the relationship I had with my lifelong best friend.

"That's bullshit," Han said. "Fighting doesn't make a relation-ship healthy. And even if we did fight, it'd be nothing like your fights with Jackie. She has no respect."

I sighed. "I thought you were making nice with her?"

"I'm trying, man." Han shook his head. "I just don't like how she talks to you. She puts these weird-ass ideas in your head."

"I don't just buy into everything she tells me..." I mumbled. I definitely didn't agree with the fighting thing.

"Good. I'll see you later."

And with that, Han left the car and went inside. At least he was trying?

I stalled in the lot for a bit before going to pick Jackie up to bring her to my parents'. I was hoping to get their permission to get married. If Han wasn't going to give my engagement his enthusiastic approval and unwavering support, maybe my par-ents could fill that gap.

Jackie's other goal, besides getting permission to get married, was to get her hands on my grandma's emerald engagement band. After her parents' divorce, she latched on to mine quicker than one of those slap bracelets. My parents weren't as enthusiastic about Jackie as she was about them, but since her own parents wouldn't give her an ounce of attention, she craved my parents' affection like a drug. I assumed that was why she wanted the ring so badly. It had been passed down for generations, and my parents offering it would be the ultimate show of accepting her into the family. So, I had to get her that ring. I took a deep breath as we parked in front of the house. I could do this.

The gated community I grew up in was a far cry from Han's and my little apartment just outside downtown Albuquerque. Both my parents made a decent living from real estate, so they'd lived comfortably in a suburban cookie-cutter home my whole life. When I was growing up, the house was only a few streets down from Han's place, though the neighborhoods were vastly different in house size and prices. And with Han's being chock-full of humans every waking moment, he spent a lot of his time at my quiet house with me and my parents. It made mine feel more lived in, and my parents loved it.

When Jackie pressed the doorbell, my mom answered almost immediately. Her face lit up when she saw me, her energy burning bright despite the constant bags under her eyes, which were the only indication she was anywhere near fifty.

"So nice to see you two! Come on in." She hugged me as if we hadn't seen each other in years, even though it had been only a few days. She was a bit over-the-top like that. Then she hugged Jackie just as tight, but it looked forced, at least on my mom's side. Her back was too stiff. She and Jackie had always gotten along superficially, but never on a deeper level. I hoped that might change someday, but I wasn't sure they'd get along if they knew each other any better. As we walked inside, my mom grabbed my arm and frowned as she inspected it.

"You're spending too much time in the sun."

I snatched my arm away. "*Mom*, it's fine." I wasn't even that tan, but my mom was always worrying that if I got too tan, I'd get skin cancer. Which totally wasn't a concern, considering I spent about as much time in the sun as a vampire.

"You need to protect your skin. Are you wearing sunscreen?"

"Yes," I lied. Why would I wear sunscreen to my parents' house?

With my mom satisfied, the three of us sat on the couch, chatting about the next party my mom planned to throw for her cousin's niece's friend's quinceañera (she was the go-to party planner for everyone who knew her) while my dad finished up the food. He always insisted on feeding anyone who came over, so it was usually best to show up hungry.

He finally came out of the kitchen carrying a plate full of mini elotes slathered in butter, mayo, chili powder, and lime juice. The smell of the fresh corn on the cob made my mouth water. Our family was pretty assimilated in every way *except* the food we ate. My dad made it a mission to cook only Mexican food and snacks, even if he got the recipes from white people online.

"Thanks, Dad," I said as I picked up a piece of corn by the stick poking out of it. I took a bite to stall the conversation. I really wasn't looking forward to this talk, so instead I reveled in the perfect mixture of sweet and spicy on my tongue.

My dad, on the other hand, didn't let the food get in the way. "So, you wanted to talk?" he asked with his mouth full, arching one of his bushy caterpillar eyebrows.

I wiped some mayo from my lips with a napkin and forced

a smile. "Yeah. Um, thanks for having us over." I felt myself speaking much more formally than I normally would with them. I could already feel my hands shaking, so I put the elote down and placed them on my lap to hide the tremble. Jackie must have noticed, because she grabbed one of my hands and moved it to her thigh, putting her own hand on top of mine. The gesture should have helped, but all I could think about were the potential consequences of this conversation. It wasn't that I needed my parents' approval to marry who I wanted, but how would Jackie react if they said no? Would she be mad at me?

Okay, out with it.

"Um, as you know, Jackie and I have been together for a really long time, and we think it's a good time to get married."

My parents shared a look before saying anything.

"Why is now the time?" my mom asked. She didn't offer to get the ring.

I couldn't say "because Jackie will break up with me if we don't get married," so I pulled away from Jackie's thigh and wrung my hands together, trying to come up with a reason they'd be satisfied with. She was the only person I had ever even been with—unless you counted the guy I hooked up with in college while Jackie and I were on a break, which I didn't acknowledge to anyone besides Han and my parents, who actually caught us in the act. But when you were with someone as long as we were, you were supposed to get married. That was, like, the law or something; everyone expected it.

Eventually, Jackie filled the awkward silence. "It just feels like good timing because Kenny's lease is about to end." That was a lie. I still had six months left. I guessed that would be when the wedding would happen, though. "And we've been waiting to move in until marriage, so it's perfect timing!" Jackie's pink-painted lips grinned as she threw her arms around me. She sure was confident. I'd give her that. I was glad she hadn't mentioned my lie about my parents insisting we get married before moving in. Jackie would not have been happy if she realized I'd made that up. My stomach dropped at the realization I'd finally have to move away from Han. We'd lived together for five years—since we were eighteen—and I'd gotten used to it.

"Are you sure you're ready for a lifelong commitment?" My dad casually took another bite of corn after the question. "You're both still young..."

He wasn't *wrong*, but he wasn't particularly right, either. At twenty-three, Jackie, Han, and I were at that age where half our friends were having kids and settling down, and the other half were partying it up or living at home. It was a weird in-between stage, but I had always thought of Jackie and me as being a part of the former group. I had to admit, though, I felt like a traitor for leaving Han behind...

"We're ready, Papi," Jackie said. She had been calling my dad Papi and my mom Mami ever since she'd heard Han use the familiar terms with them. I never stopped her, even though it felt a little strange considering she only got the terms from Han, who'd grown up with that kind of language. *I* didn't even call my parents that. Honestly, I preferred not to bring Jackie around my parents much because they were a bit judgy. But I knew if I said anything about the nicknames, she'd raise hell, since there was no way Jackie was going to let Han have something she couldn't. Even if it was different. Even if Han called my parents that because they treated him like their own son. He'd known my parents almost his whole life, while Jackie only saw them on special occasions. "We've been together forever; it's time," Jackie added when no one answered.

"Forever?" My mom shot my dad a concerned look. "I hate to bring this up, but didn't you two just get back together a few months ago?" I bit my tongue. Our most recent break was painful enough without my mom drudging it up. We were finally getting past it.

Jackie's face reddened, and I reached for her hand to ground her before she said anything she couldn't take back.

"We first got together in high school, Mami. It *has* been forever," Jackie said.

"Kenny? Do you feel ready for this?" my mom urged, but I couldn't get the words out. The silence was pummeling me into my grave, since Jackie would definitely kill me for this. I finally cleared my throat and managed to say something.

"We've been together forever." It was the closest to an "I'm ready" I could muster. All I knew was that I was light-years more ready to get married than to be alone.

"It's true that you just got back together," my dad said. "Maybe you should wait a couple of years."

"I agree," my mom added. "Statistically, couples who are together three years before marriage are less likely to divorce!"

"But we've been together since high school!" Jackie pleaded.

"In the course of a lifetime, what's another year or two?" my dad asked, and I couldn't bring myself to argue. I felt relieved, actually. If I was being honest, I wasn't in any rush, and I was happy Jackie had no power over my parents, meaning she didn't have control over how quickly we'd get married.

"A year . . ." Jackie paused, then squeezed my hand and got up to hug my parents. "Thank you so much! It might take us a year to plan a wedding anyway. Now all we need is a ring to make the engagement official!"

Shit. Jackie wasn't really supposed to know about that ring.

It was clear my mom wasn't going to offer it, and that made me think they didn't approve after all. I should have been upset about that, but I didn't know how to feel. I wasn't happy, but I also didn't feel angry like I'd expected to if they said no.

I thought Jackie might ask for the ring outright if the conversation went on any longer, so I thanked my parents for the food and their approval, then excused myself and Jackie to pick Han up from work. It was only a half lie. Han wouldn't be off work for another hour.

"Stay safe! Love you!" my mom said as she hugged me goodbye.

"Love you too."

"Love you too!" Jackie repeated enthusiastically, but instead of saying it back, my mom offered a stiff goodbye hug. Luckily, Jackie didn't seem to notice.

When we got in the car, Jackie slumped into her seat.

"I thought we were going on a date today?" She puffed out her bottom lip.

"What? We are," I said, unsure where Jackie got the idea that we weren't.

"You said you were going to pick up Han."

"Yeah, babe. I just need to get him and drop him off at home, and then we'll go on our date." I'd told Jackie the plan earlier, but she always seemed disappointed when I didn't cancel on Han.

"Why can't Han walk home?"

"Because I told him I would take him home." I didn't mention that Han still had a messed-up ankle from his high school soccer days. It wasn't too far of a drive from the restaurant to our apartment, but walking would take about an hour, and after Han's long walk yesterday, there was no way he'd be able to make another one without coming home in more pain than I ever cared to see him in.

"Well, it would mean a lot to me if we could go on our date *now*." Jackie slithered her hand onto my thigh while I drove. I made sure to keep my eyes on the road and not meet her pleading gaze.

"I can't just ditch Han." I sighed. I hated getting guilt-tripped. Like I was a bad boyfriend for being a good friend. Couldn't I be good at both?

Jackie paused, and I could feel her sizing me up. "Bryan would have never done this to me..."

I tightened my grip on the wheel. Bryan was the guy she'd cheated on me with only a few months ago, the reason we'd been on a break. We were still working through it, but Jackie bringing him up was a serious low blow.

"Besides, Han's an adult. He'll be fine." Jackie pouted and pulled her hand away from my thigh. "Seriously, I feel like you love him more than me."

My fingers tightened around the wheel again. I didn't like when she compared herself to Han. I hated the thought of having to compare two of the people I loved most. But...Han was the only person who I could really relax around. The only person who made sure I put *myself* first. How could I possibly have loved anyone more than the most consistent, loyal, trustworthy person I'd ever met?

Somewhere deep down, I knew I was wrong for that. I should have loved the girl I was going to spend the rest of my life with more than my childhood best friend...right? My lack of an answer only angered her more.

"Kenny..." she started, and I could feel her eyes once again trained on me.

I kept my own on the road.

"Kenny." She said it sternly this time. "If you had to choose between me and Han, who would you choose?" Her confident tone showed she had no idea the true answer.

"I'm not answering that, babe."

"No. You have to choose. We can go on our date, or you can pick up your little boyfriend. It's me or him. I'm serious. Who's it going to be?"

Instead of answering, I took her hand and kissed it. Anything to avoid a confrontation. But she wouldn't let me.

"Kenny, I swear to God, if you choose Han, we're breaking up."

"Jackie, I'm not going to choose!" I hadn't meant to raise my voice, but I didn't exactly appreciate another ultimatum so soon after getting engaged.

"What the hell! Are you fucking kidding me?"

"Please don't make me choose." Making decisions wasn't exactly my strong suit, and Jackie knew this. She usually picked for me so I wouldn't make the wrong choice, but was this something I was willing to let her choose? If I didn't make up my mind and she chose herself for me, then it didn't matter what my original choice would have been. If it was Han, she'd know and be bitter about it forever. If it was her, she'd never let me live down that I wasn't confident enough in our relationship to say it myself.

I started driving to Jackie's house instead of the restaurant. For the first time, maybe ever, the choice was clear.

It was as if she'd read my mind. My vision went white as Jackie's hand cracked across my cheek, causing me to swerve into traffic. Horns honked and cars swerved, but I was able to get control before hitting anyone. I clenched my jaw and put one hand on my cheek, leaving the other firmly gripping the wheel. Heat rose in my chest and face, and I struggled to push the anger down. She'd slapped me before, but never while I was *driving*. She could have gotten us both killed!

"I'm sorry," Jackie said, coaxing my hand away from my cheek to hold it in hers, then planting a soft kiss on the reddened handprint on my face. "You just make me so *mad* sometimes!"

I wished she wouldn't get so angry. I wished I didn't make her so angry.

"I'm sorry." My words came out weak and pathetic. Just like I felt. How I too often felt with Jackie.

"I see you made your choice." Jackie grinned as I pulled my car into my usual spot in her driveway. I *had* made my choice, and for the first time since we'd been together, I didn't need any reassurance to know exactly what I wanted.

"I choose Han," I said. "Please get out of my car."

CHAPTER FIVE

HAN

Who stole the soy sauce packets?" my new boss, Daniel, shouted from the walk-in pantry. The air got thick around me as Daniel marched red-faced through the kitchen. He pointed to Juan, the other new hire. "Where is the soy sauce?"

"I don't know, sir," Juan mumbled.

"I'll help you look," I offered, knowing if I didn't, someone was about to get fired for something they didn't do. I followed Daniel back into the pantry, and low and behold, the soy sauce was exactly where I'd left it. "There." I pointed.

"Why isn't it on the first shelf?" Daniel scolded.

"Oh, my mistake, sir." Shit. I could have gotten someone fired because I didn't learn where the soy sauce went fast enough.

"Fix that," Daniel said, then stormed out of the pantry and into his office.

I sighed and took the L by playing Tetris with the pantry

items to get the sauce where Daniel wanted it. I've always been shit at Tetris.

When I finally got the chance to take off my apron and put it in my locker, Daniel was yelling again.

"Just return the money you stole, and we won't have a problem!"

"I didn't steal anything. I swear!" Juan said frantically. Daniel seemed to have it out for Juan today.

If Kenny were here, he'd definitely handle it. If you only knew Kenny by how he acted with Jackie, you'd have no idea how he was when she wasn't around. Optimistic. Charismatic. A leader and an advocate.

But Kenny wasn't here. I looked around for a sympathetic face, but the only people in the kitchen were other cooks who were all just as much at risk of getting fired.

"Have you tried recounting the money?" As soon I'd said it, I felt like I'd stepped off a cliff's edge, but I kept going. "With all due respect, someone would have noticed if he walked out and stole from the register." I knew I was out of line, but I couldn't just watch Juan get fired and say nothing.

"Are you calling me a liar? I know it was him! Give me back the money or you're fired!" He pointed an accusatory finger at Juan, who had tears in his eyes by now.

"I swear, I didn't steal anything!"

"Get out of my kitchen!" Daniel slammed his palm on the counter hard enough to make me jump. "Or should I call the cops?"

My chest tightened so hard I could barely breathe. According to Kenny, I wasn't the only undocumented cook here. Daniel knew damn well what he was threatening.

The other cooks hung their heads, eyes focused on the

grease-splattered floor as Daniel grabbed Juan's arm and dragged him out the back door. I hung my head, too.

By the time I walked outside, Kenny was already waiting in his car. We spent most of the ride in silence. Something was obviously off with him, but I was still feeling too guilty to pay much attention. I wished I could have done something to help Juan, but if I'd done anything else, I'd have been dragged out the door with him. Or worse, I could have pushed Daniel to actually call the cops.

Pressure built up in my chest again, making it hard to breathe. I hated that Daniel could make one fucking phone call and ruin everyone's lives. That anyone had that kind of power made me sick. Literally. I wanted to throw up.

"Hey, you okay?" Kenny finally seemed to come out of his own fog. He spared me a concerned glance before looking back at the road.

"The other new hire got fired already. Daniel almost called the cops." It was all I needed to say, since I knew Kenny understood the gravity of that sentence. But saying it made my throat tighten.

Close your eyes. Breathe steady. Remember where you came from.

Back to polyp.

I tried to conjure up a comforting memory, but all I could think about was how hard it was to breathe.

Breathe...steady...

Back to polyp!

Instead of being taken back, my throat kept shrinking,

allowing less and less air. I grabbed at the locked handle to ground me, squeezing it tighter than my throat. I wanted out of the enclosed space of the car. Now.

As if he'd read my mind, Kenny immediately took the next exit and pulled into an empty parking lot.

"Han, there's no cops. No one's going to take you away, okay? You're safe. You're safe…" Kenny rubbed circles into my back while I gasped for air. My vision tunneled, and I felt suffocated. Instead of answering, I fumbled with the lock on the door until it clicked. I shoved it open, tumbling outside on all fours, desperately trying to suck in some air.

When my throat finally opened up, my breakfast came pouring out. I gasped in between bouts of bile spilling from my mouth. I barely noticed Kenny kneeling beside me, rubbing my back. Once I'd emptied my stomach, my throat burned like hell, but at least I could breathe. Kenny offered me a water bottle, and I quickly gulped some down.

"Thanks," I croaked, leaning into him in exhaustion. Kenny was the only one I felt comfortable having a panic attack around. Well, not *comfortable*. No panic attack was comfortable. But safe. Taken care of.

"You okay?" Kenny asked.

"I'm good." I didn't want to dwell on it. We got back in the car and rode the rest of the way home in silence, like we always did when I had a panic attack. The best thing for me to do was ignore it. Though Kenny often tried, I never wanted to talk about it.

When we got home, I quickly fed the cats, making sure to give them some extra treats before throwing myself down in the desk chair in my room. I was about to pick up my guitar and start playing when I noticed the sticky note on my laptop.

I pulled it off, the corners of my lips twitching at the red panda drawn on the sticky note with a quote bubble saying "it'll be okay." Kenny must have snuck in here while I was with the cats.

Kenny knew I wasn't one for an emotional conversation. But he must have known some part of me liked being reminded he cared, just without confronting it face-to-face.

I finally picked up my guitar to distract myself from the anxiety attack and the reason for it, plucking at the strings halfheartedly.

It wasn't long before Kenny peeked in through the open door. I jutted my chin toward my bed, letting him know he could sit. Neither of us mentioned the note. We never did. One day I would tell him I appreciated the notes, but not today.

Instead of sitting like a normal person, Kenny flopped down on the bed, not seeming bothered in the least that his head was hanging off the edge. Luna followed him in and curled up on the floor near Kenny's head. I strummed absentmindedly while I waited for Kenny to say whatever he came in to say. After forever and a day, he broke the silence.

"Jackie and I broke up."

I resisted the urge to say what I felt: *Thank God.*

Instead: "I'm sorry, bro. You okay?"

Kenny groaned. "How do you stay so detached from your relationships?" His voice sounded strained, since his head was hanging off the edge of my bed. I couldn't blame Kenny for being a little dramatic. Just yesterday he was convinced he'd marry the girl. He seemed pretty upset, so I didn't pry.

"I can't really get attached when I could get deported any day." I chuckled at the unfunny joke, keeping my fingers busy plucking at the guitar strings. Not a great way to lighten the vibe. I was never great at that, and Kenny didn't even laugh.

"Do you worry about that a lot?" he asked.

One part of me wanted to be honest and say of course I worried about it. But the other part wanted to say no, so Kenny wouldn't worry, too. I didn't want him to realize I damn near had a panic attack every time someone so much as mentioned the word "cop." I didn't want Kenny to worry about the constant reminders that I wasn't safe. Like my ankle being so messed up from high school. I couldn't go to the hospital then without risking getting thrown back into a country I hardly knew. Or that I had to walk on eggshells at my brand-new job so Daniel wouldn't call the cops. Or that I was the only one in the family I grew up with who was undocumented, so if I got sent back, I'd be sent back alone. But I also couldn't lie. "No bullshit," and all that.

"I've gotten used to it, but yeah, I do," I admitted, trying my best to water it down with my tone.

"You never talk about that." Kenny said it like a question.

"I don't want anyone worrying about me." I shrugged, still strumming to keep the vibe from getting too real. I didn't want Kenny dealing with my problems while he was going through a breakup.

"You know I already do. Of course I worry about that." Kenny looked hurt. I hated that look.

"We don't have to talk about that right now," I said. I'd much rather help Kenny deal with his Jackie issues. "You gonna be all right?"

Kenny shrugged. "I don't know. Who even *am* I without Jackie? She gets me, you know? She knows what I want and what I like and how I feel when I don't. She even picked the curtains in my room because I couldn't pick a fucking color!

Now I'm gonna think about Jackie whenever I see the damn window."

I didn't know how to answer. This felt like a bigger problem than a pep talk and a pat on the back could solve. At least there was one thing easily fixed, so I went with that. "Let's get you some new curtains, then."

Kenny thought about it for a second before responding. "Good idea. What color do you think they should be?"

"That's up to you. What's your favorite color?" When we were kids, Kenny's favorite color changed with the seasons, but back then he at least knew what he liked when he liked it.

He hesitated before responding, still not bothering to lift his head to speak. "Um, Jackie always said I look good in blue?"

I paused my strumming and looked over at Kenny, who was still hanging his head off the edge of the bed. "Can I be real with you and say something you're not gonna like?"

Kenny finally lifted his head to look at me. "No bullshit, right? Now you have to tell me."

"Right. I don't know if you remember how you were before Jackie, but you weren't like *this*."

"What do you mean?" Kenny scooted next to me so both our backs were leaning against the wall. "I've always been an expert at second-guessing myself. My low self-confidence isn't a Jackie thing."

"You might have second-guessed yourself, but you didn't need Jackie to approve your favorite fucking color. What happened to those plushies you used to sleep with? Since when were you embarrassed to sing in the shower? You never used to care about being too loud or too weird. You've been scared to be yourself for *years*, bro."

"Wait, you think I'm weird?" Kenny asked, looking worried.

"See what I mean?" I couldn't help but laugh. "You didn't used to care about that shit. *Everyone's* weird, okay? I like that you're weird, bro," I admitted, my cheeks warming a bit since I wasn't usually one to hand out compliments like that. Desperate times, though.

Kenny was quiet for a while, and when he finally spoke, I almost didn't hear him. "Periwinkle."

The fuck?

"Uh...plubberfloop," I added.

"Wait, what?" Kenny asked, an amused smile on his lips.

"Are we not saying made-up words?" Now *I* was second-guessing myself. "I thought we were doing a thing."

"It's a color," Kenny said, his grin widening. "Periwinkle... That's my favorite color."

I had my doubts, so I googled "periwinkle" on my phone to find that it was, in fact, a shade of purple.

"All right. Let's get you some periwinkle curtains, then."

Kenny's smile grew. "Thanks, Han."

I nodded. It felt like the end of a conversation, but Kenny stayed sitting beside me, which I couldn't complain about. It was nice to sometimes just sit in silence. But that wasn't something Kenny usually did, so I knew he still had something to say. Even with the small victory we'd just had, Kenny might have needed a little push to speak his mind. He'd usually cut a conversation about his feelings short unless you let him know you were still invested. Maybe he thought he was burdening me with his problems. Probably another Jackie side effect.

"What is it?" I asked. That single question was all he ever needed as reassurance that I was still in the conversation, so he didn't hesitate to open right back up. Kenny was an emotional guy, and being an open book was his natural state, no matter how hard he tried to hold back for other people's sake.

"Jackie and I were together for, like, our entire adult lives. I wanted to spend my life with her, start a family, all that. What am I supposed to do now?"

"Having kids is overrated anyway. Live your life. You're young. You got time to figure it out."

"Maybe to *you*. I *want* to be a dad. I think I'd be good at it."

"You would be good at it," I admitted. Kenny would be a great dad. I saw how he was with my baby nephew, Mateo. Kenny wasn't exactly stealth about his baby fever.

"Do you really never want kids? *Never*?" Kenny asked.

"Never. I don't want to fuck a kid up like my mom did with me. And she only had me for five years."

Kenny's eyes widened, and I feared I might have said something wrong. "You never talk about your mom."

I shrugged. How did the conversation keep getting back to me? "Anyway, you'll be okay. Look at it like this. You're finally free, right? You can do all the things Jackie never let you do. You're the most yourself when y'all are broken up. Be free."

I meant it, too. There were so many things Jackie made Kenny feel like shit about for doing or liking, or not doing or not liking. Kenny tried but failed at being this weird version of himself that was good enough for Jackie. More masculine, less expressive. But Kenny was free now, and I couldn't have been happier for him.

Even if I was a little jealous. Sure, I wasn't tied down by a relationship, but no matter which way you looked at it, I was never going to be free.

"I need a drink," Kenny said as he rolled off my bed and walked toward my door, Luna following closely behind.

"Periwinkle..." I mumbled when he got to my doorway, still a bit suspicious of the foreign word. He paused and turned around, waiting for me to say something else. I glanced down at the color on my phone screen, then looked up at Kenny. "It suits you."

✳ ✳ ✳

Now that I was alone, there was something I wanted to do. I made a mental note to join Kenny drinking in a bit. Not yet, though. First, I had a letter to write.

Even though she was barely mentioned in our conversation, I couldn't stop thinking about my mom. Those unsent letters were the most vulnerable I ever let myself be, but even in the letters, I peppered the sappy stuff with "lol"s and "lmao"s and whatnot. It always made the letters easier to write, less serious. Once I was finished, I read it one more time.

Dear Mami,

How've you been? I miss you. A lot.
I haven't been doing too hot lol. Had another panic attack today. Kenny helped. He's a real one. I don't know what I'd do without him tbh. I wish you could meet him. He'd love that. But it's not like we can visit each other, huh? It feels weird that he's so important to me and you've never met.
   My asshole boss almost called the cops today. If he did, I guess I could have gone to visit lmao.
   Then again, maybe I'll be going back soon enough.

Te quiero muchísimo,
Alejandro

This one was a shortie but a goodie. Just had to get the thoughts out of my brain.

I knew I should have gone out to drink with Kenny and keep him company after his breakup, but I was having a hard time bringing myself to do it. I preferred not to drink on bad days. That was usually my rule. Drink for fun, not to cope. I'd never had an addictive personality, but I didn't want to remind myself too much of my mom. I knew her addiction wasn't her fault, but it still sucked to think about. Besides, when I got drunk, the feelings always ended up pouring out, and I didn't exactly want that.

So, I called it a night and curled up in bed, falling asleep the moment my head hit the pillow—

—only to wake up a couple of hours later when my door swung open. Kenny's silhouette was illuminated by the hallway light behind him. Then the light was on.

"The hell, dude?" I squinted, pulling my blanket over my face to shield my eyes from the sudden brightness. Kenny's fumbling footsteps came closer, and before I knew it, he flopped down on my bed. Not next to me, but directly on top of me.

I laughed to myself as Kenny attempted to wrap his arms around my waist, but the blanket between us prevented his arms from going all the way around. Instead, he gave up and flopped his arms to his sides. Kenny was a pretty affectionate guy to begin with, but he was like a needy puppy when he was drunk. I'd gotten used to Kenny's physical touch love language thing a long time ago, so the two of us had always been comfortable with this kind of thing. If anyone else lay on top of me like this, I'd have read into it, but with Kenny, I might as well have been a couch cushion—or Luna. If it didn't mean anything with his pillow, it didn't have to mean anything with me. He was just looking for cuddles and affection.

Unfortunately, affection wasn't exactly my expertise. I reached over the blanket with one arm and patted him awkwardly on the head.

"I'm never gonna find someone else, am I?" Kenny's slurred whine was slightly muffled by the blanket in between us before he pulled it down from my face.

With one look at him, I softened up real quick. Eyes and nose red, he'd clearly been drunk-crying over Jackie.

"You'll find someone else. You're a fuckin' catch, bro."

"*You're* a catch, Han." Kenny giggled, not moving from on top of me. "Why couldn't I have dated someone like *you*?" I felt my cheeks go hot as Kenny rested his chin on my chest. I laughed awkwardly, cheeks still burning, with no idea how to respond.

Wait, was I being homophobic? I'd never had a problem with Kenny being bi before, but he always had Jackie. Did he basically just say he wanted to date me? I hated that my body was physically reacting to his affection despite my consciously being totally cool with his sexuality. Shit, I couldn't let Kenny know my stomach did a somersault at the idea of him wanting to date me.

Kenny looked up at me with big watery eyes, which wrecked me. Did he notice?

"You could do better than me, bro," I joked, trying to reassure him without letting him know I was feeling... something, about what he'd said.

Kenny shook his head. "Jackie's not... She's not *nice*. But she's all I could ever deserve..." Kenny rolled off me and sat with his back against the wall.

"Fuck that. You deserve so much better," I said, reluctantly giving up sleep to sit up next to him. I knew Kenny's self-esteem was pretty low, but it felt like a sucker punch to be reminded of it so blatantly.

"You really think so?" Kenny looked genuinely confused. "Why?"

Did he really not see it? Kenny was the kindest, most sincere guy I knew. He made people feel special. Like, he would go so far out of his way to make sure everyone around him was taken care of at all times. It was the little things, too. Like those little Post-it notes he left for me, or doing my laundry when he knew I was bummed out, or how he'd drive me anywhere, just so I wouldn't have to walk. I wanted to tell him all this and so much more, but all that came out of my mouth was "You're good people, Kenny."

Apparently that was enough, because he looked into my eyes with a smile. "You're good people, too."

My brain must have short-circuited right then, because the next thing I knew, Kenny's lips were pressed against mine. I was so surprised at first that I leaned in instinctually. His unexpectedly soft lips made my mind go completely and blissfully blank. It couldn't have been more than a second, but that second was split into hundreds of moments, all of them being the exact same thing. Me kissing Kenny. And in those hundreds of moments, I was completely helpless to the slow passage of that single second.

I must have been too tired to think straight. But, eventually, all those moments came to an abrupt end, and my brain caught up with my lips. I pulled away, letting out an awkward laugh.

"The hell are you doing, bro?" I said. There was no way that actually happened.

Kenny just stuck his lips out in a pout, and I was so flustered I had to quickly look away. "You don't want to?" Kenny slurred.

"You're drunk as hell." I laughed, but it did nothing to alleviate the burning in my cheeks. I had to remind myself there was no way the kiss meant anything. He was drunk. You didn't have to have feelings or even be attracted to someone to kiss them when you were drunk.

"Hmph, you're no fun." Kenny sloppily rolled off the bed and onto the floor, where he began crawling out of my room. "'M gonna go to the bar..."

I let out an awkward laugh and got out of bed. Kenny could barely make it to my door, much less the bar. I walked over and tried to help him to his feet, but he was all deadweight and not helping at all.

"Carry me," Kenny said, not bothering to open his eyes.

"Okay." I hoped he was too drunk to notice my blush. I did my best to unfluster myself as I scooped Kenny up in my arms and carried him to his room. He rested his head on my chest with closed eyes. A fond smile escaped my lips. He felt so vulnerable in my arms like this, but there was no way I'd drop him. I wished I could protect him from more than the floor. The ghost of his lips on mine tickled my memory. I quickly shooed the thought away. He was drunk. And besides, friends kissed sometimes, right? Just because he was the first boy I'd ever kissed didn't mean it had to be A Thing. Just because I leaned into it for a split second didn't mean I wasn't straight. Just because my cheeks burned and my stomach tossed in a way it never did kissing girls didn't mean I was ~~gay~~ homophobic. None of it had to mean anything.

Kenny's door was cracked open, so I only had to tap it with my foot to make it inside. I gently laid Kenny on his bed, making sure his head was safely resting on a pillow before pulling the blanket over him.

Even with his eyes closed, he looked sad, and that killed me. I hated that Jackie made him think he deserved her abuse, when he really deserved everything good in this world. Jesus, I was getting sappy. *Reel it in, Han.*

"Love you, Han," Kenny mumbled before a snore escaped his lips.

He probably wouldn't remember this tomorrow, which was good.

"Love you, too," I said, knowing he was too deep asleep to hear.

CHAPTER SIX

KENNY

In my dreams, Jackie and I were still together. I lay on my back in her college dorm bed, and she rested her head on my chest.

"I can feel your heart beating," she whispered, and it felt so intimate, so real. I smiled and held her closer. I'd missed this.

I leaned to kiss her forehead, but before I made contact, she pulled away and glared at me, disgust curling her upper lip.

"You're in love with Han, aren't you?"

"What? No! I'm in love with *you!*" I wanted to pull her close again and go back to the moment of peace, but it was gone. Her voice got louder and louder.

"You need to stop hanging out with him. It's him or me! What's it GONNA BE, KENNY? You little BEEP! BEEP! BEEP! BEEP! BEEP!"

She continued beep-screaming at me, then slapped me in the face, but since her hand was suddenly a pillow, it didn't hurt. This only enraged her more. "Wake UP, bro!" she shouted through the beeping as she slapped me again and again with her hand-pillow.

I woke up with a start, falling off my bed. Han stood over me holding a pillow, cracking up.

"You are one heavy-ass sleeper." He laughed and offered me his hand. I took it, letting him pull me up. "You missed your alarm. It's ten thirty. You have work at eleven, right?" Han playfully shoved my work clothes into my chest.

"Thanks," I mumbled, rubbing my head to soothe my killer headache. What the hell had happened last night? My memory was completely blank.

"You're popular today," Han said. "Your phone's been blowing up all morning."

"Huh?" I reached for my phone to see a *lot* of notifications. "Oh shit, I think I drunk-downloaded Grindr last night." I laughed. I didn't even remember doing that. What else didn't I remember from last night?

"Oh, uh . . . congrats on the interest, I guess?" Han said, but he didn't sound particularly thrilled. I was about to ask him what was wrong, but he was already leaving.

After flying through the motions to get ready, I knew I'd still make it to work on time, thanks to Han. And, bless his soul, he had Advil and my water bottle filled up and ready for me when I left my room, plus a bowl of menudo to cure my hangover. By the time I got to work, my headache was already dwindling.

"Kenny! My man!" Daniel waved from across the kitchen, and I waved back. Daniel made his way over to me and slapped a hand on my shoulder. "Got a minute?"

"Sure thing, boss."

He led me into his office, where he gestured to the chair in front of his desk, and we both took a seat.

"There's no easy way to say this…" Daniel ran a hand through his hair, and I shifted in my seat. That didn't exactly sound like the precursor to great news, and even though my headache was gone, I still wasn't on my game. Was I about to be fired? Daniel leaned forward. "Someone's been stealing money from the restaurant."

My stomach dropped. I was definitely about to be fired and for something I didn't even do. Han had mentioned this was why Juan had been fired. But if Daniel thought Juan did it, why was he bringing it up now? Was he about to accuse me? As assistant manager, I *did* handle the money more than the rest of the staff. If any went missing, I was the obvious culprit. I swallowed. This really didn't look great.

"I swear I didn't take any money," I pleaded before Daniel got the chance to say anything.

"'Course you didn't." He laughed without hesitation. I let out a breath of relief. "Just wanted to let you know. You and I need to keep an eye on the staff. There are some shady people working here, but I can't fire anyone for no reason." He winks. "So if you see any funny business, don't hesitate to bring it right to my attention, all right?"

"Yes, sir." I nodded. I knew Daniel was an overly suspicious person, especially with the cooks. I wasn't a snitch, though, at least not when it was punching down, and I wouldn't be the reason any of my co-workers lost their jobs. It was best to just smile and nod when Daniel was in one of these moods. I felt both lucky and unlucky to be his "favorite." Sure, it meant I could get away with the occasional tardiness, but it also meant I was supposed to be Daniel's watchdog. I felt almost dirty being so liked by that kind of person. But I let Daniel think we were "buds," if only to keep my job safe.

After Daniel excused me, I spent the rest of my shift working on overdrive. I needed a pick-me-up, and work was the perfect outlet. Anytime I was serving, my shift usually passed by faster. I loved face-to-face time with customers, especially the regulars. I had most of their orders memorized, and it always delighted them when I guessed what they wanted.

As much as I loved serving, I loved being assistant manager more. Really, it'd be amazing if I could land Daniel's job. I pretty much already did his job anyway, so it would have been nice to actually get paid for the amount of work I did. I knew the manager had to take care of all the angry customers, but something about making someone happy who'd been ready to raise hell gave me a sense of accomplishment I didn't get many other places. Daniel seemed to hate working here, so I'd happily wait it out until he quit.

With Jackie out of my life, I needed to find something to replace that sense of purpose that came from being needed by someone. To make myself feel useful, I spent any free moment of my shift helping the hosts. Silverware prep, cleaning menus, bussing tables, all that good stuff. Better to do silverware prep than let my mind wander after a breakup.

Being needed at work temporarily filled the hole in my chest, but it quickly swirled down the drain the second I clocked out. I drove myself home on autopilot, and as soon as I got there, I went straight to Han's room.

He was playing a game on his computer and sipping on a forty-four-ounce strawberry Fanta (the only fountain drink he tolerated). He paused his game when I walked in.

"What's up?" he asked, looking up from his screen.

"Can I vent really quick?" I knew he'd say yes, but I didn't want to take it for granted, since I knew Han didn't love talking about feelings.

"Go for it."

"I feel so useless now!" I blurted out as I began pacing Han's room. "Who am I supposed to take care of now that I'm alone?"

Han sighed and looked at me like the answer was obvious.

"What? It's not like anyone else needs me." If it were Jackie, she'd have reassured me that she did need me. But Han didn't need me. Sure, he appreciated me and cared about me and he never made me feel otherwise. But he didn't *need* me. And he wasn't one to lie to make me feel better, so he didn't say as much, either.

"You can take care of yourself for once, instead of someone else," Han said thoughtfully, then took another sip of Fanta.

"But I *like* taking care of people. I don't like feeling useless like this."

"You're not fucking useless, bro." Han almost sounded irritated by the idea. "But if you really want to take care of something, maybe we should get you an emotional support animal or something, like Luna?"

I thought on it, then shook my head. "What if Luna got jealous? I wouldn't want her thinking I had a new favorite."

"Fair enough. What about...an emotional support plant? Like a succulent. I hear those are easy to take care of. We can treat it as a real adoption, like you would with a dog. You can practice making decisions, like what to name it and picking out the right plant."

I couldn't help but feel self-conscious. "Isn't that a little childish?"

"Who gives a fuck? My favorite movie is *Coco*. Kid shit is Bibaporú for the soul." I must have looked confused since I'd never heard the word before, so he went on. "It's that all-healing ointment Mexican moms swear by."

I snapped my fingers. "Oh! Vicks VapoRub!"

"My point is, you *should* be childish. If you want to name and adopt a plant, no one's stopping you."

I let myself picture it. The possibilities were endless, however "childish" they may have been. "Let's get a cactus succulent! We can dress him up and everything!"

"Hell yeah." Han nodded. "What should we name him?"

"Hmm..." I thought for a second. I could do this. I could make a decision. "I feel like cacti have a really sophisticated vibe, but succulents are cute."

"So, a name that's both elegant and cute? For your cactus succulent son," Han said before taking another sip of Fanta.

"*Our* cactus succulent son," I corrected. "You're a part of this household, too. You can't go skirting your responsibility! Thornelius deserves two parents!"

Han burst out laughing, Fanta spraying out of his mouth. I cracked up and threw myself on his bed to avoid getting Fanta spit on me.

It took a minute for us both to calm down. Once we caught our breath, Han stood up from his desk chair.

"All right, let's go pick up Thornelius."

CHAPTER SEVEN

HAN

Thornelius proved to be a great exercise in decision-making for Kenny. He handpicked a plant at Target and chose the default "outfit" he'd be wearing (a monocle and top hat). Deciding where to put him was its own struggle, though. After fussing over the perfect spot, Kenny finally decided to set him on the kitchen table. So we could have meals "as a family."

"Luna, this is your new little brother, Thornelius!" Kenny said after situating Thornelius on the table. "Please protect and love him like a big sister should, okay?"

Luna wagged her tail in response; then Kenny's phone dinged with what I'd now come to recognize as a Grindr notification. He glanced at his phone and bit his lip while typing something out.

"I'm gonna have a guy over," Kenny said as he stood back up. "I was thinking I should get my rebound sex over with sooner than later so I can move on."

I hated that Kenny talking about rebound sex made me feel

anything less than happy for him. It shouldn't have bothered me in the least. There must have been a logical reason I was feeling this way besides being ~~jealous~~ homophobic. The main drawback was that since I'd replaced Kenny's blue curtains with his actual favorite color while he was at work, the first person to see his reaction to them would be some stranger he's fucking.

Or would he be getting fucked? I wasn't actually sure where Kenny stood with that stuff. Not that I cared, or needed to know, or was curious in any way, shape, or form.

"Do you know this guy?" I asked hesitantly.

"He's a Grindr hookup, so, not exactly."

"What if he's a serial killer? Are we really cool with giving random guys our address?"

"Ah, I'm sure we could take him." Kenny laughed and nudged me playfully, but I wasn't sure I understood the joke. "I'm gonna shower real quick before he gets here."

I sighed as Kenny went down the hall and into the bathroom. What the hell was wrong with me? Kenny moving on from Jackie was a *good* thing. I should have been happy for him. I *was* happy for him! But I also felt . . . weird.

I must have been in my head about it longer than I expected because soon enough Luna started barking at someone knocking on the door.

Shit, he was already here? I'd kind of wanted to hide in my room so I wouldn't have to deal with meeting a stranger, but Kenny was still in the shower. I groaned before dragging myself up and over to the door, not bothering to hold Luna back as I opened it. She wasn't a biter or anything, so I wasn't worried.

She immediately slipped through the open door and started sniffing the guy, who yelped and almost dropped the bag of Cane's he was carrying.

"You don't like dogs?" I asked, sizing him up. He was tall and lean with curly brown hair and a slightly cropped top. If this guy didn't like dogs, how compatible could he possibly have been with Kenny?

"No, I'm fine with dogs. I was just surprised," he said as he held the bag of food out of Luna's reach. Sure, he *said* he was fine with dogs, but he wasn't even petting her. I called her back inside. Normally, she would protest, wanting to explore the new person, but she didn't. I guess she didn't find him interesting enough. She was a good judge of character.

Red flag number one.

Once Luna was back inside, the guy waved at me with his free hand. "Kenny, right? You look different from your pictures. Not that I'm complaining..." He looked me up and down.

"Uh, no," I said, maybe a little colder than I'd intended. "Kenny's my roommate."

"Oh! Sorry, I only brought enough food for two...I'm Adam, by the way." He smiled and held his hand out. I scanned him for any suspicious serial killer signs before shaking it. "Okay...Ow."

I hadn't meant to grip his hand that hard, but I was a little on edge. "Sorry..."

He just stood there awkwardly until I realized I was supposed to let him in. "Right." I opened the door wider and stepped aside. Luna didn't even bother with him. Instead she lay by the bathroom waiting for Kenny. "Kenny's in the shower. He'll be out in a minute," I said, more to Luna than Adam.

Adam nodded as he looked around. He chuckled at the sight of Thornelius. "Cute cactus."

"He's a succulent," I corrected.

"Uh, yeah. A *cactus* succulent," he said with a smile. "Wait, did you say 'he'?" He let out another little laugh. Dick.

"Do you have a problem?" It wasn't that I was embarrassed. How could I have been embarrassed about something Kenny was so excited about? But how dare this guy look down on one of the first examples of Kenny expressing his own agency in *years*? If Kenny wanted to adopt and coparent and name an emotional support succulent, who was I to stand in his way? So what if it looked silly? Kenny *chose* this. Maybe choices were easy for most people, but they weren't for Kenny, and he still chose this specific plant. Chose his outfit. Named him. Yes, *him*. And chose to raise him with *me*. So fuck this Adam guy for laughing.

Adam raised his hands in surrender. "No, no problems here."

Finally, the running water from the bathroom came to a stop, and Adam looked almost as relieved as I felt. Thank fuck.

We both stood there awkwardly, waiting for Kenny to come out. Sure, I could have left Adam alone to go to my room, but I wasn't getting the best vibes from him. I wanted to make sure Kenny felt comfortable before leaving them alone. Kenny sometimes had a hard time putting his foot down when he was uncomfortable, especially if he felt like someone went out of their way for him. So if he changed his mind about wanting to fuck this guy, I'd kick him out in a heartbeat. With glee.

"Hey! Sorry, I must have overestimated how far away you were," Kenny said as he scrubbed his hands through his slightly wet hair, then lit up when he saw the Cane's. "Oh, you brought food! Me and Han had a *day*. I'm starving." Kenny went straight to the table, and Adam followed.

"Yeah, sorry, I only brought enough for two." Adam sounded apologetic enough, but he was obviously trying to get me to leave them alone. But if Kenny wanted to be alone just yet, he'd take Adam to his room. Since he wasn't doing that, I wasn't about to hide away in my own fucking house.

"No worries! Han can share with me," Kenny said, waving me over as he opened one of the to-go boxes.

I sat next to Kenny, and he handed me a chicken strip while he got to work on the fries.

"So, you two are really close, huh?" Adam asked after a couple of bites of chicken. I couldn't help but notice his hand resting on Kenny's thigh.

"For sure," Kenny said, hiding his full mouth behind his hand. "We've been friends since, like, first grade."

"So you're just friends, then?" he asked, glancing back and forth between me and Kenny like he was suspicious of *us*, as if *he* wasn't the potential serial killer in this situation.

"We're friends," I answered, almost too quickly. It felt wrong to call anything relating to me and Kenny "just." As if our relationship was "only" something. This "Adam" (if that was even his real name) was really starting to piss me off.

"Okay, cool," "Adam" said, then gave Kenny's thigh a little squeeze. Not that I was paying attention.

Kenny and "Adam" talked while we finished eating, "Adam" not once letting go of Kenny's thigh.

"So, should we take this somewhere more private?" "Adam" said as he gave Kenny this almost-hungry look. I didn't like that look. Not on "Adam."

"How could I say no to that?" Kenny said. While his expression mirrored "Adam's," I couldn't help but read into his response.

Kenny wasn't exactly great at saying no. Was he hinting that he needed help? I gave him a serious look, trying to telepathically ask if I should shut it down for him. He looked back at me for a second before giving an awkward laugh.

"Um, so, shall we?" "Adam" nodded toward the hallway where the bedrooms were.

"No means no, 'Adam'!" I found myself using actual finger quotes around the probably fake name.

"Wait, *are* you saying no?" "Adam" looked to Kenny.

"I said *how could I say no*," Kenny tried to explain, but somehow I doubted this "Adam" would get the hint.

"Exactly!" I said firmly. "I think you should leave."

Kenny gave me a slightly wide-eyed look that seemed like he was trying to tell me something, but I was never an expert in body language. Whatever. He could tell me after this "Adam" guy left.

"You don't have to leave!" Kenny said, which confused the hell out of me, but "Adam" was already standing. I stood, too, not knowing whether he was about to leave or pick a fight. He just laughed.

"Okay, I don't know what the hell is going on with...all *this*"—he gestured wildly to me and Kenny—"but y'all should really figure that shit out, far away from me."

"Wait!" Kenny stood up too now, but "Adam" was already storming out.

The door slammed behind him, leaving me and Kenny alone with an unexpected amount of tension in the air.

"What the *fuck*, Han?" Kenny's head snapped toward me.

I studied him before responding. Shoulders tense, brows furrowed, mouth hanging open. I wasn't an expert at reading people, but...even I could tell he wasn't happy.

"Wait, you're mad?" I asked, completely at a loss.

"Yes!" Kenny threw his hands up exasperatedly. "What the hell was that! Why are you cockblocking me?"

"I thought I was helping!"

Kenny slumped in the chair and rubbed his temples. "In what world does kicking out the guy I brought over help me get laid?" The gears turning in my head suddenly ground to a stop.

"Wait . . . you *wanted* to fuck that guy?"

"*Yes!*" Kenny yelled. "Do you have a problem with that or something?"

I sat down across from Kenny and sighed. "No, I don't have a problem with that."

"Then what the hell just happened?" Kenny asked earnestly, sounding more confused than angry at that point.

"You said 'how could I say no' when he asked to go to your room," I said plainly, but Kenny didn't look any less confused. "Did that not mean you needed help telling him to fuck off? Like, you didn't know how to tell him you changed your mind?"

"Fuck." Kenny softened up a little. "Okay, that's actually kind of sweet, but that's not at *all* what I meant!"

"You meant yes," I said, half realization, half question.

Kenny nodded, rubbing his temples again.

"Now I know, I guess. Um, sorry, bro." I hoped he wasn't too mad, but maybe I deserved it. I did fuck up his first chance at rebound sex. And in trying to keep him from getting taken advantage of, I ended up making the decision for him. Just like Jackie had always done.

Kenny sighed. "It's been a long day. Let's just go to bed." He got up and headed to his room.

"Okay," I said, and went to my own room. I stood in front of my door for a while, trying to decide whether to go knocking on Kenny's door to apologize again. I felt like shit, but it wasn't like Kenny to stay mad. And I wasn't great at apologies. Too vulnerable.

Still, maybe he needed more than just a "sorry, bro" to feel like I understood the problem. I started texting him, but before I typed much, my door swung open and Kenny rushed toward me in an unexpected hug.

"Thank you," he said, his words muffled by his face pressed against my shoulder. I was so caught off guard by the affection that it took a second for my body to react. Once my brain registered what was happening, I relaxed into the embrace.

"What? I was just gonna say sorry again..."

"For the curtains, Han. Not the cockblocking." He laughed into my shoulder and gave me one last squeeze before pulling away. "So...are you sure you don't have a problem with me bringing people over? Like, guys, specifically."

"No," I said quickly, and Kenny raised an eyebrow like he was suspicious, which made my heart practically combust. He was kind of right, but I had no idea why. The last thing I wanted to do was make Kenny feel bad for being himself. *He* was not the problem in this situation.

But...maybe I did have a problem. Maybe Kenny was somehow both at the center of it and the only imaginable cure.

No, maybe not. Definitely not.

Maybe I was just homophobic.

CHAPTER EIGHT

KENNY

Maybe it was because I didn't get laid last night, or maybe it was already written in the stars, but I could tell it was gonna be a bitch of a day. One of the only upsides was that Han and I would be sharing a shift, so we could carpool. Tatiana said it was a miracle we never got sick of each other with all the time we spent together, but I couldn't imagine a world where I didn't *want* to be around Han. Even if he sometimes accidentally cockblocked me.

I really did love my job, but the downsides to this particular day won out. First, there was the stress about a potential thief stealing money from the restaurant, which I was supposed to be keeping my eyes open for.

Today was also one of those days where I had too much energy for the amount of work I had to do. To add insult to injury, it was raining, which made the shift slower than usual. The customers who did come in all seemed to be in a bad mood, which wasn't great for tips.

After topping off the drinks of the single patron I was serving, I wandered back to the drink dispenser, where a few other servers were lingering. The only one of us who seemed truly busy was Tatiana. A couple of guys at one of her tables kept snapping their fingers at her, and it seemed like they were calling her over for every little thing. I was glad it wasn't my table, but I felt worse when she left the table and Daniel came back instead. They must have asked for the manager. I tried to ignore them and focus on my own customer, but one of the guys started making a scene.

"I want my money back!"

Daniel pointed to the man's plate, "I'm sorry, sir, but you ate the whole thing. If you didn't like it, we could have traded it out for something else, but since you ate it, there's nothing I can do."

"I won't accept that. Give me my money back, or you're stealing! I'll call the cops and tell them you robbed us." He puffed out his chest, pointing at the bar leading to the kitchen. "And I'm willing to bet you've got more illegal shit going on here than just stealing my money."

My chest tightened. Would they really call the cops over some food they didn't like?

"Sir, we have nothing to hide," Daniel insisted. Why was he egging this guy on? It was like he had zero intention of protecting his cooks, or Tatiana for that matter. Or was he just trying to call their bluff?

But it was too risky to bet on them bluffing. The scene flashed before my eyes. The cops would show up. They wouldn't be able to do anything about the "stealing" allegations, but the customer would want some kind of retribution. He'd tip off the cops about his suspicions, and they'd storm the kitchen. Han would get taken away.

I couldn't let that happen. I rushed to the kitchen. I needed to get Han out of here, but I didn't see him anywhere. He must have been on his break. I hurried to the breakroom and found him standing alone, on his phone. I grabbed his arm and pulled him in close.

"Go home," I whispered, trying not to sound too freaked out. "Get an Uber, and I'll tell Daniel I let you off early."

"What? Why?"

"Someone might call the cops."

Han's eyes widened, but he didn't hesitate to rush out the back door without another word. I wanted to cry as I watched him leave. He was safe, but my work wasn't done. Luckily, Han was the only undocumented cook in today, so with him gone, all I needed to worry about was Tatiana. Cops showing up for a call about a Black girl stealing from these guys couldn't end well. I rushed to meet the angry customers and try to calm the situation.

"I'm sorry, I can't help you," Daniel was saying again when I reached them.

"Assistant manager here. We'll refund you." I waved a hand to silence Daniel when he tried to interrupt. I was definitely crossing a line, but I didn't exactly have another choice. "We don't have to disrupt everyone's dinners, all right? Your refund is on me. Do you want us to remake your plate?"

"I don't want your disgusting food," the customer spat out, but he seemed to be cooling down.

Daniel couldn't be mad at me for using my own money to refund these guys, so it was all I could think to do. The men handed me their receipt, and I unzipped the pouch tied around my waist and took out exact change from today's tips. Bile rose in my throat when the man touched my hand to grab the money. It wasn't fair that people like him could get whatever they wanted by making threats. That kind of thing should have been illegal. Then again, I knew it wasn't a coincidence that the law benefited people like them and not people like Han or Tatiana.

I kept the thought to myself, but I knew in my heart that Daniel was a totally incompetent manager. If I'd been in charge, things wouldn't have escalated. If it wasn't for me patching up all of Daniel's fuckups, he would have driven this restaurant into the ground ages ago.

No matter how scared I was for Han when I thought the cops might have shown up, I couldn't forget that this was the first wake-up call I'd personally experienced. Han had to deal with scares like this all the time. With everything he'd done for me, all I wished was for some way to fix this for him.

When the restaurant finally closed for the night, I made it a point to check the money. I couldn't be too careful since someone had apparently been stealing. And while I liked interacting with people, it was relaxing to sit down to count money and run the numbers. The lack of noise was always soothing, and I didn't have to worry about anything but the task at hand.

This time there was no such enjoyment. Dread filled my chest as I counted once, twice, three times. Each coming up short. My suspicions had been confirmed. Juan had been fired for nothing. And if I wanted to keep from following in his footsteps, I'd have to figure out who the thief was.

CHAPTER NINE

HAN

My arms burned like hell as I fought to raise my chin to the pull-up bar. I'd placed the bar at the edge of the hallway leading to the living room so I could watch movies while working out. *Moana* was a good distraction from the pain in my arms, and the pain was a good distraction from what could have happened today and that I wouldn't know if everyone was okay until Kenny got home.

Don't think about it.

Instead of thinking, I screamed out the final words to the song as I pulled my chin to the bar for as long as the final note lasted.

Kenny jiggled the doorknob and walked in just in time for my performance. He laughed to himself as he tossed his stuff on the counter and kicked off his shoes. Then he walked to the living room, the smile wiped from his face as he gave me a worried look. I ignored it, pulling myself up again, then again.

Then Kenny's face changed from worried to amused, and he bit back a grin. "You sound like you're having sex."

One of my hands slipped from the bar, and an awkward laugh escaped as I reached back up and kept going, trying not to appear flustered. "And you...uhhn...sound like you're...ahhh... twelve."

Kenny laughed, too. "Just trying to lighten the mood."

"Lighten it from what?"

Kenny raised an eyebrow like the answer was obvious. He gestured to the TV. "Moana *and* working out? You couldn't possibly be looking for a...*pick-me-up*, could you?" Kenny grinned, proud of his not-even-that-clever pull-up pun.

"Whatever." I rolled my eyes. "Did those guys end up calling the cops?"

"Nope. I paid for their refund out of pocket."

Thank God.

Kenny plopped himself on the couch while I kept at my pull-ups. We were both quiet for a minute, minus the "sex sounds." Then Kenny gave me another solemn look. "I know you don't like talking about this, but is it okay if we do for a second?"

I dropped from the bar and switched to crunches. Exercising was a necessary buffer from things getting too real.

"Are you gonna stay now that you have another job?" Kenny asked after a moment of silence.

"What are you talking about?"

Kenny sighed shakily. "I know you were thinking about moving back to Mexico. But you have a job now! I'll send you home like I did today if anyone tries to call the cops at work. I...." He swallowed. "I don't want to lose you. Please stay."

A million thoughts swirled through my brain at once. It took a minute to pick one to say out loud. "You know it wasn't about the job, right? It was about the green card. My old job was supposed to sponsor it. *That's* why I was thinking about going back to Mexico. How did you even know about that, anyway?"

Kenny slumped his head and looked up at me through thick lashes. "When I was doing your laundry, I saw your video..."

"And you *watched* it?" I stopped doing sit-ups to meet Kenny's eyes. There was no way I heard him right.

"It was an accident! I thought it was one of your songs. I had no idea it wasn't for me to watch. I'm sorry, Han—"

"The hell, dude? That shit is private." I rubbed my temples. Kenny knew about the video, meaning he probably thought it was actually for my mom. How was I supposed to explain the truth?

"But, Han..." Kenny chewed his lip before eventually continuing. "Why *was* it private? Not the video, I mean... I'm your best friend. Shouldn't you tell me if you're thinking about moving to another country?"

I turned to meet his gaze. "Me going back to Mexico has always been a possibility. I could get deported tomorrow. You know that. I've *always* thought about going back. My whole life!"

"Do you really want to go back?" Kenny's voice shook.

"No!" I shouted, which made Kenny jump. Seeing him startle at my raised voice made me soften up, and I went back to doing crunches to ease the guilt. "This is my home," I finally added.

"I feel like a complete ass," Kenny said.

"Why?"

"Because you deal with this every day. Today was the first time I've had a real scare about it. Like, I worry all the time, but I never had to truly face your reality until today." Kenny leaned his elbows on his knees and covered his face with his hands.

Then his voice came out softer, like he was about to cry. "When I thought Daniel was gonna call the cops, it all hit me at once. And you have to deal with that fear all the time."

"What's your point, Kenny?" I probably sounded too exasperated to be polite, but I didn't care. I wasn't trying to talk about Kenny's feelings about my sad little life.

Kenny looked up at me, and I looked at the ceiling. "My point is . . . we should do something about it."

Wow. I stopped with the crunches again, sitting up and shooting Kenny a glare. "Are you gonna take down ICE all by yourself? 'Cause I don't have any other ideas." My words might have come across harsher than I'd meant them. I was just so frustrated. This was exactly the topic I wanted to avoid, and here Kenny was forcing it to the surface.

Kenny didn't look away. "Have you considered marrying someone for citizenship? Maybe Tatiana?"

"That's not an option."

"Why not?"

"For one, Tatiana and I broke up."

"Okay, but you're *you*. There's no way you don't have, like, twenty girls who would gladly line up to marry you if you asked."

"That's the thing. I can't just ask someone to stall their whole life for me. I'm not gonna use someone like that." I stood up and crossed my arms. Of course I'd thought about marrying someone for citizenship. But it wouldn't be right. How could Kenny bring this up like I've never thought about it myself?

Kenny stared intensely into my eyes before saying anything.

"Use me."

I wanted to check my ears to make sure I was hearing him right.

His eyes never left mine as he spoke. "I'm serious, Han. Use *me*. Marry me."

My face got hot. "This isn't funny. This whole thing is so fucked up, and all you have are jokes?"

"I'm not kidding," Kenny said, eyes still intensely on mine.

"I...Are you—" I couldn't get words out. Was he serious? "I can't—*we* can't just—"

Kenny interrupted, which was something he *never* did. "What if I couldn't calm those guys down today? What if it happened when I wasn't there?" I just stood there while Kenny rambled, dumbfounded and unable to form words. "Think about it. You could become a citizen! No more panic attacks. We can save on taxes. Everyone already thinks we're secretly in love." Kenny laughed, but I was having a hard time catching my brain up. "Plus, it would piss Jackie off."

Theeere it was. Kenny was always trying to distract himself with a project for someone else when he was going through something. The last time he and Jackie broke up, he helped Tatiana get her job at the restaurant. When Jackie cheated on him, he convinced his parents to do couples counseling. He's always putting other people before his own pain. But I didn't want to be his breakup charity case.

"Bro, you're not about to marry me just to make your ex jealous." I laughed, because if I didn't laugh, I might get my hopes up. I knew better than that when it came to relying on other people, even if that person was the most trustworthy guy I knew.

"I'm just saying. It could be a game changer. It's not a bad idea..." Kenny started mumbling, which meant the gears in his head were turning.

"Stop fucking with me," I said humorlessly. I still couldn't tell if Kenny was being serious. We'd joked about getting married before, but only because of that vote from high school.

"I'm not! The pros totally outweigh the cons. I'm dead serious." Kenny's dark eyes looked even bigger under his glasses, intense and unblinking as he spoke. "Han, you could stay. Like, legally, you could stay."

I couldn't lie, though, the thought of being a legal citizen was hard not to entertain. And don't get me wrong, I was totally aware that becoming a citizen was more complicated than a wedding, but getting married was a *huge* step. Still, there was no way this was a good idea.

"Han." Kenny got up and walked over so we were face-to-face, and his eyes bored into mine. "I know how serious this is. I'm serious, too. Do you really think I'd mess with you about this?"

I had to look away because meeting his eyes felt too intimate. "I guess you wouldn't, huh?"

Without hesitating, Kenny dropped down on one knee. "Han, will you fake marry me?"

I had to laugh. "Not happening."

It was a ridiculous idea. Way too risky. No way would I put Kenny at risk like that. I was sure the consequences of a fraudulent marriage weren't pretty. I'd definitely be deported, and Kenny would probably get thrown in jail or something.

"Why not?" Kenny looked disappointed.

"You'd probably go to jail if we got caught."

"We won't get caught." Kenny smirked, still on one knee. How could he be so confident?

"I'm not risking your ass just so I can have a valid ID."

Kenny finally stood up, and his eyes softened. "You know it's so much more than that."

I sighed. Of course I knew. Being a citizen was the dream, but...it was a selfish dream. Still, a small part of me (which I was trying to ignore) was intrigued by the idea of marrying Kenny. Even if it terrified me.

"It'll be okay! We won't get caught. We'll do a damn good job faking it."

"Kenny..."

"I'm just gonna keep asking..." Kenny said with an annoying look of determination.

"Ask all you want." I knew Kenny well enough to know he'd make good on that promise. I just needed to wait it out, and he'd eventually forget.

"I will!" Kenny announced, then left to grab his keys from the table. "I'll be back!"

"Where are you—" I started, but the door was already open and closed, and Kenny was gone.

Kenny really had no idea what his offer was doing to me. I lay in bed trying not to daydream about what it'd be like to marry him. It was true that my life would be a lot easier, but it felt so selfish. Kenny was only doing this because he basically lived to make other people happy. The dude was always doing nice things for me, or Jackie, or his parents, or strangers on the street. I didn't know how Kenny had the energy to live his own life when all he seemed to care about was other people.

I rolled over and reached for my guitar. Playing calmed my nerves, and I needed to shut out the intrusive citizenship fantasy, so I played some of Tío Nacho's favorite music. Nacho always wanted me to practice mariachi music so I could join his band, which I had no interest in. Music was personal for me, not something I wanted to share with complete strangers. Especially when it came to my own songs.

Before long the apartment door opened again. Kenny's footsteps came down the hall as if he was about to come into my room, but then he went away. Soon there was shuffling around the kitchen, and my curiosity got the better of me. I got up and opened my door to find a bouquet of red roses on the floor.

"Um, what are these for?" I asked.

"What are what for?" Kenny shouted from the kitchen.

"The flowers?"

"Sounds like a total mystery. Is there a note?"

I crouched down and plucked the note from the side of the bouquet.

To: Kenny's future husband, Alejandro Torres

I couldn't help but laugh. "Really, dude?"

When Kenny said he wasn't going to stop asking, he really wasn't wasting any time. I grabbed the roses and headed to the kitchen.

"I made dinner!" Kenny exclaimed proudly.

I sniffed the air, the smell of sweet batter wafting through the room.

"Pancakes?"

"You love breakfast for dinner, so...pancakes!" Kenny brought two plates over to the kitchen bar and pulled out a stool for me. I rolled my eyes playfully and sat down.

I looked down at the pancake, where *"marry me?"* was spelled out with chocolate chips.

"You are too much." I laughed.

"Soooo...have you changed your mind?" Kenny sat down next to me, looking up at me with those adorable puppy eyes.

"In the, what, *hour* it's been since you last asked?" I cut out a slice with my fork to distract from Kenny's puppy-dog eyes and took a bite. It was super crispy on the bottom.

"Sorry it's a little burned." Kenny nudged his head on my shoulder, laughing into it, all embarrassed. "Kinda took me a while to spell with the chocolate chips."

I wanted to enjoy the moment and savor his playful energy, but I couldn't.

"Kenny," I cleared my throat. "I appreciate the offer. Really. But I'm not gonna let you marry me just because you like making other people happy or to distract yourself from Jackie. This isn't a game. It's my *life*. It's *your* life! I'm not about to let you ruin it for my sake."

"The distraction is an added perk," Kenny admitted. "But I wouldn't offer if I wasn't serious. I know this isn't a game, Han. I *want* to do this. Just...think about it, okay?"

I took my time chewing before answering. There was no way he'd leave me alone if I didn't give him *something*. Even if nothing came of it.

"I'll think about it."

CHAPTER TEN

KENNY

The next morning, my alarm had me bolting upright and throwing my comforter off. There was no time to sulk about Jackie. Not today. I jumped up and stumbled over my feet to get out of my room as quickly as possible. I scrambled into the hallway to find Han also rushing out of his own room. We shared a mischievous grin before rushing down the hall to the living room.

It was *cleaning Sunday*. Han and I didn't do just any cleaning day. It was a race. A game. An opportunity to blast music and speed-clean faster than the week before . . . and reward ourselves with pizza if we won. I hurried to the TV and put on some music, watching Han's face as I pressed play.

He laughed and shook his head when "Marry You" by Bruno Mars started playing. I wasted precious time serenading Han as I folded the blanket on the couch while he pretended to ignore me.

After folding the blanket, I rushed to vacuum the floor while

Han did last night's dishes. The music was loud enough to hear over the vacuum and clinking plates. I kept singing, coaxing Han to join along, and he finally did. My future husband and I belted about drunkenly wanting to marry each other, and I let myself read into the twinkle in Han's eyes.

After a half hour of singing, dancing, and cleaning, the apartment was spotless.

"Time!" Han stopped his phone timer, and I waited in antic-ipation for the results. "Fuck yeah!" Han shouted, and we ran in celebratory circles around the room whooping and cheering before doing our overly complicated celebratory handshake, which always ended with us flopping onto the couch. Beat-ing last week's time meant pizza, and my empty stomach was already vibrating with excitement.

Sunday was my favorite day of the week. The tradition had started back when we'd moved into our first apartment together. Living in filth was freeing for a while, because it was the first time in our lives we were allowed to. Eventually, though, our limit was beyond reached, but we could only seem to clean reg-ularly if it was fun. Our cleaning day races were born, and we never looked back.

Han had just ordered the pizza when there was a knock on the door. I'd forgotten Leti was coming over to play *Smash Bros.* I glanced at Han, who was dramatically splayed out on the couch as if he'd just run a marathon and not merely cleaned an albeit messy apartment.

"Can you get that?" Han asked.

"Only if you marry me," I teased, and Han took the couch pillow from under his head and threw it at mine. I snickered as I dodged the pillow, then opened the door, revealing both Leti and Tatiana.

"Hey, Kenny!" Tatiana pulled me in for a hug.

"Oh shit," I accidentally said out loud. I liked Tatiana, but hadn't she and Han just broken up? I had to think fast to save Han from the awkward encounter. "Han's...um..."

"Tatiana! I didn't know you were coming!" Han said from behind me, making me jump. He hugged Leti, then Tatiana, and led them inside.

Welp, if Han was okay with Tatiana being here, then I wouldn't say anything. I couldn't lie though, it felt weird that he was so excited to see her. I couldn't imagine how I'd act if *Jackie* came over unannounced.

I shook the thought off as Leti and Tatiana filed inside while Han set up *Smash Bros*. I had to admit I was glad for the distraction. Anything to keep from thinking about *her*. Leti, Han, and Tatiana squeezed onto the couch while I sat with my legs crossed on the floor in front of Han. He handed me a controller, and we chose our fighters and the map, then started playing.

Unsurprisingly, I was the first to lose.

Okay, so *Smash Bros* was proving to be an insufficient distraction. My mind kept wandering to thoughts of Jackie, so I kept losing, no matter how hard I tried to concentrate.

Jackie and I had broken up before, but this time felt different. Final. And I knew it had to stay that way, but it still sucked. Jackie was my first. My only. What if no one else ever loved me again? Jackie definitely thought no one would—at least, she told me as much. What if I died alone because I didn't choose Jackie over Han?

Suddenly, I got déjà vu from the night we broke up, when I'd had pretty much these exact thoughts, only drunkenly. The memory of me trying to plant one on Han flashed before my eyes for a split second before I shooed it away. No, I must have been imagining that. Sure, I'd *thought* about kissing Han before, like, with a mouth that smoochy-looking, who wouldn't? But I definitely couldn't have been drunk enough to *do* it, right? And if I had, it didn't mean anything. Couldn't. It was one thing to use a random Grindr guy as a rebound (disastrous as that attempt was), but a completely different thing to use *Han*. He meant too much to be a rebound, so I had to be careful with those kinds of thoughts.

"Die, Kirby!!" Tatiana shouted.

"Fuck!" Han slumped forward and threw his arms around my shoulders and neck in a loose choke hold. "Losers' circle."

Tatiana gave Han a playful nudge, and he let go of me to nudge her back. I couldn't stop thinking about how cool it was that Han and Tatiana were so friendly despite being exes. I wondered if I could ever be friendly with Jackie. Then again, did I want to be? When I racked my brain, it was hard to even remember what that was like.

Even the thought of dying alone wasn't enough to make me regret the breakup. But it still hurt. She knew I'd always struggled with depression and low self-esteem. I liked to think she was helping me through it by building me up and making me feel special, but that always came crashing down when she got mad, which was more often than I wanted to admit...

After a few more distracted rounds on my part, I felt a hand squeeze my shoulder. I looked behind me to see Leti offering a comforting smile. Was I being that obvious? I shook it off and joined the game again the next round, vowing not to be the first to die again.

I failed less than ten seconds in.

Luckily, the pizza showed up right as I died. I was so in my own head I forgot we'd ordered it. I got the door and tipped the guy generously, but when I came back to put the boxes on the coffee table, the game was paused.

Leti sat on the arm of the couch now to make room for me to sit between them and Han. I put the pizza down, then took the seat. I must have looked extra pathetic given the three pairs of pitying eyes staring at me.

"Talk to us, Kenny," Leti said. "You okay?"

I sighed and let my head fall back against the edge of the couch. If I were Han, I'd make up some excuse and say I was fine, but I wasn't good at hiding my emotions. I tried for the sake of other people, but when I got confronted, I was always bursting to talk.

"Jackie and I broke up." My voice caught in my throat.

"Oh no, I'm sorry." Tatiana was the only one who seemed sympathetic.

"Thanks." I wiped my nose.

"I know breakups suck, but it's for the best. That bitch was fucking mean," Leti said.

"Don't call her a bitch..." I mumbled softly. I was such a wimp, I couldn't even properly stand up for the girl I loved.

"Fine. But you know I'm right," Leti said as they grabbed a slice. Han and Tatiana followed suit, but I wasn't hungry anymore. Leti always wanted to help, but the only kind of love they offered was the tough kind. "She treated you like shit. I'm glad you got out."

"Yeah, I know..." I felt weird admitting it. I always felt like the ins and outs of my relationship with Jackie were private, but clearly everyone else had their opinions. I wondered what that meant about how they thought of *me*.

"Why'd you stay with her for so long anyway? You could do way better," Leti said.

"I loved her." My voice was so low, I barely heard myself. I knew they wouldn't understand. They only saw the bad parts. They never saw her soft side. How her head fit perfectly in the crook of my neck, or how she was my big spoon, latching on to me like a backpack. How much she cared about her job at the shelter and all the women she helped. She was almost as physically affectionate as I was, so I never felt like I was being too much. Jackie knew me better than I knew myself and never hesitated to call me on my shit. I was indecisive about *everything*, but Jackie knew what she wanted. And she wanted *me*, of all the people in the world. That part I'd never understand.

"Do you still?" Tatiana asked.

"I . . ." Now that I thought about it, I wasn't sure if I was really in love or just lonely. "I don't know . . ." I finally said.

Han stayed noticeably quiet, which didn't surprise me one bit. It was very Han to avoid discussions about feelings. But more than anything, I wished he would forget about his machismo for one second and offer me a freaking hug or something.

"You have us if you need anything, okay?" Leti wrapped their arms around my shoulders, and I hugged them back. I really needed one. Even though Leti never liked Jackie, they were always a good friend. I felt my eyes prick with tears, and I quickly pulled away to wipe them. I felt so pathetic, crying over a breakup everyone was happy about.

"Oh, Kenny . . ." Leti cupped my face in their hands. "You deserve so much better than that b—I mean, than *her*."

I couldn't help it. The tears came back. I couldn't put it in words, so I just cried. I wasn't upset that Jackie had hurt me. I was upset that I lost her. I didn't deserve better at all. I didn't *want* to break up with Jackie. I just wanted her to get along with Han, but that would never happen. And Leti and Han were right. She treated me like crap, and I hated myself for letting her. But now that I ended it, I felt worse for missing her. Being alone scared the shit out of me.

I leaned on Han's shoulder, and he finally wrapped an arm around me.

"Let it out, bro."

"I don't want to be alone!" I blurted out as tears streamed down my face. Han rubbed my back.

"You're never alone, bro," he said as he reached for the last slice, which he *always* managed to get, ever since we were little. It used to annoy me, but now I allowed it every time. "I'm literally here with you, like, twenty-four-seven," he said through a mouthful of pizza, and I let out a laugh-cry. It was true. I wasn't *alone* alone. Han was always by my side. And maybe that was enough.

Maybe that was more than enough.

CHAPTER ELEVEN

HAN

Once Leti and Tatiana left, I hoped I'd be enough comfort if Kenny cried again. I'd been told I was like a deer in headlights when someone cried in front of me. Kenny never seemed to mind my awkward pats on his back or fumbly words, though. In fact, he was usually pretty happy with my uncomfortable attempts at soothing him.

He wasn't crying just yet, so the best I could do was keep him from being alone. I played *Spider-Man: Miles Morales* while he lay on the couch next to me with his laptop, his feet resting on my lap. Luna was curled up in a tiny ball between Kenny's legs. His preferred love language was acts of kindness—showing love to other people. But when he was on the receiving end, it was physical touch or bust, so I figured he was pretty comfortable all close to me and Luna.

Kenny had been glued to the laptop ever since Leti and Tatiana left. Curious about what was behind his screen, I paused my game. Kenny didn't use social media and rarely used that computer unless he was doing research. His brows scrunched together in concentration as he typed.

"Whatcha doin'?" I wasn't trying to be nosy, but it just came out.

Kenny startled, then cleared his throat and pushed his glasses up his nose with his index finger.

"Um, nothing! Just...research."

"For what?"

"You know..." Kenny glanced up at me with a shy smile. "Like, immigration stuff."

I blew out a frustrated breath. "What are you researching that shit for?"

He answered like he'd practiced his response already. "You could get insurance, so you can finally fix your ankle. You can go to school. Figure out what you're passionate about, and then, like *do it*. Discover your dream job. It wouldn't even be that hard, logistically. We already have proof of our life together! We have pictures from childhood. We know literally everything about each other for the USCIS interview. We have our lease, Luna, and Thornelius!" Kenny closed the laptop and adjusted himself so he was cross-legged facing me. "It's like you said before, this isn't a game. It was never a game to me, Han."

I stroked Luna nervously. I believed Kenny about him being serious, but it hadn't really clicked before. It wasn't like I didn't know everything I was missing out on, but I couldn't be mad at Kenny for bringing it up. Not since he was actually offering a solution. I had to admit, going to college was always a distant dream. When Kenny went to university and I was stuck working, it stung. I wasn't really the jealous type, but there was no denying I wanted what Kenny had. College was where people discovered their passions and nurtured them.

Well, except for Kenny. He studied nursing, and that obviously wasn't where he ended up. By the time it came to actually sticking needles in people, he realized he was squeamish around blood. At least he loved food service.

Kenny's passion was people. He was totally content at his job, where he got to please customers all day. At least when Kenny was in college I could help him with homework and shit. Not that nursing was my calling, but it was nice to pretend I had a promising career ahead of me.

I never really let myself get my hopes up for anything else. To be honest, I didn't really know what I was passionate about, and it kind of ticked me off that Kenny noticed. He knew I never got too into any one thing, because I'd never have the opportunity to pursue those dreams.

But what if I could?

And an even scarier question: What if I let myself get my hopes up just for it to fall apart? Of course I wanted this, but it was unrealistic. Kenny just wanted to make me happy. He didn't actually want to *marry me*.

"You know this isn't something you can decide on a whim when you're going through something, right? Let's say I agreed to the fake marriage thing. Then Jackie wants you back. And if it's not Jackie, you'll find another 'Adam' or someone else. What happens to me when you can't handle being alone anymore?"

"I don't care about dating anyone else. Not until you're safe. For good. It's like you said, I'm never alone. Not if you're here." He smiled, and goddammit, who gave him the right to give me *that* look while saying *those* things?

I searched his eyes for any sign of a bluff. I knew he wouldn't do that to me, not on purpose, but had he really thought this through? "You haven't been single since puberty. Do you really think you could hold out?" I almost hoped he'd cave and admit it wasn't possible, just so I wouldn't have my hopes up.

"I told you it's not a game to me! Maybe I offered a little abruptly, but I only did that because I knew, from the second it crossed my mind, that marrying you for your citizenship was a future I'd be happy with."

At that, Kenny leaned forward and grabbed me by the shoulders like he was afraid I'd slip through his fingers if he didn't hold on tight. Hell, he might have been onto something because I fully wanted to melt into the couch at his offer. His touch kept me solid, and his stare kept me hooked on every word.

"I'm not going anywhere, okay? I know it's a huge privilege to be *able* to promise you that. All I want is for you to have the option to make me the same promise someday." He finally let go of my shoulders.

"It's not that simple..." I looked away to avoid the intense staring. It made me feel naked, like my soul was laid bare only for his eyes.

"I get why you're hesitant, like, this is *me* we're talking about!" He laughed. "I'm not always confident with my choices. I can admit that. But when it comes to you? I've never hesitated. I didn't question choosing you over Jackie for a second."

"What are you talking about...?"

"That's why we broke up," Kenny admitted. "Second easiest decision of my life."

I laughed, torn between looking away to hide and searching those eyes for an ounce of uncertainty. I chose the latter, but found none. Had he really chosen me over the girl he'd been with since puberty? "Um, what was the first easiest?" I asked, if only to get the attention on something that made me question my entire existence a little less.

"Marrying you, of course." Kenny smiled.

I couldn't help but laugh. Not because it was a joke, but because I'd never felt lighter. Kenny was offering me the opportunity of a lifetime. Wouldn't I hate myself forever if I didn't take it?

"If you're serious...What the hell. Let's do it." I could feel the weight lifting from my shoulders. If we did this right, if it all worked out perfectly, I could stay...I'd thought of marrying someone for citizenship before, but it never felt right. I never wanted to put someone in that position. But Kenny *wanted* this. He was *choosing* this.

"Really?" Kenny's face lit up as he hopped off the couch to pull me into a way-too-tight hug.

"We can't tell anyone it's not real," I said.

"Of course." Kenny pretended to zip his lips.

"And we should probably set some ground rules. Figure out logistics, get our stories straight, and all that. You and Jackie just broke up, so we should have an explanation for how fast this is gonna happen."

"Good point." Kenny tapped his chin. "Well, obviously, we've been in love all along and have been in denial for fear of ruining the friendship. We tried to make it work with other people, but it was clear to everyone besides us we were meant to be." He gave me a fake lovesick look, holding his hand against his heart. "Of course, when it came down to it, our love for each other was simply undeniable. We'd been in denial our whole lives, and when we finally admitted how we felt, there was no way we could go back."

"Okay, shit. That's actually pretty good." If it weren't for Kenny's dramatic poses, I would have almost thought he was being sincere. Which was a testament to how good a cover it was.

"As far as rules go," Kenny added, "no dating other people until you're naturalized, obviously."

"Still not sure you know how to be single." I laughed.

"I won't be." Kenny winked. "I'll have you, sugarplum."

I shook my head, laughing harder. "When have you ever called a partner 'sugarplum'?"

"Should I call you 'baby' instead?" Kenny asked, cheeks flushing.

"Anything but 'sugarplum.'" I chuckled. "All right, if you think you can handle not dating for that long, I'm game."

"Hey, that means no hookups for you, either." Kenny pointed a finger at me like he was ready to give me a lecture.

"I got two hands. I'll be fine." I honestly didn't even care for hookups; they just sort of happened. Sometimes I needed something to do when Kenny was with Jackie, so I'd find my own person. Since I made it clear from the get-go I wasn't looking for anything serious, one thing usually led to another. It wasn't like I hated hookups, but I could take them or leave them. With my citizenship on the line, I could definitely leave them.

"We can divorce as soon as it's official," Kenny said. "Well, after you're naturalized. Three years of marriage, at least."

"And...you're really cool with that?" I couldn't believe he knew how long of a commitment it was and was still asking.

"Of course. The time will pass anyway."

I didn't know how else to react but laugh. It was genuine, and joyful, and a little delirious. I had half a mind to slap myself awake.

"You're still down, right?" Kenny asked this time.

"Yeah." It was me who should have been asking Kenny that. But he'd clearly made up his mind.

"Good. Anyway, we can get divorced because I want human kids and you're more of a succulent daddy. Not even a lie,"

Kenny said, as if this whole thing were that simple. But there were so many potential complications. For one, if anyone found out . . .

Kenny was reliable, but so was my paranoia. I, on the other hand, was known for being brutally honest and a bad liar. I wasn't mean exactly, but let's just say if someone had something stuck in their teeth or toilet paper on their shoe, I'd be the first to let them know. Still, this was something I absolutely had to lie about. And I'd do it convincingly. Had to. Maybe Kenny could help me in that department. He was an actor, after all.

I grabbed a couple of beers from the mini fridge by the couch and continued planning. Kenny sat up to take the beer I handed him, and Luna hopped off the couch, stretching out on the floor.

"We should get engaged publicly, so it's more believable." I popped my bottle open and took a sip. "Then we won't have to worry about telling everyone."

"You're a genius! We can do it at that drag show I'm doing with Leti!"

"Ah, so you are doing the show!" I said excitedly. Kenny didn't make it a big deal, but I knew it meant a lot to him. He'd never been able to express himself with makeup, fashion, and sure as hell not his sexuality when he was with Jackie. Doing drag was a big step.

"Of course I'm doing it!" Kenny said it like it was the only thing that made sense. And, knowing him, it did.

I laughed. "Go big or go home, I guess."

"You should be the one to propose, since you're a terrible actor, and the proposer has an excuse to trip over their words and get nervous and stuff."

Leave it to Kenny to call it "acting" instead of "lying."

"Good point. I don't know how you do it." I had to admit I was relieved by the idea. I couldn't imagine faking all the emotion that came with *being* proposed to. But with Kenny's background in theater, I was confident he'd kill it.

My breath hitched when Kenny rested a hand on my knee, and his other hand gently touched my cheek, forcing me to meet his deep brown eyes. The same eyes he used to wear green contacts to cover up. He'd stopped wearing them after high school, but his eyes were even more stunning now. Big with thick lashes and strong bone structure to frame them. Kenny leaned forward so our faces must have been less than a breath apart, but I couldn't get one out to test the theory. The eye contact was thrilling and excruciating, and I couldn't bring myself to pull away. Then Kenny grinned and sat back.

"See? Acting isn't that hard," he said, but "acting" wasn't the word I would've used. I wasn't sure what just happened, but it felt like I'd gotten swept up in some sort of spell, one that left me struggling to find my feet again.

"That didn't help at all," I said. Kenny just grinned.

"So, how about holding hands? Like in public," Kenny asked.

"Sure. Gotta sell it, right? What about...uh...kissing?" I almost wanted to tease Kenny about that drunken kiss but decided against it. I didn't need him feeling weird about this. Everything was so nerve-racking as it was. And drunken kisses aside, I was sure we'd at least kiss during the "proposal."

"That's what I was about to ask. I'm cool if you are." Kenny winked. I wished he wouldn't be so damn charming, even if he was kidding. It was making it hard to concentrate.

"I'm not really sure how we'd do a proposal without kissing," I admitted.

"Exactly. But, um, like I said...you're not the best actor."

"Oh. You think it's too risky, then?" A public proposal *was* a bit ambitious.

"I just mean...maybe we should practice? I can give you some pointers. Like, use your real emotions to fuel the fake narrative. We have to look convincing if we're kissing in public. It'd be obvious if it was the first time, you know?"

Heat rushed from my chest into my cheeks as I glanced at Kenny's lips, remembering how soft they were, even sloppy drunk.

"You want to practice kissing?"

"Don't be weird about it." Kenny was blushing now, too. "It won't work if we can't even do a practice kiss." He bit his lip. "Are you okay with that?"

I took a big gulp of my beer, then set it down and leaned forward, pressing my lips firmly and eagerly against Kenny's. It was a kiss that said "I'm sure about this." A quick kiss, one that lasted less than a second but didn't help release the heat in my cheeks. It was my first time kissing a dude on purpose, but I had no time to second-guess it. Kenny had kissed guys before, so maybe he wasn't as nervous as I was.

"Okay, that was a start." Kenny practically giggled, his cheeks red as hell. "I was thinking more like this..."

Kenny gently cupped my cheeks in his hands, and my stubble shifted under his fingers. He was moving painfully slowly, like he was showing off his acting by milking every moment. It was hard to keep my lips from twitching, since I was hoping to just get it over with. But maybe also because part of me just wanted those lips on mine.

Okay, okay, okay, maybe that "homophobia" I was so worried about was just straight homo. Minus the straight.

But that was irrelevant when it came to Kenny. Because this was all fake.

Okay, focus.

Real emotions to fuel the fake narrative. But I didn't know what kind of emotions I was supposed to use. Happiness? Passion? Love? I wasn't exactly great at channeling feelings, real or otherwise. Instead of thinking, I slid my fingers behind the nape of Kenny's neck, feeling the ends of his freshly cut hair stand up as I gripped him softly. He leaned in so our noses brushed against each other like two ships barely escaping collision. If this was a game of chicken, I sure as hell wouldn't be the first to back away. We both closed our eyes, and for a moment I thought maybe I was dreaming.

Finally, *finally*, our lips touched. And touched. And touched. Kenny's parted slightly without intruding. An invitation I gladly accepted. His soft lips turned up into a slight smile when I parted mine. His hand shifted to the back of my neck, running through my hair. I let out an unexpectedly embarrassing noise at the sensation.

Just when I felt my jeans get tight, Kenny pulled away.

"Whew! That was—great job!" He said it like he was nothing more than an acting coach and not the first man I'd ever kissed. "Let's try a proposal kiss now."

"A proposal kiss?" I asked breathlessly.

"Yes, propose to me, lover!" Kenny grabbed my hand, pulling me off the couch so I could kneel.

I managed to laugh out a proposal between fits of childlike giggles. "Kendrick Bautista, will you marry me?" The words came out easier than expected.

"I'd love nothing more from life!" Kenny swooned, wiping his tearless eyes. I stood up and hugged Kenny the way I'd seen couples do in engagement videos. We laughed and kissed again. I wasn't one for sappy confessions, but something about it being fake filled me with giddiness and giggles. Hopefully our real performance would be better than this one.

We practiced several different kisses, just to be safe. One where Kenny leapt into my arms and we kissed while I carried him. Kenny was cut, but lean and a bit shorter, so it wasn't too hard to hold him. We kissed again while pretending to cry happy tears. And another where we channeled the passion of two lovers who just got engaged. I felt myself getting lost in the performance as the acting filled me with warmth.

Once the night was over, I felt like an expert in acting, or at least in kissing Kenny.

＊ ＊ ＊

I went to bed dizzy and giddy. I was going to marry my best friend. I was getting my green card. I drifted to sleep with a smile on my face.

Then I woke up to Kenny's silhouette in the door once again. This time he was sober, but he still crawled into my bed, pulling the blanket over himself and snuggling up to me.

I let out a little laugh. "What are you doing?"

He looked at me without saying anything for a bit, and something about the intensity of his stare made me blush. Kenny had never looked at me like that before, and I couldn't quite place the emotion behind it. He looked down at my lips and bit his own.

"I think we need a little more practice, don't you?" he finally said.

At that moment, I didn't care about the logic behind it. Yes. We needed practice.

Kenny patiently waited for my answer, still looking at me with that hungry smile. I couldn't help it. I leaned forward and planted a slow, soft kiss on Kenny's sweet lips. I wanted to do a good job for him. If this was going to work, we needed to be experts, and from my experience so far, Kenny already was. I had some catching up to do.

When I pulled away, one of his hands traveled down my chest. The other found its way behind my neck, gripping me softly but protectively. I got the feeling I didn't do a good enough job the first time, so I went in for another kiss, this time following his lead and letting my hands roam his body freely.

I'd seen Kenny's body before, but I'd never *felt* it. Never took the time to appreciate the slight dips of muscle on his abs or the inviting warmth of his chest. I wanted to explore more. Wanted to feel all of him.

So I kissed him again, matching his hunger this time as I pulled him closer, meshing ourselves together so we could fill every crevice of each other's bodies. Kenny weaved one leg between mine, his hands moving to my ass and squeezing the fat, pulling me closer so my pelvis was pressed against his. As I felt his form shift under his boxers, my mouth moved on its own to his neck, and I allowed myself to enjoy the soft hum of pleasure Kenny let out at the sensation.

"Good," Kenny said approvingly. "You're so good."

The praise warmed my insides, and my blood rushed downward. Kenny gave me that smile again when he felt me harden. His fingers moved to the edge of my boxers, tugging slightly.

"Are you ready?"

I eagerly nodded.

"Han, are you ready?" he asked again.

Maybe he wanted me to say it out loud, so I did. "Yes, *please*."

The blankets got pulled off me. The light turned on. And I woke up.

CHAPTER TWELVE

KENNY

Han's eyes shot open, and he sat up so fast, he almost fell off his bed.

"Whoa, is this how you always wake up?" I laughed. It was rare I woke up before Han, so I'd definitely needed to take advantage of the opportunity to wake him up for once.

"I—I just—I was just..." Han stumbled over his words.

"Weird dream?" I asked, and he laughed awkwardly.

"You could say that."

"What was it about?" I asked, and his cheeks immediately flushed.

"I, ha ha...uh...nothing, really." I didn't buy that for one second, but I also wasn't going to force Han to talk.

"Hey, it was just a dream. Everything's fine," I said, hoping to help Han snap out of his funk.

He nodded. "Right, just a dream." Then he shook his head, as if to shake the dream from his mind, and he was suddenly normal again. "Time to get ready?"

I nodded. Han's weird mood did nothing to wipe the smile off my face. Even if today was going to be difficult—we planned to go to my parents' house and break the news that Jackie and I had broken up and let them know I was with Han now—really just the first step on the way to getting Han his papers.

I got déjà vu as I sat on my parents' living room couch eating snacks prepared by my dad to stall a difficult conversation again. This time it was a bowl of freshly cut watermelon, pineapple, cantaloupe, and mango with tajin seasoning. I stuck a toothpick into a piece of fruit and ate it. My dad was the type to get offended if you didn't eat whatever he'd prepared right away. I had to admit, the combination of sweet and tangy with a little kick helped calm my nerves. Everyone ate at least a couple of pieces of fruit before my parents started looking at us expectantly, waiting for me to say something.

"Jackie and I broke up." I finally just came out with it.

"Why?" My mom's voice was calm despite her eyebrows shooting up.

"She made me choose between her and Han..." I took a breath, then slipped my hand into Han's, and he nodded reassuringly. Whether he was acting or being supportive, he was doing a great job.

"How dare she? Why would she—oh...oh, I see." My dad's eyes shifted to my hand in Han's, then back and forth from the two of us. "Have you two been...?"

I realized the implication was that I'd cheated on Jackie. I hated that I had to let them think that if this was going to work.

"It's been Han for a while," I finally said. I looked away, feeling myself getting flustered. It was naive to think I could fool my parents when I'd just asked their permission to marry Jackie. I felt terrible about letting everyone think I'd cheated on her, especially since that information would probably reach her eventually, and I didn't want to hurt her. But if this was going to work, everyone had to believe Han and I had been in love much longer than we'd been pretending.

My mom reached for Han's hand. "I always knew it was you." Han's cheeks darkened. For all my talk about being a good actor, I couldn't find words to save my life. Luckily, my teaching seemed to have made a difference on Han, because he was going along just fine.

"I knew it was Kenny, too. I've loved him longer than I can remember." Han tenderly ran his thumb along the back of my hand and batted his eyelashes at me. I smiled. I was so proud. If Han acted this well during the engagement, we'd be golden. My parents approved of Han much more enthusiastically than they did Jackie. It wasn't coming out to my parents I was worried about. They knew I was bi, so I figured they'd approve. I just didn't think they would *buy* it.

"Are you happy?" my mom asked.

"Yes," I said without thinking. And I was. I hadn't been lying when I told Han I was sure about this. I was more than sure. I was eager, and excited, and, yes, *happy*.

"Of course he's happy. You've been inseparable since you were eight. I figured it was only a matter of time before you realized," Dad said.

"Realized? You mean you knew before he did?" Han grinned and leaned forward, ready for a story. I let go of him to cover my face. I was sure whatever they had to say would be royally embarrassing.

They proceeded to tell Han about me raving about how cool he was before we were ever friends, at the ripe young age of seven. Han looked surprised, probably because I'd gone out of my way to avoid him back then. I told myself I was jealous of how cool he was, but no, Han had definitely been my first crush. And now he knew. Lovely.

"I thought you hated me! You were such a jerk in first grade." Han laughed.

"Nah, you were a cutie," I said, trying to sound flirty, but my face must have been cherry red. Han would never let me live this down.

After we finished off the fruit, Han and I said our goodbyes, then headed out to my car. Next stop was Han's family.

"So, baby Kenny had a little crush on me, huh?" Han said when we got in the car, showing off his dimply grin.

"Shut up." I started driving and turned on the radio, but Han didn't get the hint.

"What was so cool about me?" he asked, this time no grin. He looked genuinely curious.

I sighed, embarrassed. I hadn't been shy around Han since back then.

"Remember in first grade when you got Alec out in dodgeball?" I laughed. Alec was a bully then, and when Han's dodgeball hit him in the groin, I was all heart eyes. I was infatuated for a year before we ever spoke.

"Alec?" Han asked.

"Oh my God, you don't even remember. You're breaking my heart right now." I pouted.

"Refresh my memory." Han turned in his seat to face me with a soft smile.

"In gym class. Alec pushed me, and then you threw a ball at his crotch. He didn't bother me after that."

Han grinned suspiciously big, even though he was biting it back.

"You asshole! You totally remember!"

Han laughed. "Yeah, I remember. You ignored me after that, though, so I thought you hated me."

"No, you saved me! You were, like, my hero." I took my eyes off the road for a moment to give Han a quick fluttery-lashed look.

We laughed and reminisced the rest of the ride to Han's family's house, but the laughter died when we got there. I had to admit I was nervous, and Han must have been, too.

I parked on the street, since the driveway had two cars in it. One car was Nacho's, and the other I recognized as Han's older cousin Mariana's. Han, Leti, and Mariana had been raised together as siblings ever since Han came to the States. While Mariana and Leti still lived at home, Han had gotten out right after high school.

We waited in the car for a while before heading inside. It started raining, and the patter of water hit my windshield in a soothing rhythm. I was emotionally exhausted and needed a minute before immersing myself in a household of well-intentioned people with minimal boundaries.

"You ready?" I asked Han.

"Should we do this another time?" Han asked.

"I don't think so, but we can wait here for a minute," I said, secretly grateful for an excuse to stall so I could get my shit together for Han's sake.

"Just for a minute," Han said, blowing out a slow breath.

"Hey, they love me, remember?" I showed off a toothy grin.

"You're right, you're right. Let's just rip off the Band-Aid," Han said, and we jogged to the house to keep as dry as possible from the drizzling rain. Han stood frozen in the doorway, so I knocked on the door myself.

A muffled "Come in!" came from the living room, so I opened the unlocked door and followed Han inside.

"Hey, Tío Nacho," Han said, and I waved. Nacho nodded a greeting without looking away from the football game on the TV. A timer went off as we walked into the living room, the spicy smell of chicken and green chile filling the small house.

Before I knew it, a baby was placed in my arms by Han's tía Mary. "You wanna go with your tío?" she asked in her baby voice, but I was already holding him. It felt like an honor being called the baby's tío. Mateo immediately reached for me, giving me a huge toothless smile. "Can you two watch him really quick? I gotta get the enchiladas. Hope you're hungry!" She was already back in the kitchen and carefully taking enchiladas out of the oven by the time she finished talking.

"Sure," I said redundantly. "How you doing, little man?"

"Mami! Who's here?" a voice called out from the laundry room.

"Your primos!" Tía Mary's voice boomed, even though the laundry room was connected to the kitchen. Mary and Ignacio—Nacho for short—had basically adopted me as another nephew, so I called them my tíos just like Han did.

"Oh, hey, Han! Hi, Kenny! Sorry you got stuck with my baby! I'll grab him as soon as I'm done loading the dryer."

"It's cool. I like hanging out with Mateo, isn't that right?" I asked in my baby voice, and he answered by grabbing my glasses with his sticky baby hand. "Hey, I need those to see!" I said playfully, and Han grabbed the glasses from Mateo's grip, replacing them with Nacho's car keys from the wall—Mateo's favorite toy. Han cleaned the glasses with his shirt before carefully putting them back on my face.

Leti came running out of their room and hugged Han from

behind, then took Mateo from my arms and started cooing at him. Between me, Han, Mariana, Leti, Tío Nacho, and Tía Mary, that baby must have been the most loved child in all of New Mexico.

Once the enchiladas had cooled, everyone gathered around the dinner table. I wasn't so hungry because of all the fruit I'd nervously eaten earlier, but Han's tíos weren't the type of people you could refuse a meal from either, so I ate anyway. With Mary's cooking as good as it was, I wasn't complaining.

I waited for Han to make his announcement, but he kept his mouth full, surely a strategy to keep from having to talk.

Mariana scoffed at her phone before dropping it not-so-gently back onto the table.

"What's wrong with you?" Nacho said through a mouthful of enchilada, spots of sauce clinging to his mustache.

"ICE raided a quinceañera. A fucking quinceañera! Look." She turned her phone so everyone could see a video of what should have been a party. But half the adults were being handcuffed, and the quinceañera and the rest of the kids bawled their eyes out.

"Are you kidding? Why am I not surprised?" Leti huffed. Nacho grunted and shook his head while Mary clicked her tongue. My cheeks got hot. How much more evil could you be than to use a fifteen-year-old's coming-of-age celebration to rip the family apart . . . ?

My fork trembled in my hand as I looked at Han, who hadn't even stopped eating. He didn't usually show much emotion, even if he *had* to be feeling it.

"Let's not discuss these things at the table, okay?" Mary said, her gaze set on Han, who didn't look up from his plate as he shoved a spoonful of refried beans into his mouth.

A guilty look shot across Mariana's face as she mouthed, *Sorry.* I wondered if Han would change the subject with our announcement. Any minute now. Right?

But even as everyone's plates were picked clean, nothing. It wasn't like Nacho and Mary wouldn't be accepting. They'd raised Leti, who was practically the queerest person you could raise. I texted Han in case he was having second thoughts.

Kenny: we still doing this?

Han: can you?

I reached for Han's hand under the table and squeezed, then rested our hands on his bouncing thigh, which finally slowed down. I cleared my throat.

"Um, we wanted to tell you all something," I said, then pulled Han's hand up from under the table and held it between our plates for everyone to see.

"Yes...?" Mary said with a knowing look in her eye. She glanced down at our hands and back to my eyes. I glanced over at Han, who nodded his confirmation.

"Han and I are together," I said.

Silence. Probably the first time since I'd known this family that there had been an extended moment of silence. Soon enough, Mateo broke the quiet with a shrill baby-giggle. I didn't know what I expected, but it wasn't exactly this.

Tío Nacho was the first to speak.

"Well..." he started, taking his time chewing before whatever was coming next, "I kind of figured."

"Oh, *you* kind of figured? No one else?" Mariana laughed. Had they also assumed Han and I were together?

"Good job getting this one to commit to something." Mariana squeezed Han's shoulder, then fed some baby food to Mateo. Han glared at her, his leg bouncing again.

"Thanks." I smiled, exuding faux confidence at the achievement I fake earned.

Tía Mary reached across the table and put her hand on Han's, then gave him a teary-eyed smile. "Mijo, I'm so glad you finally feel safe telling us. You know we love you no matter who you love."

Heat rose in my cheeks. Han's whole family seemed like they'd just been *waiting* for him to come out. Even though they had already come to the correct incorrect conclusion, this was a good thing for our cover. If we didn't even have to try to convince our families, then convincing strangers would be a breeze. I grinned. Maybe this would actually work.

CHAPTER THIRTEEN

HAN

The fact that my tíos, Mariana, and Leti all *expected* me to come out gave me a strange feeling. Almost like they *knew* I'd never felt anything with a woman before. Like they knew I *had* felt...something...when I kissed Kenny. I shook the thought away. I wasn't ready to question things any more than I already had.

After the socially exhausting day I'd had, I needed some time alone to chill, so I had Kenny drop me off at the park down the street from our complex. It was close enough that the walk back wouldn't be too harsh on my ankle but far enough that I could get some time to myself. I sat on the park bench and breathed. The image of the quinceañera sobbing as her father was dragged away was burned into my brain. I'd refused to get emotional at dinner, but now that I was alone, I could drop the facade. My fingers throbbed from clenching my fists. None of this was fair.

I needed to stay calm. That would never happen to me. Not if this wedding went according to plan. This was going to work. It had to.

If even one person didn't buy it, they could ruin everything. And it wasn't just me in danger anymore. My best friend was putting his freedom on the line now. Did that make me a horrible friend?

My chest tightened. Would he really go through with this? Would I ever forgive myself if he did?

Close your eyes. Breathe steady . . .

Back to polyp.

✳   ✳   ✳

By the time Kenny and I were twelve, I'd been to his house countless times, but this was the first time his parents had entrusted us to walk there on our own. I'd been used to walking around on my own, but Kenny's parents always picked him up from school, so this was a big deal for him.

I hadn't paid much attention to our walking formation, but when we turned a corner and I started switching places with Kenny, he immediately put himself between me and the road.

"What are you doing?" I asked.

"I think you should stay on the inside, and I'll walk closer to the road."

"Why?" I couldn't imagine why it mattered which side we walked on.

"You know . . ." He shrugged like the answer was obvious. "Safety."

✳   ✳   ✳

To this day, Kenny never let me walk on the side closest to traffic. I didn't understand then, but now it made sense. He wanted to protect me. He was *still* protecting me.

But a wedding was way bigger than anything he'd done for

me before. Of course he wasn't just trying to make Jackie jealous. Protecting me was in his nature, and I felt like a colossal piece of shit for letting him.

But I was selfish. I'd wanted citizenship so bad for so long, I couldn't pass up my first real opportunity to get it. And I felt awful about that.

I got out my phone and stared at Leti's name in my contacts. I wanted to vent, and I knew Leti would understand. Hell, they might have been able to help. Before I could be too tempted, my screen lit up with a WhatsApp call from my mom. So she was alive after all. She hadn't answered any of my calls for months (which, okay, I'd only called like twice), but whenever she disappeared like that, my mind went to the worst places.

As much as I wanted to talk to *someone*, I couldn't bring myself to answer. My mom was the last person I wanted to vent to. I needed to unload, not do more work. She probably wanted to ask for money. I made a mental note to send some to my *dad*, who could be trusted with it.

I hadn't told my parents about the wedding, and I wasn't ready to hear how my mom would react to the news of me marrying a man. I would tell them soon...just not yet. Not while I was still freaking out about it.

When the phone stopped ringing, I stared at Leti's contact again. Maybe they could talk me down. They were always good at that. But I couldn't break my promise of secrecy to Kenny a day after I'd made it. As I tucked my phone back into my pocket, a stray cat wandered from under the bench. It sat in front of me and stared.

"Sorry, buddy. I don't have any food on me."

The cat kept staring, as if to coax me into talking.

"You know I'm not supposed to tell anyone. I'm not gonna put that shit on Leti," I thought out loud. I was fully aware of how ridiculous I looked talking to a cat, but there was no one around to witness it, so I kept going.

"Am I doing the right thing?" I asked hopelessly. The cat answered by rubbing up against my shin. I let out a soft laugh and scratched its head. I needed to tell someone so badly, but I couldn't risk it. Not with Kenny's freedom on the line, and my status. But the cat was all ears, and there was no one else in the park.

"I'm marrying my best friend for citizenship." I said it so quickly that even I didn't fully understand the words coming out of my mouth. I laughed again. "And I'm talking to a cat."

The cat blinked slowly, a sign of trust that felt more like a sign from the universe.

Rain sprinkled down again, wetting my lashes. Or maybe that was something else. I sighed as my confidant ran to find shelter. I looked to the sky as the water hit my face, letting the tears fall with the drops so no one could tell the difference.

I closed my eyes, pushing out a few more tears. Then I heard someone approaching. I wiped my face and silently shook myself off, then turned to see Kenny walking up, shielded by an umbrella. He wore a jacket but had another tied around his waist. He untied it and handed it over, holding the umbrella out so it was hovering over me instead of him.

"Thanks," I said as I took off my bomber jacket, tying it around my own waist so I could put on the jacket Kenny brought. He sat next to me, close enough to share the umbrella.

"Can't have you getting sick on me."

I thoughtlessly leaned my head on Kenny's shoulder, and he responded by resting his head on mine.

"You okay?"

"Yeah." I shrugged.

"You want to talk about it?"

"Nah."

"Want me to leave you alone?"

"Nah, we can head back. Can't be getting sick," I said. If I got sick, I'd have to either call off work and risk getting fired or go to work and get customers sick. Which could also get me fired.

"Want to rewatch *Our Flag Means Death*?" Kenny asked, and while gay pirates were entertaining, I didn't need anything making me question myself right now—or, more realistically, I didn't need anything holding up a mirror in my face when the answer was just as easily left unsaid. So I shook my head no.

"I'm more in a kids' movie mood, you know?" A smile betrayed my brooding. The only times I ever cried in front of Kenny were when we watched kids' movies. For some reason I seemed to have a healthy range of emotions only when watching Disney or *The Land Before Time*.

"What movie?" he asked.

"*Coco*." I grinned.

Kenny chuckled. "So you're in the mood to cry, huh?"

"Hey, I've only cried three times in my life," I joked. "Twice when I was a baby, and the third time during *Coco*."

"Sure, Han." Kenny laughed and shoved my shoulder.

We walked back to the apartment, shoulders pressed together under the umbrella, Kenny dutifully walking on the outside closer to the road. Even though we had no one to pretend for, I wanted to wrap my arms around Kenny and squeeze him in gratitude. I wasn't sure I'd ever be able to put into words how much he meant to me, and I *knew* I'd never be able to repay him. Luckily, Kenny wasn't one to keep score.

CHAPTER FOURTEEN

KENNY

I closed the umbrella as we got to our building. I always let Han go up the stairs first, since I was afraid it'd be too much on his ankle, and I wanted to be able to catch him if he fell. Maybe it was an irrational fear, but the way Han slowed, his face scrunched in pain by the time he got to our floor was more than enough cause for worry.

When we got up the steps, my stomach dropped as my phone rang with a familiar tone.

Jackie.

She was probably calling to either get back at me or get back together.

Han sighed, noticing her name on my phone. I answered anyway.

"Hey," she said casually as I finally found my footing and made my way to the door, one step in front of the other. She spoke like nothing had changed. She always did when she wanted to "get over" a breakup. "I stopped by earlier, but you weren't home."

"What are you doing? We—we broke up." I hated how the sadness seeped into my voice at the words "broke up."

"Oh, come on. We both know you didn't mean that. I forgive you," she said, voice as sweet as honey.

"I—we can't...I did mean it. I—" I rubbed my neck, and Han turned around, giving me a questioning look. It was the same look he'd given me before kicking Adam out. I guess that look meant something along the lines of "Do you need help?" I knew if I'd let on that I didn't want to talk to Jackie, he'd swoop in at a moment's notice and shun her like he had Adam. He'd done it to Jackie in the past, too, making up excuses there was no chance she'd believe. It usually only made her *more* angry, though. I muted myself before answering Han, knowing he could misread any nonverbal cues if I didn't outright tell him what I needed.

"It's fine," I finally said. It was probably best for me to tell her myself instead of dragging Han into it.

Han looked suspicious, which made me feel guilty. There was no way I was getting back with Jackie, especially after agreeing to marry Han. But I could understand Han's fear. Jackie and I had a kind of pattern.

"It'll be okay." I hoped he knew I'd never betray him. We were doing this. Han nodded, and I unmuted the phone as we went inside.

"Why are you calling me?" I finally asked.

"I told you. I'm ready to get back together," she said matter-of-factly.

"Um, what if I'm n—"

"So, let's just pretend this whole thing never happened, okay?"

"I...can't do that."

I could almost hear her seething. "Why not?"

I felt my heart racing, and I realized I would have been better off letting Han make an excuse for me.

"I have to go, sorry."

"Kenny!" she shouted, but I was already pressing "end call." I backed up against the door and slid down to sit on the ground with my hand over my chest, my heart pounding with the quick rise and fall of my breath. Luna came running with her tail wagging, trying to calm me.

"Smooth," Han said without looking away from the TV, where he was scrolling through looking for *Coco*.

My phone rang again, but I ignored it. I moved to sit on the couch with Han as Luna followed, as if Han could protect me from the big scary Jackie in my phone.

"You okay?" There was no judgment in Han's tone, and he looked genuinely concerned.

I sighed, running a hand through my hair. "I meant it when I said that choice was easy, but she just . . . gets to me, you know?" I felt my voice crack as I remembered Jackie's palm striking my cheek. I envied Han's ability to keep his emotions under wrap. I couldn't even keep my voice steady because of one slap. I stopped myself before telling Han about that part. I knew he wouldn't judge, but something about telling him she slapped me in the middle of traffic felt wrong. I guess I didn't want to admit it out loud. Somehow Han seemed to get the general feeling behind my lack of words.

"She's abusive, bro. I'm glad you got out."

"She's not—" I started, but Han interrupted by flicking out the palm of his hand.

"She tried to control every part of your life. Remember senior year? If it wasn't for me and Leti, she would have completely isolated you."

I hung my head. It was true that things got particularly bad that year. That was when Jackie's parents got divorced, and she got way more controlling. I guess she needed to feel in control of *something*, and I was right there.

But Han was wrong. Jackie may have wanted me to drop Han, but she hadn't *forced* me. I could have broken up with her back then, but I couldn't bear to put her through more pain when she was already going through so much. Of course I felt terrible about distancing myself from Han, but I'd done it. Still, I hadn't been the only one.

"It was more of Leti doing an intervention for both of us, and you know it."

Han frowned. "Yeah, I was a jackass then. I should have reeled you in sooner."

Han and I'd had this conversation plenty of times before. We both felt guilty for distancing from each other. Me because of Jackie, and Han as a reaction to me distancing myself. I'd been the exception to his rule of never getting too close to anyone, and I'd blown it. He'd never admit it, but I knew it had hurt him bad enough that he didn't try to keep in touch when I pulled back.

So Leti intervened. They gave Han an intervention first, and then they both came to me. Han and I cried so hard that day. We both apologized profusely and promised to never get distant like that again. And we never did.

But I didn't know what to say now. It was all too fresh. I looked down at Luna to avoid having to look at Han. My face got hot, and my vision blurry. Han was blowing this whole abuse thing way out of proportion...How could someone whose literal job was to protect abuse victims be an abuser? Especially when I really didn't feel like a victim. But then, why was I getting so emotional?

"Hey, man, we don't have to talk about it. I'm just glad you got out." Han lightly slapped the back of my shoulder and squeezed.

The phone rang again and again.

"How long do you think before she stops calling?" I asked, and Han shrugged.

"Bet money she'll still be calling after the movie."

"Bet." We shook on it. I didn't *think* Jackie would be that persistent. Still, the bet making light of the situation calmed my nerves. Han pressed play, and *Coco* played over the sounds of my phone vibrating. She must have given up eventually, because by the second rendition of "Remember Me," I caught Han wiping away tears, completely immersed in the movie. I decided not to ruin the moment by bringing up our bet.

When we first started the tradition of watching kids' movies, Han would pretend he hadn't been crying. Over the last few years, though, he gave up the act and cried openly. I wondered what it was about them that turned Han into mush and why it was the only way he'd allow me the privilege of seeing him cry. It was so cute that I never mentioned it for fear of losing out on the precious movie reactions. I tried not to look, either, so he wouldn't get embarrassed, but a smile betrayed me every time I heard a sniffle. It was just too pure.

After the movie, I pulled out my phone and stared at Jackie's contact info. When I looked up, Han gave me a reassuring nod. With his encouragement, I blocked her number. I wished I could say I felt relief, but I just felt tired.

CHAPTER FIFTEEN

HAN

Even though Kenny and I were eager to get married ASAP, we decided to wait a couple of weeks before I asked Kenny's parents for permission. If it were up to me, we would have waited longer. But Kenny refused to let me wait.

So, here we were, sitting in Kenny's minivan, waiting for me to gather the courage to get the hell out of the car and into his parents' house.

"What if I can't do it?" I asked, hesitating to open the car door.

"You can. I'll be waiting right here," Kenny said. The proposal was all set up for that night, but before we could go through with it, I had to officially get permission from Kenny's parents. Everyone knew having their approval meant a lot to Kenny, even if this whole thing was fake. Maybe even more so because this whole thing was fake. If anyone found out Kenny got married without getting his parents' blessing, they'd clock this whole thing as a sham before we finished saying our I do's. Still, lying to them felt wrong. Not wrong enough not to go through with it—I would do whatever it took to make this work—but wrong enough to make me feel like shit.

I took a deep breath before opening the door and walking over to their house. Kenny was pretty sure they'd approve, since their condition about Jackie had been about waiting longer, and Kenny and I had known each other for almost two decades. But I thought the opposite. Since Kenny and Jackie had *just* broken up, that meant he and I couldn't have been seeing each other very long at all. Still, if I went with the story Kenny came up with, it'd seem like a slow burn that'd been brewing our entire lives, not a spontaneous ploy to get citizenship. Not that they knew about my status.

I rang the doorbell and after a moment was greeted with a kiss on the cheek by Elisa and a firm hug from Cedric.

"Han, so good to see you! Come in!" Cedric said while Elisa ushered me inside. I kicked off my shoes before joining them on the couch. "Where's Kenny?"

"It's just me today." I gave them a nervous smile. Back in high school, and while Kenny was in college, I'd sometimes drop by here by myself to wait for Kenny to be done with a class or play practice or Taekwondo, but Kenny hadn't done any of that in years, so it'd been a while.

"What a sweet surprise! So sorry for the mess. I wasn't expecting anyone," Elisa said as she quickly fluffed some couch pillows, which was the only "mess" she could seem to find, as the house was cleaner than my permanent record.

"Coffee?" Cedric asked. "I would have made something if I knew you were coming!" I knew better than to deny Kenny's parents an opportunity to provide hospitality, so I accepted the offer with a smile.

"Thanks, Papi," I said. Calling Kenny's parents Mami and Papi had started as a joke when I was much younger, but it'd grown to feel more natural calling them that than my own parents. Obviously they could never replace my parents, but it felt nice to call someone *here* mom and dad.

In no time, we all sat on the couch with coffee a bit too hot to be sipped on just yet. I grasped the warm cup to keep my hands from shaking. The AC in the Bautista house was always freezing, but that wasn't what caused the tremble.

"I wanted to talk to you guys about something really important to me," I said. I told myself I'd keep the lying to a minimum. It was like Kenny had said, acting was easier if you used real emotions, and it was true that this was very important to me. I wished Kenny were here, but the act was supposed to be that he wouldn't know anything about the proposal.

Cedric raised a bushy eyebrow, and Elisa gave a welcoming smile that made my guilt rise into my throat. I'd rehearsed what I would say so many times, I just had to get it out and over with.

"You guys know this, but Kenny is really important to me." Another non-lie, but my breath quivered. Both Cedric and Elisa were silent, allowing me time to get it out. "He's been a huge support for me my whole life, and I honestly couldn't imagine life without him. Which is why"—I gulped—"it would mean the world to me if I could get your permission to marry him." I couldn't bring myself to look them in the eye. I hadn't lied, sure, but this whole *thing* was a lie. I put my mug down, still unable to look up from the floor.

"Han, honey, you know you're like a son to us." Elisa took my hand in both of hers and leaned forward. Looking into her eyes now, I could see where Kenny got his intensity from. "But

I worry about Kenny...about both of you. I don't want to see either of you get hurt after jumping in too quickly."

"I know, and I get that, Mami," I started, trying my best to meet her gaze without disintegrating. I pulled Kenny's story back into my head. "Trust me, I would never pressure Kenny to move faster than he was comfortable with, and if I had any hint that he wasn't ready, I wouldn't be asking." I swallowed before letting my voice crack. "I know it looks like we're going fast, but...I can't even remember a time I didn't love Kenny," I admitted.

"That much has always been clear," Elisa said, squeezing my hand while Cedric nodded along.

"You guys are my family. I know how much your approval means to Kenny, but it means just as much to me." I reminded myself to only say true things to keep from wrecking myself with guilt. "I really do want this, and I know Kenny does, too."

I looked up to see Cedric with tears in his eyes. Had I upset him? Did he know I was basically using Kenny for citizenship? No, no, I wasn't using Kenny. He was perfectly willing. I had to stop thinking like that, or this would never work. We were in this together.

"I'm sorry. I'm such a sap," Cedric said, blowing his nose.

"I'll be right back." Elisa swiftly got up from the couch and made her way down the hall.

"Papi, you okay?" I asked.

"I always knew it would come to this one day. I'm more than okay. I would love to see Kenny marry someone who actually makes him happy." His mouth curved into a trembly smile.

Elisa came back then, smiling almost wildly. She reached for my hand and squeezed. It wasn't until she let go that I realized she'd placed something in my palm.

The emerald ring.

The gesture made me want to run away and call the whole thing off. I figured they'd agree to the marriage, but I wished they'd kept the ring. Saved it for when Kenny and I got divorced and he got married for real. This was too intimate. Too *real*. While this whole thing was fake. But if I refused the ring, it'd look suspicious.

"I...don't know what to say." I wished I could somehow make this all up to them. They would never forgive me if they found out.

"You'll have to get it resized of course, but please, take it." She folded my fingers over the ring.

"Thank you. Thank you so much" was all I could manage to say as I pocketed the ring.

"When are you proposing?" Elisa clapped her hands together.

"I was hoping to propose tonight." I shifted on the couch, feeling like I was under a microscope.

"Ahh! So soon! I know a guy who can resize a ring in less than an hour. You'll have to go to him if anyone's putting this on tonight!"

With all the parties, quinces, weddings, et cetera that Elisa had helped plan, I wasn't surprised she knew a ring guy. Getting this one resized would be the perfect cover for me to tell Kenny I'd be out buying a ring. "That would be perfect. Thank you so much."

"How are you doing it? We'll *have* to throw an engagement party! I'll need a couple of weeks to get everything together." She pulled out her phone to look at her calendar. "Hmmm...let's plan for the twenty-third?"

"Um—"

"Great! There's no time to waste. I'll get right on it. You two won't have to worry about a thing. And good luck tonight!" She

winked, and I wished I could disappear. "Don't worry. We won't
keep you any longer. I have a party to plan!" Elisa practically
shooed me away. I hadn't even popped the question, and she
was practically planning the honeymoon.

After saying our goodbyes, I was relieved to be back with
Kenny, except that he bombarded me the second I opened the
car door.

"What'd they say?"

I debated pulling out the ring, but I stopped myself. Kenny
was a sucker for the dramatic, which meant he'd eat it up if I
surprised him tonight.

"That we're good to go."

Kenny fist pumped. "I knew it!" He looked like he would
leap out of his seat if it weren't for his seat belt. He hugged me
tightly. When he pulled away, something soft flashed in his face
as he looked into my eyes before he shook his head, shaking
away the expression. Maybe he was feeling weird that his parents agreed so quickly for me but not Jackie. That had to hurt.
Best not to overthink it though.

"All right, let's do this."

✳   ✳   ✳

Even though Kenny was the one doing drag for the first time
tonight, I was more nervous than ever. While Leti did Kenny's
makeup, I sat on the edge of their bed, watching anxiously.

"Calm down, primo. You're making me nervous," Leti said
without looking away from the thick eyeliner they were drawing on Kenny's lids. I realized then I'd been wildly bouncing
my leg.

"I'm chill," I said, trying to convince myself more than Leti.
They knew I was proposing tonight, but they didn't know it was

all fake, and they were under the impression that Kenny was completely clueless, so they couldn't talk about it while they were doing his makeup.

"What are you so nervous about? I'm the one performing." Kenny laughed, and I resisted the urge to flick his forehead. Kenny obviously knew why I was nervous.

"Okay, so why aren't *you* nervous?" I shot back, and Kenny grinned.

"Are you kidding? I was born for this." He said it like it was the most obvious thing in the world. And, honestly, it kind of was. Now that Jackie wasn't around to suppress Kenny's expression, of course he'd end up doing something like this. "You don't need to worry about me, okay, love?" he added with a wink.

"He used to get real nervous when I first started performing, too, verdad, Ale?" Bless Leti's soul, trying to cover for me so Kenny wouldn't find out about the proposal. A twinge of guilt jammed its finger in my ribs. Everyone was going so far above and beyond for me. I'd never kept anything from Leti before. If they knew this was fake, they'd kill me and Kenny both for keeping it from them.

And it *was* fake, so why was I so nervous? I rubbed my hands on my thighs to keep them from bouncing. I'd never committed to anyone for longer than a few weeks. The prospect of asking someone to *marry* me made my legs shake, like they wanted to run away. But I couldn't run. I didn't *want* to run. I wanted to stay here, in my home, with Kenny, as long as I could. That much was real.

When we got to the venue, I had to sit alone in the audience since Leti was emceeing and Kenny was performing. I didn't mind sitting alone. I just had to try not to think about how this crowd would be watching *me* soon enough.

I tried to pay attention, but I couldn't get my mind off my nerves. Performers came and went, and they were great—probably—but I could hardly focus. My mind was all on Kenny. On *my* performance. I spent the next hour of restless jitters going over the speech I'd planned instead of watching the incredible talent before me.

Then Kenny came onstage. I honestly wouldn't have recognized him if I hadn't witnessed him getting ready myself. He waltzed out, letting the train of his red gown trail behind him. The picture-perfect embodiment of tonight's theme: royalty. There was a mantle caping down from his shoulders and a gold and ruby crown so big I wasn't sure how he was able to stand straight, much less keep his head up. Somehow, he walked with grace all the way down the runway. He kept his back perfectly straight, even when he lowered himself to the ground so the skirt of his dress spread delicately on the floor. With a gentle hand raised to the lights, he looked up at his fingertips regally.

I stood up and started whistling. The crowd clapped and cheered along. Before Kenny could walk offstage, Leti asked him to stay. That was my cue. I downed my drink, hoping it might give me the push I needed to get through this. The drink made me lighter, but it didn't help. I only thought I might be light enough to fly away.

"We have a very special announcement from a very special someone," they sang, and I knew it was now or never. I put one wobbly foot in front of the other, in complete contrast to Kenny's graceful stride moments ago. I hoped no one could tell my knees were shaking. When I got onstage, Leti handed me a mic. I had rehearsed this, but I couldn't remember the words for the life of me.

The crowd suddenly seemed bigger. Meaner. My mic-holding hand trembled as I brought it to my lips and choked.

I'd originally planned on lying as little as possible like with Kenny's parents, but I couldn't remember the true parts of my speech to save my life. Besides, I was in front of a bunch of strangers who didn't know Kenny at all—and Leti, who would probably understand one day. No harm in lying here, right?

I swallowed my nerves and focused on Kenny. Even under the thick makeup and wig, his eyes offered a familiar reassurance.

"I, um..." I cleared my throat, and a few hushed murmurs echoed around. I turned to face the crowd instead of Kenny. "I want to talk about something—someone—very important to me." I looked back to Kenny and held out my hand, which Kenny took in his, holding the other to his chest as if to say "Who, me?"

"Hi, Kenny." I decided to ignore the crowd and just talk to him. "I wish I could say I've loved you since the moment we met, but we were six, and I hated your guts." A few chuckles bounced against the walls. I had no idea where I was going, but I embraced the drama like Kenny encouraged me to. "But I love you now more than life itself..." I got on one knee and pulled the ring out of my pocket. The crowd went wild, but Kenny's reaction was better. A look of recognition flashed across his face before he covered his mouth with his hand, his eyes sparkling. "...and I'd want nothing more than to spend the rest of my life with you."

Kenny's eyes watered, and I wondered if he felt even a fraction as guilty as I did. Maybe he was using that real emotion to fuel the fake narrative.

"Kenny...will you marry me?"

Still covering his mouth, he nodded yes, actual tears tracking eyeliner down his face. I wondered how the hell he made himself cry like that, but I got up to hug him anyway. Kenny leapt into my arms, and the crowd erupted.

I was thrown back into our living room, where we practiced this exact kiss. It happened as naturally now as it did then. The cheering and the blaring lights faded away, and for a moment it was just me and Kenny, kissing like no one was watching. Just like we'd practiced.

CHAPTER SIXTEEN

KENNY

Han and I were bombarded with congratulations the second we left the stage. I recognized some people from Leti's other shows, but the vast majority didn't ring much of a bell. I wasn't really a faces person, or a names person for that matter. I just wasn't a "remembering people" type of person.

So when two guys around our age came rushing toward me and Han with tight hugs and cheek kisses, I figured they were overly enthusiastic acquaintances I was failing to remember.

"Oh my God, how many years has it been? I can't believe we ran into you here! Congratulations!" the taller one exclaimed, practically squealing with excitement. On second thought, they seemed like more than acquaintances, but most people didn't take kindly to being forgotten, so I opted not to ask who they were.

The other half of the couple looked at us pridefully, like we were his children gone off to college. "I can't believe you're getting married, too! We got engaged recently ourselves. You're both obviously invited to the wedding!"

He immediately produced a save-the-date card from his bag and handed it to Han.

"Congrats to y'all, too, then," Han said, scanning the invitation while I scanned him, hoping for some kind of hint about who these guys were and why we were close enough to be invited to their wedding. A glance down at the invitation revealed it was only weeks away, so I had to assume they were either desperately trying to get the venue filled, or they'd been saving these invites specifically for us all this time. "We'll be there for sure" was all Han said before pocketing the invite.

"Wouldn't miss it for the world," I added with a smile, hoping they didn't realize they'd been completely deleted from my brain's memory files. Luckily, Leti walked up just then, giving me the perfect stealthy way to investigate. "You have to meet Leti, emcee slash drag queen extraordinaire, also Han's cousin."

"It's an absolute honor!" the taller guy said as he reached out his hand. "Blaine."

"Zane," the other guy said.

"Smith," they both said at the same time. "No relation." Again in unison.

"What an introduction!" Leti waved Blaine's hand away to hug them both before getting swept off into another conversation.

"See you at the wedding!" Zane said as he and Blaine gave Han and me quick hugs before heading off.

"That was sweet," I said, and Han nodded.

"You wanna go?" Han asked.

"Oh, definitely!" Even if I didn't remember those guys, a gay wedding would be the perfect way to test out our new fake-relationship skills. Plus, seeing a wedding in action would surely give us some much-needed inspiration. It was actually pretty perfect.

✻   ✻   ✻

Whenever Han and I shared a shift, we usually stalled in the parking lot before work. Han liked to shoot the shit to get his pre-work jitters out of the way, but today he was unusually quiet. He just stared at WhatsApp without typing or reading anything.

"Everything okay?" I asked. We'd been sitting silently for way too long.

"Yeah," Han said, but I wasn't convinced.

I didn't say anything. With Han, the best way to get him to talk was through silence. Eventually he went on.

"I haven't told my parents yet. Still haven't even called my mom back."

"Are you nervous?" Han wasn't extremely close with his parents, but I would have thought he'd tell them about getting married.

"It's . . . complicated." Han ran a hand through his hair.

"It'll be okay. Everyone's buying it. Your parents will, too."

"I'm not worried about them buying it. I'm worried about . . . I mean, I don't need their blessing like you did with your parents, but it'd be nice. I just don't know how they feel about . . . you know, gay shit."

"Want me to be there when you tell them?"

"Nah, I think I want to do it on my own. Thanks, though."

Han's alarm went off, which meant it was time to get out of the car to start our shift. We did so hand in hand, our icebreaker to the fake relationship now that we were engaged. Tatiana and Julia, one of the older servers here, rushed over and hugged us both. Julia squeezed so hard, I thought my arm might bruise in her grip.

"Congratulations!" Tatiana said, not looking even a little jealous. I wondered if that bothered Han, but he didn't seem to notice. "I knew Jackie was onto something about you two." She tapped her nose like she had us all figured out.

"Why didn't you tell me you were getting *married*?" Julia squealed. Then she pulled out her phone and showed us a video from Instagram of our engagement. Someone apparently filmed it, and it was getting around.

"Han surprised me," I said, batting my eyelashes at Han. He looked like he was trying to hold back a smile.

"When's the wedding?" Julia asked.

"We just got engaged." Han laughed. "Still have to plan it." I realized then we'd actually have to *plan* the wedding. I'd been so focused on the immigration side, the USCIS interview and green card application, I didn't know the first thing about wedding planning.

"Well, we're celebrating after work. There's a cake in the freezer, and Daniel said we could have some ice cream for the special occasion!" She gestured to Daniel, who gave a thumbs-up from his open-door office.

The first few hours of my shift went by in a breeze. Some of my favorite customers were in, and they tipped generously. It slowed down after the lunch rush, but a couple of hours before the end of the day, *she* showed up.

With Bryan.

I rushed into the kitchen so they wouldn't see me, then peeked out from the corner, making sure to stay hidden. The two of them got seated just like any other customers. Jackie laughed at something Bryan said, then brushed a piece of his shaggy blond hair behind his ear. A pang of jealousy tugged at my gut.

Was Jackie really petty enough to bring the guy she cheated on me with to my place of work? I got her message loud and clear. If I was going to hurt her, she was going to hurt me right back. It was working.

Then again, maybe it had nothing to do with me. Maybe she'd moved on, and she was with Bryan now. Either way, I wasn't exactly prepared to face Jackie. Instead of going out to greet them, I stopped Tatiana as she brushed past me.

"Trade tables with me?" I tilted my head in Jackie's direction.

"Oh, shit..." She looked like she was holding her tongue. "Yeah, I got you."

"I owe you one," I said. There was no way I was giving Jackie the satisfaction of waiting on her. Unfortunately, I still had to wait on all the tables next to her. Which meant I needed to become an expert in avoiding eye contact, even though I could feel her glares whenever I passed by.

I put all my nervous energy into performing the relationship with Han to its fullest. Two could play at her game. I slipped Han goo-goo eyes every time I went to the kitchen to get a plate. Soon enough, I forgot all about Jackie and just focused on Han.

When I took a plate from him, I let my fingers linger on his gloved hand for a moment longer than necessary. Han bit back a grin, like he was trying not to laugh.

"Get a room," Tatiana joked as she grabbed a plate next to the one I was getting. Han retracted his hand.

"S-sorry... We were just—" He stumbled over his words.

"Just being in looove?" Julia said from behind my shoulder.

"I didn't—we weren't—" Han started, the sudden tension confusing me.

"Relax, babe... What's wrong?" I said, hoping he wasn't about to have a panic attack or something.

Then Daniel walked by, giving Han—but not me—a warning glance. And it hit me. Han was afraid of getting in trouble. So I kept my hands to myself and made it a point not to flirt when Daniel was around. When I went back out, Jackie was gone.

Before we celebrated at the end of the day, I made it a point to carefully count the money, letting out a sigh of relief when nothing was missing. With that settled, I could focus on cake. Now that we were off the clock, Han loosened up with the flirting. He even held my hand without being prompted.

Surprisingly, Daniel was one of the people who stayed for cake and ice cream, and he was weirdly supportive now that our shifts were over. He discreetly pulled me aside, wrapping a casual arm around my shoulder.

"You sure you're up for this?" His tone was hushed.

"What do you mean?" I asked, taken aback.

"I'm just going to be blunt here..." he said with a sigh. "I think Alejandro might be using you. He's sure got a lot to gain from marrying you, doesn't he?"

"He's not using me," I said firmly.

"Just trying to look out for you, buddy. That's all," he said, then took his arm off my shoulder and went back to the group like nothing happened. If Daniel was suspicious already, we really needed to be careful.

"So, how long have you two been together?" Julia asked, pulling me back into the conversation.

"Officially, a couple of weeks, but it's been a lifetime in the making. When we both finally realized we felt the same about each other, how could we wait?" I looked over to Han, who reached for my hand and smiled.

"We've done enough waiting, that's for sure." Han laughed. "We've known each other since we were six."

"Talk about a slow burn," Tatiana said.

Han's hand trembled in mine, so I gave it a supportive squeeze. Why was he so nervous? We had already performed our relationship for both our families; I would have thought our co-workers would have been no big deal.

After a bit of celebrating, Daniel kicked everyone out to lock up. When Han and I left, I almost jumped out of my skin at who was waiting on the bench outside, eating frozen yogurt. Had Jackie been waiting for me? I accidentally made eye contact with her, and she pulled Bryan in for a kiss. She kept her eyes open, staring at me through the kiss.

"Play along," I whispered, then pulled Han in for a kiss of our own. Han let out a soft noise of surprise when our lips met, then relaxed and sank into it, moving his mouth on his own. I appreciated how convincingly Han kissed me. Like we were really into each other. He even rested his hand behind my neck once the initial surprise wore off. I put my hands on his hips and pulled him in as close as our bodies could go. After I was confident Jackie had seen enough, I pulled away.

"Don't look, but Jackie's behind you."

"Wah!" Han jumped and immediately looked behind him to see Jackie staring at us, open-mouthed and wide-eyed.

Her date looked over and said under his breath, but loud enough for us to hear, "Babe, isn't that your ex?"

"Oh, I didn't notice. He doesn't matter to me anymore."

Despite all logic, my heart sank. I didn't matter to her, and I hated that I even cared. Han must have overheard, too, because he took my hand and led me to the car. Quick footsteps rushed closer.

"What are you doing?" Bryan called out.

"Fuck you!" Jackie shouted from right behind us. I flinched, then Han put a protective hand on my chest, like his arm was a seat belt protecting me from getting totaled.

"Don't come near us again, or we're getting a restraining order." Han's voice was icy and, I had to admit, a little hot. Even though it had to be an empty threat. Calling the cops wasn't Han's MO.

Before Jackie could answer, we got in the car and shut the doors.

"You can't shut me out forever!" She banged on my window, suddenly dropping the "I'm in love with Bryan" act. I backed away and sped off, leaving an angry Jackie shouting in the parking lot, completely ignoring her poor date.

CHAPTER SEVENTEEN

HAN

I should have been used to kissing Kenny by now, but my cheeks warmed all over again, every time. I tried to catch my breath without being obvious while we drove home. I reminded myself we were just pretending. That this time it was mostly for Jackie's eyes. I had to remind myself that was *okay*. That I knew Jackie seeing Kenny move on was a *good* thing. Even if Kenny did want to make her jealous, it didn't mean he *only* cared about that. He'd proven as much already.

"What do you think she wanted?" I asked.

"Probably for us to break up. But don't worry, love, I'll never leave you." Kenny grinned, but I wished he wouldn't joke about it.

"You know you can, right?" Giving Kenny an out was a dumbass move, but I had to do it.

His brows scrunched together. "What do you mean?"

"I don't want you to feel like you *have* to go through with this, you know? It's your choice."

"I know, and I'll make the same choice every time. I wouldn't bow out on you," Kenny said, a frown tugging at his lips.

"Thanks. Seriously, it means a lot, bro."

"When have I ever let you down? Don't worry, okay?" Kenny smiled, and I really did believe him. My own smile lingered, even when Kenny looked away.

✳ ✳ ✳

Dear Mami,

I'm getting married. Can you believe it? If you do, you won't believe to who. Or, maybe you will, since everyone else pretty much guessed it.

 It's Kenny! I'm marrying Kenny.
 But it's all supposed to be fake and I feel like I'm going to explode if I don't tell someone.

Love,
Han

I stared at the letter I had written days before, then at my mom's contact in WhatsApp. It'd been a week since the engagement, but I still hadn't built up the courage to tell my parents.

Even with Kenny's prodding, I could hardly bring myself to open the app, let alone call them. What if they disowned me? Part of me felt like that wouldn't matter. It wasn't like they'd raised me anyway. But even if it was just a phone call or a video chat every couple of months, I still wanted them in my life. I might not have been the best son in the world. I could call more, but, then again, so could they. Still, I didn't want to lose them altogether.

And now that I was going to get my green card, I could actually visit them. Maybe we'd get closer than ever. I hadn't seen
them or been to my hometown in so long. God, I missed Xalapa.

I found myself craving a chocolate-filled churro. My dad
used to take me to this park with a churro stand all the time.
You just couldn't find authentic filled churros in the States. I'd
definitely tried.

Luna broke me out of my reminiscing when she hopped onto
the couch next to me, resting her head on my lap. I scratched
her ears. Even if Kenny was her first priority (despite her being
my dog), she was always there for comfort when I really needed
it. And she gave me the tiny push to make the damn call.

It rang. And rang. And God, part of me didn't want her to
answer, until she didn't. Then I realized how badly I actually
wanted to talk to her. My mind immediately went to the scary
place it always went when she didn't answer before I shook it off
and called my dad instead. She was probably just busy. Before I
knew it, my dad was on the other end of a video call.

"Que pasó, mijo? Everything okay?" His concerned words
delivered another shot of guilt into my veins. I knew I didn't
call as much as I should, but I didn't want my dad's first instinct
when I did call to be that something was horribly wrong.

"Everything's fine. Where's Mami? I need to tell you guys
something."

My dad shook his head, sighing. "She's . . . not here. What did
you want to tell us?"

"I think she'll want to hear this, Papi. Should I call back
another time?"

"I don't know when she's coming back, mijo. Just tell me." I
could barely make out the details, but when my dad moved to
sit on the couch, the camera shifted, and I saw that the living

room was connected to the kitchen, unlike the one he and my mom called from last time. Had it been that long?

"You moved?" I asked.

"Staying with a friend. You know how it is," he answered, with the slightest hint of a frown.

"I don't, actually. I can send some money?" A guilty hole formed in my chest. If I had called more, I could have helped. I didn't make bank, but I could probably squeeze out an extra hundred bucks or so a month.

My dad clicked his tongue and waved me away. "Keep your money, mijo. God knows your mami can't be trusted with it."

Oh. Last time I spoke with my mom, she'd been sober for a year. But it sounded like she might have been using again.

"Is she...you know...?" I started, but I couldn't finish without my voice betraying the lump in my throat.

"Don't worry. We're working on it. So, what's your big news?"

I wanted to think she was in rehab getting better, but I knew my parents couldn't afford that. So she was using. She'd always struggled with addiction. A memory resurfaced of her desperately trying to sell me for drugs. One of my only clear memories of her. My parents acted like that never happened. Like I was too young to remember, but I remembered.

They sent me here to live with my tíos after that. They never flat-out said it, but I knew it was to protect me from my mom's negligence. But she seemed so much better the last time we spoke. Another pang of guilt tugged at my heart for not reaching out sooner. For not answering when she had called, or even calling back. I should have at least checked in.

"Talk to me, Papi. What's going on?" I wished my dad would just be up front, no matter how hard it was to talk about. Shit, I was starting to sound like Kenny. I wondered if I'd gotten my emotionally stunted habits from my dad, even if I lived without his influence most of my life. Could that kind of thing be genetic?

"There's no time, mijo. Just tell me your news."

I sighed. "Okay, I'll tell you, but please have Mami call me when she can, okay?"

"I'll have her call when she's better. So what's this news, mijo? What's bothering you?" He gave me a reassuring smile, and I relaxed a little.

"Actually, everything is really great. I'm...getting married." I forced myself to smile despite what I'd just learned about my mom. In contrast, my dad's smile didn't look forced at all.

"You really are grown now, aren't you?" he said. "Who's the lucky lady?"

"Um, well, it's Kenny."

I had introduced Kenny to my parents on video chats before, but I never explained the nature of our relationship. I'd be surprised if my parents hadn't made the same assumption as everyone else.

"This is so you can get citizenship, verdad?"

"What? No!" I said, defensive against the correct assumption. I hated how quickly he came to that conclusion.

"Mijo, I don't see why you can't just marry a nice girl," he said, and I had to resist the urge to hang up on him.

"I don't want to marry a nice girl. I want to marry Kenny. It's not just a gimmick. I..." I felt myself getting heated, but I had no words to articulate it. Just then Kenny walked into the room, giving me two thumbs-up for encouragement. "I love him..." I finally finished. I don't know; it felt like the right thing to say.

My dad put his hands up in defeat. "All right, all right. I

won't judge how you're doing it. I'm just happy you're gonna be a citizen."

"I'm not doing it for citizenship!" My dad knowing made my forehead bead with sweat. At the same time, I figured he was desperate to dismiss the idea of me marrying a man for love.

"Okay, enough of this. So what else is new in your life?"

"What else? I'm getting *married*. It's kind of a big deal." I didn't want to admit that there really wasn't anything else going on in my life. My whole life had been constant mediocrity. I was never able to do the things I really wanted to do for fear of attracting too much attention. I had to work a job I hated, skip college. Forget about living my dreams—I didn't even let myself have any. Hell, I couldn't even travel across state lines. I knew my parents sent me here so I'd be safer, but I was still constantly looking over my shoulder.

"I love him…" I repeated. Of course it was true, even if we were best friends. Still, I wasn't one to go blurting out my feelings. The guise of it being fake was freeing that way. Ironically, it allowed me to say how I really felt.

"Okay, okay, I get it," Papi said.

"I have to go." I hung up before my dad could voice any more judgment. I wasn't sure why, but his disapproval hurt more than the guilt of Elisa and Cedric's approval. The guilt from spinning all these lies melted away. Now all I felt was heat flushing my cheeks and twisting my hands into fists.

Kenny sat next to me and swung an arm over my shoulders.

"He'll come around." At least Kenny didn't say anything about my acting skills. He always seemed to know what to say to make me feel better, even without me having to tell him what was actually wrong.

I don't see why you can't just marry a nice girl.

I never planned on marrying a girl, or anyone. But I also never planned on meeting someone like Kenny. Someone willing to put everything on the line for me without blinking. Someone who didn't hesitate to marry me the moment he realized it would get me to stay for good. I wasn't one for commitment, but I had already committed most of my life to being his best friend. I really didn't know why I was so afraid of commitment in the first place. Maybe I didn't want to end up with the wrong person. And Kenny was nothing if not so fucking right in every way.

And truthfully? If I were to marry someone, for real, it would be him.

That thought scared the shit out of me.

And maybe it changed everything.

CHAPTER EIGHTEEN

KENNY

The two weeks after the engagement passed with an over-whelming amount of congratulations from anyone who'd ever met me or Han. With everything so chaotic, before I knew it, it was the day of our engagement party.

Han and I usually skipped out on my mom's parties, but since she insisted on hosting, we had to at least show up. If it were up to me, we would have skipped it anyway, but Han refused to disappoint my mom.

When I got home from work, I found Han hunched over the table, poring over his laptop and several notebooks. The bags under his eyes were visible from the door.

"You okay?" I asked as I made my way over.

"Just figuring out wedding stuff. How are we supposed to afford any of this?"

I stood behind him so I could see what he was reading. Absentmindedly, I rubbed his shoulders as I scanned the screen, and I could feel him relax into the touch.

"You know you don't have to do this by yourself, right?"

Han sighed. "I know. I just wanted to figure out some things. I don't know shit about wedding planning, and neither do you."

I sat in the chair next to Han. "I was planning on tapping my mom for help. Party planning is, like, her thing."

"Shit! The party!" Han slammed his laptop shut and rushed to his room.

"It's okay if we're a little late!" I shouted before going to my own room to change.

Before long, Han was dressed and ready to go, while I was still picking out an outfit. Han was definitely the punctual one between us. Even if I sometimes didn't feel Mexican enough, at least I had the whole "operating off Mexican time" thing going for me.

"Ten bucks says your family will be later than we are," I called out as I rolled up my long sleeves.

"Ándale pues," Han urged. "If you want my money, let's *go*."

I walked out of my room only to realize we were wearing the exact same outfit. Black jeans. Purple button-up. Sleeves rolled. We both burst out laughing, and I turned around to change again, but Han grabbed my hand.

"Don't even think about it! We're leaving."

By the time we got to the party, half the block was lined with cars belonging to my extended family, along with one car for Han's.

We walked from the car hand in hand, but when we reached the door, Han unexpectedly pulled me in for a kiss. I couldn't say I was complaining. I was starting to rather enjoy Han's kisses, expected or not. It turned out Han's family—plus Tatiana, who seemed to be there with Leti—were walking toward us, which had to be why Han was putting on a show. I kissed him back while they approached, and the warmth filling my insides protected me against the cold night air. But I was afraid if we kept kissing I wouldn't be able to stop, so I pulled away breathlessly.

I'd been worried about feeling lonely after the breakup, but so far I didn't. Was that thanks to Han? I loved Han, but I didn't want to love him in *that* way. I couldn't let myself use him as a rebound. He deserved so much better. This was too important for me to go complicating things. I just had to channel Han and ignore my feelings. Maybe we needed to cool it with the kissing. I'd have to bring it up to him after the party.

"You guys are adorable. Gross." Mariana fake gagged.

"Leave them alone!" Leti said.

"Love the matching outfits!" Tatiana said before she hugged Han while Leti hugged me; then they switched.

When we all got inside, Nacho reached over and nudged Han.

"If you keep doing pinche PDA like that, you gonna have to join the band," he said, and I laughed. No matter how many times Han told Nacho he had to work or didn't want to join the band, Nacho stayed persistent, bringing it up in the randomest moments.

"What does PDA have to do with your band?" Han didn't look annoyed. Probably because Nacho's attempts were a little endearing.

"You're in a band?" my little cousin Angelica asked, eyes wide.

"A mariachi band!" Nacho stood straight, practically singing the word "mariachi."

"Can you play a song?" Angelica asked with starry eyes.

"I'll get my instruments!" Nacho said, and it didn't escape me that he'd said "instruments" plural. Han was getting roped into the show, and I was going to enjoy every second of it. I loved hearing Han sing, but he rarely did publicly without Nacho's coaxing.

"Have you eaten?" My mom ushered Han and me into the kitchen, where chicken, carne asada, tortillas, beans, rice, and toppings like jicama slaw and salsa covered the island. I made a plate to share with Han. If I had to run around socializing, I was at least going to get some good food out of this. We went back to the living room, where Nacho was already standing with a guitar and guitarrón. He handed the guitar to Han, who slumped and groaned but took it.

"Aaaaaa-ha-ha-haaaiiii!" Nacho sang all high-pitched, and I caught Han smiling. They played a song I didn't recognize but enjoyed all the same. Han's voice was like velvet. Smooth and soft, but it carried throughout the room. Nacho's voice, on the other hand, bellowed. They complemented each other well. Listening to them sing together might have made this party worth it.

Once the song was over, Han handed the guitar back to Nacho.

"Not bad, bro!" Han said with a grin.

"Not your bro, mijo. Pero si, that was, como se dice...fire."

I shook my head, laughing. Han's inability to give a compliment without the "bro" honorific was both cute and extremely annoying when directed my way. Wait, was it okay to be thinking of Han as cute, while trying to keep him from becoming a rebound? To be fair, Han being cute was just an objective fact, right? It didn't mean I had feelings just for acknowledging it. Maybe I could think of Han as cute as long as I was being objective about it.

Nacho continued attempting to convince Han to join the

band for a couple of minutes, with no luck. Then my aunt Rachel—who came from Arizona for this party with my tío Edgar—interrupted the conversation, grabbing our attention while Nacho brought the instruments back to the car. Rachel married into the family years ago, and she was always eager to welcome anyone else who married in.

"It's so nice to finally meet you! Welcome to the family!" Rachel said, shaking Han's hand vigorously. "Are you Han's mother?" Rachel turned to Tía Mary and shook her hand next.

"Pretty much." Han smiled at his tía. "She's my tía, but she raised me."

"Where are your parents?" Rachel asked, blunt as always.

"Aunt Rachel..." I started, but Han was already answering. "Mexico."

"Oh right, I forgot!" She snapped her fingers as if remembering where she put her keys. I didn't know Rachel had any idea about Han being undocumented. I'd only told my mom once in confidence... Dammit. I should have known I couldn't trust my mom not to gossip. "Did you have to get locked in the back of a truck to cross? I saw that in a movie."

My jaw dropped at her audacity. Before I could change the subject to save Han from reliving any of that, he was already answering.

"Um, yeah, but it wasn't really like the movies..." This was not a story I'd ever been privy to, and I didn't want to hear it for the first time in front of my gossiping aunts. They were starting to gather around, and Han looked like he might run away. I wouldn't blame him if he did.

Mariana, Leti, and Han's tíos had already been pulled away to greet my parents, but Han and I were stuck with Rachel, since she kept asking follow-up questions. I wanted nothing more than to whisk Han away and tell him he didn't have to talk about any of this, ever.

Rachel took a step closer, so only me and Han could hear. "Is that why you're getting married?"

"What? Aunt Rachel, that's—" I started, but she interrupted.

"It's okay if it is," she said, miming the motion of zipping her lips.

"It's not like that," Han said.

"Don't worry. I'm just messing with you guys." She laughed. "But seriously, I'm dying to know what it was like to cross for the first time."

"Baby, you don't have to talk about this here," I interjected so Han wouldn't feel pressured to answer. "Seriously, Aunt Rachel, what about me? I haven't seen you in years. Don't you want to know what *I've* been up to?" I said, trying to sound jealous. "I have stories, too."

Han squeezed my hand.

"Right, right, I'd like to hear the story of how you asked your parents to marry someone else days before your engagement with Han!" Rachel burst out laughing.

"It was weeks apart, actually," I said, my face burning.

"What? You never told me you wanted to marry Jackie..." Han was lying, obviously. There was the slightest twitch at the corner of his mouth, and I knew exactly what he was doing. Jackie's words fluttered through my head.

Real couples fought.

"I swear I didn't want to. I just felt pressured!" I pleaded, purposefully making my voice crack like I was about to cry.

"Your parents said no, didn't they? Would you have married her if they said yes?" Han put a hand over his mouth, no doubt to hide a smile trying to break out.

"No! I changed my mind about it that night!" All true.

"Then who's to say you won't change your mind about me? Unbelievable." Han stormed off, and I ran after him. The family was crowded around, but they parted for Han as he marched out of the house. I willed myself not to blink so tears might form.

"Baby, wait! I don't love her. I swear! It's always been you!" My eyes burned, tears flowing down my cheeks as I ran after Han.

We got all the way to the car before we lost it, giggling like children now that we were out of earshot.

My eyes were still watering when we got inside my car. I turned to Han and made my chin quiver. "I'm so proud of you . . ." I said, voice purposely cracking again.

"How the hell do you do that? It's freaky." Han shook himself off like my fake crying gave him the chills.

"I just don't blink. You should try it. It's really convincing," I said, wiping my eyes under my glasses. Then my heart tugged. Han did this to get away from my aunt's prying. "I'm really sorry about Rachel. She's the freaking nosiest person I know."

"It's okay," Han said, but his eyes didn't meet mine. He had to be at least a little mad at me for letting his status slip.

"Look, you don't ever have to talk about that stuff. But you can, if that's what you need," I said. I wanted him to feel comfortable telling me anything.

"'Preciate it, bro" was all he said.

I wanted to give him a chance to talk on his own without me prying, but we passed several stoplights without a word.

"Are you mad at me?" I finally asked.

"Nah."

"Why not?"

A long pause.

"How can I be mad when you're doing this for me? I don't have the right to be mad at you."

"You have every right to be mad at me. We're equals, Han. It's okay to be mad. I'm not gonna call off the wedding just because you're rightfully pissed. I shouldn't have told my mom about your status. It was in confidence, and I didn't think she'd tell anyone, but still." I sighed and ran a hand through my hair. "Remember when she kept inviting you to go to Guanajuato for our family reunions?" I'd always felt terrible when my mom invited Han. She didn't know why he couldn't go, but my entire extended family was dying to meet him, since my parents talked about him so much.

"Yeah. It's been a while since she asked, though."

I nodded. "Right. I told her about your status so she'd stop. It was obvious how shitty you felt having to say no every time, but I should have checked in with you first. I'm really, really sorry."

Han let out a breath. "We're cool, bro."

He probably wasn't saying what he was thinking, but I couldn't force him. Still, there was something else we had to talk about.

"So, um...there's something else I've been wanting to bring up..." I thought back to how I felt kissing Han. How safe and right his lips were and how complicated that made things. "Maybe we shouldn't kiss anymore."

Han took a bit to respond, like he was processing my request. "Don't we kind of have to? Like, for our cover?"

I swallowed my nerves. It would definitely be hard not to kiss Han, but not for the reason he thought. "We don't *have* to. Plenty of couples don't kiss in public."

"But you and Jackie were so...uh, we'll say affectionate. Will anyone buy it if you're not like that with me?"

"They'll buy it *because* it's with you," I said, trying to come up with a good enough excuse. "Jackie's super physically affectionate, but anyone who's seen you with a girl knows you don't really do PDA."

Han nodded solemnly, again clearly not saying everything on his mind. "What about you, though? You're definitely the PDA type."

"Then it'll be all the more convincing, right? People who know us well will see it as a boundary you've always had. It'll show them I see you as more than a physical relationship, you know?"

Han nodded again. If he wasn't buying it, he didn't say as much, which I was grateful for. If he picked up on what was actually going on, it could change everything. If I let Han know I had any kind of feelings, he'd probably feel pressured to go along with it, since his green card would be on the line. Confusing feelings aside, I wouldn't do that to him.

CHAPTER NINETEEN

HAN

I invited Leti and Tatiana over that night so I wouldn't over-think why the hell Kenny *really* didn't want to kiss me. As soon as there was a knock on the door, I went right over to answer it.

"So you and Kenny got over your *fight* I see..." Leti said loudly enough for Kenny to hear from the living room. They put finger quotes around the word "fight."

"What do you mean *fight*?" I said, mirroring Leti's finger quotes.

Tatiana laughed. "There are less creative ways to bail from a party."

Shit. Was I that bad of a liar? If I couldn't be convincing about the fight, who was to say I'd be convincing about any part of this? Was that why Kenny didn't want to kiss me anymore? Was I not believable enough?

"What are you talking about? It was a real fight...and we...made up already..." I realized now that inviting them over wasn't the best move, but smarts weren't exactly my forte.

"Sure you did, Ale…" Leti winked.

"Was it that obvious?" I asked, giving up the charade.

"Nah, I just know you. You don't go picking fights. I'm sure Kenny's fam was convinced, though."

I sighed in relief, remembering our fake fight with amusement, trying hard not to replay the conversation afterward. No more kissing. Why the hell did that bother me, anyway?

I cleared my throat and stepped aside so they could come in. Tatiana headed for the bathroom, and I followed her down the hall. She glanced at me behind her shoulder and raised an eyebrow. I put my hands on the sides of her arms and let out a shaky breath.

"I need you to be straight with me." I lowered my voice to a whisper. "Am I a bad kisser?"

Tatiana burst out laughing. "What? *Why?*"

"You can tell me. If I am." The idea never crossed my mind before. I'd never kissed someone who didn't want to kiss me. At least, I hoped I hadn't. As far as I knew, I was a great kisser. Then again, maybe everyone was just sparing my ego.

"Did Kenny tell you you're a bad kisser or something?"

"Shh!" I glanced down the hallway to see Kenny distracted with Leti. He didn't hear. Kenny hadn't outright said it, but he might as well have. How gross of a kisser must I have been if he didn't even want to do it for my citizenship? Then again, why did I *care* so much about whether Kenny wanted to kiss me?

"Of course not. Just be real with me. You don't have to spare my feelings." I sighed, dreading the response I might get. No one seemed to have any issues in the past, but maybe I was blessed—or cursed—with polite lovers. What else was I terrible at that no one bothered to tell me?

Tatiana covered her mouth and laughed again.

"Fuck...I'm terrible, aren't I?"

"No!" she let out through a laugh. "Trust me, I would tell you. It's just funny how random this is. You're usually so confident."

Relief washed over me, but it left just as quickly. If I was a decent kisser, then why didn't Kenny want to kiss anymore?

"Well, thanks...Uh, you can go to the bathroom now." I ducked my head and went to the kitchen.

I grabbed a bottle of wine and a few glasses, then made my way to the couch and sat between Leti and Kenny. They'd already put some movie on, but I couldn't stop thinking about what I'd done to cause a full halt in such a key aspect of our fake relationship.

Kenny wasn't the type to flake for any small thing. I rubbed my temples, wondering if I'd done something to upset him. As the movie played in the background, I replayed all our recent interactions in my head, looking for a clue. What the hell had I done wrong?

After Tatiana came back to join us, Kenny moved to sit on the ground between my legs. Luna sat next to Kenny with her head in his lap, and he leaned his head against my left thigh. Would he lean his head on me like that if he was mad? Maybe I hadn't done something wrong then...but that just made the new rule make even less sense.

Once the movie and another bottle of wine were through, Leti stumbled forward when they tried to stand to reach for their keys.

"Whoa, I don't think you should drive," Kenny said.

I looked over to Tatiana, who was sound asleep on the edge of the couch. My fault for bringing out the wine.

"Why don't you stay the night? You can have my bed, Leti," I offered.

"But where would you sleep?" they slurred.

"With me, obviously." Kenny said it like it was a no-brainer. Okay, so he probably wasn't mad if he was offering to share his bed, right? We'd slept in each other's beds a bunch of times before, so it wasn't too big of a deal. Then again, that was before we were getting married. And before the no-kissing rule.

✳   ✳   ✳

When we got into Kenny's room, I stared at the bed like it was lava.

Kenny nonchalantly stripped down to his boxers.

Kenny undressing brought my mind back to that dream I'd had of us practicing a lot more than kissing, and my cheeks burned hot. This time I was under no illusions about where the burning feeling came from. Like, if I was really homophobic, wouldn't all the fake dating stuff have bothered me? But somehow being seen in that way with Kenny, however fake it was, felt more natural than ever.

The burning in my cheeks and fluttering in my stomach only happened when we were alone. Even if my romance with Kenny was an act, it didn't mean seeing him in only his boxers did nothing for me. Especially after that dream.

Kenny's eyes moved from my face, down to my sweatpants, which were still very much on (and I intended to keep them that way), and *his* cheeks went red. It wasn't like Kenny had never seen me catch a boner before, but he'd usually tease me or something. He never got flustered.

As soon as I realized this time was different, I all but threw myself on the bed facing away from Kenny.

"Um, g'night," I mumbled, quickly pulling the covers over me.

"Night." Kenny let out an awkward laugh, and then the lights were out.

I curled up as far away from Kenny as possible, pretending to sleep to avoid any potential weirdness. All I wanted was to ask what I'd done to cause the no-kissing rule, but Kenny seemed so chill. He even kept rolling over like he wanted to cuddle, but maybe that was just in his sleep? Still, other than the new rule, nothing had really changed. Maybe I was overthinking it.

Then again, Kenny wasn't always the type to willingly face confrontation. I could remember plenty of times when he was upset with Jackie and never said anything until things got monumentally worse.

But this was Kenny and *me*. I wasn't Jackie. Kenny had never been afraid of telling *me* when I'd done something to upset him, because I didn't abuse his trust.

I was *not* Jackie. And *we* would be fine.

CHAPTER TWENTY

KENNY

I was a heavy enough sleeper that I usually woke up last when people stayed over. I assumed today would be the same, but I opened my eyes to find my arms wrapped tightly around Han's leg. Somehow I'd ended up lying upside down so we were feet to head, but that didn't stop me from grabbing on to the first warm thing I could find: his calf, apparently.

Eyes still closed, I yawned and stretched out. I'd always been a restless sleeper, so I tended to wake up sore and still tired. Han, on the other hand, was usually up and doing things by the time I hit my first REM cycle.

"Hnngh." Han let out a pained groan when my outstretched foot connected with his chin.

"Shit, sorry!" I quickly unraveled myself from clinging to his calf. He looked all stiff and uncomfortable, like he'd been holding his breath or something. "Did I wake you up? Are Leti and Tatiana still here?"

"Nah, I've been awake since, like, eight. And I heard them leave about an hour ago." He laughed a little, rolling his stiff-looking shoulders. I glanced over at my phone on my nightstand to see it was already eleven.

"What are you still doing in bed?"

"My leg was your pillow." He said it like it was no big deal. "Seemed like you weren't sleeping well, so I didn't wanna wake you up."

"You're sweet, but you know how heavy a sleeper I am. There's no way moving me off your leg would have woken me up." I laughed. Han knew how hard it could be to wake me, but he still refused to disturb my sleep if he didn't have to.

"Anyway, you ready to go to Blaine and Zane's wedding tonight?" Han asked as he sat up and stretched out with his back to the wall.

"Hell yeah," I said, scooting next to him. "It's the perfect opportunity to practice before the real deal."

Han raised an eyebrow. "Are you saying I need practice?"

"Even a master must practice." I may have said it in a joking tone, but it was true.

"Okay, Obi-Wan."

I laughed. "Seriously, though! It'll be easier to get used to acting all cute if we have more opportunities to be seen together in the wild. You know, show everyone how real and in love we can be!"

"Okay, but you know I've never been in a 'real and in love' relationship before, right?" Han looked at me with an expression I didn't catch on him often. Was he shy? Maybe I just needed to make it simpler for him so he wasn't second-guessing everything down to the body language.

"Want to make a checklist?" Han loved a well-thought-out plan.

"Okay, so what are some things real in-love couples do that we can do at the wedding?" he asked.

"Hmm, maybe we can do the chivalry thing? Like opening doors and pulling out chairs for each other?"

"Sounds good, but who would be the, uh, chivalr*er*?" Han asked, and I couldn't help but smile at the made-up word.

"Good point. The chivalry thing might be a little heteronormative," I admitted, slumping my shoulders. I'd never had anyone open doors or pull chairs out for *me*, so I couldn't lie and say it didn't sound nice, even if we'd be doing it for show.

"What if we take turns?"

"Yes! That's perfect!" I immediately perked back up. "Okay, what else do real in-love couples do?"

Han looked off into space and tapped his chin. "They eat off each other's plates?"

"Definitely. We'll have to be super annoying about feeding each other."

Han laughed. "Okay, what else?"

"Oooh, we can introduce each other to strangers as 'my *fiancé*,' all proud, then add a cute compliment. That way everyone thinks we adore each other."

We continued for a while, brainstorming about things couples did on dates, which eventually turned into me reading off a list of romance tropes from Google.

"Oh my gosh, what about the doorstep kiss?" I asked, looking up from my phone to see Han's reaction.

Han raised an eyebrow like he had no idea what I was talking about.

"You know, like when the couple goes home for the night, and person A walks person B up to their doorstep, but since it's a new relationship, they don't get invited inside. They say good night, but neither of them wants the date to be over yet, so they don't move to leave until they finally lean in for a kiss! It's a classic rom-com staple!"

"Ohh, you mean the romantic-comedy-new-relationship-good-night-doorstep-kiss?" Han asked like this was something he'd thought about enough to have that mouthful of a name for it.

"Exactly! It's practically a rite of passage for a new relationship that's headed in the right direction! The moment that kiss happens, the audience is convinced they're endgame."

"Guess that explains why I've never had one of those," Han said thoughtfully. "I've never been convinced of a girl being endgame for me."

"Wait, seriously? Haven't you been on, like, a million dates? You never kissed someone good night?"

"You have to not get invited in for the doorstep kiss to happen. Guess that's my problem." Han snickered.

"Well, you *have* to experience the romance of a good night doorstep kiss——"

"A *romantic-comedy-new-relationship*-good-night-doorstep-kiss," Han corrected.

"Okay, yes, that—at least once in your life! How else will the audience be convinced we're endgame?"

Han stopped laughing and looked at me all confused. "What about the no-kissing rule?"

Shit, I'd almost forgotten about that. I did set the rule for a reason, so it was probably best to stick to it. "Right. Okay, we don't have to do that one. It's not like we'd have an audience anyway.

We have plenty of material to work with here. I'm sure we'll be completely convincing."

Han nodded his understanding. "All right, let's do it."

When it came time to get ready, Han and I decided to rewear our outfits from the engagement party. Nice outfits didn't come cheap, and Han and I weren't exactly rich. We'd only been wearing them for a couple of hours anyway, and it wasn't like anyone at our engagement party would be making an appearance at Blaine and Zane's wedding. No one had to know we were outfit repeaters.

We ordered a rideshare so we'd be able to drink without worrying about driving. As soon as our ride showed up, I didn't waste any time before playing up our romance to the fullest.

"Allow me," I said to Han as I opened the car door for him.

"Thanks, babe." Han didn't hold back his smile as he climbed inside.

Once he was safely in the car, I shut the door, jogged over to the other side, and got in. The wedding venue was super close to our apartment, so it wasn't long before we were outside the banquet hall. I reached to open the door, but Han leapt forward to stop me, grabbing my wrist before I could grab the handle.

"Allow me," he said with a smooth smile. As soon as he let go of my wrist, he rushed to open his own door, then sprinted to my side of the car and opened mine. He held out his arm for me.

"I love you," I said with a laugh as I took his arm and allowed him to help me out of the car.

We made our way to the entrance, noting the fancy welcome sign by the door.

CONGRATULATIONS ON OUR WEDDING
It's Truly an Honor for You

don't forget to tag your photos!
#ZBlaineSmithHyphenSmith

I jogged ahead to open the door for Han since it was my turn to chival, but the door turned out to be automatic. Instead of opening it, I gave Han a little bow and gestured for him to lead the way.

"After you," I said, trying to sound charming.

Han smiled and held his arm out for me to take again, so we walked in arm in arm.

People mingled in the banquet hall, standing around in groups or sitting at tables, but no dancing just yet. Before we could find somewhere to sit, we were greeted by one of the grooms, Blaine himself.

"Kenny! Han! *So* glad you came." He hugged and cheek-kissed us both.

"How could we miss the wedding of the incredible Mr. and Mr. Smith?" I said.

"Mr. and Mr. Smith *hyphen* Smith," Blaine corrected.

"Cute ship name." Han smiled. "Whose surname comes first?"

At first I thought Han was trolling, but he looked earnest enough, and Blaine's answer implied he didn't take it as a joke, either.

"Believe it or not, it's mine! I know Zane wears the pants in the relationship, but using his name first would be too heter-onormy. So, it had to be *Smith*-Smith, not Smith-*Smith*."

"The correct choice, obviously," I said, still unsure if he was joking. Maybe I'd have some context if I remembered who these guys were, but I had absolutely no idea.

"Seriously, though, we didn't think you two would show up." Blaine leaned in like his next words were top secret. "I know we've kind of been huge bitches to both of you in the past. But don't worry. There're no hard feelings anymore. Zane and I are totally over it, and we're actually so happy you're getting married, too!"

I glanced over at Han for any hint about how to respond. Who these guys were. Why they were "huge bitches" to us. Anything. But he didn't say anything. Maybe this news caught him off guard just as much as it had me.

"Oh, we're so glad to hear that," I finally answered.

"No hard feelings," Han added.

"Wonderful." Blaine smiled brightly. "Now that we're all friends again, let's just let bygones be gone, *byeeee!*"

He waved goodbye with a broken-wristed waggle of his fingers, then walked away. It wasn't until he was out of earshot that Han turned to me and spoke under his breath.

"Okay, confession: I have absolutely no idea who these guys are. Refresh my memory?"

"Me either!" I burst out cackling, throwing myself onto Han in laughter.

"How the hell do we know them?" Han asked in between laughing fits of his own.

"We may have to do some detective work."

"Okay, let's investigate." Instead of sitting down and being antisocial like Han usually was at parties when he didn't know anyone, he led the way to a cluster of strangers.

"Hi," he said, awkwardly announcing his presence to a trio who shared a striking resemblance to each other, all being blond haired and blue eyed.

"Hi, I don't believe we've met?" The woman waved politely. "We're Zane's cousins."

"We haven't!" I said, relieved we didn't have to pretend to recognize them, too. "I'm Kenny, and this is my fiancé, Han."

"Wait, no way. *The* Kenny and Han? You actually came?"

"Um, of course we came?" I said, trying not to let on how absolutely clueless we both were.

"Didn't realize we were famous," Han said. I hoped one of our new acquaintances would take the hint and tell us *why* we were famous, but they did no such thing.

"Not so famous that we know anything about you," the woman said with an eager smile.

"Well, we must fix that," I said, taking the opportunity to check something off our "things real in-love couples do" list by inserting a compliment. "Han's pretty much the strongest guy I've ever met. He can bench-press both me and our newly adopted son." They didn't need to know that the son in question was a succulent.

"I might be able to lift, but Kenny could take me in a fight hands-down. He's a black belt in Taekwondo!" Han said, playing along perfectly.

"Oh, please, all you'd have to do is flex before the kick and I'd break my foot!"

One of the guys started laughing. "You two are cute. I can see why Zane and Blaine were so jealous."

Before I could make any sense of *that*, food started being served, so Han and I found our way to our table. I reached to pull out the chair for Han, but his hand landed on top of mine. We looked up at each other, holding the gaze just a bit longer than necessary.

"It's my turn, right?" Han said, and I laughed and shook my head.

"The door was automatic! Still my turn."

Han hesitated before allowing me to pull the chair out for him. Then we spent the next half hour or so being super obnoxious about feeding each other and eating off the other's plates. The checklist didn't stand a chance.

Soon enough, it was time for the bouquet toss. Han and I eagerly joined the masses behind Blaine, who held a beautiful bunch of red roses in one hand and a microphone in the other.

"According to gayncient legend, whoever catches the flower bougay will be the next to get married!"

He winked, then turned his back to us as the crowd counted down from five before Blaine tossed the roses over his shoulder.

It felt like the roses soared through the air in slow motion, gradually making their way right into my hands. If I caught the bouquet, that could pretty much replace the doorstep kiss as the thing that would convince the audience of our ship being endgame. I stretched my arms into the air, reaching for the bouquet until I could almost touch it.

I *did* touch it.

A single rose got caught between two of my fingers, while the rest of the bouquet bounced right off. I slumped my shoulders in defeat and turned behind me to face Han, only to find the bouquet in *his* hands.

Time was still slow as we stared at each other in disbelief

and excitement. Han took my hand in his and carefully plucked the rose from between my fingers. He smiled shyly as he slid the stem behind my ear.

The crowd went wild, but I could still make out a few comments through the chaos.

"I heard they're already engaged. Isn't that so sweet?"

"How romantic!"

"Is that Kenny and Han? Zane's gonna lose his shit."

The cheering turned into chants for Han and me to kiss. He looked at me with wide eyes, and I knew he was worried about the no-kissing rule.

"We can pause the rule, just for tonight," I said quietly enough for only his ears.

That was all the reassurance he needed before he cupped my cheeks in his hands and leaned forward, smiling as he pressed his forehead against mine. We stared at each other in anticipation for just a moment before we both went in for the kiss. The crowd cheered even louder as I wrapped my arms around Han.

The music started then, a slow, romantic song. Instead of pulling apart, Han put his hands on my hips and held me close as we swayed with the bouquet crushed between our chests. The smell of roses mixed with the music and the cheers all around was exhilarating.

Slow dancing with Han was like a warm hug. I felt safe holding him, content in the knowledge that neither of us would ever let the other fall.

It wasn't until I heard our names from a familiar voice that I was pulled out of the moment, though I still didn't dare leave Han's embrace. It was Zane, and he sounded drunk, doing that talk-yell you do when you're completely unaware of how high your volume is.

"Let the record state that ZBlaine Smith-Smith got married first! Who's *most likely to get married* now, bitch? WE ARE!" He laughed and laughed, and his next words came out sounding less angry. "No, but seriously, I'm sooooo happy for them!"

Han must have heard, too, because he looked at me like he was trying his best not to crack up.

"I guess we went to high school together," I said with a giggle. Apparently Jackie wasn't the only one bitter about Han and me getting the vote for *most likely to get married* our senior year. Good for them for beating us to the punch.

"Mystery solved." Han laughed.

"Maybe we should get out of here. Stop stealing their spotlight on their big night."

Han's smile faded into a pout. "One more song?" he asked.

It took me a minute to process the fact that Han *wanted* to slow dance with me. We'd already done everything on our checklist. There was no reason for us to stay. But . . .

"One more dance," I agreed. Somehow, even though it made no sense, it made all the sense in the world.

CHAPTER TWENTY-ONE

HAN

Kenny and I didn't stop taking turns playing chivalrer after leaving the wedding. I opened the car door for him when we left the rideshare and headed up to our apartment. Kenny got the apartment door, then stepped aside with a bow.

"After you," he said in a flirty voice slightly lower than his usual.

I laughed and walked inside, greeting Luna right away. Even though I wasn't usually much of a parties guy, I had to admit the wedding had been fun. In fact, I'd had such a good time, I almost didn't want the night to end. So instead of going to my room, I took my time petting Luna, hoping Kenny might stay to hang out.

Unfortunately, he continued down the hall to his room. I sighed. Maybe it was okay that the night was over. It wasn't like it was our last chance at playing a "real in-love couple."

Kenny's door never opened. Instead, his voice called out from the hallway.

"Oh, however will I get to bed with this door in the way?" he asked playfully, and I realized he wanted me to take my turn opening his door.

I laughed and met him right outside his room. I reached for the doorknob, but I couldn't bring myself to open it and officially end the night. I pulled my hand away.

"Um, so..." Kenny looked up at me for a moment before giving a shy little lip bite. "I mean, we did already break the rule tonight, right?"

"Yeah, we did," I said breathlessly.

Kenny took a step closer. "Is there anything else you want to do? Like, before the rule goes back in place..."

Oh my God, the romantic-comedy-new-relationship-good-night-doorstep-kiss.

I didn't know why Kenny set the no-kissing rule, but I didn't want him to feel like he had to break it again just for me to check something off an arbitrary list when no one was even around to see.

"Only if you want to." I knew the hall outside our bedrooms wasn't exactly a doorstep, but that hardly mattered.

"For good luck." He smiled, then put a hand on my cheek and slid it behind my neck, pulling me down as he stood on his toes.

His lips softly pressed against mine for a tiny moment before he pulled away, leaving me leaning after him at the loss of contact.

He smiled all big. "Congratulations on losing your doorstep-kiss virginity."

"Thanks." I laughed, not bothering to correct him on the exact verbiage. "So, the rule's back on?"

Kenny nodded, but there was something to his expression I couldn't quite read.

"Okay. Good night, then," I said, trying to hold myself together enough that he wouldn't realize how desperately I wanted to do that again.

"Good night." Kenny turned, letting me open his door before disappearing into his room. I did the same, closing my door behind me and leaning my back against it.

Maybe I wanted just a little more time with the illusion before it shattered. Maybe I wanted more than just a fake version of a rom-com staple. I wasn't sure what came over me, but I swung my door back open, only to see Kenny's door swinging open, too, and we were suddenly face-to-face.

"Maybe just one more?" I asked, and at the same time Kenny said:

"It was a stupid rule."

And we crashed into each other.

This time was different. We weren't kissing to fool anyone, or to check something off a list. This time we kissed because we *wanted* to. For the first time in my life, I felt like I understood what all the hype was around kissing.

Kissing, touching, and sex had always been something I did when I had nothing better to kill the time with. I always felt like the other person was experiencing something I couldn't comprehend.

Until now.

Now I didn't know if anything made sense to me but this. In the past I'd acted like I didn't know why all my relationships with girls failed. I pretended it was simply fear of commitment, but I couldn't lie to myself anymore. The truth was I didn't really want them.

The realization hit me like a semi, and I suddenly pulled away from Kenny, whose eyes fluttered open in surprise.

"Is something wrong?"

"I just..." I wanted to give him something to go off of, but what was I supposed to say? *Sorry, I just realized I've had feelings for you this entire time?* I couldn't put that on him. Besides, I wasn't sure if I was ready to jump into anything literal seconds after realizing I was the cause of every one of my past relationships failing. And if Kenny didn't feel the same about me, I didn't want him to feel any kind of pressure for the marriage to be anything other than what we'd planned. If I wasn't careful, my stupid feelings could ruin everything. "I uh...I guess I had more to drink than I thought."

It was a horrible lie, and I felt awful for breaking our one roommate rule of not bullshitting each other, but I couldn't do this. Not yet.

"Wait, you're drunk?" Kenny asked, his eyes widening slightly. "I didn't realize—"

"It's cool." I forced a laugh. "I should go to bed though."

I didn't wait for Kenny to chivalrously open the door for me. I just turned around and went back to my room, leaving Kenny in the hallway with no explanation.

I'd hardly gotten any sleep when my alarm woke me up the next morning for Sunday cleaning. Despite barely getting any rest, I was up before Kenny, so it was my job to wake him up, no matter how much I hated doing that. There was no sleeping in on Sundays (Kenny's rule, not mine), so I went into his room and nudged his shoulder.

"No!" Kenny shouted as he bolted upright at the contact, eyes shooting open as he swung his arm and hit me right in my mouth.

I laughed despite the pulsing in my lip.

"Oh my God, I'm so sorry!" Kenny said, hand covering his mouth.

"I'm fine. It's all good," I said as I sucked in my bottom lip to check for the taste of blood. Nothing.

Kenny gently touched my lip with his index finger and inspected it. His gaze slowly rose to meet mine and then went back down to my lips. Warmth rose in my cheeks, and I swore Kenny could sense the skipped pulse in my heart with how close we were.

I cleared my throat. "So, um...about last night."

"The rule's officially back on," Kenny said with a nod, like he knew I'd want to erase that last kiss from existence. Even if I really didn't, both of us having selective amnesia about it was for the best. "Sunday cleaning, right?" he asked through a yawn.

"Yup," I answered as I helped him out of bed.

We followed our normal Sunday routine, making both our beds in record time. Then we rushed out to clean the rest of the house. After dusting and tidying everything up, we were on to our final chores. Dishes for me and vacuuming for Kenny.

"You still doing that show tonight?" I called out over the sound of clanking dishes, running water, and the Luna-repellant vacuum screaming.

"Of course," Kenny said, and I swear his face lit up at the reminder of his upcoming drag performance. Hell, I couldn't wait, either. I had to admit, seeing Kenny in his element like that was incredible. Ten out of ten, would watch anytime.

After a celebratory pizza, Kenny and I started getting ready for work. But the last place I wanted to be was alone in his car with nothing to distract from all the weirdness.

"You okay?" Kenny asked as he parked behind the restaurant. "You're all broody this morning."

Shit, I hadn't meant to be broody. I didn't want Kenny feeling anything was off after last night.

"Yeah, just tired as hell." Sure, it wasn't what was actually on my mind, but I'd barely slept last night, so it was true. I was really getting the hang of this whole acting thing, using the realness to get across the fakeness, or whatever.

"I think I have some 5-Hour Energy in here somewhere," Kenny said, shuffling through his bag, then pulling out a small bottle of the stuff.

"Gross, dude. How long has that been in there?"

"Mmm, probably like, less than two weeks?"

"I'll pass." I laughed, glad Kenny didn't seem too bothered.

We went into work holding hands again, which I was grateful for. At least we got to do that. But at the same time, I wasn't sure how I felt about PDA in front of Daniel. Getting an order wrong last week had gotten me a complaint, so I was on thin ice.

But Daniel stayed in his office for most of our shift, so I let myself loosen up. Besides, Kenny was a hard man to ignore. Especially since I wanted so badly to make up for the night before. I blew Kenny a kiss as he walked by, and he lit up as he blew one back, opening the dam.

Kenny was a little over-the-top with his flirting, but I had to admit it was fun. I liked pretending to catch the kisses he blew at me. Fake flirting with Kenny made working so much better. I hated my job, but the shift went by much faster when I let loose. I was so preoccupied, I almost missed my break. Finally able to let my hands breathe, I took off my gloves and headed for the break room.

As I walked through the kitchen, Kenny was passing by with a tray of food and blew me another kiss with his free hand. It was 100 percent overkill, but it was fun so I turned to catch the kiss midair.

"Behind you!" Julia's voice was too close, and it was too late for me to move out of the way. She dropped her tray of fountain drinks in front of me right as I turned, my bad foot stepping onto the wet floor.

Before I could fall, my ankle jerked at the wrong angle under me, reflexively trying to keep the rest of me upright. But the slippery drinks didn't allow for balance, and I fell to the ground, clutching my ankle and trying not to scream.

"Oh my gosh! Honey, are you okay?" Julia asked, and it wasn't until then that I noticed the blood on my hand from catching myself on the floor with broken drink glasses. Several dishwashers were already sweeping the mess, and Kenny rushed to my side, ignoring the warnings to stay away from the shattered glass on the floor. He helped me to my feet—well, my good foot. I let him support my weight as we hobbled over to a chair that Tatiana pulled out of the break room. My cheeks burned.

"Can you move your foot, sweetheart?" Julia asked. I tried pointing my foot, but the pain shot straight up my leg, and I let out a wounded noise.

Daniel came into the kitchen with a solemn look on his face.

"I think his ankle is broken, or at least sprained," Julia said. "He probably needs to go to the hospital."

My heart sank. For one, I was sure I was about to be fired. But then again, wasn't it illegal to fire someone for getting injured on the job? Did legality even matter when it came to me since I was undocumented? I wouldn't qualify for workers' comp, but I was probably safe from getting fired, as long as I didn't miss too much work...

And I obviously couldn't go to the hospital. I probably wouldn't even get more than the rest of the day off.

"I'm fine, really," I lied, sucking my breath in through my teeth and trying to look as fine as I could. Tatiana rushed over with paper towels to catch the blood on my hand.

"Are you okay to work?" Daniel asked. Kenny looked like he wanted to slap the dude, and I kind of wanted him to.

"He has an open wound and a broken ankle. He can't work," Kenny said, and I was grateful I didn't have to say it myself. Even if I could work on one leg the rest of my shift, my hand was busted, and even I was sure working with a bloody hand was some kind of health code violation.

Daniel sighed. "I'll call someone in. Get yourself cleaned up. I want to see you back here for your shift by Friday. We need all our cooks for the Friday-night rush."

That gave me more time than I'd expected, honestly.

"Yes, sir."

CHAPTER TWENTY-TWO

KENNY

After getting Han an Uber home, I went the rest of my shift feeling like a monumental piece of crap. If Han hadn't been so distracted by my pointless flirting, he wouldn't have fallen. I had done this, but I had only been trying to make things feel less weird after what happened the night before. Still, I might have gone a bit overboard.

After my shift was over, I didn't even bother to double-count the money for the day. I shot Leti a quick text letting them know I'd be missing the show tonight, then headed out to my car. I needed to be there for Han.

When I turned the corner, I almost shat myself when I saw Jackie leaning on my car door.

"What the hell are you doing here, Jackie?" I sounded a lot more confident than I was. I really couldn't let any of my complicated feelings for Jackie show in front of her, or she'd sink her claws in and take advantage. I had to be ice.

I tried to reach for my door, but Jackie blocked my way. "I

had to come here because you blocked my number! How else am I supposed to get ahold of you?"

"Yeah, I blocked it for a *reason*," I said through gritted teeth, but I softened up with one look at Jackie's face. Her eyes were puffy, and her nose and cheeks were red like she'd been crying. "What's wrong?"

She sniffed and wiped her nose, not meeting my eyes. "I'm pregnant."

I blinked, not sure if I was imagining things or if she'd actually just said that.

"What?" I felt my breath get thin, and the air I took in *hurt*. It was how I felt when I went for a long run in the winter. This wasn't happening. Jackie couldn't be pregnant.

"I'm pregnant," she repeated.

"No, I heard you. I . . . Is it mine?"

"Of course it's yours, you asshole." She punched my arm. I had to ask.

"How? We were so careful . . ." I clicked my keys to unlock the car so we could talk more behind the privacy of my non-tinted windows. She didn't answer until we were both sitting inside.

"I must have missed a pill."

"But we used condoms . . ." I rubbed my head, unable to wrap it around this new development. A baby. What was I going to do? I barely had any money in savings for an abortion. But then, what if she didn't want one? Not to mention there was no way I could cut ties with Jackie with a baby involved. What did this mean for me and Han? I kept rubbing my head, feeling dizzy now.

"I *know*." Jackie smacked the back of my head, sounding irritated. "You know condoms aren't a hundred percent reliable.

And stop doing that." She grabbed my wrist and pulled it away from rubbing my forehead.

"Sorry..." I felt bad for focusing on the how instead of what would happen next. And for dodging her this whole time. I felt terrible.

"What are we gonna do?" I asked.

"I don't know." She started tearing up. Not fake, nonblinking tears, either. Real ones. "I'm not ready to be a single mom! I can barely take care of myself, let alone a baby! What am I supposed to do?"

I pulled her into a hug. "It's gonna be okay. Whatever you choose, I'll be here for you," I said. I knew I had to be there for her. This was my problem just as much as hers, and if she wanted me there, I would be. I tried not to think of how that would complicate my situation with Han. Of course I would still do both no matter what, but I couldn't think about the logistics of all that right now.

"Thank you, Kenny," she said, sobbing into my chest.

"Why didn't you tell me before?"

"Did you forget you blocked my number?!" She hit my chest with an open palm. I swallowed the pain. I deserved that.

"What about that day at the restaurant?" I asked.

"I didn't know then, obviously."

"I'm so sorry..." was all I could say.

"I think I'm gonna keep it," she said, and the pain in my chest grew.

"Okay." I focused on taking deep breaths. In. Out.

"I don't know for sure yet. But if I do, you have to break it off with Han and help me raise it."

"No," I said, surprising myself with my firmness. I was just as committed to marrying Han as I was to raising this baby.

Unsurprisingly, my answer earned me a swift slap to the cheek, bringing tears to my eyes.

"I meant...I'm not breaking up with Han. But of course I'll help you raise it." My voice cracked as I turned to face Jackie. The woman who never hesitated to put her hands on me anytime I didn't do exactly what she wanted. The woman who made me feel so small I wanted to disappear. The woman who I would be spending the next eighteen-plus years raising a kid with if she decided to keep it. Telling her I wasn't breaking up with Han may have been one of the only times I'd told her no in our entire relationship.

My whole life flashed before my eyes. I couldn't bear the thought of getting slapped around like this on a daily basis. Maybe we could split custody. Maybe I wouldn't have to interact much with Jackie at all.

"I swear I'll be a good father," I found myself saying, "but I'm not breaking it off with Han." I was sure the kid would have a much healthier upbringing with Han in the picture anyway. Plus, I seemed to bring out the worst in Jackie. I didn't want my kid to grow up seeing their dad getting slapped around all the time.

"Whatever...I know you'll change your mind. We don't have to talk about it right now, though."

"Okay." I sighed in relief. I really didn't want her to try to convince me to break up with Han. I wouldn't do it no matter what she said, but I knew she'd be able to make me feel like the world's biggest asshole for it. "I'm so sorry. I shouldn't have ignored you, I just thought you were trying to get me to break up with Han. I had no idea you were pregnant."

"But I *do* want you to break up with Han!" Jackie replied angrily. "Ugh! Please just think about it? I want to raise this baby right. Two parents, you know?"

"I thought you said we didn't have to talk about it."

"You're the one who brought it back up!"

"The baby is going to have two parents whether I'm with Han or not," I said. I couldn't just dump him after everything. Not when we were so close to getting him a green card. This might have been a good excuse for us to get divorced sometime after the wedding, but not now. Not until Han was staying for good.

"You know what I mean, Kenny. Just think about it, okay?" Jackie said, then got out of the car, walked to her own, and drove away. I reluctantly unblocked her number.

I stopped at the store before going home to get some things for Han. We didn't have any ice at the apartment, so I got some, plus heat packs, an ankle brace, crutches, ibuprofen, and some Ace bandages. I channeled all my anxiety about the baby into worrying about Han instead. If I focused on that, I couldn't think about anything else.

When I got home, I rushed up the stairs, wondering how Han could have made his way up here with his ankle as messed up as it was. I hoped he didn't hurt himself even worse in the process.

When I got to the apartment, I was greeted by several stray cats eating food Han must have left out. I grinned. Of course he would still find it in him to feed the cats when he could barely stand.

Luna greeted me excitedly when I opened the door, panting and wagging her tail so hard her butt wobbled around. She jumped up on me, which she never did. She was way higher energy today than usual, which I figured had something to do with the fact that Han wasn't able to play with her or take her out after coming home. I made a note to myself to take her out after taking care of Han.

I gave Luna a kiss on the head and pet her really quick before checking on him. He was napping on the couch with an open laptop on his stomach. The slight wrinkle between his brows showed that he was in pain even in his sleep, and it made me want to punch something. It wasn't fair that he had to rely on the kind of medical help I could get at Walmart. He should have been able to go to a doctor and get an X-ray, a cast, *real* painkillers...This was why no matter what Jackie said, I wouldn't drop the wedding. I wanted Han to be safe. I wanted Han to be able to hurt himself and not face permanent consequences just because he couldn't go to the hospital.

I carefully took the laptop and set it on the coffee table, catching a glimpse of the screen. Looked like Han was studying civics for his eventual exam before he could officially get his green card. I had no doubt he'd ace that part. Maybe he was just studying because he was nervous about our interview at the immigration office the next day. Most of the work to apply for a green card came after marriage, but there was still a good amount we could get ahead on.

According to the research I'd done on my own, Han had a pretty good chance. As long as we didn't get caught pretending, we would be just fine. We had witnesses who could attest to Han and me being in love, we already lived together, both our names were on the lease, and hell, Han even cosigned on my car since he had the better credit. We'd be fine.

I closed the laptop quietly. Then I gently slipped a couple of pillows under Han's foot to elevate it, careful to lift his leg by the calf instead of the ankle to avoid hurting him.

"Ahh..." Han hissed at the movement, his lids scrunching together harder.

"Sorry, babe—I mean, Han. Sorry, Han," I stuttered. I was

so used to having someone I could refer to as "babe," and with the act we were putting on, I was getting used to calling Han that. I had almost forgotten we were only doing that in public. I hoped Han was still too far into his nap daze to have registered it. "I brought you some stuff. You should probably ice it."

"Thanks," Han muttered, finally opening his eyes, "*pumpkin.*" He smirked.

"Shut up." I laughed, glad Han wasn't taking it too seriously. "Have you eaten? Had any water?" I asked. The two of us hadn't eaten before our shift at eleven, and it was now well after eight p.m.

"Nah. Didn't want to get up." Han frowned as Luna hopped up on the couch, refusing to be ignored. "Could you take her on her walk for me?"

"Of course," I reassured him as I set my water bottle down on the coffee table for Han. "First you have to eat, though. I'll make you something."

"You're the best," Han said, though Luna didn't seem as pleased with the decision. I went to the kitchen to heat up some food.

"What do you want? Top Ramen or Hot Pockets?" Those were practically our only food options right now. We really needed to go grocery shopping. I would have gotten some groceries when I went to Walmart, but I didn't want Han to be waiting for me any longer than he needed to. It was probably for the best that I didn't, too, since Luna probably had to go soon.

"Hot Pockets," Han mumbled, and I obliged, popping a couple in the microwave on a folded paper towel so neither of us would have any dishes to wash. I leaned against the counter as they heated up.

"How bad is it, do you think?"

"My hand is fine. It's a shallow cut. But my ankle's definitely broken, or at least badly sprained. I can't put any weight on it at all."

"Shit . . . How are you gonna work on Friday?"

"On one foot." Han let out a single laughing breath, but he wasn't smiling.

The timer dinged, and I brought Han his steaming Hot Pockets, which I was sure would somehow still manage to be cold on the inside. I wished I could make something better right now. Han deserved something better. He deserved better in general. But that was why we were doing this. Whether Jackie wanted me to or not, whether she was pregnant or not, we were doing this.

Before Han took his first bite, Luna got the zoomies and started spinning around in circles. I laughed at first, until she zoomed right into the table where Thornelius was perched. He was supposed to be safely out of Luna's reach, but I never thought she'd slam into the table!

Thornelius wobbled a bit before falling to the ground. I ran to try to catch him, but it was too late. He hit the floor hard, separating from the pot and sliding toward the couch where Han sat. Thornelius's now naked bottom revealed a block of Styrofoam stuck to the base where his roots should have been. The top hat fell off, and his monocle stared off into the ceiling, the thorns behind it making a perfect *x*, confirming his death.

Han started cracking up. "Wait, he's plastic?"

I couldn't laugh, though. Instead, I fell to my knees as I stared at Thornelius through tear-blurred eyes, unable to speak. Han was usually the one to have panic attacks, but I could tell something was wrong in my chest. My throat tightened, and every breath was begging to be let out as a sob. Han stopped laughing and frantically maneuvered himself onto the floor next to Thornelius in a panic. "Hey, it's okay. Look, he's fine! Everything's fine!"

He quickly took Thornelius in his hands and put him back in the pot, then grabbed the top hat and placed it gingerly on his head, straightening the monocle, then looked up at me, nodding and smiling.

"Good as new, see?" He held Thornelius toward me, arms outstretched.

I took Thornelius in my arms and did my best to cradle him, but I couldn't help it. I just started sobbing.

"Bro, bro, bro, what's wrong?" he asked, overdoing the "bro" thing like he was desperate to take any of the intensity out of this whole situation.

"It's my fault!" I sobbed. "I should have just taken Luna on her damn walk!"

"Whoa, no, it's not your fault. She gets excited sometimes, that's all. It's no big deal, okay? Look, Luna's fine. Thornelius is fine. Everyone's happy!"

"None of this is fine, Han!" I snapped. "If I can't even take care of Luna for one fucking hour, how the hell am I supposed to take care of a baby? Thornelius isn't even *alive* and I *killed* him! What am I supposed to do with a human child?"

"Hey, hey, it's okay," Han reassured me, sounding panicked himself. "Don't worry. You're years away from that kind of responsibility."

"Jackie's pregnant!" I blurted out before Han could get any more confused.

There was a long silence before Han said anything. His brows furrowed as he seemed to put the pieces together. "Bro..."

"Yeah..."

"You're joking." Han hissed in pain as he shifted his body so he was sitting right across from where I knelt.

"Dead serious," I said. "I talked to her today."

"And you believe her?"

"*What?* Of course I believe her!"

"I'm just saying. She could be lying. Maybe she's just trying to manipulate you into getting back together with her."

"She's not." My voice was harsher than I'd meant it to be. The words came out like a warning for Han to drop it. I knew Jackie. Yes, she was capable of being manipulative at times, but Han hadn't seen her earlier. He hadn't seen her puffy eyes or her red nose. Jackie was never able to fake emotion like that.

"All right, all right. So she's pregnant. What's she gonna do?"

"Keep it, I think..." I wiped the tears pooling in my eyes.

Han took a while before responding again. "You're gonna kill it, bro."

"Han! Not helping!"

His eyes widened. "Not like that! I meant as a dad! Like, you're gonna kill it *at parenting*!"

I let out a strangled laugh that was more like a sob. "Sure, I will..."

It was all so weird. I had always wanted to be a dad, but not like this. This was *not* how it once played out in my head.

Han and I sat in silence for what felt like ages. Instead of talking more, I decided to just go ahead and take Luna on her walk already to avoid any further catastrophes. I finally got up from my knees, placing Thornelius back on the table. I went over to Han and offered him my hand, which he took so I could help him up and back onto the couch.

It only took about fifteen minutes of walking around before Luna did her business and seemed satisfied, so I headed back to find Han still on the couch, wringing his hands. It was the only outward sign he gave that said he was freaking out just like I was.

"What's wrong?" I asked, since there was clearly something else on his mind.

Han shook his head but continued wringing his hands.

"Han…"

"So I guess the plan's off then, huh…?" he said, voice low.

"What? Hell no, it's not. I made you a promise. I can take responsibility with Jackie and marry you at the same time."

Han's eyebrows knitted together, and he leaned forward, bringing his thumb to my cheek. "What happened to your face?"

"What?" I used my phone camera to look at my face. I had a couple of scratches on my cheek. "Oh, that. I…" I didn't know what to say. Jackie's nails must have gotten me. Han knew me better than anyone, but Jackie hitting me was one thing I didn't want him to know about. I just knew he'd overreact. "I tried to pet one of your cats. I guess she still has to warm up to me."

Han smiled and shook his head. "You gotta let them come to you, man."

"Yeah, well, I guess I learned that lesson." I felt bad lying to Han, but I just didn't know how to talk to him about this. Instead, I tried to make up for it by telling him something that was true. "I'm not gonna break off the wedding, but you should know, that's definitely what Jackie wants me to do."

"The fuck? Is she *ever* going to let you live your life?"

"It's not like that. She's just—"

"Abusive, Kenny. She's abusive." Han clenched his fists. "You should seriously get a restraining order or something."

"What, why?" I asked, thrown off by the sudden outburst.

"She wants to control every aspect of your life. You're not

yourself around her. It doesn't matter where she works. She's *abusive.*"

"But she's pregnant! And I'd never get a restraining order before you got naturalized. It's too risky. Besides, the baby—"

"You can't get back together with her. I'm not letting her near you. I swear to God—"

"Han! Just listen, okay?"

Han let out an aggravated breath through his nose, and I could have sworn I saw steam coming out.

"I'm not getting back together with her, all right? I learned my lesson. She's . . . Sure, she's abusive. I don't want to get back with her, even if she's pregnant. But I can't get a restraining order. Even after you get citizenship. I don't want to traumatize a kid like that." Even if Han didn't know the full story, he was right. This was the first time I had admitted to what I'd been thinking. Jackie was abusive. Even if some part of me knew it all along, I never let myself admit it before now. She slapped the shit out of me all the time, not to mention emotionally manipulated me every chance she got. Sure, some broken part of me still missed her, but it wasn't worth getting back together. I would help her raise our kid, but there was no way I was putting myself through that again. That much I knew for sure. Han stopped wringing his hands but started bouncing one of his legs instead, so I put a hand on his knee. "I'm not going anywhere. I promise. We're doing this."

"I'm not worried about that right now. I'm worried about *you*, bro." Han clenched his jaw like he did when he didn't want to look vulnerable. I wished he would let himself be more vulnerable, though, even if just a little bit. Then again, I was the one who might be a father, and I was comforting everyone but myself. But how could I not? Han was so concerned right now, it almost made me think maybe he'd seen through my lie about the cats.

"I'll be fine." My voice was too soft. Salty water blurred my vision once again.

"Hey, it's gonna be okay, bro," Han said, jaw unclenching.

"Stop calling me bro!" I burst out, surprising myself at how upset the word made me.

"Whoa, sorry, bro—I mean...sorry?" Han put his hands up in surrender.

We both stared at each other for a moment too long, not sure what to do next.

"Why are you doing this for me?" Han finally asked.

"What are you talking about?"

"You have a baby coming...Why are you still marrying me?"

I started answering without thinking. "We already talked about this. You can stay. We'll be able to save on—"

"Taxes, yeah, I know...Forget it." He waved me off. Was he having doubts? I realized then that I didn't know what I would do if Han changed his mind. I *wanted* to marry him. I wanted to kiss him again, hold his hand, be his...something. God, even *I* was annoyed with myself. I knew by now Han was more than just a rebound, but Han seemed pretty set on forgetting our post-wedding kiss. He must have wanted to stay friends, so I couldn't complicate it like that. It had to stay uncomplicated, or as uncomplicated as a fake relationship/real friendship could be.

Han didn't meet my eyes as he stared at the floor. "I know you're not doing all this just to make Jackie jealous..."

I sighed. He was right. "I know."

"So why are you doing it?"

"Well...for you, Han." I stared softly into his deep brown eyes. "I'm obviously doing it for you."

"But why? Why risk everything for me? Why now? When Jackie's pregnant? Just, why, bro? I don't get it."

There was that "bro" again. Heat rose up in my face for some reason. "Look, I know you're allergic to commitment, but this is fake, remember?" I said sharply.

Han looked like I'd just punched him in the gut. "I can commit to things."

I laughed. "That's a lie. You're so afraid of being vulnerable that you come up with an excuse to break things off the second they get real."

Shit, I'd said too much. I couldn't let Han know things were getting real. I knew I was crossing a line, but I couldn't stop. It was almost like I *wanted* Han to get mad.

"That's not true," Han said, his tone hurt. "Besides, it's *not* real." Han's tone was icy now. "You're the one who only wants to kiss me to make Jackie jealous or convince our 'audience' of something. How is that real?"

"I—I didn't—" I started, unable to form the words. That was the farthest from the truth. But I couldn't go telling Han the real reason I set the no-kissing rule. *That* would definitely make things too real. "I'm sorry..." was all I could manage to say.

"Jesus, cut it out with that shit," Han said, still sounding cool and unbothered despite his harsh words. "There's nothing to be sorry for. Kissing is back off the table. It's fine. It's fake. No big deal."

For some reason, Han's words cut deeper than Jackie's nails. "Then why do you say 'bro' at the end of everything nice you say to me? If it's fake, what's the point? We're *engaged*. You can't be calling me bro!"

"I don't get the big deal about calling you bro. It's just us." Han's cool demeanor just annoyed me even more. Why wasn't he getting mad? He *never* got mad. Even if I was being a dick. Even if I deserved it. I immediately felt bad for trying to provoke him. Han wasn't like Jackie. He would never say or do anything hurtful. No matter how bad I felt I deserved to be yelled at. I rolled my eyes. There was no point in arguing with someone who wouldn't get mad back, as annoying as it was.

"Right, it's fine. No worries...whatever," I said. Then I got up to go to bed.

"Good night. Love you, bro," Han said, a contagious grin on his face.

I grabbed a pillow from the couch and whacked him on the head with it.

✱　✱　✱

After about an hour of sulking in bed, the same pillow was thrown against my door. "What?" I called out, but Han didn't answer.

Then my phone rang. I braced myself for a call from Jackie, but it wasn't. It was Han. I laughed to myself.

"You know I can hear you if you shout, right?"

"Why would I want to shout when I can just call you? Get your ass over here."

I hung up and groaned. I didn't exactly want to get out of bed, but Han probably needed help with something, so I got up anyway. When I made my way to the living room, Han was sitting on the couch staring at his phone.

"What's up?" I asked.

"I just realized you missed your show because of me."

I raised an eyebrow. Han wasn't usually one to bring things up that might be any kind of sad, especially randomly like this and especially when there was nothing that could be done about it. "It's fine. Had to make sure you were okay, you know?"

The corner of Han's mouth twitched up into a small smile as he looked at me. "I wanna see you perform."

"What? We're too late, Han." The show was long over by now.

"You had a whole new routine planned, right?" Han asked, rubbing the back of his neck. "I know you do. I heard you practicing in your room."

"Well, yeah, but it's okay. It's too late to go now. I don't mind, really."

Han bit his lip like he was holding something back.

"What is it?" I asked.

"This is probably a bad idea. Never mind." He shook his head.

"What are you talking about?"

Han sighed. "Well, I was thinking...I know you really wanted to do your new routine. You were so excited about it..."

"It's okay, Han, I promise. I'd rather stay here," I said. I hated that Han was feeling guilty about me staying home with him. I didn't want to make him feel bad.

"What I'm saying is..." Han laughed awkwardly. "Why don't you do your show? Like, right here. Just for me. I mean, if you want to. I bet it's hella good. I'll hype you up just like an audience could, you know?"

I had to laugh. This must have been Han's way of trying to make up for our not-really-a-fight-but-the-closest-we've-ever-gotten-to-a-fight. Han was kind of doing his whole "trying not to be vulnerable" thing at the same time, but at least he wasn't saying "bro." I had to admit, I didn't hate the idea. I kind of loved it. If I couldn't dress up and do my performance at the bar, why waste it? I could do it right here, just for Han. In fact, that made it feel even more special.

"It'll be without makeup, since Leti was gonna do that part for me," I say, which was really the only bummer about it.

"I mean, I could try to do it for you. I'm sure there are You-Tube tutorials."

I had to laugh at the idea of Han attempting to do my makeup, but there was no way I was passing up that once-in-a-lifetime offer. "Let's do it."

✳ ✳ ✳

After I got dressed, I set up two chairs in the bathroom so Han could do my makeup, but Han made it a point to sit me with my back facing the mirror so I couldn't see his handiwork. Really, I could have done my makeup on my own, but I was just so curious to see how Han would do it. The YouTube tutorial played in the background as Han got to work.

"Close your eyes," Han said as he took a glue stick to my eyebrows.

I did, even though I knew he was asking me more to keep me from turning my head to look in the mirror than to protect my eyes from glue.

I almost fell asleep in the chair, but after what felt like ages of constantly pausing and restarting the YouTube video, Han finally finished.

"Okay, you can look now," he said, swiveling my chair so it was facing the mirror.

I opened my eyes.

CHAPTER TWENTY-THREE

HAN

My work here? Done. Kenny looked even more perfect than usual.

CHAPTER TWENTY-FOUR

KENNY

I looked like an eldritch monstrosity.

And I was absolutely thrilled about it. I couldn't help the laugh that burst from my lips from one look at my face. I threw my upper body onto Han's lap as I laughed to my heart's content.

"Don't put your face on me. You'll fuck it up!"

I wheezed. "Han, I love you, but I'm sorry. It's already so fucked up."

Han ran a hand through his hair. "That bad?"

I laugh-sighed, then looked up at Han and cupped his face in my palms. "Seriously, thank you for this." He had no idea how much his horrible makeup job had lifted my mood.

Han's mouth finally twitched up into a small smile, and I had to resist the urge to kiss him right then and there. He was just so goddam cute. I cleared my throat and let go of his overly kissable face.

"All right, showtime," I said, helping Han up from his chair as he grabbed the crutches from the door.

I waited in the hallway for him to take his seat on the couch.

Han played the music, and I came out as high energy as if I were doing this for real.

I was still figuring out the whole drag thing, but the idea of being a dancing queen was growing more and more appealing to me. Leti had taught me the basics of vogue, and I was using the hell out of them in this performance. Han sat on the couch, leaning forward with his elbows on his knees and a proud smile on his face.

I was so excited to show off one particular move I'd practiced to hell and back all week. The finale. I hadn't done Taekwondo in years, but a couple of weeks ago I started getting back into it to see if I could incorporate it into drag of all things. I guess I had never really been that into martial arts, but using it to express myself through drag? That was a whole other story. The move I'd practiced was a bolley kick into a shablam. As I spun in the air with my leg kicking high, I caught a glimpse of Han's face.

Eyes wide, mouth open. Impressed, as he should have been.

But that wasn't even the best part. I landed in a dip instead of standing on my kicking foot, and even though I was on the ground, I could see Han standing up on one foot, whistling and clapping loudly.

I hopped up to my feet as the music ended, rushing into a celebratory hug with Han.

"You're amazing," Han said as he held me tight, and it felt like such a gift. To be standing here with Han, having done my performance for his eyes only, and to get that kind of praise? From Han, of all people, without a single "bro" to cushion it? I was flying high.

I didn't want to let him go, but I knew if I didn't he might be onto me, so I pulled away, careful not to look up at him as I did, or I might not have been able to resist the urge to kiss him.

"So, you're like, officially a drag queen now, huh?" Han said with a grin.

And for some reason those words brought a huge smile to my face. Hell yes, I was a drag queen. I'd only done it twice so far, but it just felt *right*. When I was with Jackie, I couldn't be the least bit feminine, even though that had always been a part of me. But now, being able to do this freely? It was something I never would have even dreamed possible. And I *could* do it, as much as I wanted to. No one would try to stop me again.

Before I realized what was happening, Han's phone was pointed at my face.

"This one's for the 'gram," he said as he snapped a photo.

"You are so cringey." I shook my head, then realized what he was saying. "Wait, you want to post *this* on Instagram?" I said, gesturing wildly to my eldritch horror of a face.

"Hey! It's not *that* bad."

"Oh, it's bad." I laughed. "But you can post it. As long as you take proper credit for your makeup job."

"I will!" Han said, chest puffed out in pride as he typed away on his phone. "There. They'll be lining up at our door wanting their makeup done by the one and only Alejandro Torres."

"Sure, they will," I said, unable to wipe the smile from my face. I don't think I stopped smiling since I'd finished my routine. As I turned around to go change, I caught sight of Thornelius sitting at his usual table, and I sighed. "So...what should we do about Thornelius?"

"What do you mean?" Han asked.

"Well, he's not exactly what we expected. We can't really take care of him like we were before, like watering him and all that."

Han nodded and looked at Thornelius with a surprisingly soft expression. "Well, sure. He's not what we expected, but...no kid is, right? Besides, adopting him was my brain child and your name child. Just look at that face! He's *ours*."

"You're right." I looked Thornelius over, imagining big puppy eyes under his monocle, begging us not to abandon him for being plastic. I went over and patted him on the top hat. "Thornelius, you know it's not important to us what you've got on the inside; it's how you look on the outside that really matters."

"Exactly." Han laughed.

I grinned and turned back to the bathroom to change out of my short pink dress and wash my face. By the time I finished and came back out, the mood had somehow completely shifted.

Han was just staring at his phone solemnly.

"What?" I asked, my stomach dropping.

"I'm guessing you haven't seen Instagram since you got home?"

"Do I even have an Instagram?" I scratched my head. I vaguely remembered using it when I was in high school, but I wasn't really on social media these days.

"You do. You should really see this..."

I sat next to Han on the couch as he showed me what was on his phone screen.

It was a post from Jackie. An ultrasound.

Something fluttered in my gut, and for a moment I forgot about all the complications. That little thing on the screen was my baby. It almost brought tears to my eyes. But then the light feeling came crashing down.

"Holy shit." My handle was tagged in the post. It had hundreds of likes, which meant everyone close to me probably knew now that I'd gotten Jackie pregnant.

"Yeah..." Han said, rubbing his temples.

"Can I untag myself?" I asked, pulling my phone out even though I knew it was basically too late.

"Yeah. Here, I'll log out so you can get in yours." Han tapped his phone a few times with his thumb before handing it over. But I wasn't sure if I even knew how to log in. I hadn't used Instagram since high school. Still, there was one password I used for everything back then.

Jackie518

The date we first got together. Even if I wished that date meant nothing to me anymore, I could never forget it. I handed my phone to Han, who worked his magic. Moments later, I wasn't tagged anymore.

"God," Han said, "I hope Jackie chokes on a grape."

I shook my head, holding back my laugh. "She's *pregnant*."

"Fine. I hope she sits on a tack."

I couldn't help the grin on my face. "That, we might be able to arrange."

CHAPTER TWENTY-FIVE

HAN

All I could think about since last night was that Jackie was pregnant—so much so I hardly noticed the pain in my ankle and barely slept. I spent the entire night looking up all kinds of tutorials, from changing diapers to assembling a crib. If Kenny was going to be a dad, I knew I couldn't let him do it alone. I actually surprised myself with how eager I was to help out. I thought I'd never wanted kids, but I wasn't about to let Kenny go through this alone. I already felt fiercely protective of even the idea of Kenny's future child. It was a big decision, but I knew the choice I had to make right in my gut.

I got up early to make breakfast so I could surprise Kenny with something nice to get his mind off everything—and to get my own mind off my foot and the immigration interview later in the day. I knew the impromptu drag show the night before helped a little, but that was just to make up for Kenny having missed the real thing. Even if breakfast wouldn't get the interview off my mind, I could at least cheer Kenny up. It was going to be a long day, full of wedding planning and then the interview, and I wanted to start the day out right. Kenny loved when I cooked, but I didn't do it that often anymore. My job revolved around cooking now, so I didn't really like doing more work at home for no money. I'd make an exception for today, though. For Kenny.

I ordered ingredients from Instacart early enough that I could get started before Kenny woke up. I knew making chorizo chilaquiles on one foot would be a challenge, so I got up earlier than I normally would. I had my crutches to help me balance, but I needed to use my hands to make the chilaquiles, so I had to squeeze the crutches into my sides with my elbows and make the food like a T. rex. There was definitely a reason T. rexes didn't cook.

After way too long of a struggle, I finally made a more than halfway decent meal. Luckily, Kenny came out of his room right as I was finishing up.

"You cooked?" Kenny's face lit up with a smile as he sniffed the air like Luna. Mission accomplished.

"I did," I said as I struggled to reach for the plates without dropping my crutches. One of the crutches fell to the ground anyway, but I finished getting a couple of plates down from the cabinet before picking it up. Before I could bend to get it, Kenny was at my side, grabbing the crutch for me. He smiled wide as he handed it back.

"Thank you, Han. It smells so good."

"Thanks." I took the crutch, and Kenny grabbed the plates from out of my hands.

"I'll do the serving," Kenny said with a teasing grin. I didn't protest since it would have been really rough trying to serve breakfast with my T. rex arms. I moved to sit at the table, and

Kenny pulled my chair out for me so I wouldn't have to do it myself. He set two plates full of chilaquiles down, and a smile crept onto my lips. When I caught Kenny's eyes, a blush came over his face before he sat down in his own chair.

I held my breath as he took his first bite. The hell was I so nervous for?

"Sooo good," Kenny said through a mouthful of chilaquiles as he closed his eyes and relaxed his body. I knew I was a good cook, but I still felt a swell of pride at the compliment.

When Kenny was about halfway done with his food, his eyes trailed from his plate off to the distance, staring at nothing.

"You okay, bro?" I asked before I remembered how mad the "bro" thing made Kenny the night before. "Um, I mean, you okay...pal?"

Kenny's nose scrunched up like he'd eaten something bitter. "Ew. Not *pal.*"

"Noted. But you didn't answer the question."

"I guess I'm just not really hungry anymore." Kenny got up and took his half-eaten plate to the kitchen sink. My shoulders sank in defeat. I couldn't even get his mind off things for one meal. I really couldn't blame him. The dude had a baby on the way. A baby with the most selfish she-devil I had ever met. I wasn't sure how we would make it work. If we were going through with the wedding, we definitely needed a plan.

"Hey, I'm here for you. You know that, right?" I said, making sure to hold my tongue at the end of the sentence as I watched him clean the plates. The thought of helping with a baby scared the shit out of me, but if we were getting married, even if it was fake, I was going to do everything I could to ease Kenny's load. That was how I could begin to pay him back the impossible debt I owed.

"Yeah, I know, Han," Kenny said, giving me a forced smile.

"No, really, I'll help. Whatever I can do."

"What do you mean?"

"Like, help take care of the baby...buy diapers and shit, whatever I can."

"Han..." Kenny started, but I wasn't done.

"We'll fight for custody if we have to. Maybe we can even do this without Jackie in the picture. We can have a small wedding, something at your parents' house. That way we can use the money for baby stuff," I suggested. "Like I said, we can get custody. Me and you."

"I thought you didn't want kids," Kenny said, eyes all misty, "because of your mom..." The mention of my mom made my stomach sink. I'd gone out of my way to avoid thinking about her since my last conversation with my dad. I went to the kitchen with one crutch under my arm and put my free arm on Kenny's shoulder. To support me, but also to support him.

"Listen, I'm not my mom," I admitted, for the first time, to myself and to him. It was true. I was my own person, and I knew what *not* to do because of my mom. "I'm serious. I'm helping." I made sure to look Kenny in the eye as I said it. He slipped his arms under mine in a hug, knocking the crutch to the floor again. It was okay, though, because Kenny supported my weight so I wouldn't fall.

"I don't know what I'm gonna do," Kenny mumbled.

"We'll figure it out," I said, and Kenny pulled away, wiping his eyes before picking the crutch up off the floor. Unlike me, Kenny wasn't one to hide his emotions. When he wanted to cry, he just cried. I actually kind of admired that about him. I was jealous, even. I had no trouble crying during Disney movies or Kleenex commercials, but in real life? I was useless when it came to emotional maturity in front of other people. Kenny, on the other hand, was still openly crying. I wanted to drop everything and pull him into another hug, but instead I awkwardly patted him on the back. "Love you, bro."

"Shut *up*."

* * *

Early on, Kenny's mom had insisted on helping with the wedding planning, which was good, because it meant Kenny and I didn't have to do it all ourselves—and we had someone who actually knew what she was doing. On the ride to meet Kenny's mom at what she insisted was "the best bakery in New Mexico" for the cake-tasting appointment (which I was stoked about since I wouldn't have to cook), Kenny quizzed me on some questions we would probably be asked at the immigration office to prove the marriage wasn't fraudulent. This would be a piece of cake (heh) because all the answers were either the truth or half-truths, since Kenny and I already lived our lives similarly to how a married couple might. I didn't have to think twice about how we met (elementary school) or our dog's name (Luna) and who fed her (me).

When we got to the bakery, his mom was already sitting inside waiting for us. Kenny held the door open for me so I could get through on my crutches, and we made our way over to sit with Elisa.

"I know Han is injured right now, so I already got all the logistics taken care of with the baker! All you two need to do is pick a cake and frosting," she said with a huge grin on her face.

I frowned. I had wanted to talk with her *before* she gave wedding details to the baker, since everything was about to change. "We've been talking a lot, and we decided to have a small ceremony instead," I said, avoiding the bit about the baby, in case Kenny wasn't ready to have that talk yet. His parents probably hadn't seen Jackie's Insta-sound, since they weren't online, but I had to just hope no one had blabbed to them. It was still possible Jackie would get an abortion, and if she did that, we wouldn't have to tell anyone who didn't already see the post. Including the USCIS officer at the immigration office. I held out hope for that, knowing a baby might complicate the whole green card thing.

"What? Why?" Elisa's eyes were wide, and she looked absolutely horrified. Based on her reaction, I guessed no one had told her about the baby. But of course she was disappointed. She had been looking forward to a huge party.

"We'd rather save the money," Kenny said, refusing to meet his mother's eyes.

Elisa leaned forward, as if getting ready to tell a secret. "We were going to wait to tell you until everyone came over for Thanksgiving on Thursday, but we would love to pay for it! So don't you worry about money, all right? We want you to get to have the wedding of your dreams."

"Mami, you don't have to—" I started, but Elisa shushed me by practically shoving a piece of cake into my mouth.

"It's the least we can do, really. We're happy to do it!"

A lump formed in my throat as I swallowed the cake and tried to let that sink in. I didn't know if I'd be able to forgive myself for lying to Kenny's parents if they did this for us. It was one thing when we were paying for our own wedding, but how could I ask them to pay for something that wasn't even real? It all just felt so much more wrong now. Kenny looked at me with a huge grin on his face, but I couldn't give him one back. I just felt tense. And sick. How could I let Elisa and Cedric pay for this? How could I ever make it up to them if they did? And would they ever forgive me if they found out it was all fake?

I couldn't concentrate for the rest of the conversation, and I had a hard time enjoying the tasting while Elisa and Kenny got to work picking out a venue and got started on the guest list. I could barely hear them. All I could think was how I was betraying their trust in a way I could never make up for. But no matter how guilty that made me feel, I couldn't bring myself to speak. Kenny seemed perfectly fine with this arrangement, but I could hardly breathe.

I finally came out of my haze when Kenny kissed my cheek. "Ready, babe?"

I shook my head to get my foggy brain to focus. "For what?"

"We have to go to the immigration office, remember? It's almost time for our appointment."

Shit. How long had I been out of it? If *Kenny* was the one bringing it up, we had to be running late. I pulled out my phone to check the time. To my surprise, we still had plenty of time. I sighed in relief and nodded, glad Kenny was taking this seriously enough to break his late streak. "Yeah, let's go. Bye, Mami, love you," I said as I kissed her cheek, and we headed out.

Surprisingly enough, we didn't have to sit in the waiting room for very long before Kenny's name got called. But we did have to meet with the USCIS officer separately to answer questions. Kenny seemed pretty paranoid that they'd somehow know about the baby, but I wasn't convinced, so I bet him ten bucks on it to try to lighten the mood. Still, I bounced my good leg while Kenny got up and left me alone to freak out about every way this could possibly end up going wrong. I felt like Dr. Strange in *Infinity War*, watching millions of alternate futures playing out, with only one good outcome to latch on to. Sure, Kenny and I had practiced, but what if the officer threw us a curveball question we hadn't thought of? What if we both gave different answers? Would we be accused of fraud right then? And if we were, what next? Would I simply be denied a green card, or would the whole thing be taken more seriously? Would I get deported? Would Kenny go to jail? I cursed myself for not worrying about all this sooner. My green card wasn't worth Kenny's freedom.

But before I knew it, Kenny walked back into the waiting room. He looked happy enough, but he didn't have a chance to give me any indication of what happened in that interview. Did they know about the baby? If so, why did Kenny look so relaxed? He seemed way less nervous than he was before the interview, so maybe they didn't know? The questions couldn't have been that hard, right?

I got up on shaky legs and hobbled on my crutches through the door where the USCIS officer was waiting for me. The officer led me down a corridor into an office at the end of the hallway and sat down behind the desk.

"Have a seat." She gestured for me to sit. Right. I sat in the chair on the other side of her desk, hoping she didn't notice how shaky my hands were. I wiped my sweaty palms on my jeans.

"So, how long have you and Mr. Bautista been together?" she asked.

"Well, officially, since October, but we've been in love since high school. Well, I have. Kenny says he loved me since first grade, when I saved him from a bully by throwing a dodgeball at the kid's crotch." I chuckled nervously. I figured it'd be a good idea to give details. It was hard not to dread the whole baby question, but I forced myself to focus on what she was actually saying.

"Mm-hmm…" The woman typed something into her computer before flicking her eyes back to me. "You don't think that's a little fast to be getting married? You've only been dating a few weeks."

I shook my head, wiping my palms on my thighs again. "Like I said, it's been a long time in the making. We've been into each other longer than anyone either of us has ever dated. If anything, we should have gotten married a long time ago."

"Mm-hmm…" she said, typing something again. "And how did you two meet?"

I went on to tell the story of how we met when we were six, and how I thought Kenny hated me when really he had a crush. Most of the questions went this way for a while. They were easy enough to answer, and I was confident my answers wouldn't clash with Kenny's since they were all true. But the officer's expression never changed, and she kept typing things on her computer and "mm-hmm"ing at me. It was intimidating, and it did nothing to fix the clamminess in my hands. I had to force myself not to bounce my leg, because I didn't want to seem as nervous as I was.

"And I'm sure you're aware that we go through your social media…Do you do the same?" she asked, which threw me off a little bit until I remembered that the baby was all over Instagram. So she did know.

I nodded. "I know about the baby, if that's what you're asking," I started. Finally, I let my answer differ from what Kenny's had probably been. "Kenny might not have mentioned this, but the mom is extremely abusive. We're going to try for custody, together. It's gonna be my baby, too." I tried not to sound as nervous about that as I was. I was sure I wanted to do this, but that didn't mean it didn't still scare the hell out of me.

"Getting someone else pregnant doesn't really seem like something you do when you're in love with your fiancé, does it?"

"We didn't get engaged until after he broke up with her. Like I said, it wasn't that long ago. The way I see it, his relationship with her was so toxic, and it was just hard for him to get out. When he finally did, we knew it was the right time for us."

"Mm-hmm," she said as she typed.

Then the questions continued like before. After what felt like ages, she finally let me go.

I made my way down the hall to meet back up with Kenny, feeling pretty confident. My phone buzzed in my pocket before I got to him, and I paused to take it out to see my dad calling.

I debated whether or not I should even answer it. I was still mad about how he'd reacted to the wedding. But then again, he could be calling to give an update about my mom . . .

"Hey, Papi . . ." I finally answered, scrunching the phone between my ear and shoulder. I hoped this would be quick if it wasn't about my mom. I wasn't exactly looking forward to talking to him.

"Como estás, mijo?"

I made my way through the door and into the waiting room, where Kenny was waiting. Kenny gave me a huge grin and a double thumbs-up, and I squeezed the crutch with my arm in order to give a reluctant thumbs-up back.

"I'm good. What's up? Is Mami back? How is she?" I asked. Even if I'd tried not to think about it, I had to admit he'd really gotten me worried since that last conversation.

"Are you alone? Is this a good time?"

"Papi, what's going on?"

"Maybe you should sit down, mijo."

"Why? What's going on? Is she okay?" Kenny gave me a con-cerned look then, but I ignored it.

There was a long pause and an audible sigh over the phone. "We found her. She overdosed, and—"

"Is she okay?"

Another long pause. "Mijo, she didn't make it."

CHAPTER TWENTY-SIX

KENNY

"Han, talk to me," I begged on the car ride home. I couldn't help but worry. Han hadn't said anything after he'd gotten off the phone. He just made his way to the car like a zombie. "I heard you on the phone. Is everything okay?"

Han only shook his head and stared out the window, expressionless. I didn't want to pry and end up making things worse, so I stayed silent, too, hoping he would eventually say something. The silence stretched the entire car ride home and until we made it back to the apartment. Finally, once Han sat himself down on the couch, he spoke so softly I could barely hear it.

"She's dead."

I put a hand over my mouth. I didn't know what I was expecting him to say, but it wasn't that. "Oh my God, Han…" I sat next to him and rested a hand on his knee. "Are you okay?" I regretted the question as soon as I asked it. Of course he wasn't okay. His mom died. How could he be okay? To my surprise, Han actually answered the absurd question.

"Yeah." He scratched his chin pensively. "I'll be good."

I felt tears welling up in my own eyes instead of seeing them in Han's. I knew he and his mom weren't close, but I also knew he still cared about her deeply. If this was a gut punch for me, I couldn't imagine how Han felt. Even if he didn't let on, he still must have been hurting. I leaned into his side and rubbed his back, but he didn't react.

"What are you thinking?" I asked softly.

Han sighed. "I don't want to have a big wedding."

What? The answer took me by surprise. Why was he thinking about the wedding right now? Maybe he needed to deflect what was really wrong in order to keep from freaking out. That was fine with me. I would give him all the space he needed, if that would help.

"We should be trying to get married ASAP, and if we have a big wedding, it'll be like a year before we can even do it. I don't want to wait that long," Han said clinically, as if this were the only thing in the world that troubled him.

"I'll...talk to my parents," I said. I met Han's eyes, which surprisingly didn't look sad. They just looked tired. Too tired. I threw my arms around him and squeezed him up in a hug. "Whatever you need...just say the word, okay?"

Han let out a quick breath of air through his nose. "Thanks, bro."

I resisted the urge to roll my eyes. Even if I didn't understand Han's aversion to vulnerability, I had to respect it, at least right now.

✳   ✳   ✳

"What do you mean you don't want a big wedding?" my mom barked through the phone.

"Han's mom *died*." I whispered the word "died," as if Han would hear from his room. "Can we just give him what he wants right now?"

I could hear my mom click her tongue over the phone. "And I'm sorry about that, truly, I am, but you know how much I've always wanted my only baby to have a big fancy wedding!"

"You've wanted that, Mom, but I never did. I'm sorry. We want to get married *soon*. I don't really care for a big wedding, and Han really doesn't want one. He doesn't want you spending all your money on us, and I have to agree," I said, finally realizing as I said it that Han had probably been feeling guilty about it. I didn't want me or my family to contribute to any of Han's hardships right now. The least I could do was get my mom to back off about the wedding. "Listen, we really can't accept that money for the wedding. Please, Mom. I really appreciate all the things you do for me, and for Han, but I don't want this to be one of them."

There was a long silence on the phone before she said anything. "I think I know what this is about."

"What do you mean?"

"Would you accept the money for . . . something else?"

"Mom, what are you talking about?"

"Like, an immigration lawyer."

Did she know about our plan? She couldn't. But she did know Han was undocumented, so maybe even if she believed the wedding was genuine, she still knew the next step was to get him citizenship. And an immigration lawyer could practically guarantee this was going to work, even with Jackie's baby on the way. I didn't think we could say no to that.

"Mom, would you really do that?"

"Your dad's college roommate is an immigration lawyer now,

and he owes your dad a favor." I could almost imagine my mom's finger coming up to shush me. "So don't even worry about it. I want this to work out just like you do, and it won't work out if Han gets deported, now, will it? You can consider it a wedding gift."

"Oh my gosh, thank you!" I wanted to kiss my phone. Even with what happened to Han's mom, this news *had* to make him feel at least a little bit better.

"You and Han are still coming over on Thursday for Thanksgiving, right?" she asked.

"I don't know," I said honestly. Han always hated Thanksgiving anyway, and with everything he was going through, it felt almost cruel to subject him to that just because my mom loved every excuse to throw a party. "Han's never been a fan of Thanksgiving. You know that."

She paused for a moment, probably trying to come up with an angle for how to lure us to her party. "Well, if you two are really trying to get married as soon as possible, maybe we call it your bachelor party instead, hm?"

"I'll run it by Han," I said, knowing perfectly well the change of branding wouldn't make a difference.

When we eventually hung up, I threw myself onto my bed, staring up at the ceiling. We were getting an immigration lawyer. Our plan was pretty foolproof as it was, but now there was no way this wouldn't work. After a moment of reveling, I sprang to my feet and went over to Han's room to break the news.

"Han?" I rapped my knuckles against Han's bedroom door. I could hear him humming and playing his guitar on the other side.

"Yeah, come in," he called out.

I pushed the door open to find Han sitting cross-legged on his bed with his back against the wall, playing his guitar. My eyes wandered to Han's laptop on his desk, where my most recent red panda sticky note drawing had mysteriously disappeared, just like all the notes I'd ever left for Han. He probably threw them away, which was fine with me. As long as they brought him even the tiniest smile before he got rid of them, that was all I could ask for.

"I talked to my mom. She agreed that we can have a small wedding so we can get married sooner. And…" I paused for dramatic effect as I plopped down next to Han on the bed. Luna came wandering in, and she lay down at the foot of the mattress, since she wasn't allowed on Han's bed. "We're getting an immigration lawyer. As a wedding gift. Isn't that amazing? It's cheaper than the wedding would have cost, and my mom's happy to help!"

Han stopped strumming. "You told your parents about our plan?"

"No! No, I didn't say anything. But they know you're undocumented, remember? So, they know an immigration lawyer would be helpful for us."

Han hummed his understanding as he plucked along to some tune I didn't recognize, eyes distant. "Cool."

"Yeah. It's really cool," I said, a little bummed that Han wasn't more excited, but I also really couldn't blame him. How could I possibly think I'd be able to fix this?

"So, any news from Jackie?" Han asked, and I knew exactly what he was trying to do. He wanted to keep the topic of conversation on my problems so he wouldn't have to open up. It was a very Han tactic. And it was one that worked spectacularly on me, because I didn't want to pry.

"Nope." I sighed. As far as I knew, Jackie was still planning on keeping the baby. Which scared the hell out of me and wasn't exactly something I wanted to think about right now. "What's on your mind?" I changed the subject, using Han's technique against him. But it was for his own good. I didn't want him to go through losing his mom alone.

"Music," Han said nonchalantly.

"Music?"

"Yeah, I'm working on something." He kept strumming his guitar.

"Can I hear it?"

Han sucked in his lower lip. "It's really not that good."

"I'd love to hear it." I gave Han a reassuring look. God knew he needed *some* way of expressing himself. If he shared his music with me, I felt it was just as good as talking about his feelings.

Han stopped playing as he let out a breath and closed his eyes. It was several moments before his fingers moved against the strings again, playing the same tune as before but more pronounced. It was a slow melody, sad. Then he started singing. His beautiful, velvet voice, for once, full of emotion.

> *I left my heart at the door where I left you*
> *And now I can't find it*
> *Sometimes I forget I ever even knew you*
> *So I have no right to cry*
> *No right to cry*

CHAPTER TWENTY-SEVEN

HAN

My phone's constant buzzing on my nightstand woke me up long after the sun had risen. My body obviously needed the rest, and I wasn't about to fight it. Since I'd found out about my mom three days ago, sleep was a little harder to come by, so one in the afternoon still felt early as hell. I checked my phone to see a random number lit across the screen. In my half-asleep haze, I answered it.

"Hello?" I mumbled, my morning voice making it clear I'd just woken up.

"Hi, Alejandro? This is John Jones, Cedric's friend. I assume he told you about me?"

"John Jones?" I asked, still half asleep.

"That's right! Sorry to call on Thanksgiving. I can do pro bono for a friend, but I still have a full client list."

I rubbed my temple with my free hand. I sure as hell never heard of anyone named John Jones. I vaguely remembered Kenny telling me to expect a call today, though. As soon as the memory hit, my morning fog vanished, and I almost fumbled off the bed trying to straighten up. "You're that lawyer, right?"

A chuckle, "Right! I'm calling for our consultation. Is this a good time?"

I sat up straighter, like that might make my voice sound less groggy. "Yeah, it's a great time. Thanks so much for calling, Mr. Jones."

"Great! I have a few questions for you if you don't mind…"

Mr. Jones went on to ask me a bunch of the same questions the USCIS officer had asked the other day. About a half hour passed before I had answered all of them.

"Excellent! Excellent, excellent. You're in a great position here, Mr. Torres. You're already way ahead of the curve since you've gotten started on your application early. While there's not too much else you can do until after you're officially married, you're still in a great spot. Now, you're going to be tested on civics and your English—which I don't see you having any problem with—but other than that, you really shouldn't need me unless you run into any trouble. If I'm wrong and the process isn't as smooth as I think it'll be for you, feel free to give me a call and we can go from there, all right?"

"Wow…thank you so much. Thank you. I'll definitely do that."

"You have a great day now."

"You too…"

I could hardly believe the relief that flooded over me when I hung up. A professional immigration lawyer said we'd have no problem. A real professional told me we would be set. Even knowing about Jackie's baby. He'd actually said it looked great that we were planning on fighting for custody. This was going to work out. And more than that, it was going to be *easy*. I reached for my crutches against the wall and maneuvered myself into the living room, where Kenny was watching *Up*.

"Hey, Han..." Kenny scrambled to change the movie when he saw me come out of the room. Apparently, *Up* was too sad to expose me to right now. "How are you feeling?"

"Fine," I said automatically. "Just got off the call with your dad's lawyer friend."

Kenny raised an eyebrow. "And?"

I went over to the couch and plopped down next to Kenny, forcing Luna onto his lap so I could sit. "He said we don't need him, but to call if anything goes wrong. He seemed really optimistic about the whole thing."

"That's awesome!" Kenny's smile seemed to take over his entire face, and I grinned back.

Kenny wrapped an arm around my shoulders and squeezed me in a side hug.

"So..." He ran a hand through his hair. "I heard from Jackie..."

I lifted my head, waiting for him to go on.

"She's keeping the baby, for sure now."

I nodded. "We'll figure it out. You're not alone, okay, bro?"

Kenny rolled his eyes, but after a second he gave me a sad smile. "I know I'm not. Thanks. And...you're not alone either, okay? I mean it."

I knew where Kenny was trying to go with that, so I grabbed the remote and pulled up *Fast Five* on the TV. It was a change from the "I need to cry" kids' movies Kenny was probably expecting me to pick, but whatever. I didn't need to cry. I needed a distraction.

While the movie played, I couldn't shake the guilt welling up. Kenny was going through with the marriage, but I had to wonder if Jackie was the one he really wanted to marry. The last thing I wanted was to be the reason Kenny didn't get to have the family he'd dreamed of, even if she was the reincarnation of the devil herself. I was *glad* Kenny wasn't marrying her, obviously, but I didn't want it to be because of *me*. I wanted it to be because Kenny knew he deserved better. Maybe he did know. I hoped so. And part of me wondered if this would be something Kenny might hold against me in the future, if it would be a source of bitterness that would eventually tear us apart.

I knew I owed Kenny way more than I would ever be able to pay back, and I didn't know how to cope with that. And it wasn't like I could just talk to Kenny about it, either. No matter how guilty I felt, I desperately needed him to go through with this. I couldn't risk talking about it with him if it might make him change his mind. Besides, anything serious I would try to say would just lead to Kenny trying to get me to talk about my mom again, which I really wasn't trying to do.

It was all giving me a headache. Or maybe that was because I hadn't had my caffeine fix for the day. The second option was solvable, so I went with that one.

"Here, let me help you," Kenny said when he noticed me trying to get up.

"Nah, I got it," I said. I didn't want Kenny helping me with anything else. He helped me too much, and I had nothing to give back. The least I could do was make my own damned coffee. I used my crutches—the ones Kenny wouldn't let me pay him back for—to pull myself up. I slipped them under my arms and went over to the kitchen to make some coffee, which proved much more difficult than I'd thought. You would think something as simple as making coffee wouldn't be that hard to do on one foot. It was so much more effort than coffee should ever take, but it was worth it to not be even more indebted to Kenny.

"You sure you're up for the party tonight?" Kenny asked. "I'm sure everyone will understand if we cancel." But it sounded more like he was the one who wanted to cancel. To be honest, I would have loved to cancel. Kenny had told me about his mom's idea to switch things up and make it a "bachelor party" instead of Thanksgiving, but that didn't put me any more in the mood to go.

"I don't know. To be honest, it'd be really nice not to have to move until work tomorrow." I'd probably be stuck on the couch for the party anyway with my ankle the way it was, but going to Kenny's parents' house still meant making my way out of the apartment, down the stairs, to the car, and from the car to their living room. Then again in reverse.

"I'll tell them we're not up to it," Kenny offered, but it didn't give me the relief I'd hoped for.

I'd been ignoring everyone since I found out about my mom. I hadn't answered my phone at all, and the only reason I answered for the lawyer was because I *didn't* recognize the number. So I knew not going to the party would just make everyone that much more worried about me, and it'd be that much longer before they'd leave me alone.

Kenny typed away on his phone for a moment before putting it away. "It's canceled. We're officially good to do nothing until work tomorrow."

"Thank fuck."

After that, Kenny and I spent a couple of hours playing *Injustice* before Luna started barking at the door. Then came the knocking.

The door wasn't locked, so it opened before either me or Kenny made it over. Elisa and Cedric walked right in, carrying a Crock-Pot full of tamales.

"Surprise!" they both chanted as Cedric set the tamales down on the kitchen counter.

"What are you guys doing here?" Kenny asked, looking back and forth from me to them like he was afraid of my reaction.

"We wanted to celebrate your bachelor party with you! Since getting to us was a problem, we decided to bring the party to you!" Elisa clapped her hands in excitement, and I tried to hide the disappointment on my face. It was a sweet gesture, really. And I had to admit, the tamales smelled good.

Before I had a chance to decide how I felt about it, there was another knock on the door, followed by the distinct sound of a baby laughing behind it. Kenny and I both winced at the sound, though probably for different reasons. I recognized that laugh as Mateo's, which meant my family was here, too.

Elisa opened the door for them, and Mariana walked in, holding Mateo on her hip. Tía Mary came right behind her, carrying several to-go bags from her favorite local Mexican restaurant. Kenny got up quickly to grab the bags, then placed them on the counter next to the tamales.

Leti came in next with a bottle of tequila in one hand and Tatiana's hand in the other. Before I could react to the fact that Leti and Tatiana were now seemingly an item, Tío Nacho walked in, fully uniformed in his mariachi getup. All four other members of his band trailed behind him, singing "La Marcha de Zacatecas" at full volume, and everyone danced into formations with their arms, creating bridges for Kenny and me to walk through, as if we were at a wedding reception.

Kenny looked over at me apprehensively, like he was worried

I'd be upset, but I just laughed. That was our families for you. Kenny laughed, too, as he ducked and walked through the barely-four-person bridge. I rubbed a hand down my face but went along with it and hobbled through myself.

Then the band surrounded Kenny and me, and I didn't know what I was supposed to do. I never knew what I was supposed to do when this happened. The band would surround me and sing to me every year on my birthday, and for other special occasions. Tío Nacho was so embarrassing. By the time they finished the song, my armpit was aching from supporting myself on the crutch, so I went over to the couch to sit down again.

Tía Mary was at my side in an instant.

"How are you feeling, mijo?" She pressed a hand to my forehead, as if grief would manifest itself in the form of a high fever.

"Fine, Tía."

"Well, anything you need, you know we're here for you, okay?"

"I know, Tía. Can we not talk about this right now, though?"

"Okay, mijo." She kissed my forehead. "So, I hear you're doing the wedding in the middle of December? So soon!"

"Yeah. I was going to call you..." I suddenly felt bad for all the calls I ignored. I really should have told them.

"No te preocupes. Kenny told us everything, and I want to help! He said you still have some wedding planning to do. I want to volunteer my services for the food. I'm happy to cook."

Kenny walked up just then with a couple of plates of tamales and tacos and shot glasses of tequila. "Actually, my dad wanted to cook..." he started as he sat down on the couch next to me, but when Tía Mary gave him the meanest mal de ojo, he backtracked real quick. "I don't see any reason you can't *both* cook."

Leti raised their hand from the kitchen, where they were serving themself a plate. "I got you on the DJ front. You know Angie, from the last show y'all went to? She's down to do it for free. Plus, I just got ordained, so you don't need to pay for a priest, either."

"And obviously your tío and his band will play," Tía Mary cut in. I laughed. We would barely have to spend a dime. Mary got up to go get herself some food, and Kenny handed me one of the shot glasses, then placed a gentle hand on my knee as I looked to Leti and Tatiana, who were sitting at the table across the room with Mariana and Tía Mary.

"So, you two are dating now?" Kenny asked.

Leti kissed Tatiana's cheek and smiled. "We are."

With how well the two of them had always gotten along, even when Tatiana and I were dating, I couldn't say it really surprised me that they hit it off well enough to try things out. Leti had been single for so long they were starting to get a little bummed, so I was happy for them.

I clinked my shot glass with Kenny's, and we both downed them. I eyed the tamales, wishing I had some food to make my throat burn less. Kenny noticed almost immediately and got up to get me a plate. Soon enough he came back with the food and two more shot glasses.

"I'm good." I waved away the shot glass. I had only wanted the one shot to numb the pain in my ankle a bit. I couldn't be hobbling around drunk. That was just asking for another accident.

"You sure?" Tatiana asked. "You probably have lots of, uh, stuff to get off your mind."

Leti gave Tatiana a death glare.

"You told her?" Kenny asked protectively, but I held a hand out to calm him.

"It's fine. I'm fine, okay?" I said, annoyed that it seemed everyone and their mother knew what happened to mine. "Everyone needs to stop worrying about me."

"More for me then," Kenny said, and gulped down both shots in quick succession. If anything, Kenny was the one who had lots to get off his mind. Nothing a few shots wouldn't fix. Tatiana and Leti were quick to follow Kenny's lead so he at least wasn't drinking alone.

Kenny leaned on me and sighed, his body limp against mine. I wrapped an arm around him and rubbed his shoulder, knowing exactly why he was trying to get drunk. He was going to be a *dad*. No matter how bad his baby fever was, this was far from his ideal situation.

Then Kenny leaned into me and kissed my cheek, which got hot from the contact. I guess cheek kisses didn't count when it came to the no-kissing rule. I couldn't keep track of what we were or weren't allowed to do at this point. And I wasn't sure why the hell I wasn't used to the flirting yet, but it still gave me a fluttering feeling in my gut that I couldn't quite shake.

I leaned into Kenny's embrace and took his hands in mine. If he wasn't going to count non-mouth kisses, then I could play at that game. I brought Kenny's hand to my mouth and pressed a kiss into his palm.

The immediate blush on his face brought a smile to mine. Then again, the blush could have just been from the alcohol. Before I could think too much into it, my phone rang, and I pulled it out to see a call from my dad.

I quickly pulled myself up by my crutches and went to my room to answer the WhatsApp call, closing the door behind me for privacy.

"Hey, Papi. Everything okay?"

"As okay as it can be, mijo..." There was a long pause. I didn't break the silence because I didn't want to rudely ask *Then why are you calling me?* Finally, he continued. "I'm calling because I need to apologize to you."

"For what?" I asked, dumbfounded.

"I wasn't very supportive of you when you told me about your wedding. I just...I need to get used to this kind of thing. So...you're marrying a boy. And that's okay. I want to support you. You know you mean a lot to me, right, mijito?"

I felt the knots in my stomach unravel at those words. "Thank you, Papi."

"Even if you're just doing it for citizenship. This is none of my business—"

"I think I'm gay," I blurted out. "I'm...definitely gay."

I hadn't told anyone yet, not even Kenny. But as soon as I said it out loud, it was like all the tension I'd been holding on to just floated away.

"Bueno. I thought it might be true. I love you."

Just when I felt myself choking up, there was a knock on my door.

"Ale, mijo, don't be so antisocial!" Tía Mary's voice rang out.

"Coming!" I called out. "I gotta go, Papi. Thank you. I mean that. Love you."

"Love you too, mijo."

I made my way out of my room and back to the couch in the living room, where Kenny was still sitting.

"You're back!" Kenny exclaimed, jumping up and wrapping his arms around my neck. So, Kenny was definitely tipsy, at the very least. We both sat back down on the couch, but soon enough, Kenny got out his phone and stared at it for way too long.

"I have to go. I'll be right back," he said, then rushed out the front door without another word.

"Where'd your fiancé go?" Leti asked when they noticed Kenny walk out the door.

I felt my face get hot. I, of all people, should have known where my "fiancé" was headed, but I had no idea. All I knew was that Kenny better not have been driving anywhere, since he was drinking. In fact, I felt the need to go out and check up on him.

"I'll be right back," I said, and hoisted myself up with a crutch, then made my way to the door as quickly as I could. I didn't have to go far, though, because Kenny was sitting against the wall.

With Jackie.

I made sure to walk out and close the door behind me so no one would see her before I said anything. Even then, I didn't know what to say. I wanted to be mad that Kenny would ditch our "bachelor" party for his ex, but how could I be mad? Jackie was pregnant with his kid, and the marriage wasn't even real. I had no right.

"Han, I'll be back in a minute, I promise. We just need a second to talk. Don't tell anyone she's here," Kenny said with a pleading look in his eye.

"Are you serious?" Jackie said. "I have every right to be here. I think it'll take more than a second, don't you?"

"It's our bachelor party," Kenny said, and Jackie's face went red.

"Han. Go inside. Now. This is between me and Kenny." There was venom in her voice.

"If I'm not back in five minutes, come and get me," Kenny said, and Jackie gave him a feral look that gave me goose bumps. I knew Kenny had meant that he didn't want to lose track of time, but it made the situation feel that much more dangerous.

I didn't want to leave Kenny alone with her, but I didn't know what else to do. Someone else would come out and discover Jackie if I didn't go back inside soon.

"I'll come back in five minutes," I said and went back inside, closing the door behind me.

CHAPTER TWENTY-EIGHT

KENNY

A re you fucking kidding me? I said break up with him, not *get married!*" Jackie's voice was dangerously loud. It was a good thing Nacho and his mariachi band were playing music inside, or everyone else might have heard.

"I told you I wasn't leaving him!" I whisper-yelled. "Can you please keep it down?"

"Why, so no one sees you with me? If we have a kid together, people are going to have to see us together. You can't be embarrassed to be seen with the mother of your child."

It wasn't that I was embarrassed, but I didn't want Han's family, or mine, getting the wrong idea. I so badly wanted to just tell her to leave and go back inside with Han, but she was right. We were having a kid together, so I had to play nice with her. "I'm not embarrassed of you," I muttered.

"It sure seems like you are." She crossed her arms.

"I'm sorry," I said. I always found myself apologizing to her, even if I wasn't totally sure what I'd done wrong.

Then Jackie started crying. I just sat there for a moment, not knowing what to do.

"Will you just hold me?" she cried. I wrapped my arms around her and let her cry into my shoulder. "What are we going to do?" she asked.

"I'll get a better-paying job..." I said. "Han said he'll help out, too."

She choked on her sob. "Don't talk to me about Han right now!"

"Okay, sorry."

After a few moments of crying, she looked up from my shoulder and into my eyes. Hers were red and puffy, like this wasn't the first time she had cried over this. I felt so guilty for not having been there.

"I'll go to your appointments with you," I said, feeling my words starting to slip into each other a tiny bit.

"Are you drunk?"

"Uh, maybe a little," I admitted.

Jackie didn't answer, just kept staring intensely into my eyes. Then she leaned forward and pressed her lips against mine. I was so surprised at first that I didn't move. Her cheeks were wet with tears, and her face was warm. Warm and soft. Then the door opened.

I quickly pushed Jackie away. It was Han.

"Oh..." he started, closing the door behind him discreetly as words seemed to evade him. Jackie grinned victoriously, and in that moment I hated her all over again. Had she *wanted* Han to catch us? I knew our relationship wasn't real, but Jackie didn't know that. What she did know was that I had been drinking. She knew Han was coming back. And she kissed me anyway.

"I swear, it's not what it looks like!" I pleaded, partially to keep up with the act, but also because I didn't want Han to think anything of it. I had just told him things were over with Jackie, and if he thought I was having second thoughts, he'd freak out over the wedding.

"Looks like you two have a lot to work out. I'll leave you to it," Jackie said, then sauntered back down the hallway toward the stairs as if the night had gone exactly how she'd planned. Once she was out of earshot, I covered my face with my hands.

"I fucked up," I said.

"We said no dating other people."

"I know, I know. She just kissed me, and I wasn't expecting it. It won't happen again. I promise."

"I'm just gonna . . . go back inside," Han said, and reached for the door.

"I'll go with you!" I grabbed Han's hand. "I'm sorry I almost blew our cover. I really am," I said.

"It's fine," Han said, even though there was an edge in his tone that said otherwise. I opened the door and helped him inside before anyone could get too suspicious.

Once the door opened, the act was back on. Han's jaw unclenched, and he relaxed in my arms, leaning on me while he hopped back to the couch. I moved to kiss him before I remembered the rule I myself had set. No kissing. I hated that damn rule, but it was definitely for the best. I couldn't turn Han into a rebound. I helped him sit down, then took another shot before going to the bathroom to cool off.

What the hell had I just done? Why hadn't I stopped Jackie from kissing me? If it had been anyone but Han who walked out, it would have ruined everything. Somehow, though, Han walking out still felt like the worst possible outcome. I hadn't wanted to let him down, but that was exactly what I'd just done.

I stared at myself in the mirror, asking myself the same

question over and over again. What the hell was wrong with me? Then there was a knock on the door. I opened it, eager to make things right with Han.

"I'm so sorry Ha—Leti?"

"We need to talk." Leti grabbed my wrist and led me down the hallway. I stumbled along behind them, feeling the effects of the alcohol stuttering my steps. "In private," they said, then gestured to my bedroom door. I had a feeling this was important, so I opened the door and walked inside. They spoke as soon as the door was closed.

"What did you do?"

"What do you mean?"

"I mean why is Han brooding all of a sudden? An hour ago he said he wasn't going to drink, and now he's getting hammered. What happened when you left? What did you do to my cousin?" Leti put their hands on their hips and stared me down. I always knew they were confrontational when it came to protecting their family, but I'd never been on this side of their aggression before.

"I—I didn't do anything," I stuttered. What was I supposed to say?

"Bullshit. Why is he all sad now?"

"He's sad?" I asked. Han rarely showed his emotions, especially not when he was sad. And it usually took a lot to make him sad-drink. Though I supposed Leti was more in tune with the inner workings of Han than anyone else in the world, besides maybe me.

They just looked at me as if it was obvious. Was Han really that upset about the kiss? I hoped he trusted me enough to know I would keep my word with the wedding. With everything we'd been through, I would have hoped he'd trust me enough not to worry about that. So why was he upset enough for Leti to notice?

I wanted to tell Leti everything because I knew they would be able to give the best advice, but Han and I had decided on that first day we couldn't tell a single soul, and I wasn't about to break that promise. I wondered if I should come clean about the part of the truth I knew I could trust them with, that Han saw Jackie kissing me, and I didn't know what to do about it.

"Jackie kissed me," I finally said.

"Your ex? Did you kiss her back?"

"Not exactly . . . but I didn't stop her right away. I just kind of froze up. Han saw us," I said, the guilt in my voice 100 percent honest.

"Kenny, what the fuck?"

"I know, I know. I'm the worst."

"Shut up. Stop that. It's not about you. It's about *Han*. Do you even want to marry him?"

"*Yes*. I really, really do."

We were both quiet for a while before Leti's eyebrows shot up.

"Ohh, I think I see what's going on here."

"What?" I shook my head, trying to hide how tipsy I was.

"I mean, I think I do . . . I'm pretty sure I figured it out," they said. "You and Han. You're doing this for him, aren't you? It's not what you really want."

"What? This is what I want!" I raised my voice slightly. Even though Leti was sort of right, they were wrong about me not wanting this. I wanted Han to stay, whatever it took.

"Really? Look, I've known you as long as Han has, and I know you tend to do things for other people and not think about yourself. But marrying someone is *huge*, Kenny."

"I know..." I didn't even try to hide the annoyance in my voice. It was like they were convinced I hadn't even thought this through.

"You're doing it for his citizenship, aren't you?"

I pressed my lips together. How the hell had they figured it out so quickly? And if Leti could figure it out, who else would? I didn't say anything. I couldn't confirm, but I knew if I denied it Leti would see right through that, too.

"I know you're doing Han a huge favor, but like, if you're not sure, you need to figure that shit out. This can't be one of those decisions you let someone else make for you. You can't be second-guessing this. It's not fair to either of you. Fuck. Are you sure?"

"I'm sure!" I shouted this time.

"I'm just saying. If you're going to change your mind...it's better now than at the altar, you know?" Leti was talking so fast, it took me a few moments to put together what they were saying.

"Wait, does anyone else know?" I asked.

"I just figured it out right now, so no." Leti shrugged. "So, you're marrying Han so he can stay. It's a noble gesture, really."

"You can't tell anyone, please," I said.

"No shit. I want Han here as bad as you do. We all want it to work out. Just don't be all wishy-washy." They pointed a finger at me. "Be sure. If you're not sure, you need to tell him. Don't get his hopes up for nothing. That's fucked up."

"I said I was sure," I said, though considering I'd gotten caught with Jackie just now, I could imagine Leti wasn't buying it.

"Promise me," Leti said solemnly.

"I promise." I nodded. "Han's the one with the commitment problems. I don't know why you're worried about *me*."

"Because you always do everything for other people without thinking about what you really want. But this is too big a deal for you to figure out that you don't really want this when it's too late. It's like, all you want from life is to be of service. That's no life to live."

Leti was right. But they also weren't. Sure, maybe I wanted to be of service. But that wasn't why I was doing this. "Look, Han is the only person in my life who makes sure I put myself into the equation. He's the only one who *cares* if I actually want to do whatever I'm doing. Of course I want to marry him. I'd do anything for him." I felt myself getting emotional, and I couldn't tell if it was the alcohol or the much-too-belated realization that this whole thing might not be as fake as we had originally planned.

"Oh . . . oh no," Leti said.

"What?"

"You love him, don't you?"

"I mean, yeah. Obviously."

"No, I mean, you *love* him."

"I . . ." I started, but I'd done my best to avoid asking myself that question this whole time. But with the answer staring me in the face, there was no way I could deny it.

"Don't tell me. Tell *him*." Leti was smiling now.

"I don't want to complicate it. Han can't be a rebound."

"He's not a rebound. You've known him your whole life."

"I know, but—"

"Hey, you don't have to figure this out with me right now. Your fiancé is waiting out there for you." Leti winked and walked out of the room.

I fell down onto my bed and closed my eyes.

I was so fucked.

CHAPTER TWENTY-NINE

HAN

I splayed myself out on the couch, not caring I was making a fool of myself. I was around mostly family, plus Tatiana. She seemed like the only one who noticed me then. Everyone else was at the table eating, but I didn't want to move. Because of my ankle and because I'd had a bit too much to drink. The alcohol helped me stop overthinking everything. My brain and body just felt relaxed.

"Where did your fiancé go?" Tatiana asked.

"Where'd your Leti go?" I shot back at her, my words slurring together.

"Probably wherever your fiancé went," Tatiana said, taking a quick swig straight from the bottle of tequila and then offering it to me. I took a pretty big gulp myself. I knew I was breaking my own drinking rule, but what could I say? It was a moment of weakness. The more I drank, the less my ankle hurt and the more untangled my brain got. I couldn't complain about that. Soon enough, the pain in my ankle went from a constant fire to a distant burning, almost like it wasn't even attached to my body anymore. I'd already resigned myself to sleeping on the couch so I wouldn't get hurt on my way to bed. It would be fine.

Finally, Kenny and Leti came out from the hallway. Kenny lifted my head up from the couch cushion and sat down, placing my head back down in his lap. It was more comfortable like this than it was before. I felt like I might have been mad at Kenny, but I knew I had no right to be, so I just closed my eyes and leaned into his lap. Screw overthinking. I'd figure it out tomorrow.

"You're a comfy boy," I muttered, smiling lazily with my eyes closed. I heard Kenny laugh.

"Thanks, babe," Kenny said. I knew he was just doing it for show, but I liked when he called me that. It had a nice ring to it. I'd been called "babe" before, by lots of girls, but never by Kenny until recently. It felt different. Good. Most things with Kenny felt that way.

I wrapped my arms around Kenny's leg, using his thigh as a pillow, and closed my eyes. Right now nothing really mattered. I didn't care about the guests, or Jackie, or anything but Kenny's lap. I mumbled my goodbyes without opening my eyes as our guests trickled out of the house. I felt a few kisses on my forehead—probably from my tíos—and before I knew it, Kenny and I were alone again, just the two of us on the couch.

"Do you still love Jackie?" I asked as soon as the last person left. I didn't know where the question came from, but I didn't care.

"What? No. It's . . . complicated. But no."

"What's complicated about it?"

Kenny was quiet for what felt like a full minute, but time was moving weird, so I couldn't really be sure.

"I just miss having someone, you know?" Kenny finally said.

I frowned. "I don't know. I never really had someone. I mean, I have you, but it's different. Like you said. It's fake." I sighed, probably not doing the best job of hiding my exasperation.

"Um, right…" Kenny started playing with my hair, and I hummed at the sensation. I closed my eyes again, letting the comforting feeling on my scalp lull me to sleep.

Kenny's fingers were still sifting through my hair when I woke up with an uncontrollable urge to pee. I couldn't have been asleep for more than five minutes. Dammit, I would have to get up soon.

"Can you help me up? I have to take a piss," I said, regretting the words instantly, because they made Kenny's hands move away from my hair. He helped me sit up while I grabbed for the crutches so I could stand. It didn't take long before I realized I was still way too drunk to use them. Kenny must have noticed, because he immediately came to my side and pulled my arm around his shoulder to support me.

"Thanks," I said, careful not to say the word "bro," since that had started bothering him, even if I had no idea why. I felt almost naked without saying it. Like the word was some kind of protection spell that kept things from getting too real. Maybe it was okay if they got real with Kenny. I couldn't help but wonder if he was feeling the same way.

Kenny helped me all the way to the toilet. I wasn't one to get embarrassed, especially while we were both drunk, and I would need help getting back to the living room anyway. I appreciated that Kenny didn't make a big deal of it.

"Do you think we're still on the same page about this?" Kenny asked, staring at himself in the mirror and fixing his hair, completely unfazed by the sound of me relieving my bladder.

"What page are you on?" I asked, unwilling to admit I might not have been on the same page as I was when we made the agreement. I still wanted to go through with it. Had to. But I didn't know what page I was on when it came to relationships anymore. With Kenny in particular.

Kenny took in a breath like he was hyping himself up for something, then shook his head. "Nothing's changed," he said, and I didn't know if I should feel relief or disappointment.

"Great. Same," I said, even though it couldn't have been farther from the truth. I hopped sloppily over to the sink, and after I washed my hands, I threw an arm around Kenny's shoulder. If I couldn't have Kenny for real, at least we could enjoy the pretending. "Take me to bed, lover."

Kenny laughed. Instead of helping me walk out the door, he put an arm under my knees and hoisted me up. I was impressed he was able to carry me, considering how much taller I was than him. It was a little bit of a turn-on, if I was being honest.

Kenny started walking to my room, and when he nudged the door open with his foot, my weight must have gotten to him— or maybe the alcohol—because we both went tumbling to the floor. Kenny did some kind of superhero wrestling move midair, so I fell on top of him instead of the other way around.

Kenny smiled under me. Our faces were so close, but it didn't seem to bother either of us. I stared at Kenny's dark eyes, which, I couldn't help but notice, were staring at my lips. Kenny's eyes slowly traveled back up to meet mine, but instead of kissing, I burst out laughing, then rolled to my side.

"What?" Kenny asked, but he was laughing now, too.

I just crawled over to my bed, giggling all the way there. I climbed up and splayed out on top of the blankets, staring at the ceiling. The next moment, Kenny was cuddled up next to me.

He held up his phone to check the time, and I got a glimpse of his screensaver: a picture of him with his mom.

I didn't have a single picture of me with my mom to remember her by. Before I knew it, pressure built up behind my eyes, and drunken tears spilled out of them without warning.

"Han?" Kenny tenderly wiped my cheek with his thumb. "What's wrong?"

I shook my head and covered my face with my hands. "No. I'm not allowed to cry about this," I said, the words muffled behind my hands.

Kenny gently pulled one of my hands away from my face and held it tightly. "About what?"

"My mom!" The words came out in a sob, and more tears fell down the sides of my temples, sliding back down to my hair as I stared at the blurry ceiling.

Kenny squeezed my hand, his voice softer than ever. "Of course you're allowed to cry about it."

"Bullshit. I barely knew her. I never called. She tried calling me before she died and I ignored her. I don't deserve to cry about it," I said, but despite the words, I just cried harder. It felt good. It hurt, but I needed to get it out. I was glad the alcohol gave me the ability.

"It's not your fault," Kenny whispered, his eyes starting to water, too.

After a long moment of silence, Kenny whispered again. "Tell me about her..."

And I did. Through my tears, I told Kenny everything. I told him why I never called my parents. How my mom was barely there. How she tried to sell me for drugs. How she was the reason I felt like I had to be emotionally distant from everyone I cared about. I told him about the letters and videos I never sent her. How despite everything, I missed her, or at least the idea of what she could have meant to me. Despite everything, I wished she wasn't dead. And I felt guilty for not feeling as sad as everyone thought I should be.

I rolled to my side and looked into Kenny's teary face. He wiped his own eyes under his glasses, then cupped my cheeks in his hands and wiped my tears with his thumbs without breaking eye contact. Kenny's eyes were intense and full of understanding. I closed my own, squeezing out a few stray tears. I wanted to kiss him so badly in that moment. I almost did, but I stopped myself before our lips met.

"How did you know you were bi?" I asked. Anything to change the subject. Kenny looked taken aback.

"Um, I guess I always knew. I mean, before Jackie, lots of my crushes were dudes."

I was quiet for a while before saying anything. I stared into Kenny's eyes, which were still misty from me talking about my mom.

"I'm gay," I blurted out, relieved to finally admit it.

Kenny reached out for my hand and squeezed it. "How long have you known?"

"Since...well...since you. This." I pointed back and forth between Kenny and myself.

Kenny's cheeks reddened. "Are you saying...? Do you—"

Before I could overthink it, I closed the gap between our faces and pressed my lips firmly against Kenny's. He kissed back for a moment. A wonderful, beautiful moment, before pulling away.

"We're both drunk." He stated the obvious.

"Do you want to kiss me?" I asked, sure my eyes were just as intense as Kenny's in the moment.

"Yes."

"Did you ever want to kiss me sober? For no reason other than that you wanted to? Alcohol, audience, checklist aside, did you ever want to kiss me?"

"Yes." Kenny barely finished saying the word before pulling me back in for another hungry kiss. I felt his glasses slide down his nose, but neither of us seemed to care. I breathlessly took in the kiss as I gripped the back of his neck with one hand and wrapped the other around his waist, pressing us even closer together, as if we could share one body, one breath. My leg moved in between Kenny's, and just as I felt his jeans shift as he hardened, I yanked myself away, holding Kenny's shoulders as I met his confused gaze.

"Am I a bad kisser?" I slurred, sure that I'd ruined the moment, but I was too drunk to care.

"What?" Kenny looked surprised as he adjusted his glasses, but then he smiled. "No, you're...you're really good." I noticed how flushed Kenny's cheeks were. I wondered if it was the alcohol or the kissing.

"Oh..." So that meant Tatiana wasn't just being nice when she'd said it. Unless Kenny was just being nice? But I doubted anyone would kiss me like *that* if they weren't enthusiastic about it.

"So, I have feelings for you," Kenny said, eyes made to look even bigger and more intense underneath those glasses.

Normally, I would have been afraid to admit it, but the alcohol took away whatever superficial fears I would have had before.

"Me too." I smiled. We could worry about the implications of this in the morning. For now, I rested my head on Kenny's chest and smiled.

"Do you think this changes things?" Kenny asked.

"I don't want it to change things." I realized then that Kenny seemed a bit out of breath, and I regretfully rolled off him to let him breathe. Kenny immediately took the opportunity to roll over so our positions were switched. Now he was lying on top of me, staring at my lips again.

"Obviously I take back that no-kissing rule…"

Instead of answering, I grabbed him by the back of his neck and pulled our faces together so our lips crashed into each other. It was sloppy, and we were drunk, but it was real. At least, as real as an inebriated make-out could be. I resisted the urge to pull away and take off my clothes before continuing. I wanted this, but I also didn't want to have regrets in the morning. At least if we didn't do anything more than make out, we could write it off as a drunken mistake if Kenny changed his sobered mind.

"You're amazing…" Kenny let out breathlessly between kisses.

The praise warmed my insides. Despite my better judgment, I found myself wondering where Kenny's kinky sex backpack was at that moment. My imagination flared, and I wondered what Kenny got up to with the things inside…

"Are you a dom or a sub?" I had barely finished the thought before I was blurting it out aloud.

Kenny pulled away slightly to look at me, a smirk on his lips. "Wouldn't you like to know?" he said, licking his lips flirtatiously.

"I mean, yeah, I would," I said honestly.

He smirked again. "I'm a switch."

"A switch," I repeated thoughtfully.

"What about you?" he asked.

It wasn't until then that I realized I was completely unprepared to answer my own question. I never really thought of myself as a particularly submissive person, but I couldn't deny the warmth in my cheeks at the thought of Kenny using his handcuffs or ropes on me. I didn't think I'd let anyone else do that to me but Kenny. I knew with him I'd be taken care of. Safe.

"I think I'm a sub," I finally said. It wasn't like I wanted him to tie me up and fuck me then and there, but... "I'm...curious."

Kenny grinned. "I thought you might be. What are you curious about?"

I wouldn't have been brave enough to say it if I were sober, even if I knew Kenny felt the same way about me. But the alcohol loosened my lips, and I said what I was feeling. "Where's your sex backpack? You have ropes and stuff in there, right?"

Kenny chuckled. "It's not safe to play with bondage when you're drunk. But..." He leaned forward and kissed me again. His hands moved to find mine, and he pinned my wrists down against the bed next to my head. Something churned in my gut. I knew I was technically stronger than Kenny and could move my hands if I wanted to, but that wasn't the point. Kenny felt strong like this, in control. He pulled away from the kiss but kept his hands firmly pinning my wrists. Then he leaned forward so his breath tickled my ear as he spoke, giving me goose bumps.

"If you're still curious later, I know exactly what I want to do to you."

I let out a heavy breath as I felt myself hardening at his words, and I was at a loss for my own.

"For tonight, though, we shouldn't go any further," Kenny

said, and I couldn't help but deflate a bit. I knew it was a bad idea to do anything drunk, but God, I wanted him so badly.

"Okay," I said, and Kenny rolled off me, instead cuddling my side and rubbing his hand up and down my chest.

I felt myself dozing off soon enough, but instead of leaving me to go to his own room, Kenny pulled the covers over both of us. I scooted even closer to him, and we wrapped our arms around each other. Our legs intertwined for a moment, but the second Kenny's foot brushed my ankle, I recoiled.

"Oof, sorry," Kenny said, then scooted the lower half of his body away, leaving us only cuddling from our torsos up.

"It's okay." I chuckled awkwardly.

"Have you ever been in love?" Kenny asked after a while of silence.

"Not yet..." I felt like I was getting there, though. Like if we kept this up, I could easily fall in love with Kenny.

"What about commitment scares you so much?"

I didn't know how to answer that. I guessed it was because I felt like nothing was guaranteed. Things could be great one day and miserable the next, like they were with Jackie and Kenny. Then again, I was never really *afraid* of commitment so much as uninterested in it. I'd never felt that spark with anyone before like I felt it with Kenny. And I craved that feeling like caffeine. Was I afraid of committing to marrying Kenny? I didn't think so.

"I'm not scared right now," I said, relaxing into Kenny's arms.

"What if I told you *I'm* scared?"

"What are you scared of?" I asked, and Kenny didn't answer for another minute.

"I'm scared of hurting you. I don't want you to be a rebound. You mean too much to me. You mean everything to me."

Oh. I hadn't thought of that. Maybe I was a rebound, but I couldn't bring myself to care. Not right now. We could have tonight and worry about all of this tomorrow. Who knows? Sober, we might deny it ever happened. But for now it was real, and for the first time, I didn't want to run away from that.

"You won't hurt me. I trust you, babe."

Kenny smiled at the pet name, then kissed my neck softly. "Mmm. Love you. G'night."

Maybe Kenny was more drunk than I'd realized, since he was fast asleep before I had a chance to even respond. I didn't know what I would have said anyway, but I was suddenly wide-awake. We told each other we loved each other plenty of times before, but never after kissing. I was glad Kenny was asleep, because if he wasn't, I might have said it back and meant it. There was only so much gay awakening a guy could handle in one night. I wasn't ready to think about that.

For now I thought about kissing Kenny.

CHAPTER THIRTY

KENNY

I woke up in the middle of the night to a phone call from Jackie. The alcohol had worn off, and in place of the light floating feeling, I had a dry throat and a throbbing headache. I gently unwrapped myself from Han's embrace and rolled over to take the call.

"Are you okay?"

"I'm at Bryan's. Can you come pick me up?"

"Seriously, Jackie?" I asked before realizing I couldn't be mad about it. Even if Jackie cheated on me with Bryan, we weren't together anymore. Still, calling me to pick her up from his house was pretty inconsiderate. Then again, when had I ever known her to be considerate?

"Please, Ken…" Her voice shook like she was crying.

"What's wrong? Are you okay?"

"I'm okay. I'm drunk, and I want to leave."

"You're drunk?" I asked. I didn't know too much about pregnancy, but I did know alcohol wasn't exactly a prenatal vitamin.

After getting the address, I said, "I'm on my way," and hung up the phone. I didn't trust Bryan not to take advantage.

When I rolled back around, I met Han's worried eyes. "You good?"

"I'm good." I debated keeping my errand from Han to keep the peace, but he deserved to know. "I just need to pick up Jackie really quick. She's drunk and needs a ride."

"She's drunk?" Han asked, his voice still raspy from sleep.

I nodded.

"Okay. I trust you," he said, and I responded by giving him a quick kiss on the lips, and he smiled wide.

"Are you still drunk?" he asked.

"No. Are you?"

"No." Han kissed me again, and I sank into it, my stomach fluttering wildly. We were kissing each other sober, for absolutely no reason other than that we wanted to.

"I'll be right back," I assured Han, who went back to sleep almost immediately with a smile on his face.

Within fifteen minutes, I was knocking on Bryan's door, ready to deck the dude if I needed to. Jackie opened it. She had tears streaming down her face.

"Are you okay?" I asked, pulling her in for a hug.

"I'm okay. Let's just get out of here," she said, and we did. I noticed she was carrying my backpack over one of her shoulders. "I should probably give this back to you..." I'd forgotten I'd left it at her place the night I'd proposed to her. And clearly she'd taken it to Bryan's.

"What happened?" I asked when we got in my car, throwing the backpack into the back seat. She hadn't stopped crying. "Did he hurt you?"

"What? No. Why would you think he hurt me?"

I shook my head. I guess I worried too much. She had called me crying in the middle of the night. Maybe it was just me wanting to believe Bryan was a bad guy to make myself feel better about being cheated on.

"Why are you crying, then? What's the matter?"

"I'm pregnant and drunk. Not a good combination."

"Jackie—" I started, but she interrupted.

"Don't. I know I shouldn't drink. I had a moment of weakness. You stayed with Han, and I wanted someone who wanted me back, so I came here. And Bryan was drinking, so I started drinking. I don't know. I'm a terrible person."

"Are you sure you want to keep it?" I asked, wondering if her drinking was some kind of subconscious act of sabotaging the pregnancy.

"I'm keeping it," she muttered. "Not that you care."

"What? You know I'm going to help you, Jackie. What are you talking about?"

"You didn't break up with Haaaaan!" she wailed, tears coming out of her eyes again. "I want this baby to have two parents!"

"It will!" I shouted, frustration welling up in my chest. "Hell, it'll have three, with Han helping out."

"Shut up! God, Kenny, shut *up* about *Han*!"

I shut up, driving the rest of the way to Jackie's house in silence. When the car stopped, Jackie didn't move to get out.

"Do you need help?" I asked.

"I didn't..." She hiccuped. "I really didn't want to do this."

"Do what?"

"I've been so nice and patient with you about this whole thing, but I'm not going to put up with it anymore." She wiped the tears from her eyes. The sadness in her face was replaced with a cold, heartless expression.

"What are you talking about?"

"I could report him, you know." Her eyes narrowed in on mine. "I could call that hotline and make him go away." Her voice cracked just a tiny bit, but I didn't buy that it was real for one second. "But I don't want to do that."

"What are you saying?" My chest tightened so hard, I could barely breathe. There was no way she was implying what I thought she was.

"You know what I'm saying, Kenny. Break up with him. I don't want to have to escalate the situation, but I will."

"Are you fucking kidding me?" I was shouting now. How dare she? I had never even told her Han was undocumented. Maybe she was just bluffing? I could bluff, too. "He's a citizen. What would that even do?"

"I'm not stupid, Kenny. He's a fucking illegal."

"We have an immigration lawyer. He's getting his green card. You can't touch him."

"How do you think that'll go if I open my mouth about how you wanted to marry me right before you proposed to Han? How is it gonna go over if I tell them you're only marrying him so he can get his green card?"

"I'm not, Jackie, I swear!" Did she know? How could she know?

"It doesn't matter. You need to break it off. He can get his green card *legally*—"

"You know it's not that simple, Jackie!" I shouted.

"—*or*, I can tell them all about your lies."

"You wouldn't" was all I could bring myself to say.

She got out her phone and started dialing. I grabbed it out of her hand. She actually had the immigration and customs enforcement number saved to her contacts. How long had she been planning this?

"Break up with him, and I won't," she said, her words slurring together. I couldn't bet Han's citizenship on the fact that it was just a drunk threat and not a real one. She had the number saved.

"You know how fucked up this is, right?"

"Well, what else am I supposed to do? I told you already, this baby needs two parents. Two parents who are *together*! I don't want this kid to be split into two homes like I was. *We* should be the ones getting married, not you and Han! You really left me no choice here. So...you have to leave him. I need him out of the picture so we can raise this baby right."

I punched my steering wheel.

"Oh, come *on*, I'm not asking for anything unreasonable here. We could have a stable, happy life together. I still love you, you know. And I know you still love me. That kind of love doesn't just go away overnight." She reached for my hand, but I yanked it away.

"Don't—" I started, before deciding not to piss her off. "I'll break it off, okay?" I said. "Now, will you please get out of my car."

"Kenny, I have no other options!"

"Just leave me the fuck alone!" I cried, tears streaking down my face for the second time that night.

Jackie sighed. "You'll understand eventually." She grabbed her phone out of my hand and got out of the car, slamming the door shut.

I drove home with a lead foot, much faster than the speed limit. I wished I could have a do-over on this whole night. I couldn't break up with Han...but I couldn't let Jackie report him, either. Instead of going inside, I pulled into my parking spot and started sobbing.

CHAPTER THIRTY-ONE

HAN

I woke up with the biggest smile on my face. I felt like I could take on the world. But when I rolled over, Kenny wasn't in bed anymore. I rolled onto my back and sighed, still unable to wipe the smile from my mouth. I was a bit of a blanket hog, so maybe that's why Kenny had left.

I hugged my sheets, pressing them against my face. I felt like if I didn't grab on to something tight, I'd just float away, but I needed to stay grounded. For once, I wanted to be exactly where I was. Life was good.

When I moved to get out of bed, I realized I'd left my crutches in the living room by the couch, but that couldn't ruin my morning. Nothing could. I didn't even care that I had to go back to work today for a ten-hour shift where I'd be working on one foot. Well, I cared, but I was somehow more concerned about having to leave Kenny than having to work with a sprained ankle. What the hell was my problem? I couldn't find a fuck to give. I was *happy*.

Daniel had me scheduled for the late shift today, and since I didn't have to go to work yet, I took my time in the comfort of my bed. After a while, I decided I'd rather be with Kenny than in bed. I got up and hopped my way to the door, then to the living room, where one of my crutches was lying on the ground. Kenny was sitting on the couch drinking coffee. There was an extra mug for me on the coffee table, like always.

"Thanks, babe," I said, feeling a sense of freedom at using the nickname without witnesses or alcohol to coax it out of me. But Kenny didn't smile at the term like he had the night before.

"Are you riding home with Tatiana after work, or should I get you?" was all he said.

"We get off at the same time, so I'll just ride with Tatiana. But, um, you okay?"

Kenny just shook his head. "I don't know...I have to go lie down. I'll get up to take you to work," Kenny said, then got up and left without another word. I wondered again if I'd done something wrong.

A sense of dread washed over me as realization hit. Kenny must have been having regrets about the night before. Serious regrets. Sure, we were drunk, but it had still felt genuine to me. Maybe for Kenny it was different. Maybe it was just a drunken mistake. Embarrassment heated my cheeks, and my chest sank at the rejection.

I wasn't usually the one to want to talk things through, and today was no exception. I just sat on the couch watching *The Great British Bake Off*, but I was completely in my own head the whole time. Maybe if I didn't address it, it would just go away. I could pretend like last night hadn't happened. We could go back to being best friends and go through the wedding the way we had originally planned. It wouldn't be too bad. It wasn't like

I didn't enjoy being Kenny's friend. I *loved* being Kenny's friend. I could go back to that. I'd be happy to go back to that if it meant nothing else had to change between us. I only hoped he could write it off as a drunken mistake and not read too much into it, since he obviously didn't feel the same way.

But he didn't come out of his room until it was time for me to go to work. We had to leave a little earlier than usual, since it would take me a while to get down the stairs on my crutches. Pretty much the only conversation I got out of Kenny was him offering to hold my crutches while I used the railings to hop down, which was now my go-to method. Much faster.

Kenny still didn't say anything during the car ride.

"We're cool, right?" I asked. I couldn't take not knowing.

"Yeah, we're cool," Kenny said, but it didn't sound like we were cool.

"You sure?"

Kenny didn't answer, just gripped the steering wheel with trembling hands.

"Look, man, we were drunk last night. Let's just pretend it didn't happen." It killed me to say it, but I would much rather erase the night before than lose the relationship I already had with Kenny.

He still didn't say anything. His hands were gripping the wheel so hard that his knuckles were losing their color, and the car was going way faster than the speed limit.

"Kenny, talk to me. What's going on?"

"Fuck!" Kenny shouted. At me? Kenny yelling at me was the last thing I would have expected. I shut my mouth and looked out the window, waiting for him to say whatever was on his mind. He finally let out a sigh. "After your shift, okay?"

"What?"

"I'll tell you everything when you get home tonight."

Before I could answer, I saw red and blue lights flashing in the side mirror out the window. We were being pulled over.

"Shit..." Kenny said. I couldn't breathe. I clutched my chest, feeling it rising and falling much faster than it should.

"Just be cool. It's all right, I'll probably just get a ticket. You'll be fine," Kenny said, his voice a lot softer than it was before. But there was fear in Kenny's eyes. That wasn't fear of getting a speeding ticket. The fact that Kenny was worried made me worry even more. I closed my eyes and focused on breathing. In. Out. If I was hyperventilating, I would look suspicious. In. Out.

The officer walked up to the driver's-side window, and Kenny lowered it. I put my hands on the dashboard where the cop could see them and stared forward.

"Morning, sir," Kenny said. I kept my eyes forward. I didn't want to make eye contact with the cop or I might cry.

"Do you have any idea why I pulled you over?" the officer asked.

"No, sir," Kenny said, sounding way too innocent. Kenny told me you're supposed to say no when a cop asks if you know why you're being pulled over. Anything else would be an admission of guilt they could use against you.

"You were going twenty miles over the speed limit."

"Oh, I'm sorry, sir," Kenny said. "It won't happen again, I promise."

"I'm going to need your registration and both of your licenses," the officer said.

"But he wasn't driving," Kenny snapped, a little too harshly.

The cop raised an eyebrow. "Is there a reason you can't show me your license?" he asked directly to me.

"I don't have a driver's license, sir," I said.

"Why do you need his identification?" Kenny asked. "He wasn't driving. Here, take mine. I'm getting my registration from the glove compartment, that all right?" Kenny waited for the officer to nod before moving. He reached across and pulled out his registration, then took his license from his wallet and handed it over. He slyly reached for his phone while he got his license and started recording.

"I'm still going to need ID on both of you," the officer said.

"Why do you need ID from someone who wasn't driving?" Kenny asked, and the cop sighed. I knew exactly why. Good ol' racial profiling.

"ID, or out of the vehicle."

I felt my heart banging against my chest. I had a fake ID I could use, but I'd never tested out its validity with a cop before. If he realized it was fake, I'd definitely be arrested. The cars on the highway were already slowing down to get a good look.

Great. I would have an eager audience when it happened.

"I'm sorry, sir. I have my ID. I'll give it to you," I said, hoping to God the fake ID would be passable.

"All right, hand it over."

I focused on breathing steadily while I reached for my wallet, pulling out my fake and handing it over.

Kenny kept recording, but the screeching of wheels scraping against the highway stole his attention as a car in the lane next to us rear-ended a white Expedition, which had slowed almost to a stop to get a peek at the "show." The cop sighed. He glanced at our IDs, then at Kenny's phone, where he was being recorded. Then he handed them back to Kenny.

"I'll let you off with a warning this time."

"Thank you, sir," I said.

Kenny waited for the cop to pull over whoever rear-ended

the Expedition before he drove away. But even after we started moving again, I couldn't relax. No matter how much I focused, my breath came out ragged and quick, like I couldn't take in enough air.

"Hey, it's okay Han. It's over now," Kenny said, voice much softer than before.

"Did you have to agitate him?" I snapped, knowing I wasn't really being fair.

"I was trying to help," Kenny said, and I knew it was true. Kenny had just been trying to protect me. Still, though, he'd been snippy, and that no doubt contributed to why the cop kept insisting. If there hadn't been an accident, who knew what would have happened to me. I could have been taken to a detention center with no showers and barely any food for who knew how long. After all my years living in the States, I'd never come that close to getting caught. I felt tears pulling at my lashes, but they didn't fall. I blinked them back.

When we got to the restaurant, I rushed as quickly as I could on my crutches. When I got inside to clock in, seeing the time made me panic even more. I was fifteen minutes late.

Luckily, Daniel didn't seem to notice, or at least he didn't say anything. I powered all the way through the dinner rush without confrontation. The pain in my foot was a good distraction from the cop this morning and from my anxiety that Daniel might call me out for being late. I worked through the pain until closing time at midnight, when he finally called me into his office.

"What's up?" I said as I awkwardly sat down in the office chair. Not really knowing what to do with the crutches, I just laid them on the floor.

"I noticed you clocked in late today. What was that about?"

Dammit. So he had noticed. "Kenny and I got pulled over on our way here. We got here as soon as we could."

"You know I have a no-tolerance policy for unexcused tardiness and absences."

My breath caught in my throat, and it was hard to get the next words out. "I'm sorry, sir. I haven't been late once since I've been here. I can stay late to make up for the time I missed, or work through my break. Whatever you need. I swear it won't happen again."

"You're damn right it won't happen again."

I nodded. "I won't let you down."

Daniel gave an exasperated sigh. "No, I mean, I can literally guarantee it won't happen again."

"What do you mean?" I shifted in my seat.

"I mean you're fired, Alejandro."

CHAPTER THIRTY-TWO

KENNY

I meant to tell Han everything earlier, but how could I? There was no way I could have sent him to work stressing about it, and then after getting pulled over? Forget it. Han was already so messed up as it was. All I'd wanted to do was hug him and tell him it was going to be all right, but my guilt wouldn't let me. I knew I would have to break things off when he came home from work. I just didn't know where things would go from there.

There was no way Han would ever forgive me for this. Even if I was open about the reasoning, I knew Han would be completely broken up about it. He didn't give his trust out very easily. It had taken me a lifetime to earn it, and I was about to throw it all away. But I had to, or he would go through a lot worse than getting asked for his ID. I couldn't let that happen. I wouldn't let Jackie report him, no matter what.

I sat at the couch with my head between my knees, trying to figure out how I was going to break the news. My first instinct was to call *Han* and ask for advice. But obviously I couldn't do that this time. This was a problem I had to solve on my own. I'd already hurt Han enough.

My phone rang. Jackie. I couldn't answer it. If I had to hear her voice right now, I'd absolutely lose it. I forwarded her to voicemail, but I knew I had to text her. I couldn't risk pissing her off when she was holding Han's freedom hostage.

Kenny: I'm breaking it off today.

I tossed my phone onto the carpet next to the couch so I wouldn't have to see it. I didn't want to know what she would say to that.

A little after midnight, the sound of keys in the front door shook me out of my thoughts. Han came in, and I braced myself for what I needed to tell him. "How was work?" I asked, no idea how to ease into the conversation.

"I got fired for being late," Han said without making eye contact.

"Oh, fuck, Han. I'm so fucking sorry. I'll talk to Daniel, let him know it was my fault."

"Okay. Thanks," Han mumbled as he closed the door.

I felt like the fucking scum of the earth. How was I supposed to break up with him now? He'd just been fired, because of me. He'd just had a terrifying interaction with a cop, because of *me*. How could I possibly make this day even worse, on purpose? I was definitely a terrible person. Han would never forgive me, but all I could think was that a grudge was better than him getting deported.

"We really need to talk." I forced the words out of my mouth.

"I know. Can we please just pretend like last night never happened? I don't want it to change things," Han pleaded, and I blinked back my emotions. I couldn't do this. But I had to. At least knowing that he didn't want to act on our feelings from the night before helped. It meant he wouldn't be heartbroken and backstabbed all at once.

"Han, please, just, let me get this out," I said. I would never be able to do this if he said another word. I felt too terrible about it, and anything Han said might have made me not go through with it. But I had to.

"What is it?"

"I . . ." I let out a shaky breath. I debated whether I should be totally up front with him about Jackie's threat. She'd told me not to tell anyone, but I couldn't just let Han think I was dumping him after what happened last night. He deserved to know. It wasn't like Jackie would ever find out if I told him. I could do this. "It's Jackie. She—"

"You're getting back together." Han clenched his jaw.

I ran a hand through my hair. "It's actually worse than that."

"Stop dancing around it. Just *tell* me."

I choked up, and a small whimper came out of my mouth as I covered it with my hand. "She threatened to call ICE if I didn't break up with you . . . I . . . I'm so sorry. We can't get married." Tears started spilling out of my eyes, but Han stood there, seemingly emotionless if it weren't for the slight tremble of his chin.

"You told her I'm undocumented."

"No! She just guessed." I wondered if maybe my mom let it slip, but that wasn't possible. She didn't even like Jackie. She wouldn't go gossiping with her. Maybe it was Han's reaction to the time she tried to bring up ICE to him that tipped her off. Or maybe it was just plain old racism. Whatever it was, it didn't matter. I couldn't risk *him*. "I'm so, so sorry."

Han was silent for a while, clenching his jaw hard, but his lips still trembled.

Then it happened. He burst out crying in a way I had never seen before. Not drunk blubbering-crying, but real, grief-stricken sobbing. He dropped one of his crutches to cover his face with his hand as he whimpered into it.

"I'm sorry. I'm so, so sorry." I went over to Han to try to comfort him and put a hand on his shoulder, which only made him cry harder.

"I have to move out now, don't I?" Han asked, his voice raw and strangled.

I hadn't actually thought about that, but it was true. Jackie probably wouldn't accept our breakup if we were still living together. "One of us should. I'm sorry..." was all I managed to say. What else could I possibly say?

"I don't have a job anymore, so I guess it should be me," Han said, wiping his cheeks with the back of his hand.

I couldn't hold myself back. I pulled Han into a desperate embrace. Then we were both sobbing. "I'm sorry. I'm sorry..."

It was a while before Han calmed down enough to breathe properly. He finally pulled away from the embrace and struggled to bend down and pick up his crutches off the floor. I grabbed them and handed them over to save him the trouble.

"It's not your fault," he finally said, voice broken. But the words didn't make me feel any better. Han turned around and reached for the door.

"You're leaving already?" I asked. I had kind of hoped we could spend a little longer together. I felt like Han was slipping through my fingers right before my eyes. "Why don't we just wait until morning?"

He shook his head. "I just can't be here right now."

"At least let me drive you. Please?"

Han nodded, wiping his eyes with the back of his hand. "Okay."

We made the drive to Han's tíos' house in excruciating silence. All I wanted to do was turn the car around and take back our breakup, but I couldn't. Instead of pulling up to the driveway, I took the long way through the dirt alley to the back of the house. Since it was so late, Han didn't want to wake anyone up by knocking, and his tíos left a spare key in a potted plant in the carport. When I pulled up behind the house, Han put his hand on the door handle but hesitated to open it. He stayed frozen like that for a moment before quickly turning around and throwing his arms around me. I wrapped mine around him, rubbing his back.

"It's gonna be okay," I said, even though it really, really wasn't.

We sat there holding each other, letting out all the tears, holding off having to separate as long as we possibly could. Instead of pulling apart, Han loosened his grip and pressed his forehead against mine, closing his eyes and pushing out a couple of stray tears. I cupped his cheeks in my hands.

"I love you so much," I managed to say.

Han opened his eyes and looked into mine. "I love you, too."

And I knew I shouldn't do it, not now, but this would possibly be my last chance ever. Still, I wanted to make sure Han wanted me to.

"Kiss me?" I asked, my gaze not leaving Han's. "One last time."

Han put a hand over mine, which was still cupping his cheek. He slowly leaned forward and pressed our lips together. It was the softest kiss of my life. The saddest. As we kissed, our tears blurred together, and I wasn't sure whose they were anymore, but it didn't matter.

I was afraid to stop kissing him. If I stopped, we'd have to say goodbye. So I didn't stop, and neither did Han. It was like there was an unspoken understanding between us that once we stopped, this was really over. Jackie may have taken everything from us, but she couldn't take this moment. She couldn't make us say goodbye before we were ready.

I unbuckled my seat belt as the kiss grew deeper and more desperate. I needed to be closer. Han seemed to be on the same page, because he started climbing into the back seat. I followed eagerly. I leaned against the back door, and we held each other tight, our lips taking each other in fervently, not daring to part. His mouth slowly traveled down my neck, and I could feel my pulse softly drumming against his lips. He pulled away to tug his shirt off over his head, and I did the same. His hands rested on my chest while mine found the small of his back. He tenderly planted soft, wet kisses on my mouth, neck, collarbone.

When he finally came up for air, I noticed Han's eyes found my backpack. I'd forgotten to take it out of my back seat last night, but that was the opposite of a problem right now. Han looked at me with the question in his gaze.

I glanced over at the bag. "Do you want to—"

"Yes," he answered immediately.

He gave me a little space so I could unzip the backpack. I pulled out the box of condoms, and both me and Han reached inside, our fingers brushing together inside the box before we both froze. I hadn't even thought about how this part would work. I was a verse, but of course Han had only ever been the one wearing the condoms. He'd said he was a sub, but that didn't mean he was a bottom.

"Oh . . . I . . ." Han started.

"Do you want to . . . ?" I asked.

"I, um . . . I guess I don't really know how to do this," Han admitted, pulling a condom out of the box and staring at it thoughtfully. "I mean, I've done anal before, but I was always the one wearing the condoms, you know? I don't know if I'm ready to . . ."

"It's okay, Han," I said softly, giving him a kiss on the cheek before taking off my pants and discarding them on the car floor. I was no stranger to anal, whether it was sticking it in or being pegged, so I figured Han would be more comfortable wearing the condom this time.

He looked down at the condom, then up at me intensely. "Do you trust me?"

"More than anyone," I said as I pulled the lube out of the bag and handed it to Han while he unwrapped the condom and slipped it on through his unzipped jeans. Maybe it wasn't the ideal way for us to have sex for the first (and last) time, but it didn't matter. Nothing mattered to me in this moment except Han.

We hungrily pressed our lips against each other, our tongues slowly slipping into rhythm. We held on to each other tight until I found myself lying against the seats. Han kissed a soft spot by my knee, trailing his kisses lower down my thigh until he was between my legs. I ran one of my hands through his hair as he kissed me again and again.

I sucked in a breath when he finally took my penis in his mouth, his tongue circling the tip before pushing it slowly to the back of his throat. I let out a soft moan when his throat wrapped around my cock. His fingers, wet with lube, massaged my hole as he continued sucking. Then, just when he took me in his throat again, he slipped a finger inside me, then two. His mouth and fingers were warm.

A third finger found its way in, stretching me just enough that I was aching for more. For *him*.

He slowly, *painfully* slowly, ran his mouth up the base of my cock until he was at the tip. His tongue worked its way around two more times before he looked up at me and climbed forward, withdrawing his fingers so he could get on top. He kissed me as he lowered himself down so our bodies were completely pressed together. We held on as tight as we possibly could, because if we didn't, I was afraid he would slip right through my fingers. He was going to leave, but not yet.

This was going to end, but not yet.

"Han, *please*," I practically whimpered as I wrapped my legs around him tight.

He finally obliged. I gasped for air as he eased inside me, one hand sliding up and down my shaft. He moved slowly at first, as if he was afraid he might break me if he moved too quickly. I hoped against hope that we would never have to stop. Once we stopped, we'd have to say goodbye. Once we stopped, it was really over. But for now, I had Han, and Han had me.

"You feel so good," I let out through ragged breaths.

The praise seemed to awaken something in Han, because he let out a soft moan and started pushing himself in farther, harder. He tried slightly different angles until he hit that spot just right. Waves of pleasure racked through me as he pounded into me again and again and again.

"Right there!" I reassured him, and he took the hint, hitting the same spot again and again.

"I'm gonna come," Han said breathlessly.

Then it was like everything I had pent up was begging to burst out of me. All the pressure, the heartache, the anger, the grief and devastation. All the bad things. I couldn't hold it in any longer.

I let out a helpless cry as it all spilled out of me.

Han collapsed on top of me, and we both sobbed in each other's arms.

There was no avoiding it now. It was over.

It was all over.

CHAPTER THIRTY-THREE

HAN

Watching Kenny drive down the alley and turn the corner was the hardest thing I'd ever had to do. It was really over now. At least we'd said a hell of a goodbye.

I took my time before even looking for the spare key to figure out what the hell to tell everyone. I sent the family a group text saying I'd be coming over so they wouldn't think someone was breaking in. I knew as soon as they woke up, Tía Mary and Mariana would ask a million questions I wouldn't be able to answer. And just the thought of being asked about the breakup made me want to burst out crying all over again.

I waited until Kenny's car was long gone before finally grabbing the key from under a plant and unlocking the back door. I quietly made my way through the laundry room and into the living room, where I was surprised to see Tío Nacho still awake on his recliner watching TV. He must have seen my text and waited for me. He stood up when I came inside, quickly making his way across the room to meet me.

I felt my lip start to quiver as my tío stared curiously into my eyes, surely wondering what brought me here and why I looked like I'd been crying.

"Kenny and I . . ." I started, but I couldn't finish that sentence. Instead I covered my mouth as even more tears flowed out. It was like all the tears I'd held in over the years found their opening. Nacho immediately pulled me into a firm hug without asking any questions.

"You can stay here. You can stay here," Nacho repeated as he gave my shaking shoulders a reassuring pat before pulling away.

"I'll tell everyone not to ask," Nacho reassured me. "Will you be okay on the couch? We got rid of the extra bed in Leti's room a while ago."

I nodded. Growing up, Leti and I shared a room, but I didn't exactly want to intrude on them that way now in the middle of the night, even if I did still have my old bed. I was grateful to at least have somewhere to go.

"I'll give you some privacy for the night, then, mijo," he said as he gave me one more quick hug before turning off the TV and disappearing down the hallway.

As soon as the coast was clear, I let myself fall onto the couch for the night. When I'd left the apartment, I hadn't even thought to stop and pack some clothes or any of my stuff. I just needed to get out of there. I even left without Luna. I made a mental note to go back for Luna and my things the next day. It'd probably be best to do it while Kenny was working, so I wouldn't have to see him again.

For now, I fell asleep in my work clothes from the job I no longer had, in a house that was no longer mine.

* * *

I woke up what felt like moments later to the sound of people shuffling and the smell of bacon grease wafting through the air from the kitchen. It was already morning. I stretched out and breathed in the smell for a while, but despite how hungry I was, I wasn't ready to get up anytime soon.

As soon as she realized I was conscious, Tía Mary stopped ironing clothes and rushed over to me, pulling me into a seated position so she could hug me.

"If you need anything. To talk. To hang out. Anything, just tell us, okay? We know how hard this time is for you." I knew she was talking about my mom, but Tía Mary had no idea how right she was. All in one day, I thought I was going to be detained, I got fired, and Kenny broke off the wedding. Not to mention I had a broken ankle. I was having more than just a hard time.

I couldn't bring myself to tell her I was okay, so instead I just nodded and let her get back to her chores.

"Adiós, Mateo!" Nacho said in his baby voice. He was in his full mariachi gear, getting ready to leave for a gig as he waved goodbye to Mateo, who was sitting in Mariana's lap at the stool by the counter. Leti, I assumed, was sleeping in as usual. "Don't you have work, too, Alejandro?"

"Got fired." I said it as emotionlessly as I could so no one would feel too bad for me.

"What happened?" Tía Mary gasped from the kitchen, where she was using the part of the counter Mariana wasn't eating on to iron.

"How long do you need to stay for?" Mariana asked.

"I don't wanna get into that. And I . . . don't know." I felt heat spring into my chest. I needed some time to decompress before thinking about getting a new job. I didn't want to think about how long I needed yet, even though I knew it wasn't fair to the family.

"Tch!" Tía Mary waved Mariana's question away, "You can stay here as long as you need, okay, mijo?"

"Thanks, Tía," I said.

"If you need work, mijo, you can join the band!" Nacho didn't even turn around to see my reaction as he grabbed his keys. He must have known it was going to be a hard no, as usual.

I just groaned and closed my eyes, rolling over on the couch so I was facing the wall with the couch pillow hugged in my arms.

I must have lain like that for hours before Leti finally woke up and came out to the living room. They greeted me by pushing my legs off the couch, forcing me to sit up.

"Uy!" I hissed at the forgotten ache in my ankle. "You could just ask me to move instead of all the manhandling." I forced a laugh. I could always count on Leti not to treat me like I was delicate and breakable no matter what I was going through. I appreciated that about them.

"You wouldn't have moved," Leti said, handing me a plate of bacon and eggs, then putting another plate in their lap.

It was probably true. I was too physically and emotionally drained to move on my own right now. I could have used another couple of hours of wallowing. But I couldn't exactly demand time to sulk while I was on the living room couch in a house full of people. I picked up a piece of now-microwaved bacon and took a bite. It wasn't as good as it would have been fresh, but I appreciated the free meal.

"You still good to babysit?" Mariana asked Leti while she and Tía Mary got their bags before carpooling to work.

"Yup!" Leti shoveled the rest of the food in their mouth, then reached out their arms for Mateo to come. He happily waddled over to Leti, and they picked him up and held him in their lap. "You down to help me babysit?" Leti asked me.

I checked my phone. I still had another couple of hours before Kenny would be leaving for work and I'd have a chance to go get my stuff.

I guessed it would be nice to feel useful now that I was out of a job, so I agreed. It was a good way to help pass the time, but every time Leti went to the bathroom or went to make some food for Mateo, leaving me alone with him, it made me want to cry for some reason. I wondered if Kenny would be okay raising his baby with Jackie. I wanted to be mad at him and not care, but how could I? This whole thing was Jackie's fault, not Kenny's. I just wished there was a way I could still help with the baby, but I knew there wasn't. I didn't even know if I'd be allowed anywhere near Kenny anymore without Jackie making good on her threat.

I couldn't believe one person had the power to completely ruin everything for me. Not only could I not be with Kenny anymore, but I couldn't even get my green card. Jackie could hold that threat over me for the rest of my life, and there was nothing I could do about it.

I wished I had my laptop so I could write to my mom. But then, that might have just made me even more depressed.

I thought about channeling a jellyfish again and going back to polyp, but right now it was my mom who I wished was more like a jellyfish. If she could live forever like a jellyfish, maybe we'd have time to make things right. Maybe I'd have time to actually send her one of the many letters I'd written over the years. I hadn't written one of those letters since before she died.

Still, though...some part of me felt like I needed to write

one more. Just to find some kind of closure about everything. Since I didn't have my laptop, I went into the supply closet and grabbed an ancient half-used notebook and a pencil. I sat back down on the couch, hunched over the paper on the coffee table for several minutes before I could bring myself to write a single word, but once the first one came, the rest followed quickly. I wasn't writing to the made-up mom in my head this time. I was writing to *her*.

Dear Mami . . .

I feel like I have no right to be mad, but I am. I know your addiction wasn't your fault. I know you tried to fight it. And I'm sorry I couldn't be there for you to help you through it.
  But I'm mad.
  I'm mad we didn't have more time. I'm mad we didn't talk more while you were still here. I'm mad that you were never there for me, and I'm even more mad I wasn't for you.
  But even after everything you did or didn't do, there's one thing I want to thank you for. Thank you for sending me to Tía Mary and Tío Nacho. You knew you couldn't take care of me, but you made sure I was taken care of. If that was all you could have done for me, it was enough.
  Thank you.
  And I'm sorry.

                                                    Love,
                                                    Han

I stared at the letter for a while and let out a sad sigh. But Leti came back from the bathroom soon enough, banishing any thoughts of Kenny and my mom from my mind. It was already way past time for Kenny to head to work, so I started getting ready to go myself. I didn't really have much getting ready to do, considering all I had to wear were my work clothes from the day before.

I decided to just use one crutch today, that way I'd be able to roll a suitcase full of stuff and walk at the same time. Hopefully I'd be able to make that work. The suitcase was at my— Kenny's—apartment, so I would just pick it up when I got there.

"You sure you don't wanna wait till Mariana gets home so I can go with you?" Leti asked.

"Nah, I want to go while he's still working."

I called an Uber, since it was way too far to walk on crutches. Once I got to the apartment, I rushed out of the car. I wanted to get this over with as soon as possible.

It took me a while to make my way up the stairs with my one crutch, and I absolutely dreaded having to come back down with a suitcase in tow—I'd probably have to sit on my ass and slide down the steps one at a time—but I'd think about that later. I stuck my key in the lock and opened the door, then made eye contact with the exact person I was trying to avoid. Kenny sat on the couch in front of the TV with a deer-in-the-headlights look. He was bundled up in a blanket, hugging Thornelius in his arms like a pillow. His eyes were puffy, and his cheeks and nose were red. He'd clearly been crying.

Luna greeted me first, wagging her tail excitely like she had no idea how fucked this all was.

"Han?"

"Sorry, I thought you'd be working," I muttered as I leaned forward to pet Luna. Anything to avoid looking at him.

"Yeah, I called in." Kenny had this puppy-dog look as he

stared at me. I hated how hearing that he called in made me so angry. I was less than twenty minutes late to work and got fired, while Kenny could just call off anytime he wanted. It was such bullshit.

"I'm just here for Luna and my shit," I said, and it came out colder than Kenny deserved. I knew none of this was his fault, but that didn't make it any easier to have to see him. We'd said our goodbyes yesterday, and it was easier if we just ended things there. A clean break.

"I was gonna bring your stuff to you. I already got it all together," Kenny said, wiping his nose. "I'll help you take it down."

I sighed. I really didn't know how I was going to get all my stuff back downstairs, so no matter how shitty I felt seeing Kenny, I had to admit it made things easier. "Okay."

Kenny walked over to my room and came out a few moments later with my suitcase and a few other items. He looked at Luna like he wanted to scoop her up in a hug but stopped himself. His lip quivered just a bit, and he sniffled and wiped his nose again. "I'll get her leash."

Guilt wrapped around my throat at the thought of taking Luna away from Kenny. Yes, she was my dog, but he was clearly her favorite. Was it even fair to take her away from her home and her favorite person? Luna couldn't understand what was happening, but I knew deep down if she had to choose between me and Kenny, she'd choose Kenny. She'd be happier with him.

"Goddammit," I let out a frustrated breath. "There's no room for Luna at my tíos' house. I'll leave her here, for now."

Kenny looked up at me, eyes big and teary and confused. He wiped them and nodded, his voice shaky. "Thank you, Han."

He opened the door for me, then started lugging the bag down the stairs while I followed.

"I can drive you back?" Kenny asked, a hopeful gleam in his eye.

I wanted to say yes so badly. Wanted to spend just a little more time with him. But I couldn't. I needed to accept the fact that this was over, and so did Kenny. We couldn't be seen together.

"I'll just get an Uber." I grabbed the suitcase when we got to the bottom of the steps. I struggled to drag the suitcase to the curb while hopping with the crutch under my other arm.

"Can I at least pay for the ride?" Kenny asked.

"You can't fix this!" I snapped, and the hurt look on Kenny's face broke me. But I couldn't be feeling sorry for him right now. I needed to focus on me. I'd gotten through my whole life up to this point, and I would get through this, too.

But I hadn't gotten through a damn thing without Kenny by my side.

"Can you please just go?" I said, trying to keep my voice steady, but it was betraying me.

Kenny stared at me a moment longer with tears in his eyes. I wanted to pull him close and wipe them away. But without another word, he turned and ran up the stairs, leaving me alone on the curb.

CHAPTER THIRTY-FOUR

KENNY

I hadn't eaten since Han left last night. The only things in the fridge were a tub of ice cream and the last slice of pizza from the party, which I couldn't bring myself to eat. The last slice was for Han. The last slice was always supposed to be for Han.

You can't fix this!

Han's words echoed in my mind long after he'd left with his things. No matter what I did or said from here on out, it couldn't make up for the fact that I'd completely betrayed the most important person to me in the whole world. Even if it was Jackie who'd done the blackmailing, I couldn't help but feel responsible. I was the one who set up the whole fake marriage idea and got Han's hopes up in the first place.

But there had to be *something* I could do, right? I found myself wandering into Han's room, looking for something that maybe I'd forgotten to pack so I could bring it to him later, even though it wasn't like I could fit much more than clothes and his laptop and chargers into a suitcase. My eyes went straight for Han's desk, where his laptop usually was. Of course, that was one of the first things I'd packed for him, but it felt so weird not being able to leave him a little sticky note right now. This wasn't something my shitty drawings of red pandas could fix.

Still, I went to the hall closet looking for a sticky note anyway. Maybe I would feel better if I just pretended like everything was normal. Han would never see this note, but I still felt like I needed to write one. But I opened the closet to find I'd already used the last one.

Han must have had some in his desk, though, right? I went back to Han's room and opened the top drawer on his desk.

A sort of half whimper, half laugh escaped my mouth. There were sticky notes in here, all right. But they weren't fresh ones. I'd always thought Han had just thrown away my stickies after he'd found them, but this drawer was practically overflowing.

He'd kept them. All of them.

But I couldn't bear to look. I shut the desk drawer faster than I'd opened it. Whatever light feeling I got from seeing that Han had kept my notes came crashing down with the realization that I'd never be able to give him another one again.

I made my way back to the living room like a zombie. How could this possibly be my life? I knew I should have been working, but I couldn't bring myself to go in. Instead, I sat bundled up in a blanket burrito on the living room couch, hugging a tub of chocolate ice cream in one arm and Thornelius in the other. I had Luna cuddled in my lap while I watched *Coco* and cried my eyes out. It felt so off watching this movie without Han, but Han's favorite movie was the only thing that could bring me even an ounce of comfort right now. My phone buzzed, and I scrambled for it, almost dropping the ice cream to the ground in my frantic search.

My heart sank when I saw it wasn't Han's name displayed across the screen. I knew the chances of him calling were low, but I wanted to talk to him so badly.

Jackie again.

I had to resist the urge to throw my phone across the room. I hated her so much. She had always been terrible, even if it took me way too long to realize it, but she'd gone too far this time. And worst of all, I hated that I couldn't ignore her now, because if I pissed her off, I could risk her making good on her threat against Han, even though we'd already broken up.

"What do you want?" I asked, unable to mask the disgust in my voice.

"You should come over. I miss you . . ."

I had to take a deep breath before saying anything so I wouldn't blow up on her. "Jackie, I *just* broke things off with Han. I need time. I'm not exactly thrilled to hang out with you after what you did."

There was a long silence over the phone before she finally responded. "Do you hate me now?" Her voice was all choked up, and it just made me angrier.

I wanted so badly to shout YES! Of course I hated her. What else would she expect? But I was afraid if I said that, she would retaliate.

"I need time. Please just leave me alone for a while."

Instead of responding, she hung up on me. Thank God. I pressed play on the movie and shoved another giant spoonful of ice cream into my mouth.

Before I got too far into it, my phone rang again.

"Go to hell, Jackie!" I shouted before answering the phone,

but when I went to pick it up, I realized it was my mom calling. I took a deep breath before answering. I really needed to get my shit together for my mom.

"Hey, Mom." I tried to sound as okay as I possibly could.

"How are you?" she said.

"Um . . . good?" I answered hesitantly, not sure if I wanted to tell her about the breakup just yet. Besides, my parents usually had a reason for calling.

"Listen, if you ever need anything . . ."

Then there was a brief shuffling sound, and my dad's voice came through. "Mary told us about Han staying with the family. What's that about?"

Great. They already knew. So much for keeping it together. Just the mention of Han made my lip quiver.

"Tch!" More shuffling, then my mom again. "Did Han do something? Did he hurt you?"

"No!" I said defensively. I hated that even the mere thought of Han hurting me crossed her mind. Especially since no one ever really asked that about Jackie. Well, except for . . . "Han's perfect." My voice cracked. "This was all me."

"We're coming over."

"You don't have to—" But the call was already disconnected.

It wasn't long before my parents came knocking on my door. A sad smile was all I could manage to give them. If I was being honest, I felt embarrassed for daring to take their pity. There was no reason they should have been here, comforting *me*, when Han was the one who was wronged.

My mom looked around at the disheveled apartment, visibly biting her tongue as she slipped off her shoes by the door.

Her eyes caught the sink full of dirty dishes, which Han obviously didn't do before leaving after the shit I pulled. I knew I needed to do the dishes, but I just couldn't start. Couldn't do anything.

"Have you eaten yet today?" my mom asked.

"Does ice cream count?" I said, knowing what the answer would be.

"I'll make you something." My dad walked over to the kitchen and opened the fridge, then frowned. "Where's the food?"

My mom's eyes widened. "You don't have any groceries?"

"He doesn't have any groceries."

"What have you been eating?" She turned to me, not bothering to mask the look of concern on her face.

"Old pizza, from the looks of it," my dad said as he closed the refrigerator.

"From the party?" Her eyes got even bigger with concern. You'd think the pizza was weeks old by the look on her face, even though it'd only been a couple of days. "You can't live off leftover pizza."

"I know…" I hung my head, even more embarrassed now. I didn't ask for a lecture on the state of my fridge.

My mom seemed to soften up when I stopped meeting her gaze. "I'll be back, okay?" she said, then turned around and started putting her shoes back on.

"Where are you going?" I asked.

"To get you some groceries." Before I could protest, she was out the door.

Wow, my parents really weren't about to let me wallow, were they? I couldn't lie and say I didn't appreciate it, though. I had to admit I really didn't want to be alone in the apartment. Before they showed up, all I could think about was Han. How all I wanted to do was talk to him. To hug him. Kiss him. Take everything back. But I couldn't.

I plopped myself down on the couch, and my dad joined me.

"If it hurts to talk about it, we don't have to. We can just sit together."

I realized then how desperately I *did* want to talk about it. Tears started streaming down my face without my permission.

"I called off the wedding." The words brought a guttural sob out of me. I'd called off the wedding.

My dad started rubbing my back as the tears kept coming, waiting for me to say more. I wanted to tell him everything. About it being my fault Han got fired. My fault Han hurt his ankle. How Jackie had blackmailed me into calling off the wedding. But I was afraid if I told him, he'd try to get involved and Jackie might retaliate. I couldn't imagine my parents finding all this out and not getting involved. Maybe they'd blame me, too.

"It's all my fault" was all I managed to say.

We were silent for a while before my dad spoke up again. "Do you still want to get married?"

"Yes!" I sobbed. I could be honest about at least that. "But he's never gonna forgive me."

"Have you apologized?" he asked. "And I don't mean in the heat of the moment. Once you both calmed down, did you apologize sincerely?"

I wiped my nose. I hadn't spoken to Han since he came back for his things. I swallowed the lump in my throat as realization hit. "No, I didn't."

"Talk to him, then. Maybe he'll surprise you."

But what my dad didn't know was that an apology wouldn't mean a thing if we couldn't get married. Sure, if I apologized to Han, he would say it was fine. That it wasn't my fault. But forgiveness? I doubted it. It'd be more like denial. Denial that anything was wrong between us, but we'd be distant. We'd drift further and further apart until I eventually accepted my loss.

That fear was enough to keep me up at night.

The next morning, I ignored my Sunday cleaning alarm. Sunday, December first. The month Han and I were supposed to get married. There was no point in cleaning today. I felt like it would somehow be a betrayal. Han and I had established Sunday speed cleaning when we'd just moved in together. I would rather have a dirty apartment than have to clean alone for the first time since then. So, I stayed in bed, wallowing like the pathetic piece of shit I was.

As much as I wanted to, I knew I shouldn't call in to work two days in a row. I lay in my bed, hugging Luna as my alarm rang and rang. I hugged her harder instead of turning it off, and she licked my cheek, as if to reassure me that it would all be okay. Finally, I shut off the alarm and kissed Luna on her forehead. I still couldn't believe Han let her stay here with me, even if it was temporary. I didn't know what I would do without that dog. I felt like I'd lost everything, but at least I still had Luna and my parents.

I had half a mind to order pizza, just to make myself feel better. It was Sunday, after all. But I didn't deserve pizza. I didn't deserve any of the groceries my mom had gotten me, either. Instead, I went to work on an empty stomach.

I went through the motions at the restaurant but didn't bring my usual happy-go-lucky server charm. I knew my tips would suffer for it, but I couldn't bring myself to be cheery right now. I would never share a flirty workday with Han again. I might never share a workday with Han, period. It took all the self-control I had in me to keep from bursting out in tears in front of a customer.

"How's Han doing?" Julia asked when we were both grabbing plates from the kitchen. She sounded all concerned. "I heard he got fired. That's terrible."

I clenched my jaw. Han was probably doing worse than I was. What was I supposed to say? That I'd called off the wedding? That Han was homeless now? That I had no idea how he was doing, because he would never want to talk to me again?

"He's okay" was all I could bring myself to say.

Julia gave a solemn nod, like she knew there was more to it, but she didn't pry. Throughout the whole shift, people kept asking about Han. Everyone was worried about him.

As soon as my break came along, I knocked on Daniel's office door. I had to at least try to convince him to give Han his job back.

"Come in!" Daniel's muffled voice rang out from the other side of the door. I went inside the office, closing the door behind me before I sat down in the chair in front of Daniel's desk. "What's up, Kenny?"

"I wanted to talk to you about Han."

"What's done is done. I can't really do anything about it now."

"Just hear me out here. It was my fault he was late. I got pulled over while I was dropping him off."

"He should have prepared for that and left earlier," Daniel said without looking up from the papers in front of him. "Besides, I think we solved our little stealing problem. I've suspected it was Han for a while now. So, no need to double-count for missing money. I've got that covered now."

My face grew hot. "Are you serious? You can't just fire people on a hunch that you *think* they *might* be stealing! Han wouldn't do that! He needed his job too much. He was the best cook you've had since I've been here. He's shown you nothing but hard work. He didn't deserve to be fired and you know it."

"You're overstepping, Kenny. Unless you want to follow in your boyfriend's footsteps, I'd suggest you let it go."

Wow. Would Daniel really fire me for asking for Han's job back? Was that something I was willing to gamble on? An idea formed in my brain.

"That's discrimination."

Daniel rolled his eyes. "How is that discrimination?"

"You fire two queer people of color back to back, and you don't think that looks bad?"

Daniel finally met my eyes. I made sure to hold the gaze. It felt like a challenge, though I felt pretty confident I would win. Daniel wouldn't want to fire me after another server had just quit. He needed all the servers he had. Finally, Daniel shook his head. "Go home, Kenny. I'll *think* about calling Han. That's not a guarantee."

So much for him suspecting Han had been stealing money. I knew that had just been an excuse. "Thank you so much, Daniel. I really appreciate it! I'll work overtime, whatever you need."

"Yes, I was just about to suggest that. Now go. I have work to do," he said, shooing me away, as if he didn't want the conversation to last even as long as it already had.

I was happy to work as many hours as Daniel needed if it meant Han could get his job back. I had to do *something* to help him. I knew I'd never be able to fully make up for what I'd done—what Jackie had done—but I could at least ease some of Han's problems right now. Getting him his job back was a start.

CHAPTER THIRTY-FIVE

HAN

I was the only one in the family who wouldn't be able to go to the memorial service for my mom this week. My tíos, Mariana, Mateo, and Leti would all be leaving me alone in the house for a week while they went to my mother's memorial service in my hometown. The whole thing was so messed up, I couldn't think about it. While everyone else got their suitcases together and prepared for the road trip, I lay on the couch strumming my guitar.

Leti did their usual thing where they moved my legs so they could sit on the couch, but then set them back down on their lap once they were settled.

"I think I'm gonna stay here with you." They sighed.

I stopped strumming. "What? Why?"

"The fam over there isn't exactly thrilled about, you know...me."

Oh. I knew my grandparents and tíos over in Mexico were less supportive of the LGBT+ community than Tío Nacho and Tía Mary. If I were Leti, I guess I wouldn't really want to see them, either.

"What are you smiling for?" Leti asked, slapping my knee.

"Just glad I won't be the only one here." I knew it was selfish. But Leti being here was going to make things 99 percent less miserable.

"Yeah, that's the other reason I wanted to stay." Leti grinned. "Mexico would be so boring without you."

I laughed. I'd never thought of Xalapa as boring before. I had dreamed of going back to visit ever since I'd left. And I thought when I was marrying Kenny that I would finally be able to soon. But that wasn't going to happen anymore.

Maybe it was better if I just thought of it as boring.

I was pulled out of my thoughts by my buzzing phone, and the number for the immigration lawyer, Mr. Jones, displayed on the screen. I let it ring. There was no way I'd be able to afford that lawyer without Cedric's favor, and I assumed that with no wedding, that offer was off the table.

I sulked on the couch while everyone got ready to leave, but when all their suitcases were packed and ready to go, they didn't go out to the car. Instead, everyone gathered up in the living room, Mariana, Mateo, and Tía Mary all sitting on the couch with me, Leti and Nacho sitting on the floor.

I raised an eyebrow. "What's going on?"

Tío Nacho cleared his throat, then offered me a sad smile. "You look just like her, you know."

I forced a smile back. He used to tell me that all the time, but I always hated it. Every time someone told me I reminded them of my mom, it only made me want to distance myself from her further. I didn't want to end up like my mom. But now that she was gone, I found myself ashamed of those feelings.

"I thought we could all go around and tell some stories about her. As a celebration of her life," Tía Mary said, and I wanted to give her a hug. We were having our own little memorial, since I wouldn't be able to go with them.

"I'll go first," Mariana said, adjusting Mateo in her lap. "I *still* crave Tía Linda's arroz con leche. She used to let me help her make it whenever we went to visit. Ugh. It was amazing. She was such a good cook. And she always let me taste it first before serving the rest."

I felt a pang of jealousy at Mariana's words. She was five years older than me, and I had no memory of my mom's cooking. By the time I was old enough to remember, she'd given up cooking entirely. I didn't know the woman Mariana knew. Arroz con leche meant nothing to me, no matter how moving it was for Mariana.

"Ahh." Nacho sighed wistfully. "I've tried to learn how to make arroz con leche like Linda, but she must have had some secret recipe she never shared." He chuckled. "Have I ever told you all the story of how I chipped my tooth?" he asked, and we all shook our heads. "I tried to take turns with Linda playing with one of *my* model cars. When our mami told her to share *my* car with *me*, she threw it right in my face. My tooth's been chipped ever since." He gave a big belly laugh, as if that was somehow a *good* memory. "She's always known what she wanted and gone for it. No one could tell her anything." He wiped a bittersweet tear from his eye.

It went like that for a while. Everyone telling fun stories about my mom. Me, though? I was having trouble thinking of any stories I was fond of. I didn't have a lot of memories of her, and I hated that everyone else here seemed to, besides maybe Leti, since they were my age.

After every story, everyone would look at me like they expected me to share something, but no one dared to actually ask.

While Mary, Nacho, and Mariana all cried about their happy memories of my mom, I just sat there, jealous. Finally, when it became clear I wasn't going to say anything, they started wrapping up, hugging one another and me tightly before bringing everything outside.

I didn't get off the couch once as my tíos and Mariana all dragged their suitcases out to the truck. I knew I should have helped, but I couldn't bring myself to. I couldn't do much anyway with my ankle the way it was, but I was still trying to think of something—anything—nice to say.

I finally went out in just my shorts and socks to say my goodbyes, and the cool December air nipped at my skin. I hated watching my family leave me behind, but it was a little better than I imagined it. At least I'd have Leti here with me. We stood next to each other outside in the breeze, watching as the van drove off.

"She liked to sing," I found myself saying.

"What?" Leti asked.

"My mom. She liked to sing. She was good at it, too. She used to sing to me every night..." I trailed off. It made me wonder if maybe that was why Nacho always wanted me to sing with him in his band. Was it because of my mom?

Leti and I eventually went back inside and sat on the couch. I was in the mood to sing. Maybe for my mom, I wasn't sure. But when I picked up my guitar, all I found myself doing was ad-libbing about evil people whose only goals in life revolved around ruining mine. God, I hated Jackie so fucking much.

"So, are you gonna tell me what happened?" Leti cut in.

"What?" I stopped strumming.

"With Kenny, tonto."

Okay, so playing dumb wasn't a great way to avoid it. Obviously Leti would want to know what happened.

"Your fuck-Kenny's-ex songs are beautiful and all, but you know, if you want to actually talk about your fight with him, no one else is here. So, you can tell me."

"I'm fine," I said, even though I knew it wasn't convincing.

They stared at me, weighing my answer for a while, before standing and brushing their hands together. "All right, let's go."

"What?" I asked, keeping my fingers moving against the guitar strings.

"You haven't gotten off this couch to do anything but take a shit since you got here. We need to get you out of this house. Tatiana and I are going out tonight for Thirsty Thursday. Come with us. Get your mind off your fight with Kenny."

"I said I was fine."

"So act like it. Let's go out!"

I sighed. I really did want to do something other than mope around on the couch by myself. At the same time, though, I didn't want to do it *because* I was sad. Plus, I didn't want to ruin Leti and Tatiana's date by going as their third wheel. "I don't know if Tatiana would want me crashing your date."

"Oh, don't worry about that." Leti waved off my question. "Believe it or not, some people other than me actually care about your well-being and want you to have a good time."

I decided then that I could go just to have a good time. It didn't have to have anything to do with Kenny, or my mom.

"Drinks are on you, then," I said. I'd be broke soon without a job, and I didn't want to get broker any faster.

"Obviously." Leti winked. "Now, get your ass in the shower. You smell like pompis."

✳   ✳   ✳

After a shower and about an hour of Leti digging through all the clothes in my suitcase to find something decent enough for me to go out in, Tatiana showed up at the house. I grabbed the outfit Leti picked out for me and changed in the bathroom to give them their one moment alone for the night. Leti's outfit of choice: a nice pair of jeans, a short-sleeved blue button-up with the sleeves rolled, and a pair of their blue Old Skool Vans to match. Thank God we wore the same shoe size, so I could look halfway decent.

Getting shoes on was tough with my ankle the way it was. I kind of wished I could go out without a shoe on that foot, but Leti refused to entertain that idea. Once I got my outfit together, I splashed some water on my face and ran some pomade through my hair. For some reason, I agreed with Leti on one thing: I wanted to look good tonight. It wasn't like we were going to a fancy club or anything—we were just going to Leti's favorite bar—but still. I hadn't worn anything but basketball shorts and tank tops since I left the apartment and started staying here, and I was ready to branch out. What was the saying? If you looked good on the outside, you'll feel good on the inside? Cheesy, but it was worth a shot. Not like I could do anything else to change my situation.

"All right, let's go get that sad look off your face," Leti said as I came out the bathroom.

"I'm not sad." I rolled my eyes. I was *fine*.

"Good." Tatiana grinned as she pulled out a half-full bottle of Fireball from her bag. "Pregame?"

"Oh, hell yes! Drinks are expensive, and I'm paying for llorón over here." Leti pointed at me with their thumb as they went over to the kitchen. Tatiana followed, so I reluctantly did, too. I wasn't a fan of moving around on crutches, but I'd have to suck it up if we were going out. I was pretty sure there wouldn't be *too* much moving around—I'd do my best to just sit at the bar, alone if I had to—but I still had to be prepared, right?

Leti took out six shot glasses, and Tatiana carefully poured three of them with Fireball while Leti poured the rest with Coke.

"To Han," Leti said, holding up their glass. Tatiana held hers up, too, and both of them stared at me, waiting for me to follow.

I hesitated for a second before shrugging. What the hell. It felt kind of ridiculous, making a toast to myself, but hell if I didn't deserve *something* nice right now.

"To me." I chuckled as I clinked my glass with theirs and downed the spicy drink, immediately chasing it with Coke. I tried my best not to scrunch up my face when I took the shot. Fireball was a little strong for me, but it was better than nothing. I already felt my body relaxing, and I leaned more of my weight on the crutches instead of balancing on one foot. I was used to the crutches enough by now that I felt like being tipsy wouldn't be too much of a hazard anymore, so I gave myself permission to let loose.

"Okay, one more, and then let's go," Leti said, and this time Tatiana filled our glasses to the brim.

Before I knew better, I'd expected Leti's favorite bar to be a drag bar or at least a super-queer space, but no. Their favorite spot was just a regular old hole-in-the-wall, nothing fancy. They said it was because they liked the drinks, the prices were good, and that it was nice not running into anyone from the scene sometimes. For as extra and outgoing and dramatic and loud as Leti could be, sometimes they just wanted to be with a close circle and chill. They didn't always want to have to put on a show, and this regular old bar was a place they could go where none of the people they usually performed with would ever show up. I'd been here plenty of times with Leti, and I could definitely see why they liked it so much.

There was only one other person at the bar, which was kind of nice. It almost felt like we had it to ourselves. I had to admit, the dude looked vaguely familiar—white guy, blond hair, brown eyes—but I couldn't figure out how I knew him, so I brushed it off and sat down on one of the empty stools.

The place gave off a kind of old-school vibe, which I liked. The bar itself was made of brick with wooden barstools dotted around the rim. There was other seating around the room, too, but Leti always wanted to sit at the bar. Faster service, they said. The music was good, too. Lots of oldies: Destiny's Child, Ciara, Mariah Carey—that kind of vibe. And of course there was a dance floor that Leti would always drag me onto when they got way too drunk, but that obviously wouldn't be happening tonight.

"Hey, Dion," Leti said to the bartender when he came over to us. From what I understood, Dion was the bartender *and* the owner. He loved me and Leti, but especially Leti, since they were such a loyal patron.

"Leti!" he said in a low, friendly voice. "And Han! Good to see you, man. And I'm guessing you're Tati, right?" Dion asked, winking at Tatiana. "Leti told me all about you! Nice to finally put a face to the name. So what can I get you all to drink?"

"Do you trust me to pick a drink for you?" Leti asked Tatiana.

"Obviously." Tatiana grinned.

"Okay. We'll have three Blue Coconuts," Leti said, and Dion gave a thumbs-up as he got to work making the drinks.

"I never said I trusted you to pick *my* drink," I said under my breath, but I really couldn't complain, and I was too tipsy to care anyway. I actually liked the drink they picked and they knew it, even if my go-to was always something a bit simpler.

"I already know you trust me," Leti said with confidence, and I rolled my eyes.

Before we knew it, our drinks were ready. "We Belong Together" by Mariah Carey was playing in the background, and we all started singing along, arms around each other's shoulders, swaying side to side.

I sang my heart out, fueled by nostalgia and drunkenness, before it hit me like a punch in the gut how close to home the lyrics got. Then I sang harder, just to get the feeling out. Hell, I was drunk as hell at this point, so I couldn't have cared less who saw me crying about Kenny.

"Who else am I gonna lean on when times get rough?" I sang, shaking Leti by the shoulders. "Who, Leti?"

Leti pointed their thumbs at their chest with a huge grin.

"This guy!" they said, still swaying to the music. Leti was clearly as drunk as I was. They stood up and threw their arms around Tatiana's shoulders, then looked longingly over at the dance floor.

I sighed. I knew it would happen eventually; might as well give them permission. "Go ahead and dance. I'll be fine."

"Dance with us!" Tatiana said. I knew they weren't just forgetting about my ankle. Technically, I could have gone to the dance floor to get down with my crutches. I'd seen people do it before. But I was never that coordinated. Walking around was one thing, but with how drunk I was, dancing would just be tempting fate.

"Nah, I'm good. Y'all go have fun, though."

Leti held out a finger. "One dance," they slurred, and I shooed them away.

With them gone, I sipped my bright blue drink alone. Well, almost alone. There were a few more people now than when we'd gotten here. And that vaguely familiar guy was still sitting across the bar.

"I know you," I said, pointing a finger at him and squinting. "How do I know you?"

The guy downed the last of his drink before looking up at me. It looked like I might not have been the only one trying to drink my problems away. He got up from his stool and came over to sit next to me.

"You're Kenny's boyfriend," he said nonchalantly.

"No," I mumbled, finally admitting it was over to *someone*. Even if I didn't really know who. Then again, how did he know that?

"Sorry, *fiancé*." He raised his fingers to catch Dion's attention and asked for another drink.

"You want another, too?" Dion asked me, and I nodded and thanked him.

We were quiet while Dion made the drinks, but when he handed them to us, I finally spoke up.

"Ex-fiancé."

"Damn. I know your pain, man..." He took another swig. "Jackie?"

I looked up from my drink at that. Then it hit me. This guy did know my pain. He knew it all too well, because he was Jackie's ex. Bryan.

"Yeah, it was Jackie" was all I could bring myself to say. He didn't need to know the details. As far as he knew, our exes dumped us for each other. I was fine with him thinking that. To be honest, that was kind of what it felt like to me, too. I know, I know. It was more complicated than that. Kenny didn't have a choice. Blah, blah, blah. Still. "Fuck me," I mumbled.

Bryan held up his drink for a toast, "Fuck Jackie," he said, words a little soft around the edges. I clinked my glass to his and giggled.

"Fuck Jackie." And we both drank.

"It's probably a good thing we broke up, you know?" Bryan said with tears in his eyes, and I nodded. I didn't know how Jackie's relationship was with Bryan, but I wouldn't doubt she was abusive toward him, too. "We both got screwed over so bad."

"Yup," I said, not knowing if he meant himself and Kenny, or himself and me. Either way, it was true.

"Like, you think you know someone, and then..." Bryan's eyes got watery again, and, honestly, so did mine.

I didn't want to face what happened with Kenny here at this bar, but what else could I do with Jackie's ex staring me in the face? Kenny *left* me. It wasn't his fault, but he had. At the worst possible time. For once in my life, I'd thought everything was going to work out. That I'd get my green card and become a citizen. That I'd start a real relationship with Kenny. That I— *we*—could be happy, without having to worry about anything anymore.

But Jackie went and ruined all of it. If not for Jackie, Kenny and I would be married in a matter of weeks.

"I'm going to fucking expose her," I mumbled, not even sure what I meant by those words. I just knew I meant them.

Bryan downed another gulp, not seeming to even hear me. Then someone behind me spilled their drink, and he turned his head at the noise.

That's when I noticed it.

Scratch marks on Bryan's cheek.

"What happened to your face?" I asked.

Bryan touched his cheek, like he forgot he had a scratch. "Oh, that. She fuckin' slapped me. Used her nails and everything."

His cheek looked just like Kenny's the day he'd found out Jackie was pregnant. Anger burned my ears, balling my hands into fists on the bar. "Jackie hit you?"

Bryan sighed. "Yup. Just the one time, though. I ended it after that. She might think she can slap Kenny around like her little bitch, but she doesn't have control over me like that. I'm not gonna put up with that shit."

"Don't talk about Kenny like that," I snapped, fists squeezed so tight, I must have been breaking off my circulation. Jackie *hit Kenny*. How had I never seen that before? "None of this is Kenny's fault."

Bryan looked down at my fists, then held up his hands in surrender. "Whoa man, I didn't mean it like that. I'm not trying to get hit twice."

I unclenched my fists at that. It wasn't Bryan's fault, either. He was just another one of Jackie's victims. This was all so messed up. And I couldn't even go to Kenny and tell him what I knew. All I wanted to do was show up at the apartment and guard it from Jackie, and never let her come near Kenny again.

But I couldn't.

With the leverage Jackie had on us, there was no way to keep her from hurting Kenny again. She could use my status against Kenny for the rest of his life if she wanted to, trapping him in a cycle of abuse forever. And there wasn't a damn thing either of us could do about it.

I was still a little drunk when I woke up, and I had the worst fucking headache of my life. It was probably the seventh time I'd woken up already, but I refused to get up each time. Whenever I opened my eyes, one glimpse at the ceiling light had me shutting them real quick. I felt like one of those guys being interrogated in a dark room, where they would shove that bright light in your face so you couldn't see anything. But this time, when I swallowed, I realized how dry my throat was. I could have been stranded in the desert for days with no water for all I knew.

Okay, maybe that was all a little dramatic, but whatever. Point is, I was hungover. As hell.

I rolled over on my stomach and groaned into the couch pillow. I lay there for a while but couldn't fall back asleep. I wondered if Leti was as hungover as I was.

It was as if my thoughts of Leti summoned them, because before I knew it, they were lifting my feet up from the couch so they could sit down. I sighed and forced myself to sit up and face them. I ran a hand down my face as I tried to come up with something to say.

"I'm such an asshole" was all that came out.

Leti just frowned at me. They probably wanted me to explain why I was an asshole, but what was I supposed to say? That I was letting Kenny be held hostage in an abusive situation for my sake? God, I felt sick just thinking about it.

"I'm just a terrible person" was all I could manage to say about it.

"Stop it." Leti held up a hand to shush me, still frowning. "What are you doing, Ale? I'm worried." Their voice was softer than usual.

I wondered if they were worried because of how much I'd been drinking lately. Because of my mom. But I wasn't my mom. I'd never had an addictive personality like she did, and I'd never done anything besides drink and smoke a little weed. I was *not* my mom. Still, I knew it wasn't too healthy to drink my problems away. "I'll cool it on the alcohol for a while," I said, scratching my head.

"That's not what I'm worried about," Leti said.

"Then what?"

"*You*, Ale. Talk to me. For once in your life, tell someone what's going on in your head! You don't have to be alone in this."

"I..." I didn't know what to say. There was no way to explain the whole situation without telling Leti about Jackie's threat, which would definitely make Leti try to get involved, and I couldn't have that. "Kenny left me," I finally admitted. The words came out strangled and raw. It was the first time I'd admitted the truth to anyone. Kenny broke it off. There would be no wedding, or green card, or kissing Kenny. None of it. Maybe I couldn't tell Leti about Jackie's threat, but I also couldn't keep the breakup a secret forever. Especially with the would-have-been wedding date coming up.

"No..." The word came out Leti's mouth as if they hadn't meant to say it at all. They ran a hand through their long black hair and sighed. "I'm so fucking sorry, Ale. I... I think it's my fault he called it off."

"What? Why? What did you do?"

"At the bachelor party, I told him that if he wasn't sure about things, that he shouldn't keep stringing you along. I basically *told* him to break it off. And then he did. Fuck! I'm so fucking sorry."

I rubbed my temples. It made sense that Leti would think it was their fault, but that was the night Kenny and I admitted our feelings to each other. If anything, whatever Leti said to Kenny only made him more confident we should be together. If Jackie hadn't gotten in the way... "It's not your fault, Leti." I couldn't tell them why, but I didn't want them blaming themself for any of this. "I promise. It had nothing to do with that talk."

"Well, did he give you a reason for calling things off?" Leti asked.

"Jackie..." was all I could say. It wasn't even a lie, even if Leti was thinking something different. It was all Jackie's fault, whichever way you looked at it.

"That motherfu—"

"It's fine, Leti. I don't want to talk about Kenny anymore, okay?"

Leti shook their head, eyebrows scrunched together. "I'm really sorry."

"Yeah, me too," I mumbled. I didn't even have the energy to feel angry. Just tired. Just hopeless.

"I hate to leave you right now, but I have to go," Leti said, patting my thigh before getting up and putting their hair up in a colita.

"It's fine. Where are you going?"

But Leti seemed to be on a mission, and they either didn't hear me or ignored me. It was like they forgot they had anywhere to be until right then. They were already out the door before I had a chance to ask again.

I sighed and leaned my head back against the edge of the couch. Everything fucking sucked. I hated how helpless I felt about the whole situation. It was like no matter what I did, no matter how hard I tried, I couldn't catch a break. Jackie's threat would always be there, taunting me. How long would she keep me out of Kenny's life? Would she ever just decide to make good on it for no reason, just because she didn't like me? The thought made my skin crawl. There had to be *something* I could do to protect myself, to get her off my back. Something to free Kenny from her death grip. And to get him back in my life.

Then my drunken words from the night before came back to me, and an idea formed in my head. It was risky. I'd be risking *everything*. But this was a risk I had to take if I ever wanted to get my life back. To get Kenny back.

I'm going to fucking expose her.

CHAPTER THIRTY-SIX

KENNY

I took a double shift on my day off to please Daniel, hoping for some good news. But when I got to work, there was still no Han. It looked like I would have to wait until my break to bring it up with him again.

Every time I walked into the kitchen, I felt so off knowing Han wasn't back yet. The day dragged on and on, but once my break finally came around, I rapped my knuckles on Daniel's office door and waited until I heard an exasperated, "Come in, Kenny."

I opened the door wide enough to stick my head inside. "How'd your call with Han go?"

"I'm still not convinced it wasn't him who was stealing. I don't want to hire back a thief."

I had to bite my tongue to keep from saying something I might regret. "It wasn't him. First you thought it was Juan, but money still kept going missing. Now it's Han? Where's your evidence?"

"How do you know money kept going missing?" Daniel asked, eyes narrowing in on me.

"I've been counting it." Jesus, he was really about to accuse every damn body. "You told me to keep an eye out for suspicious activity. I've been trying to figure out who it was."

Daniel clenched his fists. "I told you to watch out for suspicious *people*, not to go behind my back double-checking my math."

Was Daniel really mad about me counting the money? "I'm sorry. I thought that's what you wanted me to do. Misunderstanding, I guess."

"I've got it handled."

"All right," I said, holding my hands up in surrender. "So . . . I hate to bring this up again, but—"

Daniel shushed me with a flick of his hand. "I said I would *think* about calling Han. I'm still thinking."

Oh. I had gone into my shift hoping he had already hired Han back. I wasn't used to not having Daniel's favor. I guess this was what it might have been like for Han working here. But no, there was no way Han would ever have enough say-so with Daniel to even *ask* for a favor. I tried to push down the swirling wave of anger. I knew Daniel was using Han as leverage to get me to pick up extra shifts. I just hoped he didn't hire another server before hiring Han back. That would mean I'd have nothing to offer in exchange for Han's job anymore.

"Well, how long do you need to think?" I asked. I wasn't exactly happy to work overtime indefinitely if Daniel wasn't going to make good on his side of the deal.

"I don't know. The more you ask me, the longer I'll need." Daniel rolled his eyes, and I let out an exasperated sigh before pretending to zip my lips shut. I would play his game as long as I needed to if it meant getting Han his job back.

"Oh, and, Kenny?" Daniel said right when I turned around to leave.

"Yeah, boss?"

"I meant what I said about going behind my back counting money. I already counted it today, and I don't need you undermining me."

"Yes, sir," I said. It was odd for Daniel to have counted the money before the day was over. Maybe he meant that he'd count it later and he misspoke. I rolled my eyes as I walked out of the kitchen. Daniel was so incompetent it hurt. So when the end of my shift came, I made it a point to sneakily count the money anyway.

And we were short.

Which made no sense. If Daniel had already counted the money and found we were short, why would he still say he suspected Han, who hadn't been in since he was fired? Did he really suspect me? Fuck, if he thought it was me, how could I possibly make things up to Han? But none of it added up—literally.

Then it hit me.

If I was right about this, it wasn't weird at all. It actually made *perfect* sense.

✳   ✳   ✳

I drove home on autopilot, stressing the whole way over what I was going to do about Daniel. Was he really stealing the money this whole time? Maybe I could use this as leverage to try to get Han his job back? But then again, I didn't have any proof, so what if I was wrong? That would *definitely* lose me my job, not to mention Han's. No, I would have to catch him in the act if I was going to make this work.

When I got to the apartment, I lazily trudged up the stairs, fumbling with my keys between my fingers. But instead of getting to finally relax for the night, when I got to the top of the steps, standing there was the last person I wanted to see, ever.

"Didn't I ask you to give me space?" I said through a sigh.

"Can we talk? Can I come in?" Jackie ignored my question.

I was too exhausted to stand outside and argue, so I reluctantly unlocked my door and led Jackie over to the couch. I wished I could just let sleep consume me right then and there, but I forced my eyes to stay open to keep from pissing Jackie off. The thought of living the entire rest of my life this way was already excruciating.

She sat down on the couch next to me and nervously ran her hands over her work skirt. I didn't bother asking her any questions. She'd get it out eventually, and the less talking, the better.

Before she could get a word in, there was another knock on the door. Well, if you could even call it a knock. It sounded like someone was banging their whole palm against the door hard enough to burst a blood vessel.

I groaned and closed my eyes. I'd *just* sat down.

"Aren't you gonna get that?" Jackie asked.

I forced myself to get up off the couch, dragging my feet as I made my way toward the door. As soon as I turned the knob, it swung open from the outside, and this time Leti marched in.

"So, let me get this straight, 'cause I *know* I must have heard something wrong. You left my cousin—" They stopped in their tracks when they saw Jackie on the couch, then gave me a look of disgust that made me want to crawl into a hole and hide forever. "Are you fucking kidding me, Kenny? You seriously left Han for this bitch? What the fuck is wrong with you?"

"I . . . It's complicated" was all I could bring myself to say.

"What the fuck did you do to him?" Leti stormed over to

Jackie and yanked her off the couch by her arm, then shoved her hard.

As much as I would have loved to see Leti kick Jackie's ass, I couldn't let it happen. I ran in between them.

"Leti, she's pregnant!"

Then Leti stopped, jaw open as the news sank in. I'd half expected Leti to have already seen it on Instagram, but then again, it's not like they followed Jackie. They hated Jackie, so much that it wasn't even fun to hate-follow her. Leti looked between me and Jackie for a few moments, dumbfounded. Then their eyebrows lifted in an *ohh* kind of expression. "And Han didn't want kids. Are you telling me it was mutual?"

Jackie scoffed. "Even if I wasn't pregnant, Kenny would have left Han for me eventually. It was just a stupid lapse in judgment that they were even together in the first place. It was all just a mistake. Right, babe?" There was a warning in her tone. I hated how territorial she got when anyone threatened our relationship. Apparently, even when we weren't together.

My cheeks went hot. I couldn't deny Jackie what she wanted right now. But I also couldn't bring myself to talk about Han that way. None of it was a mistake. How could I possibly say such a thing? Instead, I said nothing. That message must have been loud and clear for Leti.

"I don't know why you're surprised," Jackie said, rolling her eyes. "What could Han possibly offer Kenny that I can't? Han's a deadbeat. His life is never going to get any better than it is right now. Obviously Kenny was ready to come back to someone with an actual future. Who he can have a family with. He deserves better than—" Jackie finished her thought with a gasp as Leti's hand met her cheek.

Then they lunged at Jackie, and I quickly had to wrap my arms around Leti and waddle them backward toward the door.

"You fucking bitch! How fucking dare you! Kenny, get the *fuck* off me!" But Leti wasn't struggling to get closer to Jackie anymore. Instead, they turned around and strode the rest of the way to the door on their own.

Then they left, and I forced myself to close the door, the resounding silence screaming at me to open it back up and run after them, but I couldn't. Even if it meant closing the door on my relationship with Han and his entire family. I didn't have any other choice. A few tears fell down my cheeks as I turned to face Jackie.

She had tears of her own streaming down her face as she cupped her hand over where Leti had slapped her cheek. I wished I could have felt sorry for her, but all I felt was anger. She had slapped me like that so many times before, but when she got slapped herself, she wanted pity. Well, I wasn't giving it to her. Not this time.

But it wasn't just shock or fear in her teary eyes. It was anger. And I knew then exactly what that meant. Leti may have been trying to help, but they had just all but guaranteed Jackie would make good on her threat against Han.

I went to work the next day with an unbearable pit in my stomach. Luckily Daniel didn't have me working extra, so I was done after my morning shift was up. I got in my car as soon as I could, ready to fix the mess I'd made. It wasn't until I sat down in the driver's seat that I checked my phone to find a missed call and a text from Jackie.

Jackie: Come over. We need to talk.

Reading the text hollowed out my chest. She was going to do it. She was going to report Han. I shot back a quick "on my way" text before pulling out of the employee parking lot and speeding over. I had already been planning on heading over after work, so I told myself nothing had changed. I had to only hope she hadn't already made the call. I had to hurry.

The second I pulled into her driveway, I rushed to the door, but she opened it before I could ring the bell.

"You're here." She smiled at me the way she did before we broke up.

"You told me to come, so I'm here," I said, trying to hide the disgust in my tone. I was so angry with her, and I didn't know how to ever not be angry with her.

She smiled again, then walked to her living room, leaving the door open for me to follow. I trailed behind her, the lump in my throat growing with each step.

She sat down on the couch and patted the spot next to her. I sat, jaw clenched.

"I need you to know that I still love you. No matter what, okay, Kenny?" She reached for my hand, and I flinched before realizing I needed to appease her. I took her hand in mine, the touch sending a cold chill up my spine. Not the good kind of chill. It was the chill you get when you're walking through a haunted house and realize the hand you're holding doesn't belong to the person you thought. Jackie was not the person I thought.

"Then why are you doing this to me?" I asked, trying not to let my voice crack.

She squeezed my hand, but I let mine lie limp in hers. "For *us*, Kenny. Of course I'm doing this for us."

She leaned in for a kiss, and I just felt so incredibly violated that she would even try that. I turned my head so she kissed my cheek, and something snapped inside me at having her lips on my skin. "There will never be an 'us,' Jackie. You should know that."

She pulled her hand away, looking wounded for a moment. Then anger flashed in her eyes. "Then I'll just make that little phone call."

I grabbed her hand back but glared at her the whole time. "Is this what you want, Jackie? You want me to be your little bitch for the rest of my life? Because I'll do that. I'm your bitch. Are you happy? Whatever you want me to do, I'll fucking do it." Jackie looked at me with wide eyes, as if she hadn't expected her plan to actually work. "You want to fucking hold hands, fine. You want to kiss me? Go ahead. But this?" I said, holding up my hand in hers. "Will never be consensual. And no matter what you force me to do, you can't blackmail me into loving you again."

"I..." Tears welled in Jackie's eyes. "We really had something special, Ken. I think if you just give me another chance..."

I bit my tongue and shut my eyes to keep from exploding. I was pretty sure she noticed, because her demeanor changed then.

"Well, if you're going to be like that, then what's stopping me from making that call?"

That's when I pulled my hand away from hers and stood up to face her. "You think that will make me love you again? If you do that, how could I ever even *look* at you? How do you sleep at night, knowing what you're doing to Han? What you're doing to *me*? You say you love me, but look at how much pain you're putting me through. How could you treat someone you love like that? How could *I* love someone who would do this to me? I need you to really listen to me here, Jackie. I will *never* love you again."

Jackie's jaw hung open as she sputtered out her next words. "How—how can you say that? You're acting like everything we've been through means nothing to you! Are you really just gonna abandon me, like my dad did to my mom?"

"I think I get it now, actually." I couldn't help but laugh at the irony of this whole thing. I knew she was trying to make me feel like I'd be a bad father if I didn't let her walk all over me, but there was more to it than that. "You're afraid of being alone, just like I was. That's why we lasted for so long. Not because we worked, or loved each other, or made any kind of sense together whatsoever, but because neither of us wanted to be left alone. You're so scared of being left behind that you'd rather be with someone you've made to hate you than look yourself in the mirror. And I was the same way!

"I have bent over backwards at every turn just to make you happy, just so you wouldn't leave me. Fuck, I'm even doing it now, *again*. But this isn't who I am anymore, and you're stuck with a version of me that doesn't even exist. I'm not doing this because I want you to be happy. This is you bullying me and it's the only choice I can make, but you've shown me—and *Han* has shown me—that this isn't who I am anymore. So if you want to be with a ghost, then fine. But know the person you're bullying isn't the one you fell in love with or the one who fell for you. There's nothing between us, and there's nothing either of us can do to change that."

Jackie sat there, dumbfounded for a moment. She wiped an angry tear from her eye, then patted the space next to her on the couch. I stared at her in surprise.

"You're my bitch, then. Sit down."

CHAPTER THIRTY-SEVEN

HAN

This was the day I would get my life back. I woke up early (okay, okay, noon) to get ready. I *might* have been procrastinating, just a little. Hell, this plan was a complete gamble, but I was pretty sure it could work. I let out a deep breath as I opened the Uber's door and picked my crutches up from the floor. The car was gone before I knew it, so I couldn't just retreat and go back to Nacho and Mary's place. I stood there, right outside Jackie's house, hoping to God this plan would work. Just as I was about to make my way to the door, I noticed a car in the driveway, and my stomach yanked itself into a tangle of knots.

Kenny was here. The hell was Kenny doing here?

There was no way he could have already forgiven Jackie for what she'd done to me, right? I didn't want to believe that. So why was he here? I made my way to the door to find out, totally consumed by the bubbling anger at the notion that the two of them were just hanging out right now. I knew I wasn't being fair or logical, but none of that mattered in the moment.

I wasn't about to accept any of this. I rang the doorbell. I had to focus. This visit was about getting Jackie to back off, not about Kenny. And I *would* get Jackie to back off. I had to.

After a couple of minutes, there was still no answer, so I rang it again. And waited.

After what felt like ages, I finally heard Kenny's voice from behind the door. "I'll get rid of him, okay?" The fuck?

Now I really was mad. Kenny's voice was close enough to the door that it was obvious he'd already used the peephole to see it was me. I couldn't believe he had actually said that about me.

The door peeked open, showing me only a sliver of Kenny's face.

"Han, you should go. It's really not a good time right now."

And that fucker actually tried to close the door in my face! I blocked it by slipping one of my crutches through the crack in the door. "The hell it's not!" I said as I rammed my shoulder against the door and forced it open.

Kenny tried to protest, and I had to admit, if he wanted to, he could have just physically pushed me out of the house. But he didn't touch me.

"Han, I'm trying to help you," Kenny said under his breath so Jackie couldn't hear, but I just pushed past him. Kenny could explain later. For now, I was doing this. Whether he had my back or not. I had to look out for myself, now more than ever.

As soon as Jackie heard me come in, she marched over to the entrance where we were standing.

"Are you fucking kidding me? Why would you let him in? You're really not helping your case here, Ken," she said harshly.

Kenny looked absolutely horrified. His face was turning red, and his mouth just hung open as he stuttered out a frantic "I—I tried to—"

But I wasn't going to let either of them dominate this conversation. This was about me.

"I know you're gonna call ICE on me, Jackie," I interrupted, watching her face carefully for a reaction. Her head whipped over in Kenny's direction.

"You *told* him?" she shouted.

Kenny gave me a deer-in-headlights look. He had no idea what I was doing here or why I was egging Jackie on, but that didn't matter. He'd figure it out soon enough.

"So what if I do call?" Jackie seethed, her face now a blotchy red. "All you've done since I've known you is try to ruin my relationship! Why should I protect you from the consequences of your own actions?"

"Jackie, please—" Kenny pleaded, but I cut him off.

"Do it, then," I said, meeting Jackie's shocked eyes.

"What?" she and Kenny said in unison. Kenny looked even more surprised than Jackie, but he moved his body between us, as if he could shield me from whatever I was about to unleash.

"If you want to call ICE on me, then do it. I'll probably get deported, or maybe locked up for a while. Same difference to you though, right?"

"Han, what are you doing?" Kenny asked.

Jackie just stared at me like I'd been speaking gibberish. "I don't know what game you're playing, but I seriously will call them if you don't back off Kenny."

"Go ahead," I said, not daring to lose Jackie's gaze. "If you're not bluffing, then neither am I."

"What are you talking about?" She crossed her arms apprehensively. Kenny's expression finally switched from fearful to curious.

"I have posts ready to go on Instagram, Facebook, and Twitter.

Posts with your name, your picture, your job, and the whole story of how you called ICE on me to break up my marriage with Kenny. If you try anything, Leti has the go-ahead to post all of them. Your choice."

"You're not serious," she said, eyes narrowing in on me.

"Try it, then," I dared her, holding my breath. There was no way she'd try to get me deported if everyone would find out what she did. She'd no doubt lose her friends and her leverage on Kenny, and I doubted her job would take kindly to the implication that Jackie herself was an abuser. If she was going to ruin my life, I'd ruin hers right back. "Everyone will know what a racist bitch you are."

"Oh, please. It has nothing to do with racism. This is about me and Kenny."

"Then you wouldn't mind Leti posting about it? How many people do you think will see it your way?"

"I—I'm not *racist*! I...It's just..." Then she just burst into tears. "I wasn't actually gonna do it, okay? Is that what you want to hear?" When I didn't give her so much as a pitying look, she turned to Kenny. "What else was I supposed to do? You weren't listening to me! I had a fucking *baby* on the way, and you still wouldn't break up with him!" she sobbed, but even Kenny didn't give her an inch of pity.

"What do you mean *had*?" Kenny said, his voice cold.

Jackie let out a frustrated scream. "I got an abortion, okay! That's what I was trying to tell you, why I wanted to talk. I couldn't do it! I don't want to raise a kid with *Han*! I don't want to have a baby just to get you to stay with me if you're not even going to stay." Jackie's voice was almost unintelligible with how hard she was crying, but neither me nor Kenny was about to comfort her.

Kenny completely ignored Jackie as he threw his arms around me and squeezed me up in a hug, but I couldn't bring myself to hug back. Kenny pulled away and looked me in the eyes, relief washing over his features.

"So you can just abandon me like you were always going to do!" Jackie wailed, and Kenny finally turned to face her.

"You know what, Jackie? You are abusive."

"I'm not—" But Kenny didn't let her finish.

"You've always treated me like shit. You made me hate myself. You made me second-guess every move and every choice I made. You made me, like...really unhappy. You're so fucking controlling, it's suffocating!"

Jackie looked like she'd just been slapped in the face. "But you *know* why I'm like that! It's not my fault!"

"No, your parents getting divorced wasn't your fault. But you're an entire fucking adult now. What happened to you when you were a kid doesn't excuse you treating everyone around you like shit. Grow up."

I wanted to slow clap right there. I never would have thought I'd see the day when Kenny told Jackie off, but here we were. I had to admit, I was pretty damn proud of him. Sure, Kenny and I still had a ton of shit to work out, but the worst of it was over. He turned to me and nodded toward the door.

✳   ✳   ✳

"Come back home," Kenny said once we were in the safety of his car.

I swallowed. "I don't have a job to be paying rent."

Kenny didn't hesitate. "I'll work extra shifts until you find one."

I sighed. Part of me thought Daniel might have realized he

was wrong and rehired me, but if he hadn't by now, he probably wasn't going to.

"It'll be okay. I promise."

"Fine," I said. I didn't mean to sound so short with Kenny, but I was still a little caught off guard by the fact that he was at Jackie's in the first place. I trusted Kenny, and Jackie's threat was no longer holding me down, but I still felt sick to my stomach. It was like my mind and body hadn't fully processed yet that I was off the hook.

Kenny seemed to notice I wasn't as excited as he was. He kept his eyes on the road for the most part, but every now and then he spared a quick glance at me like he was trying to read my energy.

"It's a good thing I procrastinated canceling all the wedding plans." Kenny laughed.

Was the wedding still on? For some reason, the thought didn't comfort me as much as it should have. I had to admit...I was pissed. Pissed about Kenny being at Jackie's house. Pissed that I had to risk everything today in hopes Jackie would give up on her threat. Pissed about, well, this entire situation. On one hand, I could have just asked him why he was there. It was possible he had a good explanation, right? He probably did. But if he didn't, I didn't know if I could keep from showing my anger. If I admitted I was mad, would he call off the wedding again? I wished I didn't have to rely on Kenny, but I did. So, I had to just go along with it. I just had to be happy Kenny was still willing to go through with the wedding. No, I didn't have the right to be mad.

"I mean...if you still want to. I totally get if you want to sort through all the complicated feelings and everything first."

"Fuck that," I said without thinking. I knew I should have been better at talking about my feelings by now, but what was

the point? I didn't want to find out that Kenny didn't have feelings for me anymore. Didn't want to talk about Jackie. Didn't
want to talk about any of it. I obviously still had feelings for
Kenny, or I wouldn't have been upset about seeing him at Jackie's, but I wasn't sure I wanted him to know that at the moment.
Especially if things had changed for him.

"So, the wedding's still on. We're still doing this." Then he
looked at me again, and his expression fell as the car stopped in
front of a railroad crossing. "Do you not want to anymore?"

"It's not like that," I said.

Kenny paused for a while before saying anything else. "It's
okay if you're mad," he said, as if he'd just read my mind.

"I'm not mad," I lied, glancing at the train slowly making its
way by, trying to find the end, which was nowhere in sight.

"You're not?"

"You're marrying me, aren't you? I'm getting my citizenship.
Can't be mad about that."

"That's bullshit," Kenny spat. "You shouldn't have had to
go through any of this. You should be pissed. You *are* pissed, I
know you are. And you have every right to be. None of this was
fair to you."

"Why do you *want* me to be mad?" I asked.

"Because I deserve it!" Kenny shouted, gripping the wheel
tight even though we were still stopped. "Be mad!"

I balled my hands into fists. "You know what, Kenny? I am
mad. I'm pissed. This whole thing is so messed up. I want to
hate you!" I hit the car door with the side of my fist, and Kenny
flinched like he thought I was about to swing at him. "Kenny,
I wasn't gonna—I would never..." Kenny thinking I'd hit him
forced me to soften up a little. He was used to getting hit when
someone was mad.

He swallowed. "I... I know you wouldn't. Sorry, I didn't mean to react, I..." Tears came to his eyes. "I know this is what I asked for. I'm so sorry, Han. It's okay if you hate me."

"I don't hate you. I could never hate you..." *I love you*, I wanted to say. My voice softened, and it was true. Even if Kenny broke off the wedding for good, I wouldn't *hate* him. Not really. There was nothing on earth Kenny could do that would make me *hate* him. With that realization, I let out a deep sigh. I might as well ask. "Why were you at Jackie's?"

"I was—" Then his eyes widened. "Oh my gosh, it wasn't like that! Leti confronted Jackie last night, and I thought it might have made her want to make good on her threat, so I went over to do damage control. I was just trying to convince her not to do it. Which in hindsight feels kind of silly since she was apparently never going to do it in the first place..."

"Neither of us could have known that, though, and it seemed like something we couldn't risk," I said, running my hand down my face, embarrassed. "Thanks for looking out."

"I'll always look out for you," Kenny said, eyes concentrated on mine. "Still, it's okay if you're mad or if you hate me. I would still marry you. I would do anything for you, Han." Somehow, I knew he meant it. I knew the only reason he broke things off in the first place was to protect me. It still just wasn't fair.

Before I could react, Kenny got out of the car and, right there in front of the backed-up train crossing, jogged over to my side. He opened the passenger door. The hell was he doing?

Then he was down on one knee.

"Han, will you please marry me? Will you move back in? You don't have to forgive me. I get it if you're mad. But marry me? I lo—I... I want to help, Han. Please, at least let me help you get your green card. Marry me." He shouted his whole spiel over the rumbling train, but I heard it just fine. Even if half of me thought I was imagining this whole thing. Kenny, asking me to marry him one last time. How could I say no? The phrase finally made sense to me. Not because I wanted to say no but couldn't, but because I couldn't find a single bone in my body that wanted to give Kenny anything but *yes*.

"Okay," I said, feeling a little choked up. I couldn't say much. Any grateful words I wanted to say caught in my throat. I really was thankful, but I couldn't bring myself to say it. The last time I admitted my feelings to Kenny, I got burned. And I knew it wasn't his fault, but I didn't want to repeat history. I had cried more times since we admitted how we felt about each other than I had in my entire adult life, so I blinked the tears away. "Okay."

CHAPTER THIRTY-EIGHT

KENNY

I spent most of the next week working double shifts every day, and Daniel still hadn't called Han. I didn't know how much longer I could take this. I knew Han and I still had plenty to talk through, and the wedding was only four days away. I was grateful now that my mom refused to let me cancel the wedding just in case we worked things out. But I couldn't spare any extra time with all the hours I was putting in. I didn't want to tell Han I was trying to get him his job back because I wanted it to be a surprise when it finally worked out. Plus, I didn't exactly want to take credit for it, since it was my own fault Han had lost his job in the first place. But even with all my extra efforts, Daniel didn't seem to be budging.

What Daniel didn't know was that I had a backup plan. Ever since I'd suspected it was him who might have been stealing money, I'd been gathering evidence. Taking note of how much was missing each day and writing down Daniel's contradictions.

For a while, it didn't seem like much, but yesterday I'd finally hit the jackpot.

I'd made sure to count the money before *and* after Daniel had access to it. Sure enough, the totals were different. Now I had to decide what to do next. I could confront Daniel and blackmail him into giving Han his job back, but Daniel was unpredictable. Who knew how many people he'd bring down with him if he didn't want to go along with it. No, I needed to handle this myself, and I knew just how to do it.

✳ ✳ ✳

The next day, I went to work more stressed than I'd ever been. I'd done what I needed to do, and I didn't regret it, but I was still hit with waves of anxiety as I got in for my shift. I came in through the back, wondering what kind of environment I'd be walking into. Would Daniel be raising hell, trying to take everyone else down with him? Would he even be there at all?

To my surprise, Daniel was standing in the kitchen scolding one of the cooks for who knew what this time, like usual. My stomach dropped at the sight of him. Had the owner taken the info I'd given her and gone to Daniel with it, allowing him to talk his way out of it somehow? Did that mean my job was on the line now? What if Daniel knew I'd snitched...

I went the entire first hour of my shift stressing hard. Even my customers noticed I was a little anxious, and I was usually pretty good at putting on a happy face for them.

"Kenny, just the man I've been looking for!" Daniel said when I went back to the kitchen, waving me over. I forced my feet to move step by step as I made my way over to him. This was the moment of truth.

"What's up, Daniel?"

"I need you to cover for me this afternoon. I'm taking off after lunch."

I didn't know if I should be relieved or worried. He clearly still had his job, but he also seemed to have no idea anyone had tried to jeopardize it in the first place. "Yes, sir," I said. It wasn't unusual for Daniel to ask me at the last minute to cover part or all of the day as manager. It annoyed the hell out of me, but I had to admit taking over for a bit was a fun break in my regular day-to-day. I was basically doing the same legwork I did every day, only without having to serve customers on top of it and with the added bonus of Daniel not being around.

"Great." Daniel strolled on over to his office, closing the door behind him.

So he didn't know anything about what I'd done. But that also meant nothing had come of my complaint. So what exactly was happening? Maybe the owner hadn't seen it yet?

I went another couple of hours working, trying to make the time pass faster. I made it a point to be even friendlier than usual to combat the frustration and anxiety welling up inside. I wished I had some idea of what was going to happen.

At lunchtime, Daniel opened his office door with his bag in hand, ready to head out. But someone I recognized was already marching into the kitchen like she was on a mission.

"Hi, Mrs. Frederick! I'm Kenny Bautista, assistant manager." I introduced myself with enthusiasm. If Daniel was about to be fired, I wanted to make the best impression on the owner possible. It was only logical that I'd be promoted to manager with Daniel out of the picture, right? I needed her to believe that, too.

"Hillary. I got your email. Nice to meet you." Her words came out cold, and her eyes searched over the place quickly. Her brows scrunched together in a glare when her gaze found Daniel. "Excuse me," she said, then marched into his office without another word, waving him in to follow her.

"Wouldn't want to be Daniel right now." Tatiana had come to stand next to me, and the two of us nonchalantly made our way closer to the office so we might privilege ourselves to hear their conversation. My stomach tied itself into knots. I had to hope this would all work out the right way.

Before long, the door swung open, and Tatiana and I clumsily dispersed, tripping over each other trying to look occupied. I grabbed a customer's plate, but Daniel didn't acknowledge the eavesdropping. He slammed the door in Hillary's face and stomped out of the office. He raised his hand and swung it down on my plate, smashing it to the ground, making me jump. Then he stomped all the way out the back door. Hillary calmly stepped out of the office and watched him leave.

"Fuck all of you!" Daniel shouted, then slammed the door and left, hopefully never to come back again. It was unclear whether he'd been told I was the snitch or not, but with him gone, it didn't really matter.

"Nothing to see here. Get back to work, everybody. Someone clean this up," Hillary said, gesturing at the fallen plate on the floor.

"You." Hillary held up her index finger at me. "You're covering the rest of his shift." So, Daniel had been fired.

"You got it," I said, not bothering to mention that had already been the plan. Throughout my shift, I heard rumors about how he had apparently been stealing money from the restaurant. I guess I hadn't been the only one who'd suspected it. I waited for her to tell me I was the new manager, but she didn't.

I guess it made sense that she wouldn't make that decision so quickly, at least given the last manager's behavior, but I'd still hoped.

✳ ✳ ✳

The following day was my first off since I'd been trying to get Han rehired, and I was dying to spend some quality time with him before we had to go to my parents' house to help set up last-minute things for the wedding.

"What are you up to?" I asked hopefully as I made coffee for two.

Han shrugged from his spot on the couch, where he was playing *Injustice*.

"Want to watch a movie?" I asked.

"Nah." Han didn't take his eyes off the screen.

Things hadn't exactly gone back to normal between Han and me yet, and I was as anxious as ever to get back to that point. We used to be so comfortable around each other, but now I got the feeling he was walking on eggshells. He barely spoke to me anymore, and when he did, it was short and to the point.

"Okay if I join you?" I asked as I set the two cups down on the coffee table and picked up a controller, flashing Han a grin as I waved it around.

"Actually, think I'm gonna take a nap. You can play, though." Han yawned and stretched out his arms, then put the controller down and got up off the couch, heading to his room without touching the mug.

I slumped into the couch. I didn't actually want to play *Injustice*. I just wanted to hang out with Han. I sighed and got up to go to my own room, but as I passed Han's door, I overheard him talking to someone—probably Leti—on the phone.

"I don't know. I just don't think things are gonna go back to normal…"

My chest felt like it caved in on itself. I wanted more than anything to storm into Han's room and beg for things to go back to normal. It was all I wanted. But I knew I couldn't do that. If Han needed his space, I would give it to him.

I continued down the hall and sulked in my room until Han cracked my door open. I sat up so fast, it gave me a headache.

"Han, what's up?"

"It's about that time," Han said.

"Time for what?" I hoped he'd say something like "time to be friends again!" or "time to kiss again!" or "time for everything to be normal again!"

Instead he said, "Time to go to your parents' house? We still have some setting up to do. Nacho and them are gonna meet us there."

I slumped against the wall. "Right. Okay, let me just…" I pulled off my tank top and threw on an oversized sweater, noticing from the corner of my eye that Han looked the other way when I took off my tank. I adjusted my glasses and grabbed my keys from the nightstand. "Okay, I'm ready."

When we got to my parents' house, I found that while I was off working double shifts, Han and the rest of our families had been busy putting things together for the wedding. Apparently Han couldn't even use his ankle as an excuse to get out of helping. Everything looked ready except for the tables and chairs, which were all against the edge of the house in the backyard, waiting to be set up.

Leti and Mary were carrying a table out to the grass, while

Nacho followed them with six chairs, three under each arm. Impressive. Han grabbed a couple of chairs in one hand and used a crutch in his other arm, while Leti and I reached for a table and carried it together. Leti nudged Han and looked back at me, but Han just waved them off. I sighed and followed him to set up some more tables.

When we'd set up all the seating, it was time to decorate the tables with tablecloths and flowers. My mom wanted each to have one white tablecloth with two long pieces of purple cloth crossing each other in the middle and hanging off the edges.

After she demonstrated what the finished product should look like, I went to work on the table Han was at, hoping to get something as small as eye contact from him. No luck.

But when I went to set the purple cloth on the table, Han was setting his down too, and our fingers touched for a brief moment. I looked up, and Han finally met my eyes. I was immediately thrown back to #ZBlaineSmithHyphenSmith's wedding, when we'd done the same thing after forgetting whose turn it was to be chivalrous. This little touch was the most intimate thing we'd done since we'd made love. But then Han cleared his throat and pulled his hand away.

"Cheer up, you two! You're getting *married!*" Nacho put one hand on my shoulder and the other on Han's and squeezed.

Then it was like a switch flipped with Han, and the pretending started up again.

"I know. I can't wait! Can you believe it, babe? We're getting married in *two days!*" He willingly reached for my hand and squeezed. And this somehow felt a million times worse than being ignored. Han was just pretending. Any affection I got was just for show.

I played along even though it killed me. I wanted this to

be real again, but Han just kissed my cheek for a split second before going back to get more tablecloths. I brought my fingertips to my cheek, savoring the warmth. This was going to be torture.

Before Jackie ruined everything, fake flirting had been *fun*. Flirting at work or in front of family had been one of my favorite parts of the day. Now it just felt like a slap in the face. A reminder that things weren't back to normal. And I had no idea if or when they ever would be. I had no idea what I could do to make that happen.

When Han and I got in my car to head back home, the energy immediately got heavy again.

"Are we okay?" I asked.

Han nodded. "I appreciate what you're doing for me."

I ignored the fact that he didn't answer my question at all. I didn't want our whole relationship to be centered around what we were or weren't doing for each other. I just wanted things to go back to how they were before.

CHAPTER THIRTY-NINE

HAN

It was weird being back in the apartment. Different. And it was my fault. But I just couldn't bring myself to go back to how things were before. That level of intimacy, of vulnerability, wasn't easy for me. Kenny had slowly brought it out of me over all the years we'd known each other, but now it was like we were back at square one. It was true that I still loved him. That I was *in* love with him. Maybe I always had been. But that didn't help anything.

He had been picking up so many extra shifts lately that we barely had any time to talk, and even when he was home, he was constantly on his laptop working on who knows what. So, maybe he wouldn't even notice what was going on with me. Maybe I'd get over it before it really made a difference.

I shook the thoughts away as Leti opened the apartment door and came inside with a box of doughnuts.

"You haven't been eating. I can tell," they said as they set the box down on the coffee table and took their seat on the couch next to me. They had been coming over to keep me company while Kenny worked, which I really appreciated. They opened the box and smiled widely, waving their hands in the direction of the doughnuts. "Eh? Eh? I know you want one!"

Leti used their huge fake nails to pick up a chocolate cake doughnut like a claw machine at an arcade. They made a show of sniffing the doughnut and sighing happily. I laughed and picked up a chocolate sprinkled one of my own. It wasn't exactly the healthiest breakfast, but it was much better than what I'd been eating lately, which—Leti was right—was nothing.

As soon as my mouth was full of doughnut, Leti took the opportunity to catch me off guard.

"Why are you avoiding Kenny?"

I chewed slowly to keep from having to answer the question right away. The truth was, I didn't really know. Still, I couldn't help it. Maybe I just needed time to heal from all the Jackie-related stress. I knew Kenny only wanted to help me. He'd never done anything to intentionally harm me, and he didn't deserve me treating him this way. I knew that much.

But I don't know. I guess I was stubborn. Afraid. All over again.

Leti rolled their eyes. "Look, it's obvious that you two are into each other. You really just need to kiss and make up."

I choked on my doughnut. What the hell did they mean by that? "Obviously we're into each other. We're getting married!"

"I know about your whole scheme, okay?" I started to protest, but Leti waved me off with their hand. "Don't worry. I support it. But y'all are being so weird right now. It's not Kenny's fault he called things off. I know that must have hurt, but Jackie's the one to blame."

"Wait. How did you—"

"Your future husband told me everything. But I'm serious, you can't be mad at Kenny for what Jackie did."

"I know. I have no right to be mad." I sighed and ran a hand through my hair.

"I didn't say you have no right to be mad. You just shouldn't be mad *at Kenny*."

"I'm not mad at Kenny."

"Then why are you being so weird? You're getting married tomorrow. You two really need to figure this shit out."

I couldn't bring myself to answer that. The truth was, I was stumped.

"I'll tell you why," Leti said, taking another bite from their cake doughnut before continuing. "If you ignore him, you don't have to admit how you feel."

"And how would you know how I feel?" I felt my ears heating up with embarrassment.

"You're obvious. Both of you. God, why are you so allergic to admitting how you feel? I just wanna take you guys and . . ." Leti grabbed two doughnuts and smooshed them together. "KISS ALREADY!"

I slumped deeper into the couch. "We have kissed." I didn't mention that we'd done more than just kissing. Leti didn't need to know *all* my business. "But that was literally right before we broke up. I can't just forget about that."

"Because of *Jackie.*"

"I know! But . . . still."

"You're afraid of getting hurt again."

I just shrugged.

"So, are you okay with just drifting apart from Kenny forever?"

"No!" I rubbed a hand down my face. I hated how this was

all turning out. Before Jackie came along and ruined it, I really thought things between me and Kenny could be different. I thought we could really be...something. "I'm just...scared, I guess."

"What are you more scared of? Getting rejected or slowly drifting away from your best friend until you lose him for good?"

I didn't even have to answer that. Leti had a major point. I really needed to talk to Kenny.

* * *

I fell asleep before Kenny got home from work, and then we had to wake up early for our *wedding*. We made the drive over to Kenny's parents' house in silence. I sat stiff in the passenger seat, waiting for a vibe, a moment, *something*, to tell me it was okay to tell him. But the only sound in the car was the soft thrum of the radio. I tried to psych myself up again and again to tell Kenny how I felt, but I couldn't bring myself to do it.

Come on, it couldn't be that hard, could it? I just needed to say three simple words. I could do that. I could say three fucking words. But every time I tried to say them, they got lost in my throat. Before I knew it, we were at Elisa and Cedric's house, and I hadn't admitted a single thing.

"You okay?" Kenny asked.

I nodded quickly.

Say it. Just three words.

"Are *you* okay?" I flipped the question.

"I'm just happy we're finally doing this," Kenny said. He started to reach for my hand but then pulled away. Goddammit, why did he have to pull away?

Before I could say what I wanted to, a knock on the passenger-side window brought a startled noise out of Kenny.

Tía Mary was waving for us to come inside. She ushered us out of the car and into the house. Once we were inside, we signed the marriage license so we wouldn't forget later on, with Elisa and Tía Mary as the witnesses. Now all we had to do was the ceremony to make it official. My eyes got a little misty at the thought, but before anyone could see, I felt a warm hand on my shoulder.

"It's good to see you, mijo," a familiar voice said from behind me. I had to have been imagining this.

"Papi?" I whirled around to see that my ears were not playing tricks on me at all. The familiar smile lines I'd only ever seen over WhatsApp, the thick salt-and-pepper hair I'd surely inherit, and those dark brown eyes that mirrored the shape of my own. How was this possible?

It didn't matter. I didn't know who pulled who in, but before I knew it, I was in a firm embrace with my dad, neither of us daring to let go. I didn't realize I was crying until I felt him patting me on my back. His shoulders were shaking, too, so I wasn't the only one getting emotional.

"How are you here?" I asked, finally pulling away and wiping my eyes.

Papi just smiled warmly and gestured to Kenny and his parents. "You have your husband and in-laws to thank for that."

"I . . . I don't know what to say," I started. The tears came back, but I'd never cried like this before. Never been this happy. Instead of words, I just pulled the three of them into a hug, then hugged my dad one more time before Elisa pulled Kenny away from me.

"Sappy reunions will be for after the wedding!" she said.

"Don't worry, Han. I'll keep your papi company while you

get ready! You're not the only one who misses him," Tía Mary teased before pulling me in the other direction so Kenny and I could get dressed in two separate rooms.

*   *   *

While Kenny got dressed in his old bedroom, I was getting ready in Cedric and Elisa's. I stared at myself in the full-sized mirror, hardly believing what I saw. I was getting *married*. This was really happening. I was going to be a citizen, all thanks to Kenny. I still didn't understand why he was doing all this for me, especially given the way I'd been acting recently.

Before I could get too into my thoughts, there was a knock on the door.

"Can I come in, mijo?" It was my dad.

I rushed over to open the door and pull him inside. I gestured to my tux.

"How do I look?"

His smile creased the lines around his eyes. "You look good, mijo." He put a firm, congratulatory hand on my shoulder and squeezed, holding the other hand behind his back. "You look good. I brought something for you." Then he pulled his hand out from behind his back, revealing a brown envelope.

I took it in my hand, hesitating before tearing it open.

"Go ahead," my dad coaxed, and I finally opened it up.

There was a folded piece of paper inside, and a jellyfish neck-lace. I held the pendant in my palm and stared at it for way too long before all the memories came flooding back to me. This was the necklace my mom always wore. My dad started singing then, and I recognized it as the song she used to sing to me every night.

When the world feels too heavy, when the tides feel too
  strong,
Take my hand once you're ready, for we may not have
  long.
Just close your eyes, breathe steady. Remember where
  you came from.

It all made sense now. Jellyfish were *her* favorite animal. Not mine. Tears pricked at my lashes, and I wiped them away quickly.

"What's this?" I asked as I unfolded the piece of paper.

"I found it in your mom's things. When your mom was in treatment a year ago, she apparently wrote you letters every day. This is the last one she wrote. I can give you the rest if you want them."

My hands shook as I looked down at the letter. This whole time, I hadn't been the only one writing letters?

I cleared my throat and blinked away my tears so the words wouldn't be blurry. It was handwritten in blue colored pencil, which I was now remembering was her favorite color.

~~My~~ dearest Alejandro,

I don't deserve to call you mine, do I? I gave up that privilege when I said goodbye to you. Part of recovery means making amends and taking responsibility, even when it's hard. Even when an apology can never fix the pain I've caused you. My counselor today told me that children often blame themselves for their parent's addiction, but you are never to blame for this illness. I did a lot of horrible things in my sickness, but you are never to blame. I'm so sorry if you ever felt that way. You may not belong to me anymore, but you will forever be my son.

I love you.

The letter was signed with a drawing of a jellyfish.

No matter how hard I tried, I guess there were some things I could never forget.

I thought I'd forgotten her, but she was always right there. She'd never left my brain or my heart. Never could.

Just then my phone buzzed. I wiped my eyes as a little spark went off in my chest, hoping it was Kenny, ready to talk. Somehow, I felt like telling him how I felt over the phone might be easier. But when I grabbed my phone, it was only an email notification from someone named Patrice Crawford. Who the hell?

I opened it.

Dear Mr. Torres,

We have reviewed your application for the New Mexico Community College Scholarship Endowment, and we are pleased to inform you that you are the 1st place awardee, which qualifies you for a full-ride scholarship to Central New Mexico Community College.

In order for you to claim this scholarship, you must . . .

I skimmed the rest of the email. This had to be some kind of mistake. I never applied for a scholarship. I continued reading, to see if maybe there was some hint they'd emailed the wrong "Mr. Torres."

Let us know when you're available for a phone call to sort
out the details. Is 555-847-0384 still the best contact phone
number to reach you?

Kenny's number.

"Papi, I have to talk to Kenny," I said, and as soon as he nodded, I left the room and made a beeline for Kenny as quickly as
I could on crutches. I opened the door to his childhood room
without knocking, and a startled Kenny yelped and dropped
the tux jacket he was putting on. His cell phone was squeezed
between his chin and shoulder. Kenny waved me inside, but
held up a finger as he finished his call.

Sorry, I mouthed as I closed the door behind me and picked
up the jacket, handing it to Kenny with my eyes glued to the
floor.

Kenny grabbed it with a huge grin on his face, though I suspected that grin was because of his phone call. "Thank you so
much, Mrs. Frederick! I won't disappoint you...Yes...Thanks
again! Have a great day!"

Kenny hung up the phone, finally turning toward me.

"Hey, Han." He ran a hand through his slick black hair. I
stared at Kenny in his tie and white button-up, which fit just
right. I blinked myself back into the moment as Kenny spoke.

"Han, I—"

"You applied for a scholarship for me?" I blurted out. I
thought back to all the time Kenny had been spending on the
laptop recently, and it made sense.

Kenny's eyes widened, "Did you get it?"

I pulled Kenny into a tight hug, "I got it," I said before pulling
away. The corners of Kenny's full lips tugged upward. I wanted
to kiss them so bad.

"So what good news did you get?" I asked.

"What?"

"That call you took? You seemed all happy."

Kenny grinned wide again. "I got promoted! I have Daniel's old job now. *Huge* raise."

"I guess that means I get my old job back?" I sighed, partly in relief and partly in resignation. I needed that job, even though it wasn't exactly the dream job. Still, it'd be much more enjoyable working for Kenny than for Daniel.

Kenny took my hand and sat down at the edge of the bed, pulling me over to sit next to him.

"Han, I'm not giving you your job back."

I felt like I'd just been punched in the gut. All I could say was "What?"

Kenny's eyes widened, "I mean, if you really want it, then sure, it's yours. I just mean... I'll be making enough to support you through school. You can take your time and figure out what it is you really want to do, you know? Pursue your passions!"

A watery pressure built up behind my eyes.

"I... Why would you do all this for me?" I couldn't help but ask. I needed to know. I did nothing to deserve everything Kenny had done for me over the years. The scholarship. The marriage. My freaking dad. Even the sticky notes. It made no sense.

"What? It's no big deal, really. It's the least I can do," Kenny said, his eyes falling to the floor.

"Oh. Okay, then." I didn't know why I wasn't saying what I wanted to say. It was the perfect time, and yet... maybe I could tell Kenny after the wedding. I grabbed my crutch and started to get up, like the coward I was.

"Wait." Kenny touched my arm, his fingers lingering on my

sleeve even after I stopped moving. He stood up to meet me face-to-face, and when I turned back around, Kenny's eyes fluttered up under his thick lashes, his intense stare meeting my own. "I do...pretty much everything...because..." Kenny let out a shaky breath, and I stepped closer.

"Because what?"

"Because I don't want to lose you! I would do anything for you, Han. Anything for you to stay here. With me. I...That's why I broke things off when Jackie, you know. It's why I'm marrying you. Why else, Han?"

"I love you," I finally admitted. The words didn't come out smooth like I'd hoped, but they came out.

Kenny tilted his head, like he was expecting me to say something else.

"What?" I felt like I was under a microscope. Kenny wasn't saying it back.

"No 'bro'?" Kenny bit back a smile.

"No 'bro.'"

"Wait. No, bro, or no 'bro'?"

"No 'bro.'"

Kenny tilted his head. "That doesn't make it any clearer."

I shook my head, laughing, and Kenny laughed, too.

I put my hands on his shoulders for emphasis. "I'm in love with you," I said again, then closed the space between us and kissed him eagerly. I wanted him to know without question that I still felt the same as I did that night. We both sank into the kiss for a moment before I pulled away. "Is that clear enough for you?"

Kenny smiled. "I love you, too, Han."

"Glad we cleared that up." I found myself fidgeting with my tie, which was loose around my neck.

"Here, let me help you with that," Kenny said as he reached out toward my tie to adjust it himself. But instead of tightening it like I'd expected, he loosened it even more.

"What are you doing?" I asked, and Kenny looked up at me with a mischievous smirk.

"Are you still...curious?" he asked.

I bit my lip and nodded breathlessly, more than ready for whatever he had planned.

"Good, good," Kenny said thoughtfully as he turned to lock the door. "Sit down and take off your jacket."

I tossed my suit jacket as Kenny gently pushed me to sit on the bed and undid my shirt one button at a time, speaking slowly as he did.

"If you need me to stop, your color is red, understand?" Another button, and then he tightened the tie around my bare neck.

I nodded.

"If you need me to slow down or try something else, your color is yellow." Last button.

"Yes, sir," I said readily, then quickly took off the shirt and threw it on the floor, too.

"And if you like it"—he grabbed the middle of the tie and wrapped it around his hand once. Then he leaned down and gave it a firm tug, pulling me almost close enough to kiss, but didn't close the gap—"then your color is green."

"Green, green," I said breathlessly.

"Good." Kenny smiled approvingly. "And if you go nonverbal or can't talk for whatever reason, snap your fingers once for yellow and twice for red."

I nodded, wanting to melt into a puddle right then. I didn't go nonverbal very often, but I felt more than safe knowing Kenny had already considered the possibility.

"I don't have my backpack with me, so we'll have to get a little creative," Kenny said as he started to undo his own tie. "Give me your hands," he commanded. He pulled the tie off his neck and held it in both hands, then snapped it like a belt, making my insides churn.

I held my hands out together for him, and he quickly got to work tying them. The tie was snug against my wrists as he cinched it, securing my hands together tight. "Color?" he asked.

"Green."

He smiled, then let my hands fall to my lap and turned around, searching the room for something. "Pretty sure I have some lube and condoms in here somewhere," Kenny said, opening and closing dresser drawers until he finally found what he was looking for. Then he grabbed a towel that was hanging from the closet door and laid it out on the bed.

Before he could come closer and put a condom on me, I couldn't help but interrupt his thought process.

"I want you to fuck me," I blurted out.

Kenny turned toward me, raising an eyebrow. I felt so vulnerable sitting there, hands tied and shirtless with him staring at me like that.

"Please," I found myself begging.

Kenny smiled and took a step closer so he was standing over me at the edge of the bed. "I like it when you beg," he said before stealing a hungry kiss. My hands came up to touch his chest, but since they were tied together, they just got pinned against my own. There was that feeling again pulsing in my groin. God, I wanted him so bad. Needed him.

"*Please*, Kenny," I said again, my voice desperate.

Then he put a hand on my chest and pushed me down onto my back before climbing on top of me. I let out a ragged breath as he pinned my hands above my head and used what was left of the tie to secure them to the headboard.

"Color?" he asked.

"*Green*," I said enthusiastically, and he smiled again.

He got to work pulling my pants off and discarding them. Then he positioned himself in between my legs and grabbed them to spread them apart. My breath hitched as he lowered his head and licked my hole. I couldn't help but squirm as his wet tongue worked its way inside me.

Chatter from people arriving outside the door made my heart race. We could get caught. But that somehow only made this feel all the more real. More exciting. Kenny hesitated like he was about to pull away.

"Green," I said eagerly. "Don't stop. Green."

"Will you be quiet for me?" Kenny asked smoothly, and I nodded, pressing my lips together and swallowing.

Then a lubed finger replaced his tongue, and he stretched me for a while before slipping another finger inside. His other hand started stroking my cock in rhythm with his fingers. I had thought I'd be too tight for anal to work, but Kenny's fingers had a way of loosening me up. I let out a noise of pleasure that might have been loud enough for someone outside to hear, but at this moment, I couldn't bring myself to care.

Kenny looked at me disapprovingly but didn't stop. "I thought I told you to be quiet," he said as he stuck a third finger in me, as if he was testing my resolve to keep my volume down. I bit my lip, trying my hardest to keep from moaning out loud.

"Fuck me, Kenny, *please*," I begged in what was barely over a desperate whisper.

He smirked and replaced his fingers with his cock, which went much deeper than I'd expected. It took everything in me to keep from crying out in pleasure. Kenny slowly slid into me, grinding himself in and out. I wanted so badly to touch him, to touch *myself*. But all I could do was succumb to it and let Kenny do whatever he wanted with me.

He slowly stroked in and out a few times before I was loose enough for him to really go for it. Then he thrust himself inside me fully, and I couldn't hold back my moan this time.

Instead of scolding me again, Kenny moved his hand from my penis to cover my mouth firmly. "Quiet, babe," he said, then pumped himself into me even harder.

I moaned into his hand, relieved at the stifled sound that wouldn't get past the door. It was like with his hand over my mouth, the pressure to stay quiet fully dissolved, and I could finally be completely in the moment. I could fully give in to him.

Finally, Kenny started to touch me with his free hand. I couldn't hold back the muffled noises of pleasure I let out at the sensation of being stroked in two places at once. Pleasure rushed through my entire body, and I knew if it wasn't for his hand over my mouth I'd be screaming by now.

All the pressure I'd been feeling up to this point, any anxiety or stress or tension floated away somewhere far, and I sank into the mattress as Kenny sank even deeper into me. I felt a pressure building up in my groin, and I tried my hardest to keep it from erupting.

"I'm gonna come," Kenny said breathlessly.

Then he pressed himself as deep into me as he'd been, letting out a strangled exhale with the surge of warmth. I whimpered into his hand at the loss of contact when he pulled out of me. I was so close.

He immediately moved his mouth to my penis and started deep-throating me, sucking hard.

"I'm so close," I moaned as his throat enveloped my full size. I tried to hold back until he wasn't swallowing me whole, but I couldn't help it. I came right in his mouth, expecting him to be disgusted.

Instead, he swallowed it, his moving throat muscles tightening around my tip, and he didn't stop sucking until every last drop was emptied. Until all that was left inside me was a feeling of utter bliss as my whole body turned to mush.

CHAPTER FORTY

KENNY

I knew Han and I were supposed to be waiting in separate rooms for our wedding to start, but after what we'd just shared, I didn't want him to leave.

"Stay," I said softly, taking Han's newly freed wrist and kissing it tenderly. Since he'd been bound with a soft necktie, there were no rope marks. Still, I gently rubbed the skin where he'd been tied in case he was sore.

"Okay." Han didn't protest, and I was glad for it. What was the point of waiting in two separate rooms? We could hear Elisa ushering guests outside. The wedding would be starting in only fifteen minutes, and I, for one, couldn't wait.

"Can I admit something weird?" Han asked.

"Of course."

He sighed. "It feels so...I don't know...maybe naive or something. But...I'm kind of bummed there's no baby anymore."

"What do you mean?" I asked.

"Like, don't get me wrong. I'm thrilled Jackie isn't in the picture. But I don't know. I was kind of looking forward to raising a little you." He chuckled.

"Really?" I asked, and Han looked embarrassed but didn't cower away. I couldn't hide the smile on my face. Han, who'd never wanted kids before, wanted one . . . with me? Was that what he was saying? I might not have been ready to have a kid right then, but I could totally see it happening with Han at some point in the future.

"So, do you still want to get divorced after I'm naturalized?" Han asked. I chewed on my lip. Things were definitely more complicated now, but I could deal with complicated.

"Let's not worry about that right now. Right now I just want to kiss you." I pressed my lips against his one more time and felt Han chuckling under the kiss.

"I just want to actually date you," he said.

"Good thing we're getting married, then." I grinned.

Before I knew it, there were several knocks at the door.

"You boys ready?" It was my mom. We got ourselves together and opened the door, and were greeted by Tía Mary, Tío Nacho, Han's dad, and both my parents. For the first time since Han came into the room, we allowed ourselves to be separated again so we could be walked down the aisle.

One of the guys from Nacho's band played a slow acoustic version of "Cielito Lindo" as Han and I waited on opposite ends of the back of the aisle. I heard a few gasps and hushed whispers when we walked out. When our cue came, my parents and Han's dad respectively walked us toward the aisle to meet each other. I could have sworn I saw Han tearing up.

Han had just one crutch to help him walk, and the other

arm was wrapped around mine. We made our way up the aisle slowly, until we made it to the altar, every step increasing the speed at which my heart would beat.

I could hardly hear the words coming out of Leti's mouth as they said their marriage spiel—I could only look at Han, who was staring right back at me. He was smiling contagiously, and I smiled right back. Finally, after all this time, it was happening.

Han was first to say his vows, but he stopped Leti from starting him off.

"Actually, I wrote my own vows." He pulled out a folded-up piece of paper from his pocket and unfolded it shakily. He cleared his throat. "Um, I'm not great at writing speeches, so don't go thinking this is gonna be good." He let out a nervous breath of a laugh. "I just wanted to say thank you, Kenny. For everything. You've been there for me my entire life. Even when I didn't want to talk about what was wrong, you were there for me. You were there for things as small as when we were ten and I didn't make the basketball team, but also for the big things, like getting freaking *married*." He smiled through his words. "And I'm so happy to be marrying you. Like, ridiculously happy. This isn't some means to an end for me." Han smiled as he wiped a tear from his eye. "So, I vow to do everything I can to make it up to you. I want to let you in, Kenny. To be vulnerable. To be real. I want this. I want *you*, so fucking bad." He didn't clear his throat or look away when I looked into his eyes during his speech. He held my gaze earnestly, and it absolutely broke me in the best way possible. "Um. Yeah. I just wanted to say thank you. So much. Thank you, Kenny. And I love you."

I almost felt Han's pain in saying all that without uttering the word "bro" even once. I didn't realize I'd been crying until I found myself mirroring Han wiping a tear from my eye. What saps we both were.

When Leti was about to start me off for my turn, I interrupted them just like Han had.

"I wrote my own vows, too," I said, trying to hold it together long enough to say what I had to say. Instead of reading the vows from the paper I had in my pocket, I spoke from the heart. "I know everyone thinks I don't know how to make a decision to save my life. I've never been the most confident guy. I thought I needed someone else's approval before saying what I really wanted, or even daring to think it. I was so afraid of making the wrong choice, and I thought if I let someone else make the choices for me, I couldn't possibly disappoint them. Han, I told you before that marrying you was the easiest decision I've made in my life, and I meant it. I'm not afraid of being wrong. I don't care who approves or doesn't." I let out a shaky breath to avoid audibly choking up. "I vow to choose you, Han. Today, tomorrow, the next day, and every day after that. I can't wait to choose you over and over, for the rest of my life. There isn't a single alternate universe or timeline or dimension where I won't make the same choice. It's you, Han. It's always been you, and it always will be. I love you . . . *bro*." I laughed through the tears, and Han did the same.

"Bro . . ." Han laughed, shaking his head.

"Okay, now kiss, you losers!" Leti said, grabbing both our heads and pushing them together.

We kissed, and at that moment, I knew things would never go back to normal. They would never be the same, but that was okay. It was more than okay. I didn't want things to go back anymore. I wanted Han in a way I never would have thought I deserved, but now the possibilities were endless. I could be with him now. I could feel his lips on mine. We could make love and never have to say goodbye. The past with Han was incredible, but the best part? That's what comes next.

EPILOGUE

HAN

FIVE YEARS LATER...

Kenny and I stood at the doorway of a house down the street from my tíos' place. *Our* house. The Realtor had handed Kenny the keys earlier in the day, but since I was at work, he waited until dark to go inside with me, as the official new owners. We'd be bringing Luna, Thornelius, and the rest of our stuff here later, but for now we just wanted to enjoy the house as the owners as soon as we could. Kenny unlocked the door but held his hand out for me before opening it. I happily took it.

"Ready?" he asked.

"Ready," I said, and we both took a deep breath before we pushed the door open together and walked inside.

We'd already seen the house, of course, but that was before it was *ours*. Now that we knew we had it to ourselves for the foreseeable future, we both started running and skipping around like kids, excitedly yelling out ideas about what we'd do with the place.

With his free hand, Kenny gestured to the wall in the living room with the higher ceiling. "Instead of a painting, or a big mirror or something here, we can make a big blowup of your degree and hang it right there! The real copy will go in our room, of course."

We both laughed while I led Kenny out of the living room to the hallway, where the other two bedrooms were. "Our family photos can go on this wall."

Kenny squeezed my hand with a smile and skipped along, practically dragging me back into the main area. "Thornelius will go on the dining room table. Family dinner just wouldn't be the same without him."

"Of course," I said, then gestured to the walls in general. "We'll have to redo the paint."

"Oooh, can one of the walls be periwinkle?" Kenny asked, folding his hands together like he was praying for me to grant his wish.

"At *least* one of the walls."

He pulled me in for a thankful kiss, pecking his lips against mine several times in quick succession before pulling away and pointing to the wall that separated the kitchen from the living room. "We can mark up this one with how tall our kids grow! Different colors for each kid."

I beamed. We'd decided a couple of years ago that we'd adopt after I graduated. I really wanted to adopt kids who were more likely to be stuck in the system, like older kids, or siblings to keep them from being separated. I could have easily ended up in a similar system if I didn't have my tíos. Kenny loved the idea, so we started the application process as soon as I secured my first post-degree job as a substance abuse counselor.

We continued pulling each other around the house and

blurting out all our ideas, eventually making our way to the backyard. It was pretty barren save for a tree stump and a boulder in the middle of the yard. It was a bit of a fixer-upper, but we'd make it home.

"Maybe we can grow a garden out here?" I suggested.

"Yes! And we can get a fire pit and put it between the boulder and the stump!" Kenny let go of my hand and ran toward the stump, sitting down on it and grinning back at me. "Add maybe a log and another chair, and it'll be our bonfire hangout spot!"

I followed and sat across from him on the boulder. A phantom fire crackled between us under the stars, lighting his face with an imaginary orange glow, and I could picture it. This felt like home. *He* felt like home.

And I could stay as long as I wanted.

ACKNOWLEDGMENTS

I'm so incredibly grateful for all the support and help I've had in bringing this book to life and putting it in the hands of readers.

To my agent, Alexandra Levick, for never letting me give up on this story even when I wanted to burn it to the ground and never look back. To Amy Pierpont for believing in my writing enough to take a chance on me. To my editor Junessa Viloria for helping me whip *The Proposal* into shape. To Jessie Gang for designing such a swoon-worthy cover and to Charlotte Gomez for bringing it to life. To the entire team at Forever for all the incredible work you've put into bringing this book to fruition, especially Jordyn Penner, Alli Rosenthal, Dana Cuadrado, Daniela Medina, Anjuli Johnson, Penina Lopez, and Taylor Navis.

I also really want to thank Lee Call, without whom I would probably be curled up hiding in a corner somewhere procrastinating. From body doubling with me, to encouraging me to let myself be silly and ridiculous in my writing, to brainstorming some downright brilliant ideas, to putting up with me in general, I cannot stress this enough. THANK YOU!

And lastly, I want to thank all of my beta readers, especially Ana Franco, who was always my number one cheerleader and the first person I showed every single rough draft to. Even when *The Broposal* was an awful first draft, she told me it was her favorite book of mine to date. Love and miss you always, Ana. This one's for you.

READING GROUP GUIDE

AUTHOR'S NOTE

Some of the most common writing advice I've heard is to "write what you know." Even though I'm Mexican, autistic, and queer, and have experienced many of the same trials my characters do, I've never felt confident at the start of writing any story that I "knew" a single thing. I always questioned myself before starting the drafting process. Am I Mexican enough? Autistic enough? Boy enough? Queer enough?

Am I enough?

So often, the answer was something I wouldn't be able to find until after I'd told the story. Somewhere along the process of exploring all the intersecting identities and experiences that make up the characters on the pages, I found myself.

All the anxiety, longing, grief, joy, awkwardness, and love on the page were my own. With each book I write, I find myself falling deeper and deeper in love with parts of myself I thought were unlovable. I can't help but love every character I see myself in. I want them to succeed and find happiness and fall in love and have their happily-ever-afters. And in realizing that they deserved those things, I found I did, too. After each story, I find the answer is unchanging.

I am more than enough.

DISCUSSION QUESTIONS

1. In the beginning, both Han and Kenny are deep in denial over their feelings for the other. In your opinion, what was the moment for each of them that felt like the tipping point of when they *knew* they'd fallen in love?

2. While *The Broposal* focuses mostly on the lives of Han and Kenny, there are still many side characters, from family members to emotional support animals (and succulents) to Grindr hookups turned third wheels. Which character did you relate to the most and why?

3. This book is told from the points of view of two characters with intersectional identities. Both are queer and Mexican, while Kenny is also an abuse victim and Han is undocumented and autistic. Though not every reader is going to relate to every piece of these characters, what, if anything, stood out to you in their representation that felt particularly meaningful?

4. *The Broposal* is a romance, but there are also a lot of heavy issues brought to light in this story, i.e. abuse, immigration, grief, etc. How did you feel about the

balance between the sweet or lighthearted moments and the more emotional content?

5. On that note, which scene or situation made you laugh the hardest? Were there any moments that made you cry?

6. Memories and the past play a significant role in this story, particularly for Han. Why do you think it was so hard for Han to remember specific details about his mom, even when he was intentionally searching those memories for comfort? How did you feel when you found out the origin of Han's love of jellyfish and where his "close your eyes" flashback mantra came from?

7. Since this book is told in dual POV, did you feel like the personalities and voices of the two main characters contrasted or complemented each other? In what ways were they similar or different?

8. If *The Broposal* were made into a movie, who do you think would be perfect to play each character?

9. Kenny and Han were voted "most likely to get married" for their high school superlative. Out of this book's cast of characters, who would you give the winning vote to for the following superlatives, and why?

    a. Best character development

    b. Suffered the most

    c. Funniest character

    d. Most hated

    e. Most underrated

    f. The reason their therapist goes to therapy

DON'T MISS SONORA'S

NEXT CHARMING BOOK

COMING IN 2026

ABOUT THE AUTHOR

Sonora Reyes is the bestselling and award-winning author of *The Lesbiana's Guide to Catholic School* and *The Luis Ortega Survival Club*. Born and raised in Arizona, they write fiction celebrating queer and Mexican stories in a variety of genres, across ages. Sonora is also the vice president of the nonprofit organization My Galvanized Friend, an organization meant to promote and encourage the creation, dissemination, and enjoyment of LGBTQIA+ literary and artistic expression.

Outside of writing, Sonora loves breaking their body and vocal cords by playing with their baby niblings and dancing/singing karaoke at the same time.

You can learn more at:
    sonorareyes.com
    Instagram @sonora.reyes
    X @SonoraReyes
    TikTok @sonora.reyes

YOUR
BOOK
CLUB
RESOURCE

VISIT
GCPClubCar.com

to sign up for the **GCP Club Car** newsletter, featuring exclusive promotions, info on other **Club Car** titles, and more.

GRAND
CENTRAL

FOREVER

TWELVE

LEGACY
LIT

balance